A DANCE WITH DEATH

She leaned hard against his chest. Her breasts urged him through the thin layer of his sweat-dampened shirt, and he laughed. This was trouble – the good kind.

Then her head lolled back and he zoomed in on the wide, fixed points of her green eyes.

He wasn't holding her anymore; he was holding her up.

They weren't dancing now.

Colors ranged across her dark skin like a station in distress. Energetic bodies moved in and out of shadow at the edges of his sight. He touched her long hair. Wet. He pulled his fingers away. Under the flashing lights they were covered in iridescent purple.

They felt red.

The music gave one long, eternal beat.

Novels by Karin Lowachee

Warchild

BURNDIVE

KARIN LOWACHEE

WARNER BOOKS

An AOL Time Warner Company

Cover design by Don Puckey
Cover type design by Shasti O'Leary Soudant
Cover illustration by Matt Stawicki
Book design by Charles Sutherland

Warner Books, Inc.
1271 Avenue of the Americas
New York, NY 10020

Visit our Web site at www.twbookmark.com

An AOL Time Warner Company

Printed in the United States of America
First Printing: October 2003

10 9 8 7 6 5 4 3 2 1

To my parents

ACKNOWLEDGMENTS

For my difficult middle child, many props must go to:

—my readers, who gave the firstborn such a warm welcome

—Shawna McCarthy

—Jaime Levine

—Devi Pillai

—the team at Warner Aspect

—Matt Stawicki

—the guerrilla street soldiers for their clandestine operations in bookstores across the continent, many of whom are—

—my friends and family near and far (y'all do good PR)

—my fellow writers near and far, some of whom are: Sue Bee, the F.O.G.ians, the Nimvuri clan, the Sock Monkeys, the Sporks, and all m'peeps who represented on my behalf in various blogs and conversations

—particularly Angela Boord, Mike Dumas, and Helen Vorster for very helpful eleventh-hour commando feedback

—and Sensei Steve K. S. Perry, for generously assisting me once again through his expertise in bodyguard, police, and military matters (if anything sounds dumb, it's all Sid's fault)

—and the Goddess Nancy Proctor, my intrepid fellow traveler,

—for links, lightning crits, liquor research, and for loving my Boyz

—and always to Winnie Wong and Yukiko Kawakami, my sushi sisters and know-me friends, there before the world was

—and, finally, thanks to the music of 30 Seconds To Mars for providing many (loud) hours of inspiration when I needed to meet deadlines

Provehito in Altum

"Fame is nothing but the sum of all misunderstandings that gather around a new name."

—R. M. Rilke

"Outer space is no place for a person of breeding."

—Lady Violet Bonham Carter

"*Vox populi, vox galaxiae*—the voice of the people (is) the voice of the galaxy."

—slogan of the Satellite Entertainment and News Distribution (SEND) Networx

BURNDIVE

SILVER

Ryan Azarcon went to meet his dealer in Austro Station's richest, busiest shopping district, known to its younger patrons as the Market—but not for the many tech, clothing, and jewelry shops available. Here in the Market you could buy anything, or anyone, if you knew where to look or who to kiss.

It was a triple-level open-quad design, airy white and pseudo-sunlit, mocked up with reinforced stained-glass balconies, fluted ivory columns placed more for decoration than engineering, and hanging sculptures that resembled featureless cranes in flight. The Market was situated deep within Module 3, where all the wealthy citizens lived and poorer people from the general docksides and lower modules needed pre-authorized passes to visit. Shops catered specifically to affluent clientele who wanted to parade their bodies and designer labels—sometimes one and the same—which you couldn't do from your comps at home.

Ryan himself had designer eyes—two professionally cut, blue-iris jewels—thanks to Eternity Enhancements' biolabs. That vain bit of genetic tweaking had been his mother's decision before he was even born; he felt no need to flaunt them, though he used his eyes sometimes to unnerve annoying meedees. Dr. Grandma Ramcharan back on Earth said his wide blue stare could strip bark from a tree and words from a brain, especially when he was peeved. His mother called it "the Azarcon look" (despite the fact his father's eyes were brown), not usually as a compliment, since the Captain Father was not exactly well liked in Ms. Mom Lau's more polite circles.

Not that the captain cared. And neither did Ryan, who wasn't so fond of his mother's associations either.

Tweaked eyes aside, Ryan had naturally inherited his father's brown hair, which burnished to dark gold if he ever found himself under a real sun. Three months since returning from a three-year university sojourn on Earth and he still had the beach-sand color that star-squatting trendiosos paid salons to mimic. Most Austroans only saw beaches in augmented reality progs; it took cred to get to Earth from this far in the Rim, like it took cred to genetically change the color of a child's eyes. Cred was never Ryan's problem. He had a famous family and a famous smile. The complete exterior workup—a well-dressed skin over a rather slight frame—resulted in the SendTertain's latest transcast: *Young Azarcon, Austro's Hot #1 Bachelor.*

It was embarrassing, not funny. Especially when rich thirteen-year-olds in the Market eyed him up on deck like he was an item tagged for sale.

Most of the people recognized him on the white-tiled, fountain-warbling promenade, but he ignored the looks. He had *one thing* on his mind since returning from Earth in November, since waking up this early goldshift with an itch in his blood and a long, fed-up sigh:

Silver.

Footsteps going by seemed to tap out the rhythm.

Suck.

Push.

Inhale.

All the ways you could do it.

He flicked his fingers on his thigh in air-guitar patterns as he walked—one step behind his bodyguard Sid, who insisted on clearing the way in case lady-here or mister-there in their silk suits decided to mob him (not that he ever got mobbed, but try telling the bodyguard). It was tedious. Sid never had cause to draw his weapon so there seemed no point to the protocol—and it made things like doing deals exceptionally difficult.

The bodyguard, Marine Corporal Timothy Carl Sidney (sir!), was Admiral Grandpa Ashrafi's idea, who knew Sid from Earth. Sid was a pretty accessory, alert as a dog and trained as well as the German shepherds that worked with Hub Command Secret Service agents at Grandpa's estate. Sid was friendly when he was officially off the job, but brutal if disobeyed at any time. If Ryan decided to slip away, the bite out of his hide would make sitting difficult for a week. He'd learned that seven years ago, when he was twelve.

So he didn't bitch, just dutifully followed Sid to Macroplay, an overpriced tech shop frequented by everyone from burndivers to speedkids addicted to the games now popular in cybetoriums across EarthHub. Burndivers never bought off the shelf, though, just like rich kids looking to suck some Silver never went underdeck. Serious people all had backdoor contacts for illegal swack, and rich stitches didn't like to dirty their boots underdeck. It was notorious among certain kids on Austro that you could get what you wanted from the shadow management at Macroplay.

This was coveted info, strongly guarded. All that seriousness was expensive. Hard-core users were trusted if they could be depended upon to keep their holes shut; break that trust and unfortunate ailments seemed to crop up on the blabbermouths. Scandalous overdoses, suicides, those kinds of things. Ryan didn't think Sid knew, but even if he did, it was another thing altogether to prove it. The only way *he'd* found out about the shadow management was a chance discussion with Tyler Coe last month at the actor's vid premiere. Tyler always kissed his arse because he was Songlian Lau's son and Ms. Mom Lau knew everybody in PR on Austro. Public relations was important to a weed like Tyler and after a couple months back on station, floating adrift without the high, Ryan figured Tyler could jack him in with some grade-A swack. Call Tyler what you wanted, but at least he was discreet about his bad habits. And he knew how to avoid Sid.

Ryan fooled around on his comps with enough credibility to convince Sid that he needed an extension for some new aug prog that hit the market or some ware that was getting a lot of noise on the SendGame. That wasn't the market he was really interested in, though.

Sid eyeballed inside Macroplay before passing Ryan through, then stood just outside to case the traffic. Ryan left him to it and approached the counter where one live body always lingered to cater to customers, despite the infobooths dotting displays around the wide, techno-Gothic purchase space. Rich stitches didn't like to swear at inanimate objects when their answers weren't promptly forthcoming; cred bought attention and smiles, and the headwired kid behind the main scan recognized Ryan.

"Yo, Raz!"

He smiled. "Hey, Shoe. Is Fara around?"

Shoe moved his gaze left and right but he wasn't looking at anything Ryan could see. The red eyeband he wore projected data overlay to the user; it always made Ryan feel as if he were talking to a first-gen holavatar that couldn't quite interact.

"Fara's at the back, I'll cue her," Shoe said after a couple seconds of interactive burn.

"Thanks, man."

Usually Shoe required people to go to Fara, but Shoe knew as well as Ryan that Marine Boy Sid would only follow. Here in the open was less conspicuous, oddly enough.

While Shoe continued to burndive, occasionally squeaking at things only he could see, Ryan leaned his arms on the glass counter and stared down at the display items—the kind of ware you wore: cameye globes, amateur meedee headwires, and transcast spike interfaces for your own Send updates on the public facets of the networx. He usually bought only gameware; he wasn't much interested in making statements. Ninety percent of reports on the Send and all of its children networx were detritus, in his experience. Admittedly he contributed to the sound and fury when his mother forced him to sit interviews at bloody tedious fashion galas or mutual appreciation awards shows. Which were fine themselves if he didn't have to talk to transparent people who wouldn't care less what he thought if his DNA was different and he happened to be ugly.

Nobody listened to you unless you had more cred than God, or if you murdered some important people, or if you were beautiful to the right powers (or all three combined). Kingpins, pirates, and status dolls—they were the "Voices of the Galaxy."

Yawn.

Thankfully Macroplay had loud music scrolling on their wallvids instead of the ever-present political debates that seemed to consume the Send lately. Invade the strits once and for all, or leave them on their planet? War and more war, as if anything would ever really change. The Hub would always hate the strits, and the strits would always be alien. He'd heard earfuls at Admiral Grandpa's dinner functions back on Earth, forced to nod his head or walk away when his father's name inevitably came up.

Shoe and Fara called him Raz because that was his name

on the SendGame. Everyone else on Austro Station and in EarthHub as a whole knew him as Songlian Lau's and Captain Cairo Azarcon's son.

It's not your fault, Sid joked sometimes. Of *course* it wasn't his fault that strits, politicos, and deep-space pirates all hated his father. But it was never really a joke since Marine Boy was, obviously, here for his protection.

He glanced over his shoulder. Sid was still outside, looking at the people who dared walk through the door or mingle across the balcony in front of other shops. Snipers could be anywhere, apparently, even among women's lingerie.

When he looked back to the display case Fara had materialized across the counter, nudging Shoe out of the way. She could frighten anybody at first glance, all black horn-twisted hair and accentuated eyes, a typical meedee concept of a burndiver (which she was, among other things). Ryan thought she pulled the sudden appearances on purpose.

"Raaaz," she drawled. Her royal-purple, puff-injetted mouth broke into a banner of a smile.

"My girl," he said, and leaned across the counter for a kiss.

She put her talon-tipped hand in his hair and parted his lips with her tongue. He felt the usual buzz-sting from her neon-lit teeth, then the roll of the capsule from her tongue to his, wrapped in a flavor of grape. That was a Fara-only feature reserved solely for him, since his first exchange two weeks ago. She said he was a good kisser. He slipped the capsule to the inside of his cheek and kissed her for real, a thank you for this extra charade; he was her only client who had a bodyguard that would report her if they were caught.

When he leaned back Fara grinned like a ten-cred den ad and rubbed the side of his mouth with a beringed thumb. "You make me light up inside, kitten. I love it when you don't shave for a week."

It took that long for him to grow stubble, nineteen years old or not. She thought that was cute. He was resigned to the opinion since she wasn't alone in it and it got him the Silver. He was a hundred seventy centimeters in shoes and slender in build. Cute was his name from the day he was born, and he'd met enough people who reminded him of that fact (sometimes it worked to his advantage, but most of the time it irritated him). Still, he found Fara funny, sexy in a borderline repulsive way, the kind of woman his mother strongly lectured him about.

She always delivered.

"Whatcha gonna buy this time?" she asked, moving on to more prosaic business. It was just business with her, despite the kiss. Her boyfriend would shoot him, otherwise.

He needed something to make this trip worthwhile to Sid. So he pointed to a new game that he'd had his eye on for a couple weeks. It was that easy. Once he saw Sid had glanced away he spat out the Silver capsule into his palm and pocketed it in his pants.

Then it was just a matter of going home so he could sail. Because he'd run out of Silver seventy-two hours ago and seventy-two hours of unadulterated harping from Ms. Mom Lau about what he ought to do with his life gave him a headache. Rang on his nerves. So he needed to sail. He kept his hands in his flat front pockets and poked the capsule with his right index finger.

"Why so quiet?" Sid asked as they rewound their way through the perfumed stitches in the Market, toward the central bank of levs that would take them up to the executive residences.

The lights were brighter on the promenade than in the shop and Ryan squinted, shrugged. "No reason."

He'd been quiet since returning from Earth. Well, he

went out to premieres and parties and Sid shadowed him everywhere, but Sid meant quiet toward *him*. At home.

Depressed, Sid meant. Ryan knew he was worried. So Sid, being Sid, was going to feel around for a specific target to explore. Because talking always *helped*, right?

Right.

"Have you heard from Shiri lately?" Sid asked.

Shiri was Ryan's ex-girlfriend on Earth, from university. He'd met her in his Psychology of Public Opinion class; she was spritely pretty, moderately smart, and she'd asked him out for a beer at The Clover, a Georgetown pub. She hadn't known who he was and even after she found out, she hadn't much cared. For a Media and Public Affairs major that was certainly different, but then it was Earth and she hailed from one of the last small communities in some backcountry state like Montana, in America.

It was quaint to hear her accent, to point at her house on an augmap and walk through a replica of her little town and think, *This is so damn far from Austro it's practically alien.* She'd never been in space. The thought of going where you couldn't breathe "real" air frightened her. He'd thought she was joking at first. But no. He couldn't imagine never setting foot on a station, especially with Pax Terra so near Earth. Dirtsiders were an odd bunch sometimes.

Anyway, after Spring Break in Hong Kong, in his third year, she'd jettisoned him.

You've changed, she said.

Whatever the hell that meant. People changed, things never stayed the same like she wished, back there in her minuscule town with her safe ideas of what the galaxy was like. She was completely clueless about the reality of war and selfish, dangerous idiocy.

Sid thought she was sweet. But of course Sid was from Texas America.

Sure, he'd told Sid. Sweet in an ignorant kind of way.

He missed her, though. Or maybe he missed the lulling simplicity of her life. He missed the sex, of course.

"She hasn't commed me, if that's what you mean, and I haven't commed her. What's the point?"

Sid raised an eyebrow in his so-called nonjudgmental way. Maybe it wasn't judgment, but it was opinion. "I thought you two were still friends."

"Life goes on."

He felt Sid look at him sidelong. He knew he wasn't fooling anybody.

Problem with having the same bodyguard since you were twelve: you knew each other too damn well.

He did miss the way she used to hug his neck and kiss his temple, and hold his hand when they crossed roads because, she said, he wasn't used to four-lane traffic back there in his "tin can"—as she called Austro.

We have podways, he'd told her, attempting to brag. Between modules. In modules.

Sure, she'd said. But they're *designated.*

She meant regulated, which was true. Not every kid with a wild streak could hop in a pod and knock over people's fences (if Austro had fences) like kids back in her hometown apparently did for fun.

Dirtsiders.

He missed how she could drink him under the table and not break a sweat. He missed their banter.

But, well, that was before Hong Kong. And he had no real interest in talking to a girl who'd tossed him. They'd left things amicably but with the understanding that they'd never hear from each other again.

"So after Shiri you've gone to—that."

Sid meant Fara.

"Fara's a good-time gam. We flirt, it doesn't mean anything. Besides, she's a good kisser."

Sid smiled. "Have you been inoculated?"

Funny boy.

"I don't think she's safe," Sid continued.

"You're just paranoid."

"It's my job." Sid laughed, to try and get him to smile or give away a clue. Sid was suspicious and he had a right to be, but Ryan wasn't going to feed into it. He couldn't focus on that. The capsule of Silver was burning a hole in his pocket, he wanted it so bad right about now.

But they had to wait at the levs, like you always had to wait on Austro, even if you were the son of Songlian Lau and had a bodyguard who never let you walk the same route twice. Sixty thousand people on this station and some things no amount of cred could buy.

Ten other people stood by the levs, a couple talking to each other, but most everyone gazed over at the holosphere that dropped from the ceiling, hanging over the open quad. Rotating the Send news. Not that anything was particularly new. The Centralist party was up in arms again (as if they ever lowered them) because the Annexationist majority in EarthHub wasn't moving hard or fast enough against the strits. The aliens and their human sympathizers were still (like they ever *weren't*?) blowing up ships both merchant and military, not to mention stations scattered all through the Dragons and even some in the Rim, though Austro never got hit—it was too far in and too well defended by the Rim Guard.

Lucky for the commerce.

Amazing what people believed. Flak grew like fungus, and nobody was better at blue-cheese headlines than the Centralists. He knew from dinner-table conversation with EarthHub Joint Chief Admiral Grandpa that the strit attacks had actually decreased over the last few months and pirate activity had increased. But the Send never concentrated too closely on pirates. They were bad for business. Merchants from the Spokes to the Rim who took the safe, longer leap routes to get to ports delayed the exchange of goods and cred.

Plus aliens and their human symps made better enemies.

Not that regular humans didn't already corner the market on craziness. Extremists were everywhere, not only in the government or across the Demilitarized Zone.

Put them all on a moon, he'd told Admiral Grandpa one night during his first month on Earth. Away from any leap points, with no weapons or ships, and let them fend for themselves. Strit, symp, and sulking govie alike.

Would that it was so easy, Grandpa said.

No, it was never so easy.

The war dragged on and malcontents flourished, from Hubcentral to the Dragons, a spinning galactic gyroscope of violent offenders too wily to be caught.

Your father's at the top of that list, some student politico at his university had shouted, pointing a finger.

Screw you, symp, he'd said back, before knocking the kid on his arse. That had gone over well with the dean.

January 30, 2197 EHSD flashed on the holosphere in red and Ryan stared for a second. He would be into his last semester if he'd stayed in school. Weird that it was three months already since he'd left Earth and tried to reintegrate himself back into the rhythm of his homestation. Unlike Earth's days and nights, all it felt like here was one long, lethargic shift, a sleepless hour that didn't advance or retreat. A static army of time, coated in Silver.

He rubbed his eyes; they burned from fatigue even though it wasn't yet midshift. A young woman was staring at the side of his face, in his peripheral vision. He turned to glare at her. She said, in that tactless way people had when they thought they knew you just because your face was on the Send: "You look terrible, Ryan."

Using his given name, no less. He said, "I have insomnia. What's your excuse?"

Sid murmured, "Ryan."

The lev crowd all looked at him now, most of them affronted, minding his business.

The woman turned away and he slid his stare up to Sid, unapologetic. If people took liberties with him, why should he be polite? Of course Ms. Mom Lau would bleat if a little item appeared on the SendTertain tomorrow about Rude Ryan Azarcon or some such shit. She always wanted the proper face in public, but bugger it—this damn lev was never going to get here and his Silver bullet was getting too warm in his pocket.

More people joined them at the bank of levs, a few of them children holding reflective ribbons of color left over from the New Year celebration. Sid waved fingers at them and smiled and Ryan stared across the balcony to the other side of the promenade. The lev doors opened eventually and they piled in, rode up in silence. He tried to ignore everyone else, but the people who hadn't witnessed his snark at the woman insisted on engaging him now that he couldn't run. *Nice to see you back, Ryan. How's your mother, Ryan? We saw your father on the Send last week, Ryan.*

His father must've liked that, he was sure. The pug producer of the unauthorized bio segment had even tried to dig some dirt from Ryan himself, but Mom Lau screened those comms. Not that he would've said anything anyway. Left with no familial sources, they'd gussied up the captain's life by focusing on his wife and kid. Captain Cairo Azarcon of the deep-space carrier *Macedon* didn't *do* publicity. He just did Austro's Senior Public Affairs Officer Songlian Lau (all caps, baby), then left her on station with a child. That was the gist of the segment.

It was all bob. Bunch of bullshit.

Ryan didn't let himself get pulled in to any conversations. Especially not about his father. Maybe they thought he was sulking but he didn't care and didn't say good-bye when the lev opened on his floor.

He ignored Marine guard Perry outside the apartment door and went inside, while Sid lingered to talk to his opposite number.

Freedom.

Of a sort. Mom Lau came through the butterfly kitchen doors, a targeted missile. She was shorter than him, beautiful even off-cam and to the eyes of a son, with a heart-shaped face and "sweet button nose"—coined by the TrendSend—which she'd unwittingly passed to him (no gene-tampering involved in that bit of nightmare). Long dark hair and confident dark eyes. She looked younger than her forty-some Standard years, thanks to suspended aging treatments.

He knew from her face that he'd forgotten to do something.

"I asked you to organize your room," she said. "It's been months since you've come back and it's still a mess."

The eons-old complaint of every mother from the Stone Age onward.

"Nobody goes into my room but me," he said, a threat more than an observation, and headed that way across her translucent marble foyer. It was lit from beneath and cast a white glow from wall to wall, like a stage.

"Ryan, your shoes! I just had the floors cleaned!"

"Sheez, Mom, go lie down or something." He didn't stop. The Silver capsule in his pocket was a smooth comfort at the tip of his finger.

"Tim . . ." he heard her say to Sid, exasperated, then he shut the door on both of them and locked it.

He knew he was being childish and unfair. He shouldn't treat her that way. But inertia was a funny thing.

He put his back against the door and slid down, dug into his pocket and pulled out the capsule. The air vent in the wall was magnetic, so it took just a little prying before he could snake in an arm and feel around the dusty metal recess. He'd put the injet there after Sid's routine inspection of the premises earlier, and thankfully it was where he'd left it.

He thumbed open the loading tube, cracked the capsule with a bite, and shook out one 9mm round of transparent cylinder, enough to last two pushes. The liquid drug inside was the color of molten silver, like its tunnel name. A pretty shade, almost like the color of the walls in his kitchen. *Zen silver,* according to the Beautifix Design Interiors shop when his mother hired them to consult on the apartment. Zen *Silver.* That had a nice ring to it. In the cylinder it resembled a bullet. Dealers packaged them that way on purpose. Some dealers colored the tapered ends in bronze, red, or gold, depending. Marks of quality.

Fara didn't do any of that. Her Silver was a notoriously high quality. Pure. It was guaranteed to run through the cleanest labs. Fara had a reputation among Austro's elite, if you knew who to ask.

So Ryan Azarcon loaded the round into the injet and flattened the tube shut, priming it at the same time. Then he put the narrow point against the vein in his arm and pressed the trigger.

He'd never tried Earth street drugs again, but his first time sailing spacer-brand Silver had been Tyler Coe's fault. Tyler hooked an arm around his neck at the vid premiere after-party a month ago, smiled for the cam—there's one for the Send! he said—then whisked Ryan away to the bar with Sid trailing them like a loose leash. Tyler leaned down close to Ryan's cheek and Ryan smelled his sweet cocktail breath and felt it shoot into his ear to his brain like a spy bug. Tyler said, You look like shit, Azarcon, what you been doing on that dirtball? Which was Tyler's way of saying hello. Everybody had to look worse than Tyler in Tyler's world. Tyler was all about image. He had a nice image on the SendTertain but Ryan knew better. He'd known Tyler since Austro Academy; Tyler was a couple years older than he, and Tyler had been the same hypocritical flash whore then as he was now. But now he got paid big cred for it and he lived as large as Jupiter off the link sales.

Ryan had months of dark Hong Kong memories steeping in his system and no way to strain them out. From Delhi to D.C. he'd gone looking for an exorcism or an excuse, but nothing. London had been a disaster. Sid was too close, his grandparents too concerned, and school too all-consuming. He got on academic probation, then dropped out before they kicked him out—came home in shame, despite counseling initiated by Admiral Grandpa, and faced his mother's disappointment, his father's long-distance reproach. Not that they didn't *understand* what he was going through. No, everybody understood, they said. Sid understood, Sid who'd fought in conflicts from Tibet to Tel Aviv when he was younger than Ryan was now. Seeing bodies blown up was not normal by any standard, and even when you were trained for it you were never prepared.

Ryan didn't tell Tyler this, but Tyler was paid to be observant of human behavior and whispered in his ear, Let's lose the pole-ass and go somewhere. Which made Ryan think, with his five-drinks-later logic, that Tyler was hitting on him. Sid stood behind them frowning but Ryan kind of waved an arm and beckoned Sid to the private room Tyler's studio had rented along with the rest of the bijou club. Private rooms like this came equipped with expensive drinks and food and people, if you only asked. Tyler had asked, at least for the first two. Sid did a look-through to make sure it wasn't planted with bombs or tripwires or whatever, and then Ryan shut the door, shut him out, and sank down on the big pink couch for a breath of freedom.

He'd only been back on Austro for two months. It felt like a decade because it was back to routine—his mother harping, Sid shadowing, the looks and the meedees and the reports on the Send: *Ryan Azarcon drops out of Earth's George Washington University, a year from graduating with honors from their Media and Public Affairs program* . . . Not only that, but his girlfriend had dumped him.

What would the captain think?

Tyler fiddled with the wall display and it shifted from its static black to an underwater Earthscape, swimming fishes and floating plankton. Very soothing. Tyler turned up the music, grinding guitar and a heartbeat thrum from every wall that Ryan felt down into his crotch. Ahh, nice? Tyler asked. Nice, he replied, with a buzzed smile. Tyler dislodged a champagne bottle from the cold rack above the couch and poured them both glasses. It went down sweet and filled Ryan's mouth with bubbly happiness.

It wasn't like he got drunk a lot. Sid didn't let him. But maybe Sid saw he needed something, because he and Mom Lau both encouraged him to come out this night and deal with Tyler, even though they all knew Tyler wasn't necessarily an outstanding good influence. But Tyler had a reputation for being benignly social and Mom Lau and Sid both worried when Ryan spent all his time locked behind his bedroom door. What deviant private acts were going on there? Not even Sid knew, even though *he* knew Sid checked his room and his comps on a regular basis. Mostly he spent time on his mobile comp playing games or practicing the antique guitar that he'd got on Earth. Sid knew he wasn't, at least, sailing Silver. Where would he get it anyway, locked in his room?

Nobody knew Tyler sailed, which was the point, Tyler said. Austro's dealers didn't like famous clientele, and if you were famous you had better keep your mouth extra shut.

I can keep my mouth shut, Ryan said, as he downed that champagne like it was ambrosia of the gods.

Tyler didn't go further with it though. Tyler wanted to know about Songlian Lau, because, he said, their mothers were friends and it would've been nice to see Songlian this shift. What Tyler really wanted was a good downlink through the PR machine that would give him some rah-rah galaxy-wide 'casting about his new vid. Hell, Tyler would even love some words spread to the strits. Wouldn't that be funny? he said. My vids in a strit home or on a symp ship. Most of his vids were all about the superiority of EarthHub over less cultured cultures. The big symp Warboy would love that.

Mom was busy, Ryan said. Some press release to the Merchants Protection Commission. It wasn't like he paid attention. It was routine by now, what she did, and her absences. Besides, he said, I'm not your pimp.

Hey, Tyler said, since when did you become such a thorn?

Since I'm like telling the truth, he said. You want good 'cast on your vid you go work the SendTertain like all the other actor whores.

Tyler said, You sure know how to blow a boy's mood. And he smoked his cigret and refused to give Ryan a hit of it.

Well, my smart mouth, Ryan said. Sorry. Okay. I'll talk

to my mom. It wasn't a bad vid, actually. You really dating that gam, whatshername? Your costar?

No. Tyler laughed. That's just gossip.

Yeah, gossip.

Tyler said, Hey, Raz, you know you're wound tighter than a virgin's panties.

Ryan said, I wouldn't know about any virgins.

They laughed and rolled on the big couch, kicking each other like kids in a sandbox and the music drilled some more, right down Ryan's pants so he splayed back on the cushions and looked at the hot pink lightning patterns on the ceiling, glowing from the room's ambient.

So Tyler said, What was it like? That deal in Hong Kong, at EarthHub's embassy, wasn't it? Your poor face, they put it all over the Send.

Yeah, Ryan said. All over the damn Send. He didn't want to talk about it. Tyler and his lemon lollipop face came close and peered at him.

You need some bliss, Tyler said.

Ryan hauled himself forward so he could take some of the sushi rolls and cracker-caviar combos on the table. He stuffed his mouth, eyes watering from a sinus hit of wasabi. He licked his fingers and pushed his hair from his eyes, looked up as Tyler swayed to the low table-box in the corner and went to his knees as if in prayer.

What're you doing, boy?

Ssshhh, Tyler said. Before your Maureen barges in.

Ah, he won't. He thinks we're in here making out.

Tyler laughed so hard he lost his balance and had to grab the edge of the table. Ryan giggled and sipped his champagne.

Tyler dug into the drawers and came back with an injet and two bullets in the palm of his hand.

Hey, Ryan said. No, man, I better not. I don't want to get addicted or anything.

Or in trouble. Sid would kill him.

Addicted. Tyler laughed and hit his arm. I've been sailing for two years and I'm not addicted. This stuff doesn't addict you, he said, it just makes you *feel*. Like real.

I feel real, Ryan said.

No you don't, Tyler said, with all the authoritative logic of the drunken. You feel like a Send report, stamped and dated different every shift.

Maybe Tyler did know. Meedees tried to sneak optics into his bedrooms, no matter where he went. No matter what security he had. No matter how many times he complained to the public. Actors were fair game too, as well as famous sons.

So? Ryan said. And drank some more.

Tyler said, This isn't any different from alcohol.

It's illegal, Ryan said.

A small technicality, Tyler said. You want to keep seeing that embassy in your dreams? I'll make you a switch. You just try this and if you like it, drop a nice word to your mother for me. Tell her about the premiere. All the good stuff. She doesn't want you to be a hermit. I can help.

Help yourself, Ryan said.

Tyler said, Okay, whatever. You decide. And Tyler sat back and loaded a round into the injet, then rolled up his sleeve and shot himself in the arm. The injet went whoosh. Tyler's lemon lollipop face seemed to melt into something golden and his eyes fluttered a bit and he sank more into that pink couch like he was making love to a world of cotton candy. His knees widened and his tongue slipped out between his teeth. The galaxy is galactic, he said.

Ryan stared. Mr. Boy, you are so lost. But he laughed because Tyler laughed and Tyler started moving to the music except it was only his upper body and his neck bobbing up-and-down and up-and-down like someone's ass in a bed of sin, and it was the funniest damn thing Ryan had ever seen. He laughed and couldn't stop. And it had been a long time since he'd laughed like that, about anything or with anybody.

It's a damn good screw, Tyler said, with wisdom. He curved to the music like an eel in the ocean. He said, One push, an hour of bliss, then it's back to the dire shit. And again: One push, an hour of bliss, then it's back to the dire shit.

It was a rhythm. It was music. It was a single bullet on the table between the sushi and the caviar, and the injet was between him and Tyler, a small silver gun used for medicine and madness.

You could suck it in candy form.

Push it with an injet.

Or inhale it like dust.

Like ashes.

Behind his eyes were exploded people, a terrorist act to protest the Hub's "bigoted and murdering" policy against the alien strits. That kind of logic possessed believers and fanatics, like the student group across the street on the second floor of a noodle restaurant.

He'd gone walking that morning with Sid to Tai Po market and they'd bought dumplings and rice from a little stall and sparred with chopsticks. It was a hot March day and he was on Spring Break with his grandfather and his bodyguard in a foreign land, on a foreign planet more exotic than any wildlife segment he'd seen on a vid. Grandpa was there to stroke the pelts of the Chinese ministers in the Hub government, because they were always bitching about something like every other country on Earth was always bitching. One side didn't like how another side ran things, and Grandpa

Admiral of the EarthHub Joint Chiefs had to do his diplomatic duty once a year to these powers. It was going to be a great vacation because Ryan had nothing to do with any of it.

Then the students across the street launched a few rocket-propelled explosives over the high walls and into the embassy compound. Half the building went down. They'd heard it five blocks up and Ryan ran back to see—barely, through the dust—the guts of the embassy hanging to the ground, as if a giant had taken a large bite out of the cement and marble. Structural veins swung loose, blocks of stone fell in cloudy avalanches, rolling over the carpet of bodies thrown wide from the impact. People had been in the front quad, arriving or leaving for the day. Hub Marines had stood at the entrance portico. Now bodies lay scattered near and far like squashed insects on a summer sidewalk, red imprints in his memory. Empty vessels even emptied of blood, like spilled secrets you could never retract. One of them might've been his grandfather; he didn't know Grandpa had gone to a meeting across the city.

Sirens ripped the air.

He couldn't look away. A shout rose from the bottom of his throat like bile, but all he could do was cough.

Fanged heat bit through his skin and clothing, made him choke. Fire and black smoke licked the belly of the bruised sky, burning images into his eyes. He was drugged by the stench of melted steel and burnt flesh. The world slowed to a nightmare crawl. His heart clawed at his chest. Dirt and ashes blew around his face, suctioned to his skin, went into his eyes until the tears ran out and stung.

He saw torn uniforms on ragged bodies.

Grandpa.

He tried to get past the blockade of emergency airwings but the pollies grabbed him, then Sid grabbed him, dragging him off his feet to keep him back. Meedees were on the scene as if they'd had precognition of the event and they captured his face, his soul, and sent it out to deep space so even his father saw.

And everywhere he went his horrified face scrolled forever on high rolling holoboards and wide flashing Send reports. He saw that face in the mirror.

Ryan Azarcon. His famous smile and his designer eyes. Austro's Hot #1 Bachelor.

It was all bob. Everything was bob. Even Tyler was bob and this Silver was bob but he reached for it anyway, loaded the injet, pushed it in his arm, and unfurled his mental sails, sliding back on the couch for that first time, a virgin in this one thing. A virgin with his legs spread and both feet flat on the floor. It hit him hard and it hit him sweet and for an hour he forgot about everything, even his name, just like Tyler had promised.

Someone tried to open his door. It rattled, then there came a polite knock. "Ryan?" Sid's voice through the door. He wouldn't open it with his keycode unless Ryan didn't answer.

"Uh, yeah." He had gravitated to his bed from the floor and lay on it looking up at the blue ceiling, letting the last vestiges of the sail slide from his fingertips. Everything was colorful and velvety. His shirt was made of blue elastic material that wrinkled like silk between his fingers, then flattened out again to a perfect sheen. It waved up on his stomach from the way he'd lain down so that he spent some time inspecting the smooth ridges of his ribs. He'd lost weight in the past year. He used to have more muscle, not a lot, but the kind a small-framed person developed from regular activity—like trying to beat Sid in the powerball decacourts. He'd also taken up winter sports on Earth and slid himself down mountains every season. But that had stopped after Hong Kong too.

Everything just—stopped. Frozen on that image in his head of cartoon massacre that was all too real to dismiss as vid magic.

He'd smelled the charred bodies. It had gone up his nose and into his mind like cult indoctrination.

"Ryan?"

"Yeah, I'm there."

He pulled himself up, one side and then the other, and shuffled to the door. He squinted at the code display. It took a few pokes on the pad to unlock it.

Sid looked at him with raised eyebrows.

"I was sleeping," he said, rubbing an eye.

Sid slipped in and shut the door. "Your mother wants to know about the party."

Her New Year's Eve bash. Her *second* New Year's Eve bash, to appease their Chinese ancestors, and because Austro needed no excuse to throw consecutive station-wide parties.

Happening in a couple weeks, February 17 if the shop windows were correct. Ms. Mom Lau always did things ahead of time.

Oh, yeah.

It was the Year of the Rooster. Wake up. Cock-a-doodle-doo.

He started to laugh.

"Ryan?" Sid's eyes narrowed.

Oh, bad. Bad if he got caught. So he stifled the giggles, sniffed and went to his guitar and picked it up, plucking a few strings at random. "I'm going to die if I have to sit through her friends again, Sid. Don't tell me you want another few hours of"—he pitched his voice—*"Isn't he so handsome? What a nice young man. Fetch me that wine, would you, nice young man?"*

Sid didn't look enthusiastic about the prospect. He might've loved Mom Lau, but her friends were another matter. "I was thinking. Miyasake—remember him? He's a friend of your father's—he told me last week that his flash is open to us if we wanted." Sid grinned.

Ryan smiled back and stopped fussing with the guitar, wrapping his arms around it instead, like a lover. "You're beautiful. I'd kiss you if it wouldn't make my mother jealous."

Sid and his mother were sleeping together. They had been since before Earth, since he was fourteen in fact. It was a scab on his and Sid's friendship and the more he picked at it, the more it bled. And the deeper the scar. So he'd learned not to pick at it—too much. Even though he doubted the scab would ever fall away. It was a permanent mark on his inner skin and maybe Sid saw it when they were together. When had they not been together in the last seven years? It got to the point where people who didn't know why Sid followed him around would ask if they were a couple. It had stopped being funny after Sid and Mom Lau got together and Sid started to get impatient with misunderstandings.

Maybe Sid had learned to overlook the scab. At least Sid seemed able to sleep in off-shifts, and sleep with Mom Lau without a complaint. So good for Sid, good for Mom Lau who complained about the captain's absence, and good for Ryan that he didn't make himself bleed with anger, otherwise he'd drive himself mad just thinking about it.

Five years of them and maybe he was getting used to it. Being pissed all the time when he had to look at them twenty-four seven was just too much effort. Half the time he hated them for it, but then he just couldn't be bothered for the other half. Sid was good-looking, young, and accessible.

His mother was good-looking, young-looking, and accessible. His father was one of the most feared captains in the Hub fleet but both of them seemed capable of overlooking that fact too.

The sex must be outstanding.

Ah, dammit. Sometimes he couldn't control his thoughts in a sail. They buffeted his brain and he just rolled with them.

He couldn't remember if Sid had said anything in the last five minutes. Sid was looking at him a bit suspiciously.

"Ryan, maybe I should take you to the doctor. You really need to—Are you still not sleeping?"

Sleeplessness made him silly. So did Silver, but he didn't tell that to his bodyguard.

He was zoning again. He smiled at Sid and held out his arms, holding the guitar by its neck. "Cuddle with me, Timmy. I don't think Mom would mind."

He still liked to tease Sid about it sometimes, just so Sid didn't mistake his bodyguard job for a parenting one.

Sid said, half serious, "Shut up with that, okay? So this is the plan: I convince your mother about the flash and you behave."

Behave? That was funny.

He let his arms drop and pouted. "Be my prince, Sid. Please? I can't live another day without you."

"Turn on your comp, your grandmother's on comm for you."

"Ugh, LO Lau?"

Grandmother Lau was the Austro-Earth Liaison Officer. He didn't like her as much as Dr. Grandma Ramcharan on Earth, Admiral Grandpa's wife.

Sid frowned at him. "You don't say that to her face, do you?"

"Of course not. Please."

"It's the admiral's wife. Go on, she's waiting."

"Well, you can leave first."

Sid walked out, all Marine about it, shutting the door. He did that when he was offended or fed up. Ryan laughed so hard he had to sit down. He missed the edge of the bed by a hand span, but saved the guitar on his lap.

He had to compose himself. Before Grandma saw him and recommended more shrink sessions.

He set the guitar on its stand and went over to the desk for his mobile comp, where he'd left it last shift. He hooked it behind his ear and slid down the eyeband. In seconds his optical implants (a sweet sixteen birthday present from Mom Lau) connected to the activation icon and he dived to the red cross symbol that was his grandmother's avatar and blinked an open code to it. Dr. Grandma's face bloomed in his field of vision, live, all the way from Earth, darting in coded quantum teleportations of light across the span of space, only a few moments lapsed.

The arcing wire with its InterFace bud attached to the eyeband sent his own image across to his grandmother's comp. He hoped he didn't look high.

"Hello, Ryan." She smiled, polished from the gray-lined hair pulled back from her face to her dark green suit tapered perfectly to her long frame.

He could tell from the tight smile that this wasn't just a social comm. And she was in her office, judging from the high leather chair behind her shoulders.

"What's wrong, Grandma? Is Grandpa all right?"

She dropped the edges of the smile. "Yes, he's fine. He's in London right now for a meeting."

The pause came unexpectedly when they both lit on the same thought. London had memories, most of them unpleasant. Ryan scratched his cheek, glad that Sid had left the room.

"Ah . . . that's good."

She didn't dwell on it. "He wanted me to tell you something before it hits the Send, since he's caught up right now." She leaned forward. "We got word a couple days ago that *Macedon* was attacked out at the Meridia mines. By pirates. She took heavy damage."

A couple days ago. His father's ship. That could mean this had happened weeks ago, out in deep space, in the Dragons, where time and ships in constant motion operated at a different relative rate from Earth or even Austro Station—any fixed object. Leaps cut the gaps but not enough to obliterate their effects. Meridia was nearer to the Dragons than the Rim, even though technically they called it a Rim colony. But it wasn't Austro.

Macedon hardly ever came this far into the Rim. So if she was damaged, or killed, that would be it. He'd never see his father again and the news would be too little too late.

It was the last thing he expected to hear. Even though his father fought with strits, symps, and pirates, it seemed a done deal that the captain of *Macedon* would always win his battles. Because he always had.

Ryan took a breath. "Heavy damage?"

"She's still spaceworthy, but she was boarded and it's pretty severe. Your grandfather had sent *Trinity* and *Arabia* out for a rendezvous but they didn't quite get there in time." She stared at him as if she expected a wall to come down.

He didn't know what to say. It wasn't like he could do anything, or like his father had even commed. His father hadn't commed for months, station time.

Was she leading up to something?

A curious numbness began to spread inside of him. From the sail, maybe. Dregs of the bullet ran through his bloodstream.

"Is he—all right?"

"They lost contact," she said, sounding almost apologetic. "He might be silent running or his comms might be out. *Trinity* says he leaped."

"Leaped? In a damaged ship?" Even *he* knew that was just shy of insane.

Grandma laced her fingers on the desk, her worried pose, when she didn't want to *look* worried. "He went after the pirates. One of the attacking ships was *Genghis Khan*."

He wracked his brain. Ah. The *Khan*. The pirate captain of that ship—Falcone, was it?—kept the Send occupied almost as much as the sympathizer leader, the Warboy, did. Falcone liked to follow in the wake of strit and symp attacks and steal people and resources for dealing on the black market, when he wasn't launching attacks himself and running the slave trade. Ryan's father, the captain of *Macedon*, hated the man and that was no secret.

But still—it was madness. What was his father thinking, leaping in a damaged ship just to get some criminals?

There was dedication and duty, and then there was obsession.

"Why doesn't the admiral—?" But he cut the thought before it could flower. He knew the answer already. Grandma knew it too; he watched her mouth tighten in chagrin. Grandpa couldn't tell the captain a thing from Earth's vantage, and in all likelihood his father wouldn't listen anyway. That was part of the reason Hub govies looked on deep-space captains with such suspicion and nervousness. People with ships full of deadly weapons who chose what orders they wanted to follow made great warriors but mercurial subordinates.

All well and good if strits were kept in their place by such captains, but it wasn't conducive to govie agendas sometimes. Or govie pride that hated to think they'd lost control of their star soldiers, or that anyone other than themselves was above the rules.

"The Send knows?" Ryan thought to ask, figuring what his mother must be doing now if she also knew.

And what was going to happen the moment he stepped into a public place.

"We got tipped that it's going to be 'casted in an hour. A leak on Earth's end, I don't know, but your grandfather's pretty angry."

He would be. He didn't like deep-space operations to be on transcasts. Unfortunately, Captain Azarcon was a favorite among meedees and the more he blew them off, the more they scrabbled after him.

"Why does my father *do* these things? Doesn't he realize how it looks?" The irritation came through without his logical consent, and he couldn't stop it. "Taking a beat-up ship into a leap just makes him look crazy. Kill his crew with it and he'll be court-martialed. I don't get him, Grandma."

Killing himself would be—

Selfish.

The thought angered Ryan. Beyond reason.

"Sweetheart," she said with a little sigh, "sometimes I don't understand him either. And I've known him since he was eighteen."

His father was adopted. Maybe that explained why the grandparents were sane and their son wasn't.

"Did you tell Mom?"

Please say yes.

But Dr. Grandma shook her head. "I thought it'd be better coming from you."

His grandparents didn't like dropping info about the captain on Mom Lau because it usually ended in virulent argument. With the captain inaccessible, the admiral often got the brunt of his mother's frustrations.

So they dumped it on him. They said they wanted him to take more emotional responsibility. Whatever that meant.

Denial wasn't healthy, Dr. Grandma had said.

Yeah, he'd answered. But it works.

They couldn't force him in some things, so they urged him in others.

Talk with your mother, they said.

He had to deal with Sid and Mom Lau.

Stop avoiding your father, Sid said.

His father who didn't have the decency to be around, or not to leap a damaged ship after pirates. So now what choice did anybody have but to worry and to blame?

Better not to know. Better not to wallow in it.

He said, Leave me the hell alone.

He just wanted to forget.

Dinner was always a sit-down affair, if Mom Lau wasn't working, in the dining room with the teardrop chandelier giving a golden glow. It warmed the gloss-striped, Wedgewood-blue walls. No Send (especially now), just soft music from the unit in the living room and little sounds from the kitchen as the cook prepared the dishes, then brought them out to the table.

Sid always ate with them as long as Mom Lau was there, sat usually on her right side, and Ryan slouched across from Sid on her left and played with his fork, looking at the two of them. Sid wore an expensive pale brown shirt that matched his eyes and smiled a lot at Mom Lau. They did that all the time now since he and Sid came back from Earth. They didn't even bother trying to hide it around him anymore. Three years away was too long for no bed business, Ryan supposed.

Sid caught him watching and leaned back in his seat. He had the good grace to look a bit bashful.

Ryan mouthed to him, Flash. And stuck his fork into his sirloin steak.

Sid owed him. Sid had better be convincing. He wanted to go to that party instead of suffering at home in *wei-lu* with a boring brigade of his mother's friends, and Sid had better do his job or he was going to make Sid's life difficult.

"Song, about New Year's Eve," Sid said. "I was thinking I could take Ryan to a flash house instead. He'll be bored here and I can run a team to scope the place beforehand. We'll make sure it's clean." He didn't mean clean like the apartment core, all open door chic, that new style bally-hooed on the TrendSend; he meant clean like *no assassins* clean.

"Do you think it'd be safe?" Mom Lau asked Sid, except she called him *Tim. Tim, do you think it would be safe for my endangered nineteen-year-old son?* Endangered like all those fuzzy animals on Earth with exotic eyes and woebegone faces.

Never mind he'd never been violently accosted by anyone in his whole life, not even by panhandlers on the pedway or protesters on the steps of Parliament, back on Earth. That thing at Hong Kong hadn't been because of him or even his grandfather. It was just because of the Hub in general. Like the dock bombing a few years ago, that sympathizer protest. Isolated incidents, mostly.

"I'll make it safe. He's just going to sulk if he's stuck here," Sid continued, the real reason Mom Lau would agree to let him out of his box. Nobody liked an insolent son around their colleagues.

"With what's been on the Send lately? I don't know if that's a good idea, Tim." She sipped her red wine.

They liked to talk around the fact of his father. Mom Lau had predictably blown up (in private) at the captain's actions, but by the time she had to make a statement on the Send, she'd acquired her proper face.

My husband has been a successful deep-space captain in this war for over a decade. I trust his judgment, especially where it concerns his own ship, and so should the Hub.

"New Year's isn't for another two weeks," Ryan said. "Things'll die down by then."

"What's wrong with spending the evening with your family? Your grandmother will be here."

LO Lau. That was supposed to be incentive?

He made a face. "I don't like the way she always blames me for the messed-up state of the universe."

His mother stared at him. "Don't be absurd."

"In absentia of the captain. You know it, Mom." His vegetables had gone soft on the warming center of the plate. He hated gooey vegetables and mashed the peas and string beans with the flat of his fork until they looked like guacamole. "She gives you a headache too. I don't even know why you bother to invite her. She doesn't like us. She hasn't liked you since you married the captain, isn't that right?"

He was pissed. He didn't know exactly why, but lately all he had to do was look at his mother and he wanted to—

Jump off a balcony, or something.

Push her face into the salad.

His mother glared at him like she was halfway to throwing something at his head.

Sid nudged his ankle under the table and widened his eyes at him. This wasn't helping, he meant.

But it was true. It was all true. It was so true it was pathetic.

"Your grandmother," Mom Lau said, "to whom you owe respect, is your blood." And if that wasn't bad enough, she added, "And mine."

Unlike Admiral Ashrafi and Dr. Hannah Ramcharan.

It was a good thing their families were separated by stars and planets.

"She went to Earth when I was there, Mom, and didn't once contact me. Tell me why I owe her anything."

Sid stepped on the toe of Ryan's right shoe. "About the flash," Sid murmured. "Song . . ."

She still looked at Ryan, one hand on her wineglass and shards of chandelier light in her eyes. "It's not a good idea. I want you here."

"Well, I don't want to be here. So I'm going. Sid's going to do his Marine thing and we'll have fun. You can ward off Grandmother's insinuations with vodka and caviar. Thanks."

"He means to ask politely," Sid said, kicking his foot this time.

His mother didn't believe that. "All you've done since coming back from Earth is go to parties or hole up in your room, Ryan. You won't register with Austro University to finish your courses and I'm tired of you just flopping around the residence with no thoughts of the future."

He looked up at the molded ceiling. White angel images and curlicues swirled above his head.

"I don't ask for much, Ryan. This isn't a large thing to do—it's being with your family and talking with my friends. Considerately."

Her friends. Not his friends.

She knew he had no real friends.

And she wanted Sid around for it. They never did anything in public but they still liked to orbit each other.

Except Sid was only twenty-seven and he preferred flash houses too. Of course he would never *say* that.

"Mom. I'm going to that flash. Don't try to order me around." He finished his wine and got up from the table.

"Where are you going?" she and Sid asked.

"Away. While I can."

"Sit down," his mother said, meaning it. Her eyes were hard.

Sid got up too, depositing his napkin on the table. Ryan was sure they exchanged looks, but he had his back to them. The cook stood in the dining-room doorway with a platter of fruit slices for dessert. Ryan took the other entrance into the living room, going for the foyer.

"Ryan." Sid followed him.

"You're my bodyguard, not my keeper."

"Hold on, at least. Take your jacket. I won't stop you, but I'm coming with you."

He breathed out. He took the jacket Sid offered him and tried not to hit Sid or the other Marine that stood by the doors like a statue. The third Marine that they lived with must've been in the security office, monitoring traffic outside of the residence.

Everywhere he went people watched. Except for in his bedroom and bathroom. But if he stayed there all the time he was going to go crazy.

He had a bloody right to take a walk if he wanted, dammit, without having to worry about what people thought or what people might do, or if it pleased his mother or not.

"This isn't a good idea," Sid said, watching him like he was going to explode any second.

But he didn't explode. He opened the door and walked out.

"She doesn't understand," Sid said as they rode the lev down to the bottom of the executive tower. "You need to tell her about Earth. About London."

Ryan folded his arms. "Just shut up, okay? You're here because you have to be, not because I want to talk. Better yet, why don't you go back upstairs and bang her while I'm out?"

Sid grabbed his shoulder, twisting the red silk of his jacket. Ryan shoved at him and both of them ended up slamming into the mirrored lev walls. He got a swipe across Sid's cheek but Sid jammed a forearm up under his chin and shook him once, hard.

"Settle down!"

His head rang. The doors opened. Three people stood there waiting, and stared. Their eyes darted.

He broke from Sid's grip, pushed him aside, and strode out. Fixed his jacket and shoved his hair from his face. At least no meedees were waiting in ambush, but he'd give it time. Footsteps came up behind him and Sid slipped a hand around his right elbow, firm.

"Don't do that again. You don't run off from me in public, understand?"

His heart was thudding in his ears. He stared at the crowd going past him to offices and shops, flowing around the tall fountain that poured noise and water into its faux-stone basin. He wanted to disappear among it all.

It could all disappear so easily. Stations were vulnerable. All a symp terrorist or pirate had to do was muck up one of the many systems critical for supporting life. Sid had run it down for him years ago. Cut the heat and freeze people; slip a toxic gas into the ventilation system; cut oxygen so people would die of asphyxiation or carbon monoxide poisoning. Mess with the gravity. Plant a bomb near the energy towers.

And that would be it. Bodies everywhere. A dead puckered station for the Send to memorialize.

He had nightmares of it.

Sid squeezed his arm. "Ryan."

He looked up at his bodyguard. "I only want one thing, Sid. And you can't even do that."

He didn't mean the flash.

He started to walk, knowing his bodyguard would follow, and ignored the frozen hurt that impacted Sid's face just as sure as if he'd hit him.

They didn't get far before a Send holoboard scrolled a story about his father's recent activities. What they knew of it, which was just enough to create sufficient flak and piranhalike interest. People started to stare—from café tables lining the concourse, from small square public playgrounds surrounded by security and filled with nannies and their charges. The station was alive one way or another, on gold or blueshifts depending on where you worked, and the Send never went to sleep.

Neither did meedees. Sid saw them coming from branch corridors and propelled him around the fountain's wall-side, away from sight. He sat there behind some variegated greenery while Sid stood watch.

Alone, at least, though sound traveled through the leaves.

"Sources from the Dragons-Rim military depot, Meridia, say that two Komodo-class pirate ships attacked Captain Azarcon's *Macedon* from around the dark side of the Meridia moon. The spacecarrier sustained heavy damage, including substantial fire on their bay doors and escape pods, through which the pirate outriders boarded the Earth-Hub ship. This perhaps comes as no surprise to many that have been following the captain's career of late. Captain Azarcon has gone on record declaring pirates an equal menace to EarthHub's security as the sympathizer Warboy and the strits themselves. For the past few months, EarthHub Standard, he has targeted pirate ships, caches, and sinkholes—while relegating normal patrol routes along the Demilitarized Zone to other Hub ships. Does this give the Warboy and his strit benefactors free rein on our deep-space routes and free access to our deep-space stations? Later we will be speaking to EarthHub Centralist First Minister and presidential candidate Judy Damiani about her views on the captain's latest—"

They knew how to write those scripts, all right. Mention the Warboy and that moved everyone's mild interest into paranoid defense. The human sympathizer captain, stritified more than any other human symp in the galaxy (if you believed the Send), had been terrorizing deep space and half of the Hub's Rimstations for more than a decade. The fact that particular symp was still flying free incensed Centralists—everyone, really—although it was more than rhetoric to the people living in the cross fire.

Hatred begat hatred, as the old saying went.

Nobody ever shut up about it, as if talking about the war made it any better for anybody. As if talking about his father made the captain change his behavior.

Maybe it was better for people with agendas, like that vitriolic Damiani woman who fashioned herself one of the revered signers of the EarthHub Coalition. Meanwhile, Admiral Grandpa had told *him* that people in EarthHub Command suspected the Family of Humanity terrorist organization had ties to Centralists on Earth and elsewhere.

If he had to draw a map of all the layers of politics that weighed down his family, he'd run out of comp memory.

Sid knew. Sid was watching him every other glance, while watching the passersby, probably wondering when he wanted to leave.

He could leave. If there was actually somewhere better to go.

Back up to the residence meant facing off with Mom Lau again and he couldn't look at her. Half the time he confused her, the other half he probably infuriated her. It went both ways, and he couldn't bring himself to talk to her, explain anything, or even move from his misty spot near this Gaia-inspired stone fountain.

It hid him from most of the concourse traffic, but also drowned out a lot of the ambient noise.

So he didn't hear the man approach, just saw Sid move suddenly in front of him and put out a hand to keep somebody back.

"Ryan!" the man called. "Ryan Azarcon, please, just a few questions."

"Step back, sir." Sid had a hand inside his jacket and the other on the man's chest.

"It's not about the transcast," the man insisted. An old man who nevertheless tried to step around Sid's tall body.

Ryan stood but didn't approach.

Sid was a wall. "Step *back,* sir. I won't ask again."

The man held up his empty hands in a casual gesture of goodwill. "Easy, Corporal. I know you have his best interests at heart, but I'm not armed. My name is Arthur Pompeo, I'm writing a biography on Cairo Azarcon and I'd like to—"

Ryan said, "You're what?" Which he shouldn't have done because it gave Sid mixed signals. Let the man talk to him or not?

He'd heard of Arthur Pompeo. An old era meedee who'd shipped out with carriers (but never *Macedon*) more than two decades ago, at the height of the deep-space war. He wasn't some earnest segment producer for the SendTertain. He had a mantle of award statues behind his name.

And, damn it all, he was researching the captain?

"Ryan," Pompeo said, standing his ground despite Sid's blocking shoulder. "Just ten minutes of your time, that's all I ask."

His mother would kill him. The captain would put a bounty on his head. He didn't even entertain the thought.

"Sid, let's go." He walked around the greenery and headed back to the levs at the base of their tower.

"Ryan, listen to me, you can shed some light on your father's actions. You can help him!"

"Not with your words," he said over his shoulder. Sid walked close behind him, at a clip.

"You should know that your grandmother Yvonne Lau has already spoken to me. I offer you the opportunity to refute her."

Bastard.

Bitch.

Ryan stopped, pushed Sid aside, and walked back. "What did she say?"

Pompeo's pale gray eyes evaluated him. "Sit with me and we can go over it. And I'll take anything you want me to have, on or off the record."

Sid said, "Ryan, we're leaving. Now."

Ryan watched the old man. A war dog maybe as much as any captain. "Did you speak to my mother?"

"Not yet."

Sid said, "You'll have to go through her office, Mr. Pompeo, and we'd appreciate it if you didn't harass Mr. Azarcon outside of official channels."

Ryan thought, Mr. Azarcon can speak for himself.

"I'm available anytime," Pompeo said to him, ignoring Sid. "Here's my comm number." He held out a finger-sized chipsheet.

Ryan knew he'd have to give something up if he wanted to know what LO Lau had said. And that was out of the question. Pompeo didn't offer a talk out of any sense of fair play. It was all just to get his story.

And why should Ryan care what was said anyway? It was the captain's problem. And the captain was in deep space.

Where he couldn't get harassed except by strits and pirates, but maybe he preferred them, over all, to meedees.

Never mind his family, who got the brunt of people like Pompeo.

Never mind them at all.

Because Mom Lau could handle meedees, that was her job, and Ryan Azarcon was incidental to that equation.

Talk to your father, his family liked to tell him.

But just not over the Send.

He didn't take the chipsheet. He turned his back on Pompeo and felt the old man's annoyance all the way up to the apartment.

Sid must have worked some sexy voodoo on Mom Lau during their sleepshift because she approached Ryan at breakfast next shift, dressed for her day in a subdued cream-and-chocolate-colored outfit, her demeanor equally subdued. She brought her caff to the table nook under the high umbrella of fake morning light, and sat across from him and his slate, which he liked to read while he ate so people didn't talk to him.

"Ryan," she said, smoothing a long lock of dark hair from her cheek and resting an elbow on the gray tabletop. "About New Year's Eve . . ."

He tried to remember if he'd moved his injet with its half a capsule of Silver from the airvent to under his mattress. Sid would be doing his goldshift inspection of the premises right now.

" . . . I think it'll be fine if you went to the flash with Sid, but only if you promise not to ditch him."

She wasn't joking.

"I won't ditch him, Mom. Maybe I'll get him laid, you know, to loosen him up."

She frowned, then hid it behind her mug.

"Besides," he said, "I planned on going anyway. Just so you know."

He wouldn't be controlled as if he were twelve again. Time his mother caught up to that fact.

She looked into his face. He thought she'd argue with him or verbally knock him down, but instead she just seemed kind of tired.

Wistful.

He caught her looking at him like that sometimes, ever since they discovered he was now a head taller and she could no longer comfortably put her hands on his shoulders.

He looked down at his slate.

"Tim told me Arthur Pompeo approached you last shift," she said, without addressing his declaration of emancipation.

He wasn't sure if that annoyed him or not. So he just answered her. "Yeah. Ambushed." He tapped his slate to flip the screen. On it was the tour schedule of one of his favorite music artists. Of course Austro would be a stop.

"Don't give him any quotes," she said. "Let me handle him."

"Maybe you should be telling Grandmother Lau."

"Oh, I'll be speaking with her this shift." She leaned back and crossed her legs.

His mother had married the captain against LO Lau's explicit wishes. LO Lau hadn't liked the captain's attitude. *If you think he's a bastard now, you should've seen him when he was younger,* Grandmother Lau had told Ryan on his nineteenth birthday. *No respect whatsoever for superiors.* Grandma Ramcharan had said a different thing: *He only respects people he thinks deserve it.*

The marriage had taken a certain amount of rebellion on his mother's part, but she paid for it now. LO Lau barely spoke to them and used her busy work schedule as an excuse. But it seemed she had time to speak to meedees like Arthur Pompeo.

The look on his mother's face now said it all. The captain was *her* territory and no matter their arguments in private, Mom Lau didn't want their problems in the public sphere.

"Does this mean you're uninviting Grandmother Lau for *wei-lu*?" He couldn't help it; he smiled from under his brows.

It was difficult for her to resist his smiles; he'd learned that early.

She laughed, stood, and rubbed his hair as she passed him toward the zap counter where the breakfast omelet sat, fragrant from warmth. She'd picked up that gesture from Sid, who messed up Ryan's appearance at every opportunity.

"Don't push it, Ryan. She's still my mother and I have to respect that."

He bit down lightly on the tines of his fork and watched his mother's attention shift as Sid walked into the kitchen. Her smile widened and the affection in her voice didn't go away when she greeted him. Like a girl.

Grandmother Lau's defiant daughter; she'd been that long before she'd been his mother.

She didn't seem like his mother when she lit up for Sid, who was nearly twenty years her junior, despite the fact they *looked* the same age.

Mom Lau was a person too. At least, that was what Sid would like him to think. A woman fed up with an absentee husband.

And Ryan couldn't help it. Sometimes he saw it despite himself.

Damn them.

Ryan dreamed he was back in Hong Kong, before the embassy attack, when he and Sid had gone to the district of

Tsuen Wan to visit the Yuen Yuen Institute. It was a monastery complex unlike anything on Austro Station or anywhere in space, he'd bet. It was rooted into the earth, old like the religions here were old, born long before humans had ever set foot off their planet and started to debate whether aliens were also creations of God. In the Great Temple hand-carved statues stood in representation of the three historic philosophies of the city: Taoism, Buddhism, and Confucianism. He didn't really know anything about any of them, but the statues overpowered him, made him feel small, fragile, and ephemeral. He would never outlast the ages like these man-made creations; he'd never stand for anything that profound. Incense weighted the air, the pungent smell of this land. He wondered if he could get high off it.

In his dream he saw ancient marching armies in the lines of rising smoke.

He and Sid held slender, fragrant sticks and waved them around like they later would with chopsticks on a market street. Ribbon tails of incense trailed in their wake, drifting for the ancient generals that lined the walls in the temple to step on. Images of deified men, old war heroes with severe faces and funny outfits, and he thought of his father up on that wall, smelling all this incense. He wondered if his father would step down from the wall and follow him and Sid around the city, begging for offerings.

But no, the captain never begged, and he would never follow his son anywhere.

Not even when the temple blew up and the ashes and incense stifled him, pushed him to the ground and onto his back as if a demon sat on his chest. He tried to take a full breath and couldn't, tried to move or open his eyes or call out to Sid, but he couldn't do anything except let that demon dig through his shirt and his body and clamp a fist around his heart.

It felt like some stone force was crushing his world beneath an unrelenting pestle of accusation.

Ryan, what did you do to yourself?

He thought he felt tiles under his back and heard tap water running. Smelled the sharp perfume of hotel soap. Dim slits of light bled into his eyes.

He needed to wake up.

Pounding drove him into the double layer of his mattress.

Eyes opened on his familiar blue ceiling, high and blurry, clouded by round white lights. His fists twisted his clothing and slowly, slowly he began to feel the fabric beneath his fingers. The worn T-shirt. The damp skin of his stomach grazing his knuckles. The hard length of the injet stuck beneath his left leg.

That hadn't been a smooth sail at all. It had started so sweet, like all the times before, dripping bliss through his limbs and down his pants.

But then he'd dreamed.

It took several deep breaths to slow his heart, but the pounding didn't stop.

It was at his door.

It was New Year's Eve again and he was going to a flash.

"Ryan! I need you out here!"

His mother.

"Yeah," he said, hoarse, and then louder, "okay!"

"I want you to clean up before the guests arrive!" she harped. "I want you to *help* me this shift, Ryan."

"I'm going to the flash!" he shouted back, through the door because he couldn't move yet, his brain felt wrapped in dirty sheets.

"You're going to help me while Sid checks with

Miyasake. Now get your ass out here, it's already oh-nine-thirty."

In his goldshift. He'd eaten breakfast at 0800 because Mom Lau insisted, and then gone right back to bed. To sail.

He rolled over and pushed his nose into the pillow. It didn't smell like anything but his own shampoo.

He missed Shiri's flowery scent, of a sudden.

"Ryan!"

Sid this time. Sid who had the keycode and wasn't afraid to use it.

"All right! You bunch of slavers."

He hauled himself up and went to the door, stumbling on the edge of the rug. He managed to get it open and confronted Sid's spic-and-span appearance.

"I was asleep," he said. "Or trying to."

Sid stared at him. A long second.

Damn.

Sid said quietly, "Go wash your face, then come out here and help your mother."

He didn't have the strength to argue even if he wanted to. So he went to his bathroom and told the lights *emphatically* to stay at a comfortable forty percent, and bent over his sink while the tap ran. The water slid off his nose in pale silver drops.

After, he went out to the hallway and shuffled down to the lit foyer to meet Mom Lau. She stood waiting for him while Marine Perry kept watch by the ceiling-high hibiscus plant, not looking at anything in particular.

The guards stayed out of domestic arguments.

Mom Lau looked at him in the way only mothers could. *I gave birth to you and I'll remind you of it when it's convenient.*

She had a whole work ethic mania. *The privileged should*

still participate. Hard labor and all that so nobody felt guilty about those poor people in the belt mines.

"Start in the kitchen," she said. "Lars is in there, he'll tell you what needs to be done. The caterers are due any minute and I need to tend to that."

She had a slate propped against her hip, so she took it and her annoyance to the living room where she was finalizing dining details over comm. Just left him there in the foyer with Marine Perry and the plant. She didn't understand why he was wasting away his life.

He hadn't told her about his dreams. Maybe Sid had. Not that it would've made a difference.

"Sid's gone to the flash house?" he asked Marine Perry.

"Yes, sir," Perry said.

"He didn't take you?"

Perry said, "He went plainclothes with other Marines from the barracks."

Better that than putting barracks Marines in the residence. Perry and Finlay, Sid's direct subordinates, were used to the household's dynamic.

They weren't going to help set up for the party, that was for sure. That was *his* job. So he spent a couple hours walking domed trays, silver cutlery, and linen napkins back and forth from the kitchen to the dining corner, where a long glossy table of food sat waiting for the devouring mouths of Austro's rich elite. Carved duck, roast pork. Quack and oink. Appropriate.

Most of the apartment scheme wasn't quite battleship gray, but it was close. It all went with the Zen silver in the kitchen. Color 11905 in Austro's Beautifix Design Interiors shop. Nice young men who went to Austro Academy as a kid knew these things, especially when they lived with mothers who liked to scroll catalogues over breakfast tea.

The apartment shone like bleached teeth, frenzily cleaned to sweep away ill fortune this shift. Chinese tradition.

The Send scrolled on the long gold-lit wall above the faux fireplace, for background visual ambience. It was linked to the Dharma music 'cast and had a lot of calm imagery of rotating planets, fields of green, slowmo twirling children. Everything that had nothing to do with a station in the Rim, or a war going on in the Dragons. Or anything in life that Ryan was aware of.

Eventually his Silver-soaked dislocation went away, leaving only an airy buzz reverberating through his system. When he was done with the drone-help routine he ran and slid on sock feet to the end of the hall, skidding to the middle of the bedroom until he shored up against the rug. Apartment surfing. (Quickest way to get shot? Wear shoes on his mother's marble floors.) The overheads automatically popped up, on eighty percent, glowy white.

Just like heaven.

"Music, track five. Eighty-five volume."

The kind his mother hated.

Chinese New Year's Eve. *Kung hei fat choy.* Everyone was going glittered out and glossed. Some even costumed. All the rich stitches would get the best new clothes and haircuts and parade on the decks like the flash whores they were. He got invited places, of course, but nobody expected him to orbit them all. Not when Sid orbited him for more than just show. Vid stars had designer bodyguards and wore them like high fashion, but his was for real because Admiral Grandpa thought something might actually happen to him, Captain Azarcon's son. Nothing had, of course, except nosey meedees and frivolity on the TrendSend, but nobody found that invasive enough for military action.

Meanwhile, his father was still out there making enemies.

Sometimes he asked Sid to demonstrate how to work that bodyguard sidearm, but Sid never agreed. Too much glass and marble in the apartment, maybe.

For the flash he dressed in white, with a silver dragon writhing up one leg to mirror the elaborate dancers on the main concourse this time of year. Sid couldn't miss him in a crowd if he was blind, but it wasn't so glitter that it would stand out. Ryan knew that would be a consideration. It was always a consideration.

He zipped himself up just as Sid walked in the room as if he had conjugal rights, not even knocking on the door. His was the only door in the apartment, a condition he insisted upon when he returned from Earth. Everywhere else was partitions, the chic open concept he hated, with funhouse mirror-grid that tossed his distorted image back at him everywhere he went. As if he needed the reminder.

The maid had a mantra, a proverb from her Spokes colony culture, which she always made a point of telling him, especially when he locked her out of his room: *Privacy is what you shut your mouth about. Denial is what you shut your eyes against.*

The help saw everything. He was sure his old nanny, long released except from a confidentiality agreement, could make multimillions if she dared.

Who knew what the guards thought.

Well, he could guess what Sid thought. And knew.

Sid looked him up and down and gestured to his head. "What'd you do now?"

His hair. He liked to experiment. Right now it was bright blond and shaped at a sharp angle so it fell over one side of his face. He'd decided on it in the bathroom, even cut it himself. Nobody would recognize him at first glance.

"Thought you'd like it, Timmy. I did it just for you."

Sid pursed his lips and chose not to answer.

Down the hall, tinkly party music dripped from the walls, all air and ice. Like his mother. Sid folded his arms, leaned on the wall as Ryan put on his shoes, and half yawned. "I cleared the flash house for Your Highness, and cleared it with Her Majesty. Actually I cleared about five flashes, so I hope you didn't blab to anyone where you were going to be."

"Of course I didn't. I don't talk to anyone besides you, don't you know?"

Which was depressingly close to the truth.

Sid handed him a silver panic ring, just in case, with a tiny white contact pad where a gem might've been, if the ring weren't designed to alert Sid and his security if Ryan hit it in distress. A nice reminder that they were not just two guys going out to celebrate like the rest of the station.

They made it to the front doors before his mother emerged from the kitchen to bid them farewell. She kissed his cheek (and thankfully didn't kiss Sid). "Enjoy your party. Come back by oh-one-hundred, okay?"

"I'll take that as a joke," Ryan said.

At least she didn't say anything about the shoes and her marble floors. Or his hair. But she was used to the things he did to his hair.

An exodus of partyers from neighboring residences walked the plush green and gold corridors of the executive level res ring in Module 3, where they lived, heading out to their own dates and clubs. Festive red decorations plastered the walls and doors. Security guard Sam greeted them at the bank of mirrored levs in their wing and said hello to Ryan, to Sid. Hello to the crowd of twenty people, in their jewelry and silk.

Ryan ignored them and they got the message.

They waited for the lev.

And waited.

It was a tall tower.

A transparent plexpane wall separated this outer ring from the module's core towers, separated them from the ped and podway ramparts that connected the residency rings to the commercial center. The view was nice enough through the panes, with a suicidal drop. The three core towers were lit around the windows in all colors, blinking. If the lights spoke they'd say, *Xin Nien Kuai Le.* Happy New Year. They really should've said, Get drunk and laid. Because that was the plan.

The flash was at the Dojo, a Module 7 club down by one of the primary dockrings and in Austro's main concourse, easy access for ships. It was kind of a walk to get there.

The lev finally arrived and everyone jostled in. It was so secure they didn't feel the drop.

"We could've taken your mother's pod," Sid said when they eventually exited the lev into the echoing public pod terminal.

"I'd rather walk."

It gave Sid (and his plainclothes coterie of fellow guards) more work to do but at this time of year, out for the blueshift, Ryan liked to see the performers in their martial-moving, serpentine dragon and lion costumes, with their rich embroidery and snapping jaws. Some free-floating holo images of the same animals sank and soared over the heads of everyone. Lions brought good luck and warded off evil. It was a quaint thought, a familiar sight from consecutive years of celebrations. An explosion of people on deck, like festive confetti, made him just another partyer. He could be normal here, despite bodyguard attachments, and just *walking* was more normal than being whisked in private pods here and there at odd unexpected times.

A parade of peacocked citizens and visitors streamed by, some of them trailing lit streamers behind them like children. They were loud, a constant rumble in Ryan's ears to match the twin public pods that riproared through the tunnels. The pods swallowed up the crowd and disgorged them in a steady rhythm of lights and noise. All the chrome and steel of the terminal reflected the energy and rainbow festivity, a sea of mangled faces in mirrors.

"You're not into anything you shouldn't be, are you?" Sid asked, just under the racket of the pods and people.

"What?"

Sid liked to blindside him. He said, while his gaze roamed around for enemies: "Ryan, you aren't doing anything stupid, are you?"

"You mean out for the shift with you instead of a pretty girl?"

Sid looked at him for a flat moment, his Marine face, not his co-conspirator face. "Don't screw with me in this, all right?"

He had a retort behind his teeth about screwing and with whom. But he didn't say it.

"I'm good, Sid. Okay?"

Sid locked his glance and made it a stare. "You are."

"I am. Really. Stop worrying."

Sid touched his back briefly. "I do worry, you know."

He meant above and beyond his job. Ryan knew it. In quiet moments it made him both pleased and depressed, because Sid was supposed to be there for him like he had been when Ryan was twelve, when the only thing between them had been Sid's duty.

He was fourteen when he heard the noises for the first time, in that open-door chic apartment, the soft voices from behind his mother's partition. He went to the kitchen for some water, which meant going by Sid's bedroom, which was next to his, and when he looked in Sid's bed was empty. Then he passed his mother's room and recognized the low voices. The next morning there were empty wineglasses in the sink—two.

It became this ugly thing between them, a squatting spider nobody wanted to kill.

Yet Sid still worried, maybe out of guilt, maybe out of true affection, Ryan didn't count on anything anymore, and Sid made it a point to spend off-duty time with him after Spring Break, had even taught him how to ride horses, and there had been some respite in that.

But reality and the Send had a way of intruding. And ultimately nobody was reliable, not for the important things.

Sid's concern gnawed at him. Fatigued him. He didn't feel like going to the flash anymore, thanks to Sid's sudden need for honesty, even though Fara might be there and Fara could jack him in. Surely Tyler could, even though he got tired of dealing with Tyler, that was why he went straight to Fara now.

But that last sail had been bad. Maybe he needed to lay off for a while. Maybe the Silver contributed to his inertia. He didn't want to end up like some strung-out tunnel kid, like the ones who dotted the podways like specks of dirt. You saw them everywhere if you looked.

"Gotta eat," one kid said, hunched down by the wall looking up at Ryan as he passed. The kid's eyes were blue, his face curiously cherubic. A little homeless angel, like in the charity ads that sometimes mugged him on the concourse.

"Sorry," Ryan said. "I—"

Sid propelled him into the pod. "Don't talk to them."

"Or what?" Ryan tugged out of his hold and sat. Sid held one of the vertical bars and sank down beside him as the pod racketed forward.

"Let me do my job," he said. The commstud in his ear

linked him back to the home Marines. Maybe they had the music on, otherwise what was he listening to all the time?

Eventually they changed from pod to lev and dropped down the station core. Then they walked some more, through wide corridors flanked by darkened offices, then shops and restaurants littered with holo-ads and the mosh scents of people and food. The concourse in Module 7 was even more crowded for Chinese New Year's Eve than normal, with all of the ship crews and Austro citizens mingled together in general revelry. Sid kept close, one hand hovering at Ryan's back as if someone was going to snatch him out of midair. Things got more crowded the closer they got to the multilevel den district.

Citizens called this district the Red River. It sat at the bottom of a spiraling ramp, a descent into sin. Stark fluorescence from the main level disappeared into seductive shadow. The doors were opaque glass, lit by signs and symbols, the names and stamps of the individual clubs and dens. Marks of the Beast, all the religiosos said. People flowed in and out, hopping the blueshift, releasing a blur of music into the corridors. Heavy bass. Echoing voices. The complicated dance rhythms of wild drums. Ryan's gut shivered as half-naked women brushed by, smelling of cigret smoke and citric perfume. Some of them smiled at him but Sid moved him along. They weren't going to cruise, even though he was hardly recognizable in the skittering darkness.

Caution. Always caution.

The Dojo was near the end of the lower district arm. After a walk through the security arch (Sid beeped with his gun, but he'd arranged to get passed through) they entered on the heels of a group of kids dressed all in black and white. In the brighter entrance light Ryan recognized some faces—kid celebrities famous across the Hub and older socialites that liked them young. Tyler Coe, leaning against a fish tank post with two women on either side of him, jerked his chin when their eyes met. Ryan knew he was jacked for the party, if only he could dodge Sid long enough. One small push of Silver shouldn't be so bad.

Images blinked from the walls, actors in ancient Earth battle scenes, melding and shifting in real time on a fabricated digiset. Lights lanced down, moving all around the dancers on both tiers. Silver and gold. Blue and purple. Red. He caught glimpses of costumes among the regular flashwear: animals from Earth, bizarre robots, exaggerated uniforms, opposite genders, and a couple brave souls dressed as strits with white faces and coiled clothing like those dead Egyptians he'd read about in primary school. If they were lucky some drunk patron wouldn't mistake them for the real aliens and try to kill them.

But the war was far from this flash house, and far from him.

Scoping the crowd, feeling the music start to animate his limbs, he caught the unnaturally green eyes of a cat. Lenses or implants, who knew, but he couldn't mistake which way she looked. She smiled at him, tongue between her teeth. Her costume was skintight black, with a diamond choker and a tail like a whip. Tiger stripes of black paint flared on her forehead and teased the delicate lines of her exposed collarbone.

"Mee-*yow*," he said, elbowing Sid. "No way she's hiding anything in that, huh." There wasn't anywhere to hide a thought in that outfit, much less a weapon.

Sid laughed just under the music and bent to his ear. "Stay near the edges so I can see you." Then Sid gave his back a little push toward the girl and Ryan went, grinning.

She met him halfway and hooked a long, gold-tipped finger into the backwaist of his pants, reaching around him all familiar. Pretty soon he was up against her breasts and the firm plane of her stomach, dancing the way you did when you knew how the song would end. The sweet smoke of her perfume wrapped around his head and made him thirsty. So he kissed her openmouthed and she tasted like her scent.

Who needed Silver when you had women?

It was all perfect with potential.

She leaned hard against his chest. Her breasts urged him through the thin layer of his sweat-dampened shirt, and he laughed. This was trouble—the good kind.

Then her head lolled back and he zoomed on the wide, fixed points of her green eyes.

He wasn't holding her anymore; he was holding her up.

They weren't dancing now.

Colors ranged across her dark skin like a station in distress. Energetic bodies moved in and out of shadow at the edges of his sight. He touched her hair. Wet. He pulled his fingers away. Under the flashing lights they were covered in iridescent purple.

They felt red.

The music gave one long, eternal beat.

His arms gave way.

He looked down where she'd slid from his body to the floor.

One moment to the next, a blink or a breath, and a small part of him disappeared up into the lights and smoke.

Again.

And again.

A slow fall.

A crumbled building. A tumbled body.

Blood spread from beneath her head, reaching to him like claws. Pointing in accusation.

This should be him.

He knew it like he knew his own name.

Blood on his hands. Lights in his eyes. A dead girl lay at his feet but he was the one who was supposed to be there, like that.

Nobody noticed yet in the high and happy air of celebration. Arms above their heads, hair swinging, hips grinding in a mirror of sexual abandonment—the flash crowd just kept dancing.

He tapped his panic ring. Twice. Five times.

The music thrummed like the blood beneath his skin, drumming away from him. And she was on the floor, arms cast to the side as if she waited. For something. Somebody knocked him in the back and he pitched forward, slipped, went down with one knee on the girl, his hand by her head where it was wet.

He recoiled, wiped at his shirt. Fast. Just a drink he spilled, maybe. Just a drink. He rubbed his cheek to swipe the sweat but felt it get stickier. So then he rubbed with the back of his hand, smudging what was there. Tears. He knew they weren't tears but he told himself they were tears.

"Sid," he said aloud. But not loud enough.

This music.

This music wouldn't stop.

If someone was shooting at him, nobody would hear it.

"Sid—"

The lights cut down in wild patterns. Somebody stepped on his hand. He yelped and shoved, staggered up and turned. Looking.

"Sid!"

Sid had watched him dance with the cat. Ryan had seen him leaning at the bar, smiling. He'd watched with a gun under his jacket and Ryan was safe in the way you were safe when you took your life for granted.

He twisted in the crowd, looked up at the second level. Nothing but shadows and wild lights. Some people stared down in his direction, or not, it was impossible to see clearly. Tubes of drink could've been guns, he didn't know. The music pounded out of sync with his heartbeat. A frenzied dancer brushed his shoulder, eyes blown wide by Silver and alcohol. Ryan backed up, hit someone else, and turned full around in defense. The dancer saw the woman on the floor, even through the drugs. He looked at Ryan as if it were his fault.

Ryan twisted and pushed against the gyrating bodies. Hot, slick arms. Bare shoulders and muscled backs, moving him away from his direction. Shouts rose up but it was lost in the music. Or it was the music. He couldn't see Sid; his bodyguard was nowhere in this hell. It was loud and long and he was alone in it.

For seconds. Minutes. Hours.

Heartbeats.

Then Sid materialized, clawing forward through a writhing flow of people. Stupid oblivious people.

A light exploded above Ryan. It was louder than the music. It punctured the beat.

And he was down.

Down with his arms over his head and breath shooting out so fast he felt deflated, on the verge of darting about the room.

Everyone ran now, stepping over one another like colorful insects in an upended colony.

Someone yelled, "Shots fired! Shots fired!"

It might've been Sid. He couldn't tell.

The music stopped midbeat, sudden death. Screams and steps of panic rose up like balloons. On the verge of bursting.

Bombs on this station. It had happened before.

"Ryan!"

His sight flickered in and out as another light exploded in

shards of red glass, falling around in a glittering blood storm.

Someonewithagun went through his head, chased by the face of the girl and the feel of her hair—

Sticky.

Wet.

If he shut his eyes maybe he'd disappear.

"Ryan!"

Feet cleared from around him. His eyes locked with the girl's green stare.

That was how dead people looked.

They looked at you. They looked like you.

Sound melted through his ears, ran down his skin, and pooled at his feet.

"Ryan, dammit!"

He couldn't move. His insides shook. His fear was a gasp that couldn't get out.

He smelled charred bodies. Saw fallen concrete and marble. Smoke licked his eyes. Ashes. Sirens went off in his head.

A hand yanked him up. He collided against a chest, struggling, but it was Sid in extreme close up, smelling of cigrets and sweat. His fingers dug through Ryan's shirt, straight to the bone. Ryan saw the smooth length of a gun and a sear of red light reflected on the barrel. It looked hot to touch.

Sid's gun. That was okay. One to protect.

Sid was yelling at somebody. The exits, he said. And a jumble of words, codes Ryan couldn't decipher.

Sharp pops ricocheted overhead. He flinched, unsteady as Sid dragged him—somewhere. He didn't know. Out. Over people fallen on the dance floor.

Dead people.

He just wanted to be blind.

"Ryan, c'mon—"

A crowd milled outside the flash house in sudden bright light, packed all the way up the ramp, blocking the doors of the other clubs on the River strip. Dull gray uniforms eeled through the bombardment of party colors, using riot sticks to clear the way, pushing against the press. One of the grays stopped Sid with a hand on his shoulder. They recognized him. Another uniform, as tall as Sid, shored up at Ryan's side and took his arm. They recognized *him*.

"Let me go!"

He tried to move but he was crushed. Pinned. The crowd surged like they were blown in a planetary wind. Sid didn't let go of his arm and the pollies shouted, telling everyone to be orderly in this clogged throat of corridor.

"Get your hand off of him," Sid said, distinct, hard, a tone Ryan had never heard before.

"Where do you think you're going?" the polly asked.

"I'm taking him home. Get your hand *off* him."

Sid reached across. The *thwap* of a fist meeting flesh poked the air by Ryan's ear. He shrank down, felt Sid's jacket zipper digging into his cheek.

The polly let go.

They jostled him. Now three pollies held Sid in that crush with another one by Ryan's side, cloned. They moved fast when it was one of their own threatened. Sid's voice talked above his head, trying to convince the pollies he had authority to remove Ryan from a crime scene. But they didn't care. Everybody—everybody, they said, was going to security until this got sorted out.

"So settle down!" the lead polly yelled, at the top of the spiraling ramp.

They couldn't even sort the snipers from this crowd and they wanted to sort everything else?

"Get out of our way," Sid said to the nearest polly, "before I shoot you."

And he would. As if seven years of shadowing had only been a dress rehearsal.

But they seized Sid's arms and his gun, another grabbed Ryan and shoved both of them out from the crowd, up the lit red-edged ramp, past the openmouthed entrance of the multilevel den district where pollies propagated like bot-knitters on a gaping wound. Uniforms everywhere.

Uniforms.

Riot sticks.

Guns.

"Sid, I don't feel so good."

In the brighter lights he saw blood on the front of his white shirt, large swaths of it, blurry fingers of it.

Cool air swept down and sank its teeth through his skin. He couldn't stop shaking.

"Are you all right? Ryan?" Sid wrenched from the pollies and grabbed him, checking for wounds. Sid's eyes were wide, pale brown, right up close. "Ryan?"

"It's not mine. That girl—"

The relief blared from Sid's face, so intense that for a moment Ryan couldn't speak.

A polly said, "We want to ask you some questions, Corporal, just standard procedure."

The news traveled already. People in holiday costumes milled around on the main concourse, lion and dragon dancers with their masters exposed, craning their necks for a glimpse of tragedy downramp. Meedee lights winked.

They wanted his face on a holoboard. Again.

Even in this mess. Especially in this mess. He tried to get behind Sid's shoulder.

The pollies caved in and began to steer them to the levs.

"Ow!" Damn polly with a grip like teeth. Ryan kicked.

"Quit it, kid!" The polly dug fingers where his shoulder met his neck. Pain, right there, making his knees curl.

Sid: *"Get off him now!"*

A hand caught his collar and pulled him back. Polly fell on the deck—hard—and winced, holding his elbow. Sid was a barrier, with his gun back in his hand, however he'd got it, aimed at a polly. Aimed at the polly who talked, a woman with hooded eyes. The rank on her collar meant lieutenant.

"Corporal, we don't want trouble. You can comm who you need to comm but you're both coming with us. Now."

"Damn Marine dog," one of them muttered from behind.

Sid said, in that calm voice Ryan had never heard him use in this way: "You all keep your distance. You're manhandling Ms. Lau's son."

"Bring Ms. Lau's son peaceably to the offices and we won't have to manhandle him. Or you."

Sid tugged him behind a structural column and commed home, alerted Marine Perry and told his mother to stay put with the guards because the situation wasn't stable. He had to tell her or she'd barrel down and attract more attention. Then Sid commed the Marine barracks commander and requested a Marine escort to the polly precinct, since his own unit was still back at the flash. The pollies didn't like that. No matter what the lieutenant said, they didn't like waiting while Sid made his comms. Sid watched all around—the pollies, the festival-garbed concourse, the people held back and away by a fence of security, out of sight line. Sid's eyes ranged to the upper levels. Sometimes he spoke into his wire, code to his unit, getting updates.

Ryan stayed behind Sid and told himself to keep standing. Even though all he wanted was to find a wall and meld to it.

They waited, and damn the pollies anyway.

Two Marines promptly showed up in full dark blue battle dress, holding rifles, and the pollies looked ill-clad and clawless beside them. Everyone walked in a herd. The two

Marines flanked him and Sid all the way to the precinct and past a writhing, living body of uniforms separated haphazardly by desks and tinted plexwalls. Busy, noisy, bright lights.

Eyes.

The first thing the lieutenant polly said was, Put him in a cell.

Him.

"No," Sid said.

They couldn't. He wasn't a criminal.

Maybe that was why they didn't care. Maybe they wouldn't suggest it if he was anybody else, but here they made a point of treating him like he was common.

But he wasn't common.

Sid had a gun, people were dead in the middle of a New Year's flash and the pollies didn't care that Sid was an EarthHub Marine on special assignment from Commandant Gutierrez and Admiral Ashrafi of the EarthHub Joint Chiefs of Staff.

Those names were back on Earth, not here in the Rim.

Ryan didn't like to drop names but he yelled it in their faces. "Ashrafi's my *grandfather*!"

Polly said, "He can be Allah for all I care. You're going in holding like everybody else until we sort this."

"Listen to me," Sid said. But they didn't.

The lieutenant said, You had a gun, Corporal, in a club that screens its patrons.

Sid shouted, "I'm his bodyguard! Miyasake, the owner, he cleared me. Ask him!"

The polly said, Regardless.

The polly said, He'll be safe in the cell and you can leave one of your men with him if you wish.

Sid said, "Damn right I won't leave him alone with you people."

This polly lieutenant with hooded eyes and a blank, practiced face. This polly didn't like him. Ryan had never seen her before in his life, but the polly didn't like him.

Maybe because he was rich, or famous, or protected. Or maybe the polly was just a bitch.

Sid looked at the Marines. "Make sure he's all right while I deal with these idiots."

One of the idiots escorted Ryan, with the two Marines in tow. He looked back, and Sid looked at him.

Sid didn't say it, but his hand signed: *You're okay.*

Liar.

They put him in a cell. Maybe they got a clue because he was alone, but adjacent to another cell in the row of cells, with only steel double-mesh to separate them. The two Marines stood outside, one looking down the blue-gray concrete hall toward the bright main room, the other looking into the other cells filled by people from the flash house. More suspects.

The wall was cold against his back, the floor etched with scars made by boots and pulse shots. Rebellion management protocol, maybe even aimed at soljets on leave from his father's ship, once upon a time.

His father might as well have been on Earth.

He sat in the corner, trying to forget his name.

Since he was a child he'd always been vaguely aware that the fact his father was a captain of a deep-space carrier—*the* captain of *the* deep-space carrier—brought trouble to their home.

He met his father in person for the first time when he was four years old. *Macedon* only came insystem once every four or five stationyears, and that was usually how the arguments began. You're not here, his mother would say. Don't dictate to me.

His father would say, You knew what you were getting into.

Ryan understood when he was older. They were talking about marriage.

He was four and he'd talk to his father over comm about the silly things children found so important—the latest toys and games, who was beating up on whom in school, and a lot of "Mommy makes me eat those yucky vegetables." He had no idea about the war, sheltered in his executive tower with his school, playgroup, screened entertainment facilities, and security-infested shops.

The war. Aliens were bad. Humans who sided with aliens were bad. Everybody else was good. Except pirates. But none of those things really touched Austro Station, which was three colors removed from Earth on the galactic map that glowed in the corner of his room like a big transparent ball. Earth, the tiny blue marble; Hubcentral, Earth's yellow solar system; the Spoke worlds and colonies, random white points on his chart; the red Rim, where Austro was; and the green Dragons, where his father lived most of the time. Where the war raged, the war that he kept hearing about when his mother interrupted his vid cartoons so she could watch the news. Austro wasn't anywhere near that, or at least not the Austro Ryan knew.

Austro was a lot of parties that his mother went to on late blueshifts, dressed up and sparkly. Austro was meedees. That first meeting with his father had been a prearranged transcast op that his mother okayed without his father's knowledge. She held Ryan's hand and walked him from the residence with a guard of station security gray, down levs and through back corridors of all the modules between them and the main one until they got to the military docksides in Module 7, which were restricted. Except for the authorized few meedees who stood offside to capture some images to be later 'casted on the Send.

Publicity-hating Cairo Azarcon, taking a break from the war out there in the Dragons. The meedees practically salivated over the opportunity to get his face from the Dragons to Hubcentral.

Mommy, why are all these people here?

Daddy's coming down the ramp right now, Ryan. Wave hi.

Meedees hovered their cam-orbs at him, with lights.

A tall figure came toward him, dressed in a black uniform, with two serious soljets just behind holding big guns. The tall figure came right up and said over Ryan's head to Mommy: Are you mad? He said, How could you bring him here in public?

Oh, and the anger. Ryan looked up at the pale face and the dark eyes and all the anger in the universe seemed to funnel into this man, who was his father. His father's voice was soft, but his anger was a hard diamond point.

His mother said, He's perfectly safe. This station is safe. Now smile and don't make a scene.

(This was before the dock bombing.)

His father said, I'm not going to damn well smile for this bloody charade.

This is your *first* time visiting the family since he was born, his mother said. People want to see your face.

People can go to hell, his father said.

They were talking with anger but their faces hardly moved.

One of the serious men behind his father looked ready to shoot somebody.

Ryan started to cry.

His father looked down at him, finally. And his father

picked him up, one fast move that gave his world a sudden new perspective.

His mother never lifted him once he could run, and she never let anyone else. But he felt safe. This tall man had a solid grip, a sturdy shoulder, and a warm chest. Ryan's arms went around his father's neck and his cheek against the soft dark hair. The captain smelled like Mommy's green tea before she put it in her cup, but sharper like it was frozen cold in space, and his black shirt was smooth in Ryan's fist like fabric got when it was well used. He rubbed Ryan's back. Behind him, one of the men made funny faces. Ryan stopped crying, laughed, and a smart meedee captured the moment.

It became one of the most transcasted images on the Send that year—the ruthless captain with his son in his arms, while a soljet holding a battered rifle stuck out his tongue behind his commanding officer's back.

Songlian Lau got her moment.

But Ryan remembered the arguments at home, every shift his father was there.

They recognized him. He heard the buildup of whispers on the other side of the steel mesh that separated him from every drunk or disturbed person the pollies had reeled in for questioning. Azarcon, they whispered. Ryan Azarcon. Whisper whisper.

Violence invaded their good living, and they wanted somebody to blame.

"Hey," one of them said, pressing against the mesh. Ryan looked up. It was Tyler Coe. His Silver sib. His sometime friend. And even that was overstating the matter. "Hey, yo. Azarcon, why're you in luxury all by yourself?"

Snorts of laughter. This happened when you put a load of

Silver-soaked drunks in the same space and didn't update or entertain them.

"Yo, Azarcon! You too good to talk to us?"

Tyler wouldn't like being in common lockup with the other dross. Why hadn't *he* been identified and either been segregated or let go?

Maybe because his manager wasn't fast enough. Maybe because he was sailing quicker than a solar ship across the sun.

Tyler said, "Ryan, c'mon," in his nice voice. In his let's-make-a-switch voice.

Ryan stayed on the floor with his back to the wall, knees pulled up and arms against his chest, wishing he had a cigret so he had something to do with his hands. He kept them in so nobody saw them shaking.

"Azarcon! Help me out here!"

The younger of the two Marines said, "Shut your hole, drunk."

Tyler told the Marine where to go, in precise detail.

"Hey, boy in blue," another voice said to the young Marine, a girl this time. "Don't stand there lookin' all soldier. Come in here and keep me warm."

"I ain't vaccinated for it," the Marine said. This one had been around station dross before.

The other, older Marine looked in at Ryan. "You okay?"

He nodded, wished he could wash his hands. Take a shower. Go to the bathroom without twenty eyes looking. His leg twitched, nervous habit. "What's going on with Sid?"

"Want me to check?"

"Yeah. Please." That would leave only one of them to defend his honor, but whatever.

The older Marine went to the end of the hall, to the main room, and barked at a polly. Ryan thought that Marine's name was McGregor. He'd seen him before, when Sid had visited the barracks on their way to Austro Academy one time. Ages ago, when he was a kid. McGregor might've thought he was a brat. Most of Sid's friends did. Ryan heard them call him PJ once, the Porcelain John. Pretty to sit on but a waste to guard.

He didn't recognize the younger one standing outside the cell, the one who had mouthed off to the girl. But he looked barely legal.

"How come he gets a cell all by himself, and the rest of us are crammed in here?" Tyler said.

"Because you're ugly," the young Marine said, since McGregor was still down the hall with the polly on guard. "And you can't act."

"Were they shooting at you, Ryan? Is that blood on your shirt? Ah, shit. Ah, man. Look, you have to get me out. Talk to your Maureen."

He didn't answer. He wished Tyler would shut up.

Tyler kept talking nice, but it wore thin fast. Then he said, "They were shooting at you, weren't they, Azarcon? You or your daddy?"

Somebody who dressed like drug addict dross even though he made millions should've kept his mouth shut.

"Daddy's out in deep space. Sniper's got rotten aim," a new voice said from behind Tyler.

"How'd they get a sniper in the flash, anyway?"

Here came the theories, surrounded by blame.

"My boyfriend was shot!" burst another voice, genuinely upset. "Because of this wad!"

"Shut it down," the Marine said, this time with a tilt of his rifle.

But it was too late. That one accusation unplugged the toilet.

"Tell your mama to lock you up," they said. "We don't need more targets on this station. War's bad enough."

"Where was your pretty bodyguard, anyway?"

"Guardin' his body. While everybody else got shoved in the cross fire."

Oh, had he ruined the party? Had he messed up Tyler's chances of getting laid? So sorry. A girl died in his arms, he had her blood all over himself, but poor Tyler wasn't getting screwed right now. Tyler Coe. Second-rate script reader with the charisma of an eggplant.

"Who's your daddy pissin' off now, Azarcon?"

"I hear it's pirates."

"Nah, man. Strits. He's always pissin' off strits."

"We don't wanna die for you or your daddy's politics!"

That made him look up. They shifted and coiled against the mesh like a large, restless snake. So right in their accusations and their judgments. As if any of them linked on the Send for something more than fashion.

He thought about shutting them up.

With a gun.

But he had no weapons. Just blood on his clothes.

He bit down on the inside of his cheek. Hard.

Then Tyler said, "It's govies, I bet. His daddy's rogue, crazy sumbast tailin' after pirates like he don't care about his own crew or all the cits he *oughtta* be defending, and not even Grandpa can fix him. I bet Ops is behind this. Gotta put the dog outta his misery."

Ryan got up and rushed to the mesh wall, banging it with his fist. The move drove them back in shock and shook the wire.

He pointed at Tyler's nose. "Come in here and say that, you dumb little shit!"

"Sir," the Marine said. "Stand back. Ignore them."

"This," Tyler Coe said, finding his target, leaning to the

mesh because he knew he was safe. "This is what we call 'righteous indignation'! All hail Caesar Azarcon!" His bloodshot eyes found Ryan's through the pockets of white light and dusty shadow. "So tell us, Azarcon. That bomb down at the docks a few years ago. That wasn't a symp protest against *military* treatment of POWs?"

As if the symps and strits didn't torture human prisoners. "I don't know, Tyler. You tell me, you being such an advocate of symps and all."

"We all know your father's reputation. If anybody makes this war worse, it's him. And guess who gets it? Not *el capitan* out there lording it over deep space with his guns."

Tyler wanted a fight. He was pissed Ryan didn't ask the Marine to get him out. As if the Marine could do anything when Ryan himself was in jail. Stupid weed.

Deep breath.

It was going to take a dozen of them.

Ryan folded his arms against his chest, felt the chill of his hands through his shirt. He rubbed his cheek where it itched and flakes of blood came off in his palm. His gut threatened to revolt in a most embarrassing way. He closed his fist and stared through the mesh. "Maybe they were shooting at you, Tyler. I hear your vid bombed the big one."

That struck a chord. "You son of a PR whore!"

He wanted to order the Marine to shoot Tyler Coe and deprive the vid industry of future slush.

But he saw everyone behind and around Tyler, watching. His mother spoke in his ear from memory. Everything he did in public was a potential story on the Send. *The meedees are your friends, but the kind you hide your silverware from. Never create scandal, even when faced with idiots.*

So he turned his back, just breathing, because if he concentrated on more than that he was going to murder somebody. He walked to the far wall. He slid down and sat on the floor, knees up, elbows in.

"What d'you say now, Azarcon? You got what you deserve! Hear that? Just a matter of time! Your papa brings this on himself!"

On and on. The young Marine couldn't do anything but shout, and Tyler was one in a row of dozens.

Flash crowd. If any of them paid attention to politics it would be a first. He knew them. If it weren't for his family tree he'd be just as oblivious and proud of it.

He put his arms over his ears, tucked down. Somewhere, some kids were crying, wailing about their boyfriends, girlfriends, whoever didn't leave the flash alive. Fear and anger, alcohol and drugs fueled the shouts. This wasn't a few dockworkers on a slow shift getting their limbs blown apart. This was a sniper in one of Austro's most ruby clubs, targeting multi-mill-cred bodies.

Targeting his body. Everybody else was collateral damage.

The mesh of the cages rattled, trying to get his attention. Crazy, murderous monkeys.

Marine McGregor finally came back to the cell with a cautious look on his face. He reported: "The corporal's working on it still."

Sid must've been one step short of shooting somebody.

In a few minutes Sid came in the holding pen flanked by two pollies, the lieutenant with the flat expression among them. The lieutenant opened the cell, come-hithered Ryan sharply, so he stood and squeezed out. Sid immediately put a hand on his arm and gave him a look that said, *No questions.* They left Tyler Coe and the other noisemakers behind, thankfully, back out to the offices and the busy uniforms, comps, and bleeping comms.

But instead of heading to the exit, Sid directed him to an interrogation room that had a long sign on the door: NO ADMITTANCE. During torture, Ryan figured. They lost the Marines and the pollies, even the lieutenant, and Sid sat him down and pulled up a chair, close beside him in that small, high-ceiling room. It was depressingly bare and beige. The walls would be more institutional if they were padded, but that was about it. Metal chairs on a concrete floor, and a wide stained table with cuffs attached, were the only furniture. How many murderers had sat in this same seat and lied?

"Are they spying on us?" Ryan asked, glancing at the little black squares in the walls where the optics sat.

"No. Just the Marines to make sure no pollies walk in. I got ten minutes with you before they bear down. Look at me, Ryan."

He dragged his eyes from the dented table to Sid's serious face.

Sid half blinked, then put a hand around his wrist. "Three people are dead. Eleven others injured. I want to know if anybody other than my team and Miyasake and his security knew you were going to be at the Dojo."

"Mom knew."

"Someone other than our circle, Ryan."

"No, then."

"Ryan. This isn't a time for lies. I'm not going to get mad but I need you to tell me the truth."

He yanked his arm from Sid's grip. "Stop talking to me like I'm a kid. I said I didn't tell anybody!"

"Tyler didn't know?"

"Why would I tell that weed?"

"Ryan, are you sailing?"

He squinted at Sid but Sid's eyes were laser sights, spot on.

"I keep checking your room but I can't find the para-phernalia. Your friends hide their evidence real well too. But I want you to tell me the truth, Ryan. All of it. Now."

"Nobody was shooting at me for *that*."

Sid's mouth tightened. Disappointment at the confirma-tion, though he didn't seem surprised. Ryan stared down at the table before he realized he was doing it, like a guilty per-son. Like he had to hide from his decisions.

"Listen to me, Ryan. I'm going to need the names of all your contacts."

"If I do that, they *will* shoot at me."

Sid slammed his fist on the table, a thunderous metallic bang. "*Don't* fuck around with this!"

Ryan looked at him in alarm, his heart up his throat. It didn't make a difference to his bodyguard.

"You're going to give me those names, Ryan. You're going to draw me a damn map if I ask for it, because this is your *life,* do you get that? I know I messed up letting you go on when I knew—after London—dammit—" He took a breath. Settled. His voice lowered. "This is partly my fault, I didn't push you hard enough to come clean. You kept changing where you stashed the swack, didn't you?"

"Yes," he said, because his walls were starting to come down no matter how fast he moved to restack them. He was crumbling.

"I have to look at all the sides, Ryan. So do the pollies. Maybe it had to do with your father or maybe it was some dealer who didn't get paid on time. Maybe that girl had a jealous boyfriend. I need to know what I can from *you* so we can narrow it down."

"Okay. Okay."

Sid handed over a slate that he pulled from an inner pocket. He made Ryan write down all the people he knew. Fara. Shoe. Tyler. Anyone else he happened to sail with, even once. How much he paid, how the bullets were passed, how frequently he bought and from where.

Everything Ryan knew he should never say, or his life would be in danger.

But his life was in danger already. Maybe he was just compounding it. He compounded it the first time he went to deal without going through Tyler.

Sid looked at him in silence all through it. After, Sid grabbed him suddenly at the side of his neck and pulled him close. He thought it was a hug and reached up to touch Sid's back, but Sid's hands dipped into his pockets, then up and down his ribs and legs.

"Stop it!" He tried to shove away.

Sid came up empty, looked at him in half apology. "I'm sorry, but I had to check. They were going to."

Ryan got up, blind, tipping the chair over. He went for the door. Sid grabbed his arm and then he found himself engulfed. A brief, hard embrace that seemed to shore up his outer defenses at the same time it chipped him away from the inside. Sid touched his hair, a simple stroke, before letting him go. When he looked up he saw his bodyguard, not a friend.

"Fix your face, Mr. Azarcon. The pollies want to talk to us together."

They went to the lieutenant's office cube on the upper level of the precinct, where she waited. Sid nodded to the two Marines to stand outside. The lieutenant ordered her plexpane walls to tint dusk and suddenly they were private. Maybe even gun-proof.

"Have a seat, Mr. Azarcon," she said.

The office was lived in, as if most of her time was spent in this square space. Shelves stood along one wall, a comp console lay flat on her crowded desk, and a water dispenser hid in one corner, all bland earth-tone colors. The only brightness came from the lieutenant's medals and citation plaques mounted strategically behind her head, so anybody on the opposite side of her desk couldn't help but notice them. Gold and ribbons.

Ryan sat on one of the creaky metal-and-faux-leather seats, glanced at Sid and his blank Marine expression, then back at the polly as she eased her whipcord frame into her chair, tilting back a bit and drumming her fingers on the desktop. Next to her hand was, of all things, a kitschy snow globe of some Earth city holding down a long transparent chipsheet.

"I'm Lieutenant Plodovic. As I was telling your body-guard here, we're investigating the deaths at the Dojo club and we would appreciate your full cooperation. Which *includes*—listen to me, young man—"

He let his jaw snap shut. He hated it when they took that adult tone with him, as if he hadn't had his majority for three years, getting it like every other sixteen-year-old across the Hub.

Bristle down, he thought. And give her attitude only if she keeps looking at you like that.

She said, "Which *includes* staying here under question with Corporal Sidney—"

"You're arresting us?"

Plodovic didn't blink. "You're not under arrest. I'd just like your cooperation. We all want to find out what happened, so I'm going to need a statement from you."

Fara liked to say, Always cover your ass, especially with hostile pollies in murder investigations.

You just never knew what could jump back at you when you weren't looking. Innocence was no defense unless it came with an attorney.

Probably the one thing Fara and his mother would agree on.

He said, "I'll talk when my lawyer gets here."

Sid said, "I've commed her."

"You're not under arrest," Plodovic said. "You're not accused of anything."

Funny how pollies said you weren't under arrest but then treated you like a criminal.

Ryan said, "By the time you people get done the sniper will be off station."

"Ships have been halted. So I suggest you cooperate quickly," Plodovic said.

Ships in dock, burning cred when they needed to be in space, and guess who would get blamed once the story hit the Send? *Snipers at the Dojo, shooting at Ryan Azarcon . . .* He saw the scroll in his mind's eye. The ships waiting to undock and those waiting to port would think his mother or his father's reputation created the lockdown, because when an Azarcon sneezed the galaxy had to injet the antihistamine.

That was how it was going to read. Never mind innocent people were killed and any murder, much less a multiple homicide, was enough cause to halt ships until they established that the perp wasn't headed outbound.

Perp. Sniper. Maybe more than one.

Snipers that missed. On purpose?

For a second he almost smelled the dead girl's hair. The sweet smoke. As if he weren't sitting in a polly's office being benignly interrogated.

The lieutenant was talking, a flood of words that made sense to surface thoughts.

"Your bodyguard has to remain here, anyway, until we can clear him. He and his unit were the only patrons in there with guns."

"What about their security?"

"The only *patrons*," she said again, with a squint.

"What, so you think he'd shoot at me?" He didn't quite laugh in her face but he made her think it.

"You tell me. Would Corporal Sidney have a reason to shoot at you?"

"Yeah, sure. Because he's my *bodyguard*."

"Ryan," Sid said. Shut up. Wait for the lawyer.

"There have been rumors," Plodovic said, "with regard to your bodyguard's relationship with your mother. You might be inconvenient in a scenario like that, Mr. Azarcon."

For a second he didn't believe he'd heard right.

This was a whole other area of questioning.

He looked that polly in the eyes and didn't glance once at Sid. "So this department bases their investigations on gossip? I'll make sure and let my mother know that."

"We examine all possibilities. Is there any truth to it?"

He kept the stare. "We're not answering your questions. Especially the stupid ones."

"You bring a lawyer in here and it becomes adversarial. We're all on the same side."

"Not at this desk."

"Who are your drug contacts, Mr. Azarcon? Tyler Coe?"

Did she think she was going to kill two crimes with one interrogation? "This isn't just about the people in that flash, is it."

"You were in that flash, Mr. Azarcon. The girl you were dancing with, according to witnesses, was the first to be killed. So this is partly about you. Isn't it?"

He said nothing. Sid said nothing. They all looked at one another like mutes.

Plodovic's deskcomm buzzed. She lingered a glare on them for a silent moment, then tapped it. Another female voice said, "Lieutenant, I think you better link to the Send."

That was all they needed. Fluff about him, Austro's Hot #1 Bachelor, in the midst of a murder investigation.

He twisted the bottom of his shirt, tried to warm up his hands. Told himself Plodovic was just doing her job and it had nothing to do with the fact of his parents' or anybody's political views. He and Sid were going to walk out of here and go home and—

Except the fact of his family could be why someone shot at him in the first place, like Admiral Grandpa feared.

Or maybe it was his Silver habit.

Maybe the girl had enemies.

Maybe Fara's boyfriend finally got jealous.

Plodovic tapped off from her secretary, then poked her screen a couple times. Ryan leaned to get a view, despite himself. Images popped up—a block of live footage, a scroll of words, a split screen of a meedee woman on a station dockside.

Not Austro.

In the livecast block was his father, flanked by black-uniformed soljets.

The meedee said, ". . . from Chaos Station in the Dragons, where Captain Cairo Azarcon"—his face appeared in close up on screen—"finally lifted a communications blackout of the Chaos Port Authority. Then in a shocking statement he announced a cease-fire and the commencement of peace negotiations with the aliens and their sympathizers, headed by the Warboy, who we have just learned has been docked at the station for three full shifts—"

The strits.

The Warboy.

And his father.

Ryan's whole body froze and his heart gave a heavy thump.

Austro seemed to flip on its axis.

*   *   *

He was twelve when Marine Corporal Timothy Carl Sidney arrived on station, a gift from Admiral Grandpa back on Earth. Sid was tall, twenty, tanned, and dark blond, despite a month of space training on Pax Terra Station. He'd been an American Marine since he was seventeen and looked down at Ryan there in the apartment, a single drab-olive duffel at his shiny booted feet, decked head to toe in streamlined dress blues. *EarthHub* Marine blues. He'd survived numerous interviews and sweet-talked a load of signatures to get himself transferred from a dirtside unit to the space one. He had to be good; a move like that was notoriously difficult to swing, no matter what country you served before.

He was good. Good-looking, good-humored, and good with guns.

Sid's mother was an EarthHub Marine colonel, he told Mom Lau, there in the foyer with all his "yes ma'ams" and "no ma'ams." He said, Colonel Ann Sidney served with Admiral Ashrafi on *Trinity,* way back when.

Ah. So it wasn't all professional prowess that landed him this sweet assignment.

How fortuitous for us, Mom Lau said, with a big smile unwarranted by the situation.

It all started then.

It didn't take Ryan long to figure out that his grandfather had sent Sid this far, not only for Ryan's safety, but for his education. Sid didn't patronize him or gloss over anything, or tie up the truth in neat bows and ribbons.

Sid sat him down in the kitchen that first shift and looked at Ryan with all the force of his gold-flecked eyes. Sid fit right in with the kind of people Mom Lau liked to orbit, the pretty kind of people she invited to parties who either fawned over him or ignored him. Except Sid didn't talk like them and it wasn't all his Earth accent.

"Just want to get a couple things straight," he said, sliding over a cup of milk. Ryan watched him, didn't touch it, and waited. "First, call me Sid, not sir, and I'll call you Ryan, not kid. Second, your grandfather trusts me a great deal to send me here and I don't intend to let him down. The admiral did me a favor because I wanted off Earth."

Why?

"It was too much."

Ryan later discovered that Sid was burnt-out from dirt-side conflicts. Burnt-out at twenty. EarthHub might've presented a united front to the galaxy, but Earth itself was another matter. Countries squabbled, old hatreds flared up every other year or never really died, and Sid had stepped through more than one massacre in his life, seen more than one atrocity in more than one nation, and a request from his colonel mother to Ryan's grandfather got him as far away from that as possible. To space. To an important assignment that didn't require battlefields.

A twelve-year-old kid.

He said to Ryan, "So I want you to know that I'll work to build your trust. I know it's not an overnight thing. I'm here to protect you—and your mom—and I'm not going to bullshit you. So that means I want you to have an understanding of your situation."

What situation?

Sid said, "About your father. And your grandfather. About your mother."

Oh. You mean how they hardly talk and practically never see each other?

Sid paused. And kind of smiled. Not like a baby-sitter, but an ally. As if the behavior of the parental species was a mystery indeed. Ryan didn't want to, but he started to like Sid then. Even though he didn't show it, no way. He didn't expect Sid to really answer his point.

But Sid said, "Your father's a deep-space captain facing

the brunt of the war, and your grandfather's colleagues back in Hubcentral don't like how independent he is. Not to mention the fact your grandfather supports him and that ruffles a lot of feathers . . . and your mother and her mother are always on the Send talking for Austro and parading you about, and you're in the middle of it, a target."

Me a target?

"Not everyone likes your family, Ryan. Strits and symps really don't. Some factions of the goverment don't. And they might just go through you to make a point, now that you aren't a kid anymore."

That was the first he'd heard of it. Or at least heard of it that bluntly.

Sid added, "Your dad has it in for pirates too, right? He makes enemies kind of easily."

He'd never thought of his father in that light. His father was just—there. Or, really, not there.

Sid ended up drinking the milk. Then he patted Ryan's shoulder and said, "I better go scope out your security system. And I'm going to want to talk to you later about your user protocol for the Send."

The residence *felt* different with Sid there. It sounded different with his heavier male footsteps going from one room to the next, and his deep voice issuing orders even to Mom Lau.

And Ryan sat alone in the kitchen thinking, Everything's changed.

Everything changed with that one Send report.

The lieutenant wasn't looking at the screen now. She looked at him. He read it on her expression: *Azarcons.*

It wasn't supportive.

The meedee jabbered on about why wasn't there anything official coming from EarthHub Command yet, and did that mean the captain was (no surprise) acting independently? What authority did he have to sit down with the strits, to *let strits* dock at an EarthHub station, to announce to everybody in the Hub that we were now going to *talk* to those strits and their human traitor sympathizers?

The meedee didn't say it in so many words, but it was implicit.

Ryan bit down, stared right back at the lieutenant, who seemed like she wanted to ask *him* that question.

And it was a valid question. The Send transcasted fast reactions from station governors, and while the deep-space citizens seemed almost relieved, the closer the 'casts got to Hubcentral and Earth, the louder the diatribes.

Governor Ng from Austro said, "As far as I'm concerned we are still at war until EarthHub Command declares otherwise. There will be no strit ships docking at our station, no matter what any deep-space captain says, until that point."

Lieutenant Plodovic let it run, but she wasn't watching the screen. She watched Ryan's face.

He and Sid said nothing. Only listened. The office seemed to get warmer with every second, with every new blurb from the Send.

One moderate meedee talked about the dilation factor, and captains who were used to making crucial decisions on the spot without a lot of hassling, brass channel verifications. Maybe Hub Command hadn't got the news at exactly the same time that it had happened. Communication was virtually instantaneous but travel wasn't, even with leap points scattered throughout the Hub. Getting to them still took time, transit inside a leap still took time. And for Chaos Station, way in the Dragons, time certainly moved at a different rate from Earth's perspective looking out.

Events in deep space came with drag time and you just got used to it. A father roaming the Dragons commed his son, thinking he had just talked to the kid a week ago (and for him, he *had*), but for the boy it was a month. So while an eight-hour shift passed on Chaos Station and a simple cease-fire changed somehow to allowing the Warboy docking privilege at a Hub station, three weeks could've spun out on Earth before they heard what was happening, and that was assuming the captain had promptly commed them.

Which was assuming a lot, considering his track record.

It must've been written on Ryan's face, the same thing he saw on Plodovic's, even though he didn't want to show it.

What was his father *thinking*?

The meedee equivocated with, "A belatedly authorized move of this kind may well provide Centralist presidential candidate Judy Damiani with all the firepower she needs to convince a Hub majority that harsher restrictions need to be enforced on the deep-space arm of our military. Forcing the government's hand with a move this decisive sets a dangerous precedent indeed."

Admiral Grandpa was going to have to address that, since he was in charge of the Navy Space Corps.

The captain was going to have to justify his actions, whatever his intentions or the outcome.

People weren't just going to trust it. Not when the strits might've been lulling the Hub into a false sense of security.

Like pollies preferred to do.

"Well," Plodovic said finally, "it makes you wonder who else knew about your father's move before we did."

Ryan stared at her. "Excuse me?"

She looked almost smug. "It's just now hitting the Send and, apparently, Earth. He had a blackout on Chaos Station's Port Authority for three full shifts. Seventy-two hours *their* time. They couldn't release who was in dock, but they *knew*. Makes me wonder how airtight that blackout was, and maybe someone not in accordance with your father's decision decided to . . . protest. Sent a comm under the wire."

His father had many enemies, Sid had said way back when.

Symps, govies, pirates—any of them could've had backdoor contacts to the Dragons, especially on a station the size of Austro, where you could easily lose yourself if you didn't happen to be famous. A whisper of the peace talks could've got ahead of the captain, the meedees, and swept insystem where everybody knew Ryan Azarcon lived—

You linked on the Send every shift, and for every peacehawk from the Dragons to Hubcentral that wanted an end to the war, there was a raging political group or a racist paramilitary organization that thought the symps were traitors fit to be executed and strits an abomination to humanity. Or people who'd lost families through the fighting were simply unable to forgive, or forget, and would rather avenge. They devoted time, cred, and weapons to the cause.

Oh, everybody had a Cause. And they all thought their points were best made with bombs.

He didn't feel Sid's hand right away, only when the fingers clenched on his arm and the pain brought him back.

To blood on his shirt.

To the deaths in the Dojo—his fault. His name. His very existence.

He twisted the hem of his shirt, out of sight of the lieutenant and her accusatory eyes. "I need to get out of these clothes."

"I don't think you'll be going anywhere." She tapped her comp.

A block on her screen changed. It showed the outside of the precinct; a swarm of meedees descended with blinking lights and cam-orbs. Waiting for him to emerge.

Vultures. Scavenging cannibals.

"Get rid of them!" he snapped. Sid touched his back but he twitched it off.

The lieutenant said, "Don't be alarmed, Mr. Azarcon, they won't get in."

He turned to Sid, but Sid's eyes had disconnected. His commstud was talking to him. Then he looked at Ryan.

"Jo's caught in a press at the base of your tower."

Plodovic called it up on her comp. An image of his mother's lawyer, Joanne Martin, severely lit by white meedee lights and surrounded by satellites of floating cams that softly whirred. Recording, transcasting.

"I don't know any more than you do," she said. "Now if you could please get out of my way, I need to attend to Ms. Lau's son."

"Ms. Lau had no knowledge of her husband's actions before it hit the Send?" a meedee shouted. A faceless voice out of frame.

"I need to get to the precinct," Jo said, pushing forward when her aide cleared a cone of space.

"What does she think of it? Ms. Martin! Has she been in contact with the captain?"

"Ms. Martin! Have you spoken to Ryan yet? Was he injured in the flash house attack?"

They continued to ask, despite a lack of answers. They wanted to know if he was dead, if the pollies had confirmed the murders were indeed an assassination attempt on his life, if the captain had commed in, if he knew his son was being held. If, if, if.

The captain might've got this transcast at the same time they were getting his.

"Sit down, Ryan," Sid said quietly.

He didn't know he was standing.

The heaviness in the pit of his stomach made him sink back to the chair.

The lieutenant commed her secretary. "Send some people to ward off the crowd. Ms. Martin will be joining us shortly and I don't want a melee outside." She looked back at Ryan as if it were his fault, but didn't say anything.

They made her job more stressful. Imagine.

He was covered in blood but she was stressed.

They didn't speak for long minutes.

Eventually the secretary came on again, a disembodied voice: "Ms. Martin is finally here, Lieutenant."

"Send her in."

Jo looked displeased and didn't even bother to nod politely at Plodovic. Some strands of dark hair flew loosely from her upsweep. A slight dampness from overcompensation in the bright lights and cool air ringed her eyes. Her voice was a whip as she took a seat on Ryan's right.

"What have you got?"

Plodovic said, "A flash house with guarded entrances and exits, even the maintenance tunnels are laser-tripped, albeit only enough to dissuade drunk patrons from hiding out and doing illegal things. Miyasake's security cleared. And then there's Mr. Azarcon's bodyguard. He cleared the flash before it opened."

Sid looked at Jo. "I left plainclothes units on site while Ryan and I were at the residence. They were also there when the shots started."

"I need Mr. Azarcon to make a statement for the record," Plodovic said.

"I'd like a word before," Jo said. "In private."

That didn't make Plodovic any happier. But she wasn't going to win against Songlian Lau's lawyer. She got up and left them alone, shutting the door.

Ryan knew his mother must have applied pressure somewhere. Otherwise they'd all be in an interro room without the pretense of politeness.

He wanted to be home, in bed, with a single light on and his door shut and locked. Music turned up. He wanted to be in different clothes.

Maybe in a different skin.

The silver embroidered dragon on his leg was coming undone. He tugged at a thread and wound it around his index finger until the skin puffed purple and then white. He let go of the thread, looked beyond his knee. The corners of the polly's desk were edged raw, as if it had taken too many hits over the years. Hits of what? The front panel was scuffed, perhaps by boots kicking in rebellion. The floor around the legs of the desk was layered with dust and grime.

He tried to pay attention but with the polly gone his mind sank, giving blurred flashes of memory. Lights, the feel of the girl under his hands, then the feel of her blood. He blinked. The heaviness in his stomach spread to his limbs, his eyelids, and sleep oblivion sang in his ear. If only. Just to wipe it all out.

Facts slid across his lap in two directions.

Ryan, are you listening?

Sid had talked to his CO on the station, briefed him on events, while Ryan had been in lockup. His CO had talked to Plodovic. Sid wasn't going to answer rumors. The pollies were just fishing for motive, but now with the captain's transcast they had plenty, and it had nothing to do with Songlian. Still, this lieutenant didn't like the Azarcons or Songlian Lau.

Sid was already running checks on Plodovic's political affiliations. Could be she just didn't like rich people. Could be she'd crossed words with Songlian at some point in the past. Who knew.

Ryan, are you listening?

Sid had seen glimpses of suspicious-moving, dark-clad

forms on the catwalks. His other units had reported the same. Two, maybe three.

Shots fired? Jo asked.

Sid said, Our side used paralysis only and it was tricky with all the people running. Whoever died in there was the sniper's doing. It had to be a damn good sniper to get off a shot like that under those conditions—varied lights, moving bodies, some smoke. Most snipers would never take a shot like that.

Ryan thought, That's why the girl's dead and not me. They missed.

He felt sick.

Great, Jo said. So whoever did it was either real desperate or real pressured to do the job.

Sid agreed. Pollies said the girl Ryan was dancing with took a laser bolt to the back of the head—

Ryan wanted to shut them out, but he couldn't.

Sid said: My number two, Proctor, stayed behind to talk to Miyasake's people. I don't think they got off any shots.

The other patrons who died? Jo asked.

Preliminary checks landed all but one on the legal side.

Jo sat forward. And that one?

Underdeck kid, prior arrests for assault and theft. Nobody knew how he'd got into the flash. No weapon on the body.

So it wasn't confirmed that kid was the sniper.

No, but if it quacked like a duck . . .

What about Miyasake?

Sid said, The captain knows him. He's a friend.

"Ryan," Jo said, and waited until he looked at her. Waited until he seemed to pay attention. "When Plodovic comes back in I want you just to tell her what happened as the shots started. Anything else she might ask you let me handle. All right?"

She meant if Plodovic asked more questions about his mother's bedmates or his mother's reaction to events.

Jo looked out for his mother, first. He was a necessary by-product. Of course, no message came from his mother either. Nothing that she might've thought to transmit through her lawyer, any show of concern or a small word of comfort. She might as well have been in deep space too.

He shut his eyes for just a second and the dead girl's face materialized amid dots of red. Echoes of music pulsed in his heart. He opened his eyes and it all shrank back from the here and now.

But he knew that would change as soon as he tried to sleep.

Sid went to the door and opened it. In a few seconds Ryan heard footsteps and then Plodovic sat back behind her desk, looking at them.

"How are you now, Mr. Azarcon?" Plodovic asked, as if she cared.

He put his hands in his lap. "Fine," he muttered, the kind of answer you gave meedees because anything more was an invitation. "Except I'd like to go home and change."

She poked a recorder bud on her desk. "Tell me what happened in the flash house."

He had to; it would help. Even though, after that transcast, Plodovic might have more motive to target him. Because targeting him might mess up the captain.

It was an old thought. He'd just never paid it any attention until now.

Would a polly really do that?

He knew. Not even pollies were always that clean. Not even his father.

He was so tired he couldn't hold a thought. He wanted to dive under something and never come up.

He wanted to cry—out of exhaustion or remembrance or

plain, cowardly weakness, but all of his urges simply shored up against the dull edges of his emotions.

Like the dregs of a long sail.

"Mr. Azarcon," Plodovic said.

All that about Sid and Silver was a mask. They all knew it. Out there in the Dragons a hated captain and a hated terrorist symp were sitting down to shake hands.

He had blood on his shirt and a polly with an agenda.

So he relived it.

The polly wanted Sid to be available for further questioning. She also promised to update Sid on their progress but she didn't even try to hide the insincerity of her words. It didn't matter. Ryan knew Sid would keep on her arse. And conduct his own investigation.

Finally, after a half hour of detail confirmation, she let them go. Sid, the two Marine escorts, and Ryan. While Jo Martin distracted the meedees in front of the polly precinct with a few answers-not-answers, they went through the back. A pod waited in the executive terminal, called by Marine McGregor. It was a robotic passage of time as they darted along the podway. Sid accessed the Send in the pod's unit and they watched repetitious scrolls of info—repetitious because the captain wasn't giving any press conferences yet.

It said, A pirate named Vincenzo Falcone was murdered by a symp from the Warboy's ship, and now the symp was aboard *Macedon*. Under *Macedon*'s protection.

Sid told the volume to increase. It filled the pod's cabin.

A symp. Aboard *Macedon*.

Macedon had captured Falcone after the scuffle out by Meridia, had in fact leaped after Falcone's ship *Genghis Khan,* right into the DMZ. So the captain had got his pirate prey. The government had intended to extradite Falcone to

Earth because he'd been a Hub carrier captain a bazillion years ago. A corner of the screen ran data on the man, this dead pirate leader, and the fact not all of his senior crew were accounted for. A source aboard the battleship *Arabia* said some pirates were captured, most were killed when *Macedon* shot the *Khan*, but Falcone's lieutenant as well as his protégé had been on a planet on the strit side of the DMZ called Slavepoint doing black-market deals. When *Mac*'s jets landed, the place was empty of overseers.

Helped by symps, perhaps?

And yet a symp had killed Falcone.

Ryan slumped back in his seat, forced to listen, but paid most of his attention to the central square where the meedee woman stood just outside the main dock on Chaos Station.

"Captain Azarcon won't release the name of the sympathizer who murdered Falcone, and all cams and citizens have been banned from the conference rooms and walkroutes that Azarcon and the Warboy have taken to begin their negotiations. So far the entire process has been kept under wraps, leading many to wonder if these overtures of peace are indeed sanctioned by EarthHub Command."

The screen split again. His father stood outside *Macedon*'s main airlock, an archived transcast at this point.

"Safety is the primary issue," he said. "Safety for Captain S'tlian and his interpreter, and safety for myself so these talks can go forward. We all realize there are fanatics in the Hub who would rather this cease-fire fail. I am not one of them and neither is the president or his Joint Chiefs. I'll be issuing a statement after I've had a chance to speak more in depth with Captain S'tlian, but I've been told that Admiral Ashrafi and President James will both be speaking shortly on the matter. That's all. I have a meeting to prepare for, thank you."

He called the Warboy by the symp's actual name, S'tlian.

Called him *captain.* As if they were equals. As if he respected the symp.

The Hub was going to love that.

The image rolled full again to the meedee at the dockside doors, where she tried to imply she was in the know about what was going to happen next. But in truth they knew nothing.

"What does this pirate Falcone have to do with the ceasefire?" McGregor said.

Sid waved the volume low and frowned. "I don't know. It said *Macedon* was delivering him to custody on Chaos. The Hub ships all ended up on the strit side after *Mac* leaped, so . . . maybe the Warboy helped the captain capture Falcone?"

McGregor's eyebrows went up. "Why would the Warboy do that?"

Sid shrugged. "Maybe he didn't like the fact *Macedon* found the pirate on the strit side of the DMZ. Maybe Falcone likes to kidnap symps too? This other symp that they aren't talking about—he up and killed Falcone on dockside. All they have are eyewitnesses, no cam proof. It's all a little strange . . ."

Ryan thought, No damn joke.

McGregor said, "Has the admiral gone on 'cast yet?"

Sid searched for the report on the Send archive but it didn't pop up. So that statement from the Hub president hadn't been issued either.

Sid said, "I think if they got wind of what happened in the Dojo already, things might be a bit in flux."

An understatement. Ryan stared out the window as the tunnel fled by in a blur of gray and black.

The pod deposited them by the Module 7 executive levs; no common stroll on the return route, meanwhile the party still went on stationwide, galactic politics notwithstanding.

Sid held his arm all the way back up to their module, to the tower, and into the lev where security from their wing escorted them out to the residency doors. Marine Perry stood guard there. McGregor and his partner faded away, back to their barracks, and suddenly Ryan was inside, home, and his mother rushed up from the living pit in her heels and black evening dress to smother him in her arms.

"Ryan, sweetie." Her fingers ran through his hair, down the edges of his face, and her eyes swept over him head to toe. Her hands avoided the blood. "Are you all right?"

Why did people ask that when it was obvious that you weren't? Anyway, Sid would have told her. Jo would have told her. She could've asked herself a few hours ago. "Yeah. Yeah, just let me change, okay?"

Then he saw over her shoulder—Grandmother Lau. Typically looking as if she'd been born with a lemon in her mouth. Her black hair was swept back from her face as if she'd caught the ends in a vacuum.

"What have they learned so far, Ryan?" she asked. "This move from your father, is your mother also a target?"

Such a show of concern truly overwhelmed him.

Mom Lau glanced over her shoulder, then turned back to him. She had the same thought. "Go on to your room, Ryan."

Food sat on the long table with half-empty glasses of wine and crumbs from expensive hors d'oeuvres. As if someone had pressed a button in the middle of the party and deleted the guests. The vid sprawled mute on the walls, a visual of his father's face, talking without sound. The recycled transcast.

Grandmother Lau saw where he looked, and frowned. "We know who to thank," she said.

He opened his mouth.

"Ryan," his mother said, on a deep breath. "Go and change out of those clothes, sweetie."

Before he said something he wouldn't regret.

Sid gave him a quick look and a small smile, code for him to just leave it alone, so he went to his room. Before he reached the bathroom he heard them behind in the hall and paused just inside his bedroom door.

"Why weren't you guarding him?" his mother asked.

"I was. My eyes never left him. He went onto the floor to dance and then the shots started." Sid sounded like he was giving a report.

"You should've been closer to him!"

"Lower your voice, Song. He can hear you."

"Don't talk to me like I'm ill. You have a job to do. If you can't do it I'll send you back to Earth, I don't give a damn what the admiral says."

"Doesn't look like he's saying much," Grandmother Lau put in. "It's all just Azarcon."

"These peace negotiations—" Sid said.

"I don't want to talk about that! You nearly got my son killed! If you want to be useful, Corporal Sidney, go sit outside his room."

"Song," LO Lau said. "In all fairness, it's the captain you ought to be yelling at."

"Mother. I think you should leave now. Thank you."

A pause. Then the sound of the front doors opening and closing.

Ryan shut himself in the bathroom and turned up the lights. Reflections poked at his eyes and he squinted, stared down. Just gripped the edge of his sink and concentrated on the cold ceramic beneath his hands.

Then came a tap on the door.

"Do you need anything?"

His bodyguard's voice held that flat distance, the kind

that masked a deep hurt. But he was here and asking, when Mom Lau wasn't. Ryan wanted to open the door, except— he couldn't.

He took off the bloodstained shirt and held it in his hands, looked at the pattern of red on white like some weird work of art. Like a masochist he looked at it, and into the mirror where smudges of blood marred his cheek and across his nose. It matched the red, sick look in his eyes. His image was a smudge.

"Ryan?"

"I'm okay," he said through the door, and in the tiled room his voice echoed the lie.

Eventually he heard Sid go away, and eventually he showered, got on clean clothes, and fell into bed.

Blessed oblivion. He didn't sleep for long, and when he awoke it felt like he never had.

Moonlike glow from the lowlights filled the room, with a shadow standing by the side of the bed.

His heart kick-started, painful.

"Mom?" His eyes adjusted slowly. It was too large a shape to be his mother. And the hair was short.

"It's me," Sid said. He sat on the unoccupied half of the bed. "How're you feeling?"

"Where's Mom?"

"Working. The station's in an uproar. And the comm won't stop bleating."

The comm was never going to stop now.

He rolled over and put his face back in the pillow.

"Ryan," his bodyguard said. "Do you want to talk about what happened?"

"Not really."

"I think maybe you should."

A hand on his shoulder made him turn back. Sid looked

disheveled and weary. His eyes checked Ryan's face and all over, like Ryan was damaged or something.

He'd got all the blood off his face, but maybe it still showed—that it felt as if he hadn't.

"I don't have any more Silver in the room."

Sid breathed out. "Ryan—"

"Look, I know it was stupid. I know." His voice cracked a little and he sniffed. Stifled it. Looked up at Sid with what he hoped was steady control. "But it doesn't matter now, right? You got all the names. I won't be—going anywhere for a while. Just . . . don't arrest them, okay?"

"Don't *arrest* them? I've got half a mind to hunt them down and shoot them." His eyes flicked to Ryan's and his hand twitched, halfway to a thought before forgetting it. "Or maybe I ought to just kick your ass."

"Sid. Are they really the priority right now?"

"No. But if you ever sail again I *will* personally nail your butt to the wall. And the next time I see Tyler I'll—"

"Sid." It was nice the way he made an issue of it. With that half smile to take the edge off.

But he meant it. The unblinking stare said so.

"You can look through my stuff if you don't trust me," Ryan offered.

Sid said, "Don't worry, I will."

He looked past Sid's shoulder to the wall where his framed *Battlemech Bear* prints hung, residue from his childhood. Gifts from his father, when his mother refused to shell out cred for it. "Did you have something else to tell me?"

Sid breathed out, was silent a minute as if trying to gauge his words before he said them. "My unit at the scene's been talking to the pollies . . . by the placement of the shots and who got killed, we think there were two shooters on the catwalks. Maybe three. The tunnel kid, we think maybe he was one of the shooters. So that means at least one is running loose."

One. On a station of thousands.

They were never going to let him out of this apartment.

"But how'd they get *in* the Dojo?" However it was, they must've got out the same way. "You had the place secured. You checked in advance."

He didn't mean to sound accusatory.

Sid stared a bit at the bed's curving headboard. "We did . . . we did. We had blueprints of that area from the planning commission and nobody else had accessed them lately. But no matter what we do, no matter what systems are in place, there's always the chance that somebody—a trained somebody—can get through. It's actually . . . not that hard. If you know what you're doing. We took necessary precautions, Ryan, but—like I had to tell your mother—those maintenance tunnels . . . they're *meant* for people to pass through them. The Dojo isn't a military base."

It wasn't the impenetrable cocoon that he had to live in now.

"Proctor checked out the maintenance accesses. They've got laser triggers, but if you're connected you might be able to find ways to disable them. It's not unheard of."

"Connected?"

"To some of the more . . . willful . . . underdeck activity. The second sniper, and if there was a third . . . they both could've escaped through there too. The problem is none of the accesses looked like they were breached. So they're either really well trained or . . ."

"Or?"

"It was an inside job. But I highly doubt that. Miyasake's people are good. I know them. The captain knows them. But we're still checking out the station's maintenance crew in charge of that sector . . . if I was planning a hit on somebody I'd—co-opt an existing asset and use them."

Interrogate some poor sot of a tunnel worker? Kill them even?

Sid would think of that. Sid had to think that way, that such a thing was possible and perhaps even easy.

Sometimes he forgot Sid had a job, and training, above and beyond just following him around the station.

"But *who* ultimately? Like, who shot at me? And how did they know I would be at that flash?" He didn't want to ask it, but had to: "How come they missed? All of them *missed*."

Sid looked chagrined. "I hate to say it, but they could've followed us. If they just assumed you'd be out for the parties, they could've tailed us from this tower and we just didn't catch them. As for who . . . the dead kid certainly wasn't working alone, he must've been hired. We don't know by whom, yet. But . . . with this news just now— about your father—anything's possible. Terrorists like the Family of Humanity don't usually target just one person but . . . this thing with the pirates. I don't know. One of their leaders is dead."

And pirates could infiltrate underdeck a lot easier than any legit organization. Refugees, criminals, homeless, and poor . . . Austro liked to pretend their unaccounted citizens weren't as big a problem as they were. Occasional sweeps of those tunnels only scattered the wily ones further into the shadows. As soon as the light receded, they skittered back out to their business.

Business like assassinations, maybe.

Pirates held grudges, the Send reported. And everybody knew Cairo Azarcon hated them. Hunted them.

Sid said, "The flash was crowded. It was a difficult shot. Or maybe it was just a warning and that's why they missed."

He couldn't talk about it anymore. But his mind refused to let it go.

Tunnel kids trained in high-security infiltration? This wasn't a local thing, or even a drug thing. If not pirates, then maybe govies. Maybe even people his grandfather worked with. Maybe some Centralist fanatics with access to terrorist resources.

Too many maybes.

He pulled himself to sit up.

Sid's back straightened, instantly aware. "You all right?"

"Just feeling a little sick."

He was a blister. Sore and ready to burst.

"You might want to stay off the Send for a while," Sid said, looking across the bedroom to the prints on the wall.

"That bad?"

"Just take some time. I'll get you a glass of water and something for the nausea." He stood.

"Sid."

"Yeah?"

Pressure built up in his sinuses, with a spike beating behind his left eye.

"Do you know her name?" The girl he'd danced with. "Did you find out?"

Sid paused by the door, arms at his sides. "You sure you want to know?"

Ryan didn't say anything. Maybe he was a coward, but he let his bodyguard walk out without an answer.

Sid was as good as his word. He brought some foul-tasting medicine to help Ryan's upset stomach, a glass of water, and upturned the bedroom and bathroom for Silver. He found none, just the empty injet, so he took that and shut the door. Ryan sat on his bed trying not to throw up the meds, holding the empty glass, suctioned together in his bubble of silence.

He tried not to think of the dead girl.

Or dead people. On the ground. Under a planet-blue sky. He couldn't sail.

So he cleaned his room. He unpacked the cases that had sat for three months full of some of his clothes and junk that he'd taken to or bought on Earth. Little bits of memory. Stickers from concerts in the city, souvenirs from countries he'd visited—one or two hand-carved Buddha statuettes from China—image cubes of him and Shiri . . . he thought he'd left those behind, but maybe Sid had thrown them in during the hurried stages of packing three years of his life.

His cases looked like they'd disgorged themselves all over his floor and bed when the door opened and his mother came in.

She stopped before her manicured feet hit a tumble of shoes. Her eyes took it all in with a determination not to comment.

"I'm cleaning," Ryan told her, holding one of the Union Jack shirts he'd bought in England that he could've sworn he'd lost.

"I see." She stepped over the land mines and stopped in front of him, putting a hand flat on his chest. "I'm sorry I haven't been around the past couple hours . . . Tim told me you were feeling ill?"

"I'm okay." He folded the shirt, even though it probably needed a wash, and stuffed it into one of his dresser drawers.

"Ryan, I know I haven't exactly been attentive—"

"Mom." The last thing he wanted was a heart-to-heart, all because he'd been shot at. He looked at her, not inviting it.

"I just want you to understand . . . please, can you sit down?"

She wanted to act like his mother now, full of concern for his well-being and emotions, when at the end of the shift she was going straight into Sid's bed. Or he into hers. Whichever. She had to talk to her son to make herself feel better, or because there was a lull in her work, or maybe it finally hit her that he didn't have a bodyguard just for her own personal enjoyment.

She'd never slept with her security. Just the one who guarded her son.

He thought he'd dealt with the idea, but here it jumped back on him and the anger still felt new. As if he didn't have better things to think about.

"This isn't a good time, Mom."

"Ryan, just sit." She stood in front of him. "Please."

So he sat. He picked up his guitar, ran his fingers along the red and black hieroglyphs on the body. It gave his hands something to do.

"I'm worried about you, Ryan."

His hand stopped moving.

"I know I haven't exactly been the model of motherhood, especially about Tim . . ."

He played an open note, high on the neck. His light E string was too loose.

"We've never talked about it," she said. Soft.

She wondered why? But now they should, right, because now he might be killed tomorrow. And this was what he wanted to talk about, naturally.

"We've never really discussed what happened on Earth," she said. "I guess that's my fault."

He chewed his lip and stared down at the instrument, his one real indulgence. He couldn't play in front of her, so he just plucked a note here and there. He couldn't speak.

Words were too open and heavy.

"Maybe I should've explained," she said, "about Tim and me."

She kept pausing as if she waited for him to jump in with

a maudlin confession or a strong assurance that everything was going to be okay. She wanted to trade. Her explanation for his, except he had none that he cared to let fly.

She said, "We didn't plan for it to happen, you know."

Now he began to imagine stock characters moving around a basic digiset, spinning complicated tales of betrayal and lust. Even her heart to heart talks couldn't sound genuine. Maybe she'd written it all beforehand, memorized it, practiced it in front of the mirror.

He could hate her for doing this to him, coming here now and wanting some kind of intimacy when all he wanted was to be left alone. Didn't she see that? He couldn't even look up. He didn't want to feel this way, any which way; he didn't want to feel. And yet she still pushed.

She went on about how lonely she was, how his father had little sympathy for their situation on the station, how she had always thought, after they were married, that the captain would take a little more interest. And why had they gotten married in the first place? Perhaps they were young and dreamy, perhaps she'd convinced him of it, or he had honestly thought it could be worked out even though they came from, and lived in, two completely different worlds.

This and that and a few more tears.

Sid was a sweet distraction, but she'd never wanted to get in the way of his job. Now she was afraid she had, that it was somehow her fault that Sid had *allowed* someone to shoot at him, that through her power and her beauty she had somehow lured the young Marine from his place of honor—

It was too much. She wanted to share, she wanted him to spill his soul and she tried to touch his hair and stroke it like he was eight years old again and it wasn't going to happen. He wasn't going to sit here and cry in front of her.

The words fell out of his mouth and before he knew it they were in the air and flying. "Mom, why're you blaming *him*?" He put his palm against the guitar strings. "Or the captain, for that matter? Or yourself? You think short of locking me in this room for the rest of my life that any sort of protection is total and absolute? It's not like anyone *tried* before, either. So just—stop it. I swear. I know why you and Sid sleep together."

"Ryan," she said, as if she didn't want to hear it from his mouth.

But he waved her silent. "It's a good bang, I understand that. Maybe you're both lonely. Maybe you really love each other, I don't know. But unless you plan on divorcing the captain and marrying Sid, he'll just go back to Earth eventually when I don't need him anymore and that'll be it. That's all. Have you thought of that? So I don't know why you're going on about it. Screw him if you want, I don't care."

Her expression was stark, as if she had ice cubes in her mouth.

He knew how good he was at shutting people out, and shutting them down. He had plenty of practice with meedees.

He strummed a few hollow chords.

"Your father," she said finally, "is on comm for you."

He looked up, but she left the room.

A black knot tightened in his stomach. She hadn't deserved that, maybe. And maybe she'd just had an earful from the captain. Maybe he should've opened his door and called her back and apologized, and let her hug him if that was what she wanted.

But his father waited on comm, and it was too late anyway. From down the hall he heard her tell Sid she was going to her office.

It was too tiring to deal with parents. When he wanted

them they weren't around, and when he wanted to be alone, they showed up.

Before Sid came in with an order he set the guitar on the bed and reached to his bedside table for his mobile. He slipped it on, linked to the designated, highly secured private comm, and leaned back as his father's real-time face bloomed in his vision.

"What took you so long?" the captain asked, with that odd spacer accent, tendrils of which Ryan had heard in England. It gave a clue to where his father's family might have come from, ancestrally . . . not that they ever discussed it.

Ryan said, "Mom was talking to me."

The man on the other end of the comm studied him, silent in the way teachers and parents could be when they knew the weight of the conversation rested on their shoulders. Somewhere near Chaos Station the satellite leapfrogged the captain's signal in quantum acrobatics, traveling light coded with imagery and words until it was netted by Austro's node and sent down a direct link to Ryan's safe unit. It had a couple seconds of drag, hardly noticeable.

His face was the same unreadable expression Ryan remembered since—forever. Young and a bit jarring at first, even though he knew to expect it because the captain was a born deep spacer. Except for a few short years on Earth with Grandpa Ashrafi he'd lived his entire life in the Rim or farther, near strit territory, constantly on the move.

That was about all Ryan knew. His father's past was as much of a mystery to him, and to his mother, as it was to the Send. The admiral had adopted the captain for some reason when the captain was eighteen years old and already an adult. For all appearances he looked maybe ten years older than that, like a brother, not a parent. His features were almost pretty in their regularity and fineness, though his chin was a bit too strong and his nose too long to carry that impression. His eyes were the kind of deep dark that gave nothing and saw everything. It wasn't a face Ryan equated with his own, despite their shared genetics. He remembered that face mostly from pictures and comms.

"I'm going to be there in a couple weeks," the captain said, after some mutual scrutiny.

Ryan ran it through his mind a few times. "What?"

"It's a hard push in leaps but that doesn't matter. In the meantime I don't want you leaving the residence. Is that clear?"

"Yeah. Yes." Something about that tone always made him snap to, even when he was determined not to be another of his father's soljets. "How can you afford to come here? Aren't you, like, kibbitzing with strits?"

Don't you have any idea how this is playing to the public?

His father said, without any sort of shame, "I'm the one conducting these negotiations, so I can take a leave of absence to see my son if I damn well please. Besides, when I commed your grandfather about the talks he got on the first flight out to the deep. He'll be here soon."

"So you did actually comm Hubcentral."

"I commed your grandfather. Long before anything hit the Send, which is the way it ought to be."

Ryan stared into his father's eyes but couldn't see a single private thought. "Don't you think you should've *asked*? Before you went ahead—?"

The man didn't even blink. "Why?"

"Because . . ." He couldn't believe his father didn't see it. Or chose not to see it. "The govies on Earth kind of run the Hub. You don't."

"Not from where I sit. I don't see President James out here getting his ass shot off. Govies need to be told what to do or they'd never get anything done. Nothing worthwhile, anyway."

He couldn't get into this with the captain. There would be no point. It was like arguing with a wall and he'd rather leave that up to his mother.

Instead he said, "I'm doing okay, too, thanks for asking."

"I could see for myself. And your mother briefed me. But since you mention it, *are* you okay?"

"I'm fine."

One eyebrow arched. "Like after Hong Kong?"

Trust his father to bring that up out of nowhere. He said what everyone wanted to hear. "I was fine then too."

"Don't lie to me, Ryan, or worse yet to yourself."

He had no reply to that, even though the captain waited for one. He didn't say a thing. He wondered how the hell the captain saw anything in his answers when the captain barely saw him, period.

Eventually his father said, "That boy who was killed in the Dojo, the tunnel kid. One of my crew has a contact in Austro's underdeck that's looking into his activities. I'm going to let the corporal know what I find out."

"Okay." He stared at a blinking happy face icon at the corner of his field of vision. An incoming message.

"Are you listening to me?"

"Don't you want to talk to Sid?"

The captain leaned forward slightly. He was in his office. Ryan recognized the span of gray bulkhead behind his shoulders and head. "I want to talk to *you*, Ryan. This concerns you. You shouldn't be in the dark about it."

"So what're you doing with a symp on your ship? And what does the Warboy look like up close?"

"The symp on my ship happens to be helping in this investigation. It's *his* underdeck contact. And if you meet Captain S'tlian I would appreciate it if you didn't call him the Warboy. That's a Hub label and it's quite insulting to him."

"You're not serious. The man's a terrorist." He took a long look at the captain's face. "Never mind."

"He's not a terrorist, he's a war leader, and despite what the Send says, there is a difference. You'd do well to learn it. But we'll talk more when I get there, I don't want to be on comm too long. Just pay attention to what Corporal Sidney says and . . . be careful."

Don't be stupid, he meant. Maybe Sid had told him about the Silver.

"I'll live," he said, a lame joke.

The captain reached for the disconnect on his console. "You'd better. I love you, despite the atrocity you did to your hair. See you in a couple weeks."

He'd seen his father three times in person, when he was four, eight, and twelve. He would've seen him when he was sixteen but he'd left for Earth before *Macedon*'s scheduled visit.

He remembered, at twelve, how the captain never stayed in the same room with Mom Lau for more than a few minutes, and instead spent most of his time taking Ryan around Austro. His ship was in dock for a major resupply, repairs, and recruitment, which meant he was on station for about a week at least. Every hour or so he got a comm and talked to people on *Macedon*. He took Ryan to dinner once. Ryan sat across from him in Siam Star, the posh Thai restaurant on the third level concourse in Module 7. Ryan resisted tossing a chopstick at his father's head and that bloody comm.

Ryan said, What's with you and Mom anyway?

Oh, the question. The one that his mother never quite answered except to imply it was his father's fault. They sat with their green coconut curry and sticky rice, quiet sounds of cutlery hitting plates all around their little private corner, which was shaded by plants and soft lighting and a considerable payment to keep the waiter away until called for, all so civilized and rich. Except Ryan wanted to go to a game restaurant where it wouldn't be out of place to drop sauce all over himself and laugh out loud.

But that was too public so here they were.

Away from Mom.

His father didn't answer the question. He drank his water instead.

Ryan wondered how long it would take to eat his dinner one rice grain at a time. He played a game with himself while his father sat in silence, probably watching him, but Ryan wasn't sure because he didn't look up, he just concentrated on picking up his rice one grain at a time. Eating, listening to the low murmur all around him, voices he couldn't quite understand. He didn't know what to say to his father and maybe his father didn't know what to say to him past all the regular questions that they'd covered over comms. What do you like in school. Who are your friends. What vids have you seen lately. What are you reading.

They didn't have much of a conversation for the rest of the dinner. The waiter came by and the captain said, Do you want dessert, Ryan? So Ryan nodded because he was here and he might as well get what he could from it, so he ordered the creamiest thing on the menu, which was some sort of pudding. He looked all around at the greenery and artifacts set in low-lit cubbyholes in the walls, things from Earth or replicas of things from Earth, from Asia he assumed. He knew where Asia was, they'd had tests on it in his Earth Origins class in school.

Is there somewhere you wanted to go after this? his father asked.

Ryan looked at his watch. Sid's going to take me to the decacourts at seven.

Ah. His father glanced down at his lap and picked up his napkin and folded it, then set it on the table in a neat pile by his empty dessert bowl.

I told him to meet me here, Ryan said. I didn't know how long we'd take.

Of course, his father said. That's fine.

Ryan knew his father was looking at him now, with those dark eyes and that serious face, and he really wanted to know why his parents didn't get along. But he didn't get answers, just the pudding, and after that his father ran the cred through in the table and they got up and went by the other tables to the exit, and people stared. They weren't meedees and his father ignored them all anyway, but Ryan turned to one woman and stuck his tongue out, fast, just as if nothing had happened. The woman's eyes widened and her back straightened before he breezed on by with his father out of the restaurant.

Sid was waiting. He always showed up early to things. He said, Captain. Ryan's father said, Corporal. Ryan smiled at Sid because Sid was going to show him how to do a double rebound with the powerball and he wanted to get it down so he could show up Tyler Coe in gym class tomorrow, because Tyler was older and thought he was better. Sid messed up his hair by habit, then smoothed it out, the way he liked to greet Ryan, and the captain said, I want to take a picture before you go.

The captain fished out a cam-orb from his jacket pocket and set its height and distance and let it go, and the orb whirred in the air and positioned itself in front of them. Sid stepped out of frame even though Ryan would've liked him in the shot. They stood in front of the one-way glass of the restaurant with all the neon lettering behind and the holo-prog menu and the captain draped an arm around Ryan's neck and hugged him to his side.

Smile, Ryan, Sid said, grinning at him off-cam.

So he smiled and the cam flashed, then announced it had taken the shot, but the captain didn't let go for a few seconds. Instead he put his other arm around Ryan and patted his back and his hair, and it was strange to feel those arms around him. It wasn't playful like the way Sid hugged him sometimes, or brief, the way his mother did. The captain held on as if Ryan was going to fight him, but Ryan didn't, you didn't make scenes like that in public. So he stood still and kind of slapped his arms around the captain's back, then the captain let him go.

Have fun, his father said, smiling even though his eyes were somber.

I will, Ryan said. Thanks, Captain.

Sid said, Thank you, Captain, all formal like an adult, then nudged Ryan's shoulder as they headed down the concourse.

Ryan didn't look back. He didn't think of it. His mind was already on the powerball game.

Sid must've had orders from the captain to keep Ryan informed of The Situation, because every goldshift Sid woke him up with a report. Get up, Ryan, I've talked to Otter today.

Otter was the symp's underdeck contact, the symp that was aboard *Macedon* that the captain seemed to trust but refused to talk about. The Send speculated. Some apparent eyewitnesses claimed it was a teenager, or a scary beast with a white assassin face, or something altogether more fierce and inhuman, although why a symp would have it in for Falcone enough to murder him was anybody's guess (as if anyone needed an outstanding good reason to want a pirate dead).

The timeline of events, like any aspect of time in deep space, was spurious to the general populace of Hubcentral. Had the captain really captured Falcone before proposing this treaty with the strits, or was it vice versa? Did one have much to do with the other? Was *that* the significance of this assassin symp? And had that symp been under orders of the biggest symp of all, the Warboy? Weren't the strits and sympathizers working with the pirates?

Because, you know, all baddies had to be in cahoots, didn't they?

While all of that raged on the Send, this tunnel kid Otter ran intel on the drama at the Dojo. Through what resources Ryan didn't know, but if Otter was a friend of the symps, then possibly the lines went deep indeed—to the sympathizer network across the Hub, which nobody liked to talk about but everybody knew existed.

All of this before Ryan even had breakfast.

He was a powerball hauled from bed every goldshift. He bounced to the bathroom to shit and shower, bounced to his wardrobe to dress, then careened to the kitchen for food. Nobody left him alone. If it wasn't Admiral Grandpa on the comm somewhere in transit from Hubcentral to Chaos Station, it was the president of EarthHub on the Send (finally), condemning the actions of those who would attempt to assassinate an innocent young man. (No word on if he condemned the innocent young man's father, but that wouldn't be politic anyway.) At any rate, no amount of threats would discourage the peace talks. The government refused to be bullied by assassins.

That was all fine for the government, but *he* still couldn't leave his apartment.

On the unofficial links, on the secured comms between

Earth and Austro and *Macedon* and Austro, his family and Sid talked about those old-body Centralist factions, with First Minister and presidential candidate Judy Damiani their vocal advocate. Colonies and stations from the edges of the Rim toward the Dragons were behind the cease-fire, but every corner had fringes and flames that were fanned by groups like the Family of Humanity. And they were louder than the silencing of guns.

Not that the guns were completely silenced. One ship in the Hub fleet and one or two ships in the Warboy's fleet didn't control the entire fleets on both sides of the Demilitarized Zone, especially in the distances of space. While word trickled down that you weren't supposed to engage "the enemy," the Send still reported "misunderstandings" and "nervous captains" all across the Dragons and the Rim. Those ships were soundly reprimanded by their superiors, in public, but for two weeks the ripples still rolled.

Pirates raided ships whose routes ran as far as the inner Spokes, as if in retaliation for an affront too severe to let go.

Captain Azarcon went ahead anyway, with the official blessings of EarthHub Command, no matter who grumbled in the shadows. Admiral Grandpa and a platoon of governmental suits that included the Minister of Alien Affairs were on a transport to meet with the captain and the Warboy (the Send still called him the Warboy, not Captain S'tlian, because it drew more hits). They had orders from the president and the Hub Council on Deep-Space Affairs, although what exactly those orders were beside the political "do your best" was the Send's guess. Damiani was not at all happy with those chosen (Annexationist) negotiators, and she bitched about it.

"Fair representation of all EarthHub citizens . . . are the Annexationists going to ignore protesters on their own doorstep?"

Captain Azarcon didn't respond, the Send said. He was still on his way to Austro. Because his son had been shot at. It played well on the Send, Mom Lau said. A captain who would drop even unprecedented negotiations with an enemy war leader so he could be with his son played *very* well to the public. The man had a heart after all, it wasn't all cold fusion making him run.

Ryan was so happy to be useful. He was so happy that nearly getting his head blown off and watching a girl die in his arms benefited somebody.

Which was why Admiral Grandpa was going to Chaos, at least that was the official word. To cover the talks while *Macedon* went insystem. Even though Grandpa had already launched from Earth before the assassination attempt. Sid said the admiral was really going to Chaos because Hub-central wanted a non-deep spacer to oversee the captain. Admiral Ashrafi was the natural choice (despite Damiani's bleating), as a representative of the EarthHub Joint Chiefs and the one in charge of the Hub's deep-space military affairs. He was also the only one who *seemed* able to control the captain. Because who knew what funkiness the captain would create with the Warboy, since the captain was half rogue himself.

The hyperbole. No matter where the captain went he seemed to attract debris, and its comet tail picked up his family in the process.

It made Ryan's head hurt. He retreated to his bedroom and locked the door, played his guitar until his fingers ached and thought about the Silver he no longer had. He fell asleep sideways, in his clothes more often than not, until twelve full shifts after the Dojo when Sid came in and shook him awake. He said, Get up, Ryan, Otter's traced that tunnel kid. He wasn't Ops or a terrorist, he was paid by the pirates. And a body turned up underdeck. DNA analysis said it belongs to one of Austro's tunnel maintenance engineers. A single guy with no family on station.

So somebody had used the man's ID.

Sid said the pollies were still looking for the second sniper. They thought now there were only two.

Only.

The sniper had gone to the trouble of murdering a man to gain access codes to the restricted, laser-tripped parts of the tunnels by the den district. But he hadn't followed through with the assassination.

Easy to miss in that environment, Sid said.

Be grateful, Mom Lau said. We don't need to know why the sniper missed.

At least, she implied, Ryan didn't need to know. It was too disturbing. She was already worried about him and how much time he spent sleeping. Sid was worried. Sid dragged him around the residence, to keep him "informed" so Ryan didn't have time to just zone out or hide himself for too long in his room.

Like he had after Hong Kong. In London. Claiming fatigue so Sid left him alone in the hotel room, with access to room service and a couple guards outside his door.

Except he didn't really sleep, not then and not now. In the late blueshift when his mother finally went to bed and Sid padded around the rooms on security checks before joining her, Ryan lay awake listening to the activity die.

He thought about the alcohol in his mother's cold drawer. Thought for a while, and to make sure Sid wasn't going to get up again he climbed out of bed and slipped down the hall until he stood just outside the closed partition that separated his mother's room from the rest of the apartment. Behind the screen he heard soft, impatient crying, and Sid murmuring, "It's going to be all right."

"It's not a large thing to ask, but for some reason he can never *do* it. It's his damn pride."

"He's uncompromising. But that doesn't mean he doesn't care about you or Ryan. Let's not go over this again, Song."

"You're so good to Ryan. You're so good to me, Tim, even when I complain about—"

"I'm not all that good," Ryan heard his bodyguard say.

And then he felt ashamed to be standing there, even though *he* wasn't breaking anybody's trust, and moved on toward the kitchen.

He remembered that first conversation over comm with the captain after he'd discovered his mother and Sid were having an affair. He was fourteen and the captain treated him like an adult, even long distance. The captain talked to him about the war if he asked, or girls if he wanted to know (since talking to Sid about sex, and Sid and his mother were doing it, was just too—weird), or anything that didn't infringe on the captain's own line of privacy.

And Ryan wondered how his father could know so much about nearly everything, but have no clue about his own wife.

How's your mother, the captain would ask.

Fine. Busy.

And how's Sid?

Fine. Busy.

And he thought with his one-tone answer, only two shifts after seeing those wineglasses in the sink and his mother and his bodyguard at breakfast, all smiles, that the captain would have to be blind, deaf, and dumb not to know what was going on. Just by looking at his son.

Maybe the captain knew, but maybe the captain didn't care. Not enough to do something about it. And Ryan never understood that.

This is our family, he'd thought.

But maybe that was a word that didn't apply to them, not when one parent lived on a ship in deep space and the other lived in front of cams most of the time.

Not when his mother slept with another man and her husband looked the other way. And nothing was ever talked about.

Everything else was more important than their son's concept of family. Perhaps even more important than the son.

So he hadn't told his father then, or ever, and it was tiring to be mad at them all the time.

It was too exhausting to love someone so much you let them hurt you, in silence.

Two weeks after the Dojo hit, the authorities on Austro had to let ships go or they were going to get railed by the Merchants Protection Commission and half a dozen agencies that had business interests elsewhere. Mom Lau didn't want ships moving if the sniper who'd shot at her son could get away, but she had to cave under practicalities. Anyway, Ryan wasn't going anywhere, locked in his room. And the customs officials took extra care with who embarked and disembarked. People bitched. Things were too slow. Mom Lau had to put a reasonable face on that too.

His father's ship got delayed a leap from Austro, out by the Persian Gate point. Something about military regulations, a backlash of pirate activity and a traffic jam of battleships and convoys and who-knew-what-else that took a while for even the captain of *Macedon* to untangle.

So instead of his father arriving on schedule to interrupt Ryan's routine, he got a comm from Earth. Two comms. One from Dr. Grandma Ramcharan, expressing concern, wanting a reply, which he sent out on a delay because he wasn't in the mood to talk live.

The other comm was from Shiri.

He'd avoided his comp with its personal link, he didn't quite know why, until now. The last thing he wanted to hear were pseudo-friends concerned for his well-being, or worse yet, people who were genuinely concerned. But eventually he checked, or Sid would, so he slipped on his mobile, blinked to connect to the full display, and there flashed a series of happy face icons with tail markers that ultimately ended with Hubcentral, Earth. He eye-flicked to the latest message and it spiraled open on Shiri's face.

She was still pretty. Her eyes looked doubly dark and large in the slight distortion of the mobile interface. She'd cut her hair to just above her shoulders, a straight fall of highlighted brown. Her skin was tanned, her voice that low timbre he remembered. Wake up, Ryan, she'd say, a morning whisper in his ear as the sunlight warmed the pillow near his nose.

Now she said in a worried flurry, "Ryan, I really hope you get this, I'm going crazy after seeing the Send. Just tell me you're okay, it doesn't have to be anything huge or long, I'll understand, I just need to hear your voice and know you're okay." Then she paused. "I still think about you."

The message died in a dispersal of image dust and a query for a reply window.

He sat on his bed staring at a blank corner of the display while the query nudged him vocally every fifteen seconds. One eye movement would connect him to the message window that would connect him to her. She'd sent a comm every day since the news had hit the Send, asking if he was all right.

He voiced for the reply and verbally input: *I'm okay.*

He didn't know what else to say, and that sounded so cheap compared to her dozen messages. She'd been a semester ahead of him, so he asked: *Did you graduate yet?* And that still sounded impersonal, but he didn't want to

admit that it would feel so good if she were here. That sometimes he thought about those first winter months when all
the dirtsiders complained, but she had joined him in the
parks so he could run around in the snow, because stations
didn't have weather and she wanted to see him experience
it.

Those words would accomplish nothing because they
were separated by a large expanse of stars. Mutually.

Anyway, it was the trauma. He hadn't intended to ever
talk to her again before all of this happened. So getting shot
at shouldn't have changed a thing.

So he sent the message as-is. Blinked out and pulled off
the mobile. And thought about what a coldhearted bastard
he could be, like father like son.

"I want you to make a statement," his mother said, sitting
on the side of his bed in a way she hadn't done since he was
eight years old.

He had a headache. It had grown over the last couple
days, since Shiri's comm, and now it was a near-blinding
pain behind his left eye. Worse yet, it seemed every time he
took a shower more of his hair fell out from stress, although
Sid said he looked the same. Maybe his mother saw something else. Weren't mothers supposed to notice?

She came into his neat blue room, perched on his bed so
the sheets hardly wrinkled, and told him he had to go in
front of the meedees completely stone-cold sober and say
something coherent.

And why?

"Because the station and the Hub need to see you're a
victim in this, we're not the enemy, your father isn't the
enemy, and it wasn't your fault those people were shot in the
Dojo."

Oh. Just that?

But it *was* his fault.

"It wasn't your fault, Ryan. You don't control what pirates do."

"So I'm a victim. That's fantastic. I want to go on the Send and declare to all the galaxy what a victim I am."

She frowned. Her eyes tightened and wrinkles appeared around her mouth. It made her look her forty-plus years.

"You won't have to leave the apartment. I've arranged for a crew to come here. Tim will check them out. You only have to make a short statement, Ryan. Two minutes, five at the most." She watched his face. "Look, things are far more public now because of the cease-fire." *And your father's involvement.* She didn't say it but he read it easily enough. "It's not acceptable to hide behind silence. It doesn't help *him.*"

Oh, so now they were doing the captain a favor? "He never wants me on the Send."

"He doesn't live on station," his mother said, and stood. "I'll show you the statement by the end of the shift. The crew's scheduled to 'cast at twenty-hundred hours. All right?"

"It's going to be live?"

"Everything is live at this point. Please, just do this one thing. It's not like you've never been in front of cams before. Okay, Ryan?"

No, it wasn't okay. He wasn't okay. He wanted to kill something.

But putting on a face for the public was his unofficial job. Putting on a face for his family was old habit. He'd been born into both.

So he smiled at his mother to reassure her that after two weeks he didn't still have nightmares of that flash—and Hong Kong, his arms covered in sweat and ash, revisited like some garish fashion, some apocalyptic, interactive vid.

Two weeks was enough for dragging around the apartment, she implied. Just because he was confined here didn't mean he couldn't do some work, make some statements, be actively involved in his own well-being. She was up and running, after all, full power. Life went on. Politics propelled action.

The Warboy was talking to Admiral Ashrafi and suits from Hubcentral. It was painstaking but promising. Every cycle of the Send showed shots of the Chaos military dock-side doors (because cams weren't allowed in) and interviewed citizens or visitors who might've caught a glimpse of the famous Warboy, since nobody had ever captured his image. Eyewitnesses were unreliable and it became glaringly obvious. He was tall, he wasn't so tall. He was strit-looking, he seemed human enough. Austro ran all those reports side by side with updates on Captain Azarcon's progress through the leap points.

They said, Ryan Azarcon hasn't been seen in public since the incident at the flash house.

Because he was a victim in all of this.

He got dressed in a black suit with white cuffs and a high collar, muted style his mother approved. He combed his hair down, a bright blond sheen that the carefully angled key light softened to a golden glow. With the new hair he didn't overtly resemble his father. He sat on the couch with his hands in his lap, but they shot him from the chest up, anyway.

His mother stood by the crew, with Sid, her arms folded and her eyes intent. She practically mouthed the words of the script she'd written. He told the galaxy how—

He will never forget the shock of that late shift.

He is deeply sorry for the lives lost.

He is grateful for the support and concern expressed, the cards and gifts that were sent (but were confiscated by security, which he didn't mention. Most of the concern was from infatuated teenagers anyway.)

He was appalled at the hyperbole that implied he was to blame for the murders, as if he could ever want something so tragic to happen. (His eyes watered here. He didn't have to fake it, even though they came down without the accompanying tightness in his chest. Even his tears felt far away.) Who can think him such a monster?

He supported his father and looked forward to seeing him, and hoped that all of the Hub would seek a peaceful resolution to the years of violence. He said there was enough death. Surely one generation of children should grow without knowing war.

The cams held on his face even after the script had run out, but he couldn't face the red live eye like usual. He looked down at his hands, saw them clenched tightly together, and wondered even then how that would play to the audience.

He sat there until the segment director called it clear.

The crew packed up and left, thanking him and his mother for how smooth it went. He ignored them. His mother linked to the Send, there on the sprawling wall screen, where he saw the cycle of his face and his big blue eyes, heard his soft voice. His mother turned to him and said, as he still sat on the couch, You did good, Ryan.

Sympathy index for the Azarcons shot up, like a hit of Silver straight to the vein.

Poor Ryan Azarcon. Innocent victim Ryan Azarcon. And look how his father rushes to his side.

Sid said, Do you want anything, Ryan?

Solitude, he thought. A shower.

He got up and stepped around the coffee table and went up the steps from the living pit, onto the lit marble floor that glowed from end to end like a stage. He headed back to his bedroom where he shut the door and locked it, for what good it did against Sid's key, and locked his bathroom door, and turned up the lights so he could see his face in the broad, unflinching mirror. He wiped his eyes just under the lashes. Took a breath. Washed his face of the non-gloss powder. Then he undressed.

He got down to his suit pants, barefoot, no shirt, and sat on the lid of the toilet seat with his arms against his stomach, suddenly shaky, suddenly so angry it made his muscles curl.

His blurry gaze fell on the floor. The overheads reflected sun puddles on the black tiles at his feet, like spotlights.

BURN

S id shook him awake in the middle of his late blueshift. Get up, Ryan, your father's here.

He rolled over. Sid stood over him in old green fatigues and a black T-shirt. He wore his serious face like a uniform, but his hair was all askew.

The captain had arrived on station during Ryan's sleepshift. Typical. Maybe he'd hustled the ship after seeing that transcast. I never want his face on the Send, the captain had said on every visit, on numerous comms to Mom Lau.

So much for that.

"Ryan," Sid said, shaking him again.

"I'm up. I know. He's here."

"No," Sid said. "He's *here*. In the living room with your mother."

What, and no breaking furniture?

"Get dressed." Sid left.

Now Ryan vaguely remembered an earlier knocking on his door. Sid calling through it that *Macedon* had docked. Was he up? And Ryan yelled in his sleep, I'm up, okay, I'm up. And then rolled back over.

He looked at the glowing time stamp on his wall. 0200.

He rubbed his eyes and lay squinting up at the cotton-white haze of the lights.

His father was here. Get up.

He dressed in worn pants and a pro powerball logo T-shirt, not the neat turnout his father might expect, but he was half asleep, so bugger it. He scratched his arm with the feeling that he was forgetting something, and on a whim checked the local Send report on his mobile. Furious items shot by his vision, all talking about *Macedon*'s arrival and how the captain had not yet disembarked though some of his crew seemed to be taking brief liberty.

A clandestine approach, then, to avoid the hubbub. He wasn't surprised.

He dumped the mobile and opened his door. Marine Finlay stood by the main entrance, voluntarily deaf and expressionless as Ryan approached. Voices talked from the living pit. Reasonable, low voices discussing how the Rim Guard wouldn't listen to logic, they had orders to regulate traffic because of the pirate backlash of attacks on merchants—and the conversation immediately ceased as soon as he stepped in view.

His parents sat on opposite sides of the long burgundy couch, a cushion between them. Sid stood by the arm of one chair, and against the wall behind the couch leaned a man and a woman, casually turned out. The captain's jet escort, probably.

The captain himself wore a gray, threadbare hooded sweater and faded black pants. Ryan would have passed him in a corridor and not looked twice, which was the point. He seemed thinner and paler than the comm images, than Ryan's memories of his last live visit. He sat with his elbows on his knees, leaning forward, and looked up at Ryan with eyes made darker by the shadows beneath them.

Then he stood and it all poured from his shoulders, an unthinking authority that bent every eye in the room to his stature. Except the jets. The jets watched Ryan, watched everything, he saw their eyes shift from one corner to another in the apartment and he felt unsafe in his own home. Felt the atmosphere change as soon as he appeared, as if he'd walked in on a secret meeting.

"I'm sorry to wake you," the captain said, sounding genuine about it. He didn't approach.

Ryan stepped down to the floor of the living pit, feeling the soft warmth of the rug under his feet. He tried to read their faces to know what to expect, but they were all reserved. Sid was a mask. And his mother was silent, unusual in itself.

The captain motioned him forward with a flick of fingers, so he went, suddenly wooden. *Just don't touch me.* He got close enough he smelled the ship off the captain's clothes, a scent completely non-Austroan, something steel and cold and deep that penetrated past outerwear. It came off the captain's skin, underscored by the contradictory fragrance of raw tea leaves that Ryan remembered from the first time they'd met, when his father had picked him up in his arms.

He still felt small beside the man, as if he hadn't grown since their last meeting when he was twelve. But of course he had.

The captain put a hand on his shoulder and squeezed, peering into his face as if he expected to find a map there. For a stressful second Ryan thought he was going to get embraced right in front of everybody, but the captain didn't do it. Just held his shoulder and looked into him for such a long second he had to shift his gaze. He saw his mother, still sitting on the couch, dressed immaculately in a cream shirt and brown silk pants, as if her sleep hadn't been interrupted. Maybe it hadn't. But he knew her expressions. Beneath the reservation boiled an old anger.

Sid was still a mask. In the presence of the captain, he wasn't going to be anything but a Marine.

The captain turned away, looked at Mom Lau, and said in

that soft, accented voice, "I want to take him aboard *Macedon.*"

The antique clock in the corner tick-ticked, loud.

Ryan blinked. *I'm sorry to wake you up and I want to take you on my ship?*

He stared at the side of the captain's face, thinking he must have lost the ability to understand language, because none of that had made any sense.

"What?" Mom Lau said, neither soft nor accented. It came through in clear Austroan, a voice so familiar to Ryan he felt his back straighten just hearing her tone.

The captain still spoke to her, not to Ryan, "We have to return to Chaos Station. And he's coming with me."

This was someone else's bad dream.

"What are you talking about?" his mother said. "Ryan can't go on your ship."

"It's the only place where I can guarantee his safety."

"Ryan's not going on your ship, Cairo!" She stood now, and the rage was plain.

The jets shifted, straightened from their seemingly relaxed poses and walked around the couch, closer. Sid moved to stand beside Mom Lau, to give her support or maybe haul her back if she decided to physically attack the captain. Her eyes blazed wide and her face slammed shut.

"Calm down," the captain said. "And listen to me."

"No," she said. "You bastard."

"Corporal Sidney," the captain said. "Help Ryan pack some things."

"Stay where you are, Tim," his mother said.

His father's gaze became fixed.

"Wait." Ryan snagged the captain's arm, made him look. "You can't be serious. I'm not leaving Austro."

The female jet stepped forward as if Ryan intended to assault the captain, but stopped at the captain's glance.

"Don't argue with me," he said to Ryan. "It won't help you."

"I'm nineteen. You can't order me around!"

"Ryan, you're coming on my ship one way or another. That sniper is still at large and I'm not leaving you on this station."

"I've *been* on this station!"

His mother said, "Cairo, I'm telling you. Leave Ryan out of your games."

"You think I'm playing games, Songlian?"

"Don't stand there and tell me our son will be safer aboard a warship with a strit spy—out there in the Dragons with all the pirates, no less!"

"I don't have any spies or pirates on my ship, despite what the Send says."

"That you know of."

"Song, he's going. I think he needs to go."

Ryan said, "How do you know what I need?"

The captain turned to him, a slow regard. "Obviously you don't know what you need, so I think you ought to be told."

That ignited such a rage in him that he couldn't form a response.

The captain faced Mom Lau again. Unblinking. "Ryan's been out of control since returning from Earth. He's sailing Silver, which you seem to do nothing about. So I'm *taking* him with me. Corporal Sidney, I gave you an order. Why aren't you on it?"

Sid gripped his arm. Ryan jerked.

"I said *stay where you are,* Tim!" his mother said.

But Sid ignored her. He was an EarthHub Marine and there stood a captain of an EarthHub carrier, so he propelled Ryan up the steps to the foyer.

Ryan heard his own voice as if through a long tunnel. "I'm not going. You can let go of me."

"You can't guarantee his safety here," the captain was saying to Mom Lau, even as Sid took him down the hall to his bedroom.

"He's safer here than on a warship!"

"My ship is the safest in the Hub. And away from snipers. Sidney," he called, "pack your own gear. You'll be accompanying him."

The grip on Ryan's arm got painful.

"No," his mother said.

"Song," the captain said. "I'm not here to ask."

Sid shut the bedroom door.

Ryan yanked his arm free. "You go ahead and pack but I'm staying right here. He can order his jets to put me in a barrel."

"Don't think he won't," Sid said.

"This is ridiculous!"

"Is it? You were shot at."

"His ship gets shot at too! Wasn't it just attacked by pirates? How am I safer there?"

"You'd be under his eye. And he was right about the Silver."

The Silver. "Did you tell him that?"

Sid started to gather his cases, annoyingly calm. "No, but he isn't stupid. He could've talked to Tyler for all I know. Or Miyasake, he's seen you two enough in the flash circuit. I have no idea what your father does."

"Evidently."

"We have no choice. Open your dresser."

"I have a choice! I'm not one of his jets!"

"No, you're his son."

Which was worse? He didn't move. The voices rose from outside his door. He was no longer a child, no matter what they had in mind, and they couldn't carry on arguments above his head anymore. He opened the door and headed down the hall, shoved off Sid when he followed, and went right back to stand at the top of the steps.

"Why aren't you packing?" the captain said. Some of his cool exterior showed hairline fractures, especially in the brittle dark of his eyes.

"I'm not your slave. I don't want to live on your ship. Austro is my home. Do you get that?"

"I do. But that hasn't changed my mind."

His mother said, quieter, "Don't take him away from me, Cairo."

A simple request. A final entreaty.

But the captain said, "Do you want our son alive?"

"You are a low-blow son of a bitch," she said.

It was going to descend into gutter drama. Ryan waved a hand at them. "Talk to *me*, dammit. I'm the one you're arguing about!"

The captain swept them both in with a look. "Unless you plan on never leaving this residence, there *is* nowhere safer but on my ship. Get it through your skull—these pirates don't play around and they *won't* miss twice. I'm not going to let you put your life in danger just because you're bloody stubborn! *Now pack your gear!*"

The shout echoed from the floor to the high ceiling. It sent silent ripples through the air and struck Ryan through. He tried not to feel it but his fingers clenched to stop the shaking. The jets had their hands inside their jackets, primed to react.

His mother didn't say a word, in that silence.

"Take my son to his room," the captain said in a normal voice. "Quickly."

The two jets peeled away like separate wings of the same raptor, and came up to flank him.

"Let's go," the woman said. Up close her eyes were wide blue, uncompromising.

He went.

He didn't think. His head felt feverish as he tossed one thing and another into the cases he'd recently unpacked, while the jets looked on and Sid went to pack his own life. The captain was dragging Sid off this station too and Ryan knew only one reason the man would do that.

Not for his son's comfort, although that might have been the conscious reasoning.

He'd drawn a line, finally, and who was Mom Lau to argue? She was guilty after all.

Ryan got halfway through the third case, silence buzzing in his ears and an odd disconnection between his sight and his movements, when the door behind him opened and he heard his mother say, "Leave us alone."

He turned around. The jets left, surprisingly without argument.

His mother came over and sat a bit heavily at the foot of the bed, crossing her legs.

"There's no sense disagreeing with him," she said, and lit a cigret.

He'd never seen her smoke. But she pulled a thin gold case and a finger lighter from her pocket, and snapped the end of the cig until it lit.

A sharp, herbal scent lifted to the ceiling.

"Mom," he said.

"He can wait," she said. "Sit here with me a moment."

He stepped over the cases and sat beside her on the bed. She looked at him, all over his face and into his eyes, and raised the hand holding her cig and rubbed his hair.

"Oh, Ryan, this horrible color."

He didn't know what to do, but the gesture made his eyes suddenly fill. So he looked at the floor.

She said, "Maybe this won't be so bad after all."

"What," he said. "My hair?"

"Don't be like that."

"Why should we listen to him? Why do you listen to him? You never did before."

"Because those were battles. This is a war and I—" She smiled, took a delicate drag from the cigret, and breathed out a cloud. "I can't win wars against your father. Look what he does for a living."

"Why did you *marry* him?"

He'd often asked, and never got an answer. He thought she owed him one now. Or his father did. But she was here.

"I was in love with him," she said.

"Amazing. I don't think he cares if anybody even likes him."

She gave him a look. "He was in love with *me*. Is that so hard to believe?"

"You're asking that now?"

She sighed, a resignation he'd never seen in her. "We were both possessive people. Young and territorial. I didn't want him to go anywhere else and when it came down to it, he didn't want me to go anywhere else—with anyone else. So we lived apart, that was understood because of our jobs, but ultimately we had something keeping us together. Marriage, and then you. That was the theory, anyway. It wasn't a good one and my mother—" Now she laughed, but it was a tired kind of amusement. "She thought I was ruining my life with an unknown quantity. He had quite a reputation in the military even then. A hunter-killer pilot, you know. And ruthless. So to my mother . . . it was worse that I even got a child with him. I guess maybe I did it just a little bit out of spite . . ."

He wondered if she realized what she'd just said. But she smoked and watched the door and he knew she had no idea. She didn't even look at him to examine the fallout.

Even her confessions couldn't do anything but build

another wall. He wished he could grab her arms and yell, Don't you want me? Why don't you make him listen so I don't have to go? But she had made him go to Earth too, had stood behind him and pushed him to that planet "for his education" and here she was again, letting him go.

Maybe it was easier for her to love him if he wasn't always around, a reminder of her own actions and the battles she kept losing.

She wasn't looking at him, even though she must have felt his stare on the side of her face.

Mom, he thought. Mom.

"My mother really despised the fact your father had no past," she said to herself. "She was suspicious of it."

The old elite families on Austro, of which LO Lau was a part, liked a solid say in who their children brought into the lineage. His mother could've chosen any number of rich businessmen or politicians, but instead she'd gone slumming. He'd heard it enough times, in various disguises, from Grandmother Lau. He knew his mother had loved the captain to put herself in that position to be ostracized. Any respect paid her by the elite of Austro Station was earned. But what had happened to the love his parents had shared over time? Damaged only by distance?

"Haven't you asked him?" He was tired. His sleep had been interrupted. She seemed tired too, sitting here with honesty and without agenda. Without Sid. "About his past?"

"He only lets me know what he wants me to know," she said.

At the end of it not even a son kept her solely as the captain's. And maybe the captain had lovers on the ship too.

He guessed he'd find out now.

"You're going to comm," she said finally, as if giving in. "Promise me."

She hadn't exacted an oath when he'd left for Earth three years ago.

He had to touch her hand. Just lightly. "I'm going to come back, Mom."

She didn't answer. Maybe that was her fear. That ship had swallowed a husband, after all.

She hugged him in private and kissed him on his cheeks more than once, both hands in his hair as if she wanted to shake him with her emotion. But she didn't. Her hold slipped from his face and she kept herself in, then she helped him pack the rest of his cases and his guitar. He tried not to stare at her smaller hands packing his private wear into the cases. Her rings shone, but the skin on the backs of her hands was thin, the veins showing through in narrow blue channels, like water under ice.

It was a quicker job with both of them packing, though he didn't care to rush for his father. His mother didn't say anything now; they took his gear out to the foyer where the captain waited with his two jets and Sid, who was looking at everything but at the captain.

The captain scrutinized Ryan's five cases next to Sid's single duffel and said, "Are you mad? Pick *one*."

One?

One case. One carryable thing to place his whole life in.

"Cairo," his mother said, "give him a break."

"He'll only need one. The ship has everything else."

The hell it did. He wanted to pick up one of his cases and throw it into his father's chest, but instead he took them all back to his room and dumped things out and exchanged other things until he had his one case, the one with his underwear. He lifted that and his guitar case and went back out and glared at the captain, but the captain wasn't looking at him.

His mother said, "If anything happens to him on your boat . . ."

The captain said, "I'll comm you."

"I suppose you'll be incommunicado, and I'll have to explain to people where my son is."

"Song, it's not anybody's business where he is. Lie if you want."

"I can't lie straight out to the public."

"Can't you?"

They stared at each other. The male, blond jet said, "Sir."

"Go ahead," the captain said.

The jets opened the doors and went out, then the captain motioned Ryan out. He glanced behind him, over the captain's shoulder and past Sid at his mother as she stood on her marble floors and watched him, arms folded. Controlled and contained. Sid looked back, following the captain, and Ryan saw his mother's eyes shift.

Tears.

Then the Marines shut the doors and Ryan turned around.

"What about her?" he said to the captain. "She needs to be safe too."

"She'll have double the security, trust me. Besides, you think I could convince her to come aboard *Macedon*?"

He doubted his father would *want* her about the ship. It was barely believable that his father wanted *him* there.

They walked down the plush hallway, rode the lev in silence. His father pulled up his hood and handed Ryan a black cap. It needed no explanation. Ryan put it on and tilted the brim low, so by the time they exited the lev they looked like a bunch of low-merch crew returning home from a long layover.

He stared at the jets' backs, the man and the woman, the man with his blond ponytail and the woman's spiked tousle, talking together as if they weren't paying attention to every person that passed by, moved, or stood in a hundred meter radius. Ryan's gaze dropped to the deck and he tried to breathe normally, tried not to think of a gun aimed at his back or his head, or a girl at his feet with blood running out in little rivers toward him. The lance of lights and the smell of smoke and ash, a crumbled building and the heavy beat of music. He blinked. He breathed. He stared at the deck. It was his last glimpse of Austro for who knew how long, but he kept his eyes about a meter in front of his feet.

He wanted to sail. He needed to sail for this.

His father took the case from him, walking abreast, so Ryan just held his guitar, a black heavy shape in his hand that he could swing if anybody came too close. He listened to the people around him, but he didn't hear a word they said.

He felt abducted.

Eventually they passed a squad of meedees idling on the concourse in Module 7. Waiting with caffs and booze and close equipment to capture faces unawares. The transsteel arch of the general dockside entrance stood opposite the meedees, trafficked by citizenry and maintenance workers and merchant crews. Military personnel didn't often pass through these doors. There were closer exits on the military docksides, around the ring, where most of the meedees probably checked on a regular basis. Especially now.

Their undercover group walked, unhurried. And he wanted to run. His palm burned from his grip on the guitar case handle. One word to reveal them and the meedees would stampede. They passed the ramped locks of a dozen different merchant ships and cruiser lines. And nobody stopped them.

He couldn't feel relieved—yet. Not until they reached the military sector and stopped by the two station Marines that stood at the entrance. It was illegal for anyone to loiter here, so they were free of meedees. The jets flashed their ship tattoos and passed their right wrists over a handheld scan to authenticate the nanocodes in the tats. Then the captain did the same and spoke to one of the Marines in a low voice. The Marine looked at his scan, then across at Ryan and waved him forward. Ryan glanced back as Sid followed and ran one of his tags through, even though they knew him on sight.

Sid met his eyes for the first time since leaving the residence and Ryan was selfishly glad his bodyguard was with him. One familiar face. Even though that face right now was as blank as a stranger's; he didn't want to be here either.

Then it was up *Macedon*'s ramp. Two jets on guard met them and nodded to the captain. Jets in uniform, armor, and holding rifles. They didn't look human, animated, or capable of laughter. Ryan moved on leaden feet through the outer lock, a dark green maw with paint-chipped gold and laser scars marring the edges. The inner lock looked much the same and he tried not to trip on the thresholds. Finally he landed up in a long corridor on the main deck of his father's ship.

The smell hit him first. Cold, recycled air with a spike of metal and rubber. The perfume of deep space.

The corridor winding on either side of him was an unending snake of gray and black, jungle-striped at the levs by yellow. No markings anywhere else to tell what was what, unless you counted the paint code on the intestinal ceiling. It was a narrow world, a bullet that encased and confined him.

The cold air went up his nose, down his throat, and swirled in his gut.

The captain said, "Take Corporal Sidney to jetdeck and get him squared away."

Sid moved to the jets. Ryan stared after him but Sid

didn't look back like he usually did. Ryan felt his father standing beside him, watching him watch Sid.

It sparked him enough to face the captain. "So where do I go, sir?"

"With me," the captain said, without comment or reaction to the tag, which Ryan hadn't meant with respect. They started to walk. The captain still carried the case.

Ryan thought about turning around and running back out the airlock and down the ramp. But it was the kind of thought you had when you knew you'd never do it.

He followed his father into the lev at the end of the corridor. The light was stark white and unflattering even to the walls. His father said, "Command crew deck," and Ryan stared at the red bar above the door as it blinked, and refused to talk. If he opened his mouth there'd be an outpouring of profanity.

The captain didn't initiate conversation anyway.

They listened to the hydraulic whine as the lev ascended the decks. It was a noisy, irritating beat, unlike the cushioned silence of station levs. The doors opened with a growl. The deck on the new corridor was a well-worn sheen separated in squares by black gripmat. They passed two and three people in black battle fatigues, but none of them looked at him, only nodded to the captain. These were his new neighbors.

The captain stopped at a door, pulled out his tags, and ran one through the lock slot. When the door opened into the room Ryan saw a blue couch, a coffee table, a small kitchen to the left. All about the size of his closet on station. It was his father's room.

Quarters. And the walls weren't walls, they were bulkheads. And this wasn't a door, it was a hatch.

A door was a door, dammit, you opened it and walked through it, and damn it all anyway.

"I'm staying here?" He didn't follow the captain inside.

"You can sleep here or out in the corridor, your choice."

"Why can't I stay with Sid? On jetdeck?"

His father set down the case by the kitchen island counter and looked at him. "Because you're staying here. Jetdeck isn't a good place for you to be right now."

"Why not? Too many symps running around?"

He couldn't stop his mouth. His father stared at him, standing so still in the middle of that small living space that Ryan expected him to lash out any second from an eruption of restrained energy.

But he didn't say anything. He went instead to the shiny kitchen and detached a bottle of dark pink juice from the cold shelf clamps on the wall. "Do you want a drink?"

"How come your own ship isn't safe?"

"I didn't say it wasn't safe." He poured a glass. "I just said jetdeck wasn't a good place for you to be right now."

"Why not? Sid's there."

"I want you *here*, Ryan. Not among my jets."

"What, you think they'd be a bad influence on me?"

His father sipped, then set the glass down on the counter. "No, I think you'd irritate them to the point of violence. They aren't as patient as I am. Now are you going to stand in the corridor until dock break?"

"I don't know. Does it have bathrooms?"

"I'm going to go on bridge in five minutes. When I leave I'll be locking my hatch. So you either get your butt in here or stay outside until I come back."

He picked up his guitar case and stepped inside, *over* the damn raised threshold, and pushed the hatch shut behind him. And looked at the captain to be told when to breathe. He put that all on his face and he watched his father read it.

"You can have my bedroom. It's there." His father pointed toward a black sliding screen. "Bathroom's also behind there. Feel free. We've already been here a few hours but I want a quick turnaround. I plan to break dock in a half hour and I expect you to stay here for that, in bed and secure. You'll know when it's safe to move."

He wondered if he ought to raise his hand before asking a question. "What am I supposed to do?"

"You brought your mobile, didn't you? Play with that for the time being."

"What, no dollhouse?"

His father set the juice bottle back in its clamps, opened a drawer and placed the used glass in, upside down on a rack, then shut it and slid down a lock.

"There's food as well. Whatever you use, you clean." He went to the hatch.

"If I have the bedroom, where are you going to sleep?"

Maybe it was a dumb question, but it had only one right answer as far as he was concerned, and he wanted to hear it.

The captain actually laughed at him. Out loud. "Don't look so worried, I'll take the couch for the time being."

"Don't let me inconvenience you."

His father opened the hatch and looked at him, paused. "You're not an inconvenience, Ryan." He stepped out, said over his shoulder, "For your own safety, don't wander the corridors until I get back or you'll get lost."

The hatch shut.

Ryan stared at it.

The silence on a docked ship could crush you into the deck.

It felt like somebody else was standing here, because it wasn't him, there was nothing familiar, not even the emotions battling through his chest—the tight feeling of absolute loneliness and lack of purpose. The dislocated absence of thought.

This ship was nothing like the cruiselines he'd leaped in

when he went to Earth and back. No accommodating officers whose only job was to see to your comfort. No cabinet full of exotic liqueurs.

Or were there?

He set down his guitar case, glanced around at the plain blue furniture, the faux wood, the colorful art prints bolted to the bulkheads, and the tiny space he now had to share with his father for an indefinite amount of time.

Booze would be good.

He went to the kitchen to hunt, tapping open drawers and cupboards. The captain had a disappointing lack of junk food, but Ryan found a quarter-used bottle of vodka at the back of the cold rack and spun it around so he could dislodge it. And the pink juice too. He poured the juice into the vodka bottle and shook it up a bit, sipped. The hit went straight to his brain, burned all the way down like a streaking meteor through a planet well, with a tangy-fruit aftertaste. He coughed, sniffed, and wiped his eyes. Took another smaller sip and coughed a little less. It would do.

But he needed to sit. Exhaustion threaded through his limbs. He sank down on the couch and put his feet on the edge of the table. For a long while he just sipped and peered absently between his knees at the objects on the table until he finally began to see them.

An image cube and some miniatures—three pyramids and a sphinx. Egyptian. Cairo. That was the association.

Funny.

He nudged the larger pyramid with his left boot. It seemed to adhere to the table by magnet. Odd. Then he remembered that a ship in battle could lose gravity if the nodes were damaged, more easily than a station the size of Austro ever would.

The image cube was lit from below. He leaned over and

plucked it from the table, and looked inside at the three-dimensional images.

They were all of him. Him and the captain. He remembered that one outside of Siam Star. How his father had hugged him as if he were going to run off.

He tossed the cube on the couch and got up, bottle under his arm, and took his cases into the bedroom. The second closet. Was there a difference? His *bathroom* at home was bigger than this room, which had just enough space to squeeze from one side of the bed to another in order to get to the bathroom door. The bed was a double, at least, with a surprising set of dark blue silk covers and pillowcases.

Oh, so the captain liked his bit of luxury after all.

Ryan wedged his case and guitar by the drawer tower, sipped from the bottle, and snooped the corners of his new den. So what? His father expected him to live here and be happy about it, he had a right to do what he pleased. He pawed open the black drawers and riffled through the neat stacks of clothing, the shirts and sweaters and underclothes, some of them quite fine and unexpectedly stylish, even expensive quality. More surprise. The pants and uniforms hung in a long dresser, the black battle fatigues as well as the dress suits. Ryan flicked from shoulder to shoulder, glanced at the pins and ribbons, then shut all the doors and drawers and went to the bedside table. He put the bottle down and tapped open the drawer.

A gun and a dagger sat on top, both housed in black leather sheaths. Real leather, by the smell. Scarred, rubbed-raw leather. He wondered what kinds of people his father slept with to need these things so close. Underneath them were a locked metal box, an old slate, some info cubes, and a cam-orb. Nothing scandalous. So he sat at the edge of the bed and took out the dagger, slid it from its sheath. The hilt was smoke-colored steel and engraved with what looked like a stout horse, reared back on its hind legs with a flaring mane and sharp hooves. He checked the gun and it had the same symbol on its handle. Familiar, somehow, but he couldn't think of where he'd ever seen it. He knew it wasn't *Macedon*'s symbol.

"Find anything?"

Ryan nearly dropped the gun shoving it back into the bedside table. He shut the drawer and looked at his father. His heart gave a couple frantic thumps before he forced it to settle.

"Vodka," he said, picking up the bottle as he got to his feet. Staying by the bed since that was all the room he had.

The captain stood just inside the open screen. His eyes slid to the bottle, then up. Not a word. He brushed past and pulled off the hooded sweater, his back to Ryan, and went to the drawer tower Ryan had just inspected and took out a uniform, plain black fatigues like a jet's. He started to change clothes right there with the unabashed casualness of someone long used to military living.

Ryan sat on the bed to put more room between them and looked at the wall, drinking from the bottle. His eyes watered and he blinked.

"I'm not going to be in here very much, I have to be on bridge," the captain said as he dressed. "I need to get us back to Chaos as soon as possible, you can figure. So I'm trusting you in my quarters. Whatever you touch, I expect it to stay where you found it. If you're looking for drugs you won't find any. And I suggest you don't play with the guns. I don't want blood on my sheets. As for the alcohol"—he rolled up his sleeves half way, tossed the used clothing over a rack on the wall, and went to the screen—"if I ever find you rolling around drunk on my deck, you'll sleep it off in the brig. Copy that?"

Ryan looked him in the eyes and took a deliberate swig

from the bottle. Chances were nobody had ever defied him that openly. He didn't react to it so Ryan took a second pull. "Why don't you just put me in a spare quarters? Don't you have diplomatic suites or something?"

"Are you a diplomat?"

"A spare quarters, then. Somewhere."

The captain said, kind of soft, "I don't want you somewhere. I want you here."

Ryan looked at the screen. "Can I see Sid?"

A pause, as if he waited for Ryan to look back at him. Ryan didn't. Refused. The captain said, impatient now, "After dock break. Stay on the bed and strap yourself in."

"You say that to all your dates?"

His father frowned at him. Ryan slid back on the sheets, up against the headboard, and finished two-thirds of the vodka. His father watched him drink it. He saw him out of the corners of his eyes.

Come over here and take the bottle from me. Do it if you so disapprove.

"You shouldn't drink before a leap," the captain said instead.

"You didn't tell me we were leaping."

"We're going back to Chaos. How did you think we'd get there, by foot?"

"That would be pretty pio—pio-neer-ing of us, wouldn't it?" He moved to set the bottle on the bedside table, but missed it. Luckily he still strangled its neck. He fumbled at the drawer with his other hand. "What's that gun and knife anyway?"

"Personal." Suddenly the captain leaned near the bed and tried to pry the bottle from him.

He pulled it out of reach. "I think it looks familiar."

"I think you should lie down now. I have to go soon."

"So? What else is new? I don't wanna be here. Let me go home."

"I can't."

Ryan felt the hand on his shoulder. It wouldn't go away even when he tried to dodge. "Let me go!"

"I need you to lie down, Ryan." The hand went after the vodka bottle again.

Ryan couldn't stop him. The bottle went away. He reached for it but the captain pushed him back. Hard.

The pillows were there. The silence formed a thick wall around his head. He hadn't had enough sleep this shift. This year. He hadn't had enough time to just wipe out.

And then he was lying down with his legs stretched out, staring up at his father's face. "Why're you doing this to me?"

The question seemed to surprise the captain. He paused from whatever he was doing at the side of the bed. Ryan couldn't see and had no volition to lean and look.

"I want you safe," the captain said.

Ryan looked toward the bathroom, away. "It won't work."

"You're going to be safe, Ryan."

Like on Earth? Like on Austro?

A black web came over his chest.

"What's that?" Too late to struggle; he couldn't move his arms. "Stop it!"

"We're leaping. I don't want you tumbling about if something goes wrong."

It was hard to breathe. Then his father put a hand on his forehead, just lightly, sliding fingers into his hair. "Calm down. Just calm down."

"Let me go."

"I won't."

He sniffed. The captain didn't say a word. It was the

drink, or the immobility, or the way his father sat with him
until he could breathe, until he'd slid into the half-awake
state of drunken fatigue.

He didn't know if he dreamed it or not, the dampness at
the corners of his eyes and how his father wiped it away,
gently.

He thought he could hear the vodka slosh in his veins.
Certainly it seemed to slosh in his stomach and insulate his
brain. Memories battered against the fog, to be let out, to
evaporate, but they swirled and cycled in his mind instead,
thick eddies that flowed in on the tail end of drunken mus-
ings about the low ceiling he was forced to stare at. The ceiling that seemed determined to lower and crush his face from
the nose inward. Gray, flat panels, bars of light accompanied
by the sound effects of the airvents, hissing softly. It was a
box of a room and his father had shut the lid.

He remembered lying on this bed years ago. Had he been
eight? Seven? He'd only seen his father twice more, at four
and at twelve. The regularity of a deep-space carrier.

Ryan looked up at the man standing in the residence
foyer and thought, Daddy, and had Daddy in his head with
comm images and conversations where Daddy smiled at
him a lot and said he missed him and he was going to see
him soon. And here he was, soon. Ryan wanted to be all
grown up when he talked to Daddy so he called him Captain. He said, It's nice to see you, Captain, like he was one
of the security guards at the levs. Mommy kissed the captain
and hugged him a long time, and then the captain picked
him up and hugged him. He said, Put me down. He was too
old to be carted around like a bag of beans.

Mommy and the captain sat in the kitchen with drinks and
talked about adult things that Ryan listened to for about five
minutes before he got bored, so he tugged on the captain's

arm to show him the Battlemech Bear stuff he'd just got for Christmas. So the captain went and sat on the bedroom floor with him and listened to all the adventures of the great bear and said, He's very brave. The captain met all the bear's friends like Lizzi the Reptile Pilot, and Kit the Cat Commando, and the captain met the great bear himself in all his armor that lit up and morphed when you touched it. Then the captain said, Would you like to see some real stuff?

What real stuff?

A real gun and a real ship and real armor.

Like Battlemech Bear's armor?

No, the captain laughed. Not quite like that. It doesn't move around. But it looks pretty good, all black.

Ryan looked up where his mother stood near the partition to his bedroom and said, Mommy, can I? Please?

Mommy frowned. She said, Cairo, is that a good idea?

The captain said, It's my ship, Song. Nothing's going to happen to him.

Daddy owned a ship. That was right.

The captain said, Let's go, Ryan. He didn't ask Mommy for permission. He took Ryan's hand and led him out, and they hopped a pod and walked some more with the captain's soljets trailing them. The captain led him right up the long steel ramp where two more soljets stood guard, tall and stiff and serious, and Ryan made faces at them as he passed to see what they would do. One of them refused to blink or even acknowledge him, which was disappointing, but the other soljet with the wicked eyes and bright blond hair—he winked and snarled, making a monster face, and Ryan laughed.

The captain said, As you were, Private.

The soljet wiggled his half-gloved fingers as Ryan went along with the captain through the airlocks and onto the deck. Ryan waved back, one hand, since the captain held his other.

All the doorways and the walls were high, and everyone they passed was tall and uniformed, serious when they nodded to the captain, though most of them smiled when they looked down at Ryan.

He's adorable, sir, one woman said, on the lev ride going down. She had spiky dark hair and a red tattoo on her neck. Ryan pointed to it but his father pushed his hand down. The woman laughed and said, He looks like a fistful.

He keeps me humble, the captain said.

Ryan didn't know what humble meant but he stepped on the captain's boots and tilted back, stuck with a hand in the captain's so he wouldn't fall over, and arched his neck back to look at the spiky-haired woman upside down.

Do you work with my father?

She folded her arms loosely, her teeth showing white against her dark skin. She said, I do. And what's your name?

Ry-an Az-arcon. Just like how he said it when he wrote it. What's yours?

Ndili Hunsou. It's nice to meet you, Ry-an. She said it like he did, and he giggled.

The captain took his other hand and balanced him from both sides now, and when the lev door opened the captain walked him out just like that, with his feet still on the captain's boots and his view of the world all topsy-turvy.

Bye-bye. He raised his chin just enough to see Hunsou-with-the-red-tattoo before flopping back.

Bye-bye, she said. And, I'll have that report to you by the end of the shift, sir.

That's fine, the captain said over his shoulder. The lev door shut. The captain pulled Ryan up and over his shoulder in one smooth move and suddenly Ryan found himself looking at the deck at his father's heels, moving as the captain walked. He yelped.

Sir, what do you have there?

Ryan couldn't see who his father talked to, but it was another man. He kicked his feet. Put me down!

The captain held on tighter and patted Ryan's bottom. He said, It's my loot. I raided Austro.

Don't look like much gain, the strange man said.

Indeed, the captain said.

Ryan grabbed the back of the captain's shirt and yanked, but only got slapped on the bottom for it, not hard.

Footsteps passed and Ryan caught a glimpse of black boots.

Looks like you can clean the deck with it at least, sir. All that hair.

I might try that, thank you, Commander.

They were laughing at him. Ryan pounded on the captain's back but the captain didn't set him down until they came to a hatch. He bounced Ryan onto his feet, then hugged him against his chest, rubbing his back briefly.

Ryan wasn't really angry, it had been a fun ride, even though they wanted to use his head as a mop. He turned around as the captain poked a pad high up on the hatch, revealing a wide gray room full of robots.

They looked like robots, but as Ryan stepped in and up to the lines of dark shapes, he saw they were empty and hung on racks. They were black bits of armor, displayed as if people stood in them, hitched securely to the wall. They were big and broad and didn't seem to cover the entire body like Battlemech Bear's. Some of them were dented, others crisscrossed by white scars. Some had stickers on them or painted pictures of animals, or symbols he didn't understand. Some of the images were scary, toothy and red.

Ryan backed up a bit until he felt his father behind him.

They were all old armor, not like the Bear's.

They aren't old, they're just used, the captain said. They protect my soljets. Keep them alive.

What are those pictures for?

With the captain behind him, holding his shoulder, he stepped forward and reached up to one smooth black thigh and touched the paw print painted there in scuffed gold.

The jets put those on, his father said. It's like a mark, it's theirs. They're all different.

They were. After a while they didn't seem scary at all. They were like the red tattoo on that woman Hunsou's neck. Or the tattoo on the captain's wrist that Ryan saw when the captain reached over him and slid some of the armor back so Ryan could get a better look.

Do you have one too? Ryan touched his father's wrist, then the armor.

Yes, but it's not here.

Can I see it?

All right.

They went back out, except Ryan walked this time on his own, looking up at the ceiling way above with all of its colorful pipes and strips of lights. The walls were cold when he trailed his fingers along them.

They went in another lev and Ryan leaned against the wall with his hands behind him and watched as a couple other people, a man and a woman, came in. One was dressed like a jet, the other in gray coveralls. They nodded to the captain and looked at Ryan curiously, but didn't say anything. The captain didn't say anything either, just looked down at Ryan and grinned quickly, as if daring him to smile back.

Ryan puckered his lips and didn't smile. He could win it.

Then the lev door opened with a clang and the captain strode out. Ryan ran after him and glanced back before the doors shut again. The man and the woman stared after him, looking somewhat surprised, so he waved at them before chasing after his father to catch up.

How come those two didn't talk to you?

The captain shrugged. They probably weren't comfortable.

Why?

I haven't really had occasion to speak to them very often. So they might be a bit intimidated.

In-tim-i-dated.

Scared, his father said.

Why? Were you mean to them?

The captain laughed. No. Do you know how many people are on my ship?

Five hundred?

Higher.

Six hundred?

The captain stopped by a hatch that looked a lot like all the others, heavy and gray, and took out his tags from inside his shirt and opened the hatch with one of them, sliding it through a little box that beeped. A tiny image of his face was on the tag, with numbers and symbols all over it front and back. He tucked it back in his shirt before Ryan could get a better look and took Ryan inside.

Not six hundred, the captain said. Six thousand and twenty-one people live and work on this ship.

Ryan stared up at him. That was almost as much as Austro.

The captain laughed again and led Ryan through a tiny living room to a bedroom that was half the size of the living room. This was where his father lived, like how he and Mommy lived in the residence. But both rooms here were barely the size of Ryan's bedroom alone. It didn't seem right that his father should live somewhere smaller than *his* home.

Austro has about sixty thousand people, the captain said. It's much larger than *Macedon*. Here, have a seat.

Ryan plopped on the bed and took off his shoes and pulled his feet up, sliding back on the soft blanket. It was a big thick bed and it felt good to just lie there. He took one of the pillows since the captain didn't have any stuffies anywhere and hugged it. It was soft and slippery but he gripped it tight and watched his father open a tall cabinet against the wall. Inside were more uniforms and the captain moved them aside and dislodged something heavier. He turned around and showed Ryan. It was a torso piece of black armor and it shone so much the lights overhead reflected in them. But it was still used, like the others, even though it was shiny. Scratches were all over it.

You wear that?

The captain said, Sometimes. Rarely, now.

Ryan blinked, his cheek on the pillow. He tried to imagine his father in that, all done up like Battlemech Bear, but he couldn't see it. His father was too tall and too skinny and he'd never seen him with a gun.

He drifted and didn't know where his father went in the room. Once he opened his eyes halfway, sleepy, and saw his father changing clothes. He didn't have a shirt on. He didn't look so skinny without his shirt and that was strange. And it was stranger, the thing on his chest. The black tattoo that Ryan couldn't quite make out in the dim light. But it looked like some sort of animal. A smaller version was on his arm, near the inside of his elbow, above the wrist tattoo that was the tattoo of the captain's ship. He'd seen that one lots of times. But not the animal one. Then the captain put on a shirt and he couldn't see it anymore.

He fell asleep again. And woke up again, a little, and the captain was beside him on the bed, reading a slate under a small circle of light. It felt later, and like bedtime, so he just rolled over and shut his eyes.

He heard voices. Maybe it was later. It was his father on the comm, talking to Mommy back on station. He heard his mother say, Keep him until the next sleepshift.

Ryan kept his eyes tightly shut. If he woke up his mother would want to talk to him and it might get loud. So he lay still and quiet and slept some more, for the last time that shift, in the absolute silence of a small room tucked inside a large, motionless ship.

Ryan vaguely heard someone from the intercom announce dock break, a voice from on high, but he didn't feel anything, doubly cushioned by alcohol and grav-nodes. He wasn't going to feel anything when the ship eased its way from dock and out of the station vicinity, he knew that much. So he floated, thirsty and tired, half in memory and half in denial that he was actually lying on his father's bed, strapped down like a child. Then later, when his bladder was beginning to send up alarms, the same woman announced the imminent leap. The drives screamed, violent. It reverberated through his veins.

Suck.

Push.

Inhale.

It suctioned his insides to his skin and he blacked out.

He woke up to find himself free, with a mighty pain in his gut and the urge to wet the bed. He scrambled to his feet, banged a shoulder against the tower drawer, and tilted to the bathroom, half-blind from headrush, past his father, not even sliding the door shut.

Ah, sweet relief.

No sooner was he done with one end that he dropped to

his knees and threw up. The sound of it hitting the insides of the toilet made him retch the more until his lungs, heart, and stomach throbbed with pain. His throat burned, it was all over his mouth, down his shirt. He gripped the stainless-steel rim, fingers cold, eyes shut tightly. Tears streamed and he thought of blue skies and green fields.

Blue.

Skies.

Green.

Fields.

He coughed, his nose running by now. *You pathetic sack of shit, get up.*

But he didn't want to move.

He'd done this to himself. He was just doing it all to himself.

The sick was all over his shirt like the blood had been.

He didn't hear his father approach, just felt the hand land lightly on his shoulder.

He jerked away, yanked free some tissue paper from the wall attachment, and wiped his mouth, struggling to his feet with barely enough room to maneuver because his father didn't back out. The toilet flushed with a roar as soon as he let it go and moved away. "You want to watch?"

"What made you drink before a leap, Ryan?"

He waved on the water in the sink. It tasted metallic but he swished and spat anyway, and splashed his face.

His father offered a towel.

Ryan snatched it. "What do you *want*?" The fast movement forced him to lean on the sink. His eyesight dimmed, then cleared, and for a second he caught his father's eyes in the mirror.

He looked away when the captain said, "We're at the Persian Gate. Shower and get dressed."

The door slid shut.

It took several deep breaths and more cold water on his face to settle his insides. It was temporary. He tried to clean up the mess and halfway through he had to spill again. Every orifice seemed to revolt on him for what felt like hours. Half crying, half retching from the sight of his own vomit, finally he was sucked dry. Empty. Shivering. He wanted to die, the ultimate cop-out in the midst of physical misery. The bathroom tiles were smooth ice under his feet. He would lie down on it if it wouldn't make him sicker, or make him remember waking up in another bathroom with a different kind of pain.

Everything seemed far away, even his hands as he mopped and scrubbed. He found antiseptic spray in the cabinet and used that until he started to sneeze from the sharp scent.

Then he stripped off his clothes, dumping them on the floor. He'd find an incinerator later.

In the narrow shower stall he peered at the water selection pads, leaned one hand on the small tiles and waved at the sensors with his other hand to get the right temperature and strength of spray. It was an older system and took more movement to get the proper combination. The sudden blast of cold water on his body scared the cobwebs from his mind and a few profane words from his mouth. With his teeth chattering he balanced it out and straightened up under the little waterfall, wiping his hair back, then grinding the heels of his hands into his eyes.

He could stay in here forever. He wouldn't have to go out and talk to his father or deal with this ship or anything.

He leaned in the tiny space for long minutes, nearly falling asleep standing up and with his eyes open. Colors seemed a little off, washed out, and his chest burned. But it was a lot better than just an hour before.

Eventually he came out feeling half human, at least, and hungry. Amazing that food entered his mind.

He was going to have to face his father. Part of his brain was still in that bathroom, even back on station. It felt like someone else's hands dressed him. Underwear, pants, hooded sweater. One leg then the other. One arm and then the next. It made him feel ten years old.

He put one cold hand in his pocket and pulled the screen aside with the other.

Sid was in the outer room talking to the captain.

Plates of noodles and dumplings sat on the kitchen counter, keeping warm on zap burners. His stomach growled, loudly, announcing him before he got out a word.

"It's alive," the captain said, standing by the counter, shooting him a glance. "Here, eat something."

"Hey," Sid said, straightening from where he leaned against the sink. "You look awful."

What had they been talking about? Sid showed no scars so he supposed it was civil. Of course the captain didn't let on whether he knew about Sid and Mom Lau, he just picked up his plate and went to his couch and sat, where glasses of drinks stood waiting. Water.

Ryan followed Sid to the cushioned seats, with his food, eating the little dumplings on the way. His tongue got scalded but he didn't care. His gut eased, surprisingly. And he didn't trip.

"Don't do that again," the captain said. "We've got another leap to ride and it'll be rougher if you don't recover now."

He didn't trust himself to talk just yet. If he started he might not stop, might even start yelling that he hated it here already. And that would make a scene and Sid would kick him, so better to be quiet.

The captain hadn't taken the bottle from him until it was

nearly empty, until he knew Ryan was drunk enough that he could wrestle it away. The man must have known what was going to happen and made Ryan endure it.

Meanwhile Sid and the captain both looked like they'd had a nice stroll through a sunny park. No half-lidded eyes, no shaking hands. It was worse because Sid was a dirtsider. That put Ryan to shame.

"What'd you do?" Sid said, not seeming particularly surprised, whatever the answer.

Ryan turned his shoulder to him. He cleared his throat, soothed it with water. "So how long are we at the Gate?"

"An hour or so," the captain said. "Corporal Sidney's had a tour of the ship so he can show you around."

Be the shadow, the captain meant. After the vodka fiasco he was going to get escorted everywhere.

"Sir." Sid grinned a bit self-consciously. "One commando tour certainly won't save me from getting lost."

"I have faith in your ability to keep your bearings."

"We can drop breadcrumbs," Ryan said.

His father ignored that. "Until we get back to Chaos Station and you can begin your training, it might benefit both of you to explore together. My people have assignments and no time to baby-sit. I trust you won't be planting bombs on our drive towers."

Ryan wanted to pretend he hadn't heard all of that. But Sid said, "Training, sir?"

"Yes." The captain sipped his water, said almost offhandedly, "All the crew are required to go through jet recruit training, so you know the protocols in the event of an attack. Since you obviously have experience in some areas it might seem redundant, but you've never served on a ship and there are procedures specific to a ship environment."

Sid nodded like he understood.

Ryan said, "I don't have to do that. Do I?"

"Yes," the captain said. "You do."

"I don't want to." He'd seen enough vids of military training. He knew that he didn't want some tall-brawn to verbally abuse him while kicking him in the arse.

"Ryan, you of all people would need this training. You have no military experience whatsoever."

He set the plate on the table. It made a clatter. His hands were sweating, more aftereffect from the leap, he had no idea. "There's a reason for that. I'm not a soldier. I don't want to be a soldier."

"You're on my ship and that's the rule. What good would it be if something happened and someone put a rifle in your hands and you didn't know what to do with it?"

"So when you invite dignitaries on board you make them do jet training?"

"No, because their stay is temporary."

"Mine's temporary."

Sid said, "Ryan."

"No," the captain said, eating with perfection, as if they sat around a formal dining table. "Your stay is more than temporary."

"I'm not *living* here, *sir.*"

"We had this discussion on Austro."

"We *didn't* have this discussion. You just ordered us about like a bunch of slaves!"

"Indeed?"

Something in his father's tone made him stop, lose thought.

"Ryan, this isn't the worst place you can be, it's just a place that won't put up with your attitude or your demands. I know you understand why you're here. The only reason you're chafing about it is because you won't be able to run Corporal Sidney in circles or sneak off from your mother and sail."

He had a knife in his hand. He thought about it, a flight of fancy. "You don't understand a thing."

"Indeed? Enlighten me."

Sid was watching him with a face that said, *Shut up now.*

He stared into his father's eyes, a jumble of words in his head. Accusations. Assertions. But they died where they were, at the tip of his tongue.

"Yes?" the captain said, with a straight dark gaze.

Ryan blinked, looked down at his glass, and picked it up. Wishing it were vodka and all of this be damned.

"Never mind," he said. "Just—never mind."

The meal didn't last long after the argument so Sid took him down to jetdeck. Sid's quarters were there and Ryan asked to see them, screw restrictions. He wanted to be away from his father. Sid didn't argue with him and hadn't opened his mouth much in the captain's quarters either.

Jetdeck seemed exactly like the command deck and maindeck to Ryan's eyes, except noisier, somehow darker with the profusion of black uniforms and baser languages. The people here were all jets, as far as he could tell, and they all made rude sounds at Sid as they passed. The jets called him Marine Boy and Sweet Thing, and one jet said, "Show me how to gloss those shiny boots." Word had spread, evidently. Sid ignored them. Left without a response, the jets focused on Ryan. Just staring, which was creepy enough.

Their progress halted as black uniforms clogged the corridor outside of what looked like a lounge. Ryan caught a glimpse in the room of round tables and couches and a gaggle of more uniforms playing sim games, talking and eating snacks. He and Sid edged past the doorway, not very far before they were stopped by three male jets who slid from the group and quickly maneuvered them into the center of a uniformed triangle. The other jets gave these ones room in the corridor. That couldn't be good. Ryan felt Sid's hand touch the middle of his back, signal to keep his mouth shut.

"Excuse us," Sid said to the lead jet.

The man had long black hair tied back at the top, making his broad forehead and angular eyes look vaguely foxlike. He bared straight white teeth at them in a friendly smile, though his eyes didn't change from their flat appraisal.

"A Marine," he said, looking over Ryan's head. "I swear, Bucher, first it's a symp, then a little pirate, and now this ferry fleetman. Our ship is really sinking lately."

Jets didn't like Marines, or at the very least they saw them as poorer cousins. One of the jets behind them answered, "Maybe we need to vent some of this refuse."

If Sid couldn't say a word without getting hit, Ryan knew at least they wouldn't touch *him*. Not their captain's son. Right?

He glanced at the lead jet's namepatch. "Maybe you need to get out of our way, Sanchez."

"Marines," Sanchez continued, ignoring him, "do nothing but sit their asses on stations playing dominoes while citizens get attacked by strits. Ain't that right, ferry fleetman?"

This sounded more like a grudge than a teasing superiority. Ryan said, "What's your bone? And why's it stuck up your arse?"

"Ryan," Sid said behind him.

"Yeah," Sanchez said. "Keep Cap's litter out of this."

That went one step too far. He'd had it with this ship. He kicked at the jet's knee, fists raised to balance and on their way to a few punches.

But Sanchez moved surprisingly fast and grabbed the front of his sweater.

An arm came down between them—Sid's. His bodyguard had dodged to Sanchez's flank and elbowed the jet into the bulkhead, freeing Ryan to the middle of the corridor.

Sanchez's two buddies burned their way between him and Sid with hot words and fiery fists. A hand clamped on his face and pushed him against the bulkhead. He saw a blur of Sid's back struggling between Sanchez and one of the jets before the third jet hauled him around, warding off his wild blows with calm, dismissive slaps. He just grabbed a fistful of uniform sleeve before something seized the back of his sweater and yanked him nearly off his feet and out of the way.

It wasn't any of the three enemy jets. He spun in time to see a blond figure breeze by him and attack Sanchez's ally with brutal speed. The jet went down to his knees with a yelp of pain, holding his ribs. That stopped the other two as if someone had pressed the pause button, with Sid locked between them disheveled and white with anger.

The blond one—a jet, judging by his black attire and the Corps patch on his arm—stood with his back to Ryan. He said in a low conversational tone, "Sanchez, mano, you must be mad-crazy to let your puppies lay their paws on the captain's son."

Ryan felt someone encircle his upper arm with long fingers, turned and saw the blue-eyed female jet who had escorted him from the residence. The blond one was her companion from his father's escort, and they were both now in uniforms.

All of the other jets in the corridor had cleared a space five meters on either side of the scuffle, and none of them spoke.

Sanchez said, "Junior's all right. It's his leash getting in my way."

"Let him go," the blond jet said, no longer conversational.

"Or what?" Sanchez's lip curled. "Cap put this fleetman down here, what'd he expect?"

"Maybe to test you, not him," the blond said, and stepped closer.

Sanchez released Sid abruptly and the blond jet paused. Sid turned to Sanchez, but Ryan said, "Sid."

Sanchez's buddy—Bucher, his patch said—had a hand resting somewhere at his backwaist and the air in the corridor suddenly seemed to drop a few degrees and become thin.

Sid walked by Bucher, then the blond jet, toward him. Ryan recognized the look on his face; he'd seen it in the polly precinct. He didn't realize he was holding his breath until Sid came up to his side and he released it at the same time the female jet let go of his arm. Sid was a much more welcome presence at this proximity.

"What're you going to do, Dorr," Sanchez said to the blond jet. "Tell on me?"

Dorr reached inside one of his cargo pockets, in no apparent hurry. In a couple seconds he held a burning cigret between his fingers. "I don't gotta waste words where you're concerned, mano. My gun'll speak for me."

Sanchez's smirk didn't quite reach the corners of his mouth. It died as his eyes shifted on Dorr.

"Good-bye," Dorr said.

Whatever threat the slighter, paler jet posed to Sanchez must have been enough, or maybe even considerable; Sanchez gathered his flock around him and brushed past their group without another comment. The other silent, gathered jets in the corridor made way for him, then started to disperse as Dorr turned around, grazing his eyes upon them all.

Quite suddenly he smiled at Ryan, blowing out a fast stream of pale smoke. His deep dimples were incongruous to the hard steel of his eyes. "Baby Az, you look like crap. Didja have a rough leap?"

Dorr saved them from a beating so felt free to take liberties with his name?

Sid said, "We appreciate the help, but Ryan and I didn't come aboard to get harassed by some gym class bullies. If those three get in my way again, I will kill them."

"That's fine, Maroon," Dorr said, with a shrug. "Sanchez can afford to be brought down a few pegs."

"What's his problem?" Ryan said.

The woman jet went around to stand beside Dorr and casually lifted his cigret from his fingers and took a puff before handing it back. Her name patch said Hartman and Ryan wasn't sure, but her rank insignia might've indicated an officer. "Sanchez's always been a little stiff. It got worse since the war got suspended."

"He's got a thing against strits and symps," Dorr added. "And pirates. And boys in blue like you, Maroon. And maybe even pets and old people, who knows. He just all around angry."

They seemed to find it more amusing than threatening. Sid said, "Why isn't he kicked off this ship by now?"

"Well he might be soon," Hartman said, glancing once at Ryan.

"I won't cry if he was," he answered.

"I can report on him," Dorr said, "if I felt like it. But it's better to leave jetdeck to jetdeck. Cap's got enough to worry about. Besides, I'd rather Sanchez and his cronies where I can see 'em, or at least spy on 'em. Where're you two off to, anyway? I heard Baby Az ain't supposed to be down here."

"He was giving me a tour of the ship," Ryan said. "Mr. Door."

Dorr looked at him closer, and laughed. "You're cute. But

don't push it. I can't be around all the time to save your sweet ass."

"Jet," Sid said.

"Or yours neither, Maroon. It's a sweet ass too."

Sid stared. Ryan didn't move, even though he wanted to quit this corridor and these jets and the sudden empty and echoing nature of their environment. Nobody loitered and if Dorr and Hartman decided to give them a hard time, he highly doubted Sanchez would come back to help.

"I wouldn't wander around here if I were you," Hartman said. "Despite Daddy's orders."

"No sense temptin' the wildlife," Dorr added, with his grin. He drifted closer to Sid.

"We're going to my quarters," Sid said, and put a hand on Ryan's shoulder. "Now."

Ryan started off without encouragement, feeling his skin crawl as Dorr started to laugh. Sid was a solid presence at his back. They walked without hurrying, even as Dorr's voice floated after them.

"What, not even a kiss of gratitude? It would make my little life so complete!"

They were a good distance away and about to turn the corner. He didn't know what it was in him that couldn't let things slide, but that last comment made him look back. Dorr and Hartman still stood where they'd left them, watching. Dorr with his predatory smile as if he'd only got rid of Sanchez so he could himself lay claim.

"I only kiss with my fist," Ryan cast into that long stretch of corridor between them.

Sid's fist closed around his collar.

Dorr laughed, a bark of surprise. "That works for me too."

Sid shoved Ryan around the corner and shook him once before letting go.

"Don't encourage them, dammit."

"What're they going to do?" He made his voice nonchalant. "They can't touch me."

"No, but they can touch *me*. And I don't fancy getting on their bad side because you can't keep your mouth shut."

"You're already on their bad side, Sid. You wear a different uniform. Worse yet, you're a dirtsider."

"Damn pack animals." It bothered Sid, all right, being treated as a second-class citizen. He didn't have backup on a ship like this. "Jets *evolved* from Marines, don't they know that?"

"They wouldn't care. And you know my father put you here so you can suffer."

Here on jetdeck. Here on the ship. Away from Mom Lau.

Sid didn't answer. Maybe he thought he deserved it.

And maybe he did.

Ryan said, "Are we really going to your quarters?" He didn't want to bump into any more jets.

Sid murmured, "Yes. Unless you want to go back to your father."

Sid knew which he'd prefer.

By the time they got there Ryan was thoroughly lost. Too many twists and turns in gray corridors that only differed in their level of disrepair. Some passageways were coated with laser pulse scars and what appeared to be explosion damage. Hatches were destroyed altogether in some parts, the rooms inside half melted, half imploded.

"They battled at Meridia," Sid said. His tone was somber. "Pirates boarded her."

Ryan remembered the Send reports. But the ship must've been safe to travel, despite the look of the interior. Or else his father never would have brought him on board. He hoped.

Unless his father was crazy, which was always a possibility.

Inside Sid's quarters he appropriated one of the bunks and stretched out, his limbs feeling drained of animation. Feedback from the leap, he wasn't sure. He looked around from that vantage.

"Are you supposed to hang your clothes in here and sleep outside?"

Sid didn't comment. The joke had too much truth in it. Six cots, only one dressed with sheets and blankets, piled three on either side in a narrow gray room—it would seem a miracle for six people to get around in here. No wonder jets were a little mad. The pillow smelled like it had been through ten cycles of detergent. He supposed that was better than it smelling like someone else's hair.

And where were the other five occupants? Empty bunks must've meant dead jets.

He ran from that thought and watched as Sid dug around in his duffel. Sid pulled out his comp and opened it up, then sat on the opposite bunk and tapped at it.

Ryan tucked his arms behind his head. "Can't you give it a rest?"

"I want to see if your mother's on 'cast."

"It'd be old. We rode a leap, remember?"

A few hours for them, maybe a few days for Austro.

Sid muttered, "I still want to check."

Ryan couldn't see the screen but he heard the transcast. He pictured his mother caught in numerous camlights, maybe standing outside her office, or maybe it was a closed announcement *in* her office, without a live audience . . . but that wasn't like her. She'd want a press conference out of it. She'd allow questions because to hide from them would seem suspicious. She'd cut them off when she'd had enough, with some indisputable excuse—she missed her son, she had to comm her husband, she had to limit her public time for security reasons (that would go over well, especially as the public would see her taking a *risk* to speak to them).

"My priority right now," he heard her say, "is my son's safety. My husband feels the same way, that's why *Macedon* came to Austro."

"Ms. Lau!" someone called out.

So she probably 'casted in front of her outer office in the PA wing, with a phalanx of security and the press corps.

"Ms. Lau, the captain didn't stay for long on station. What did he say to you and Ryan? And has he returned to Chaos Station to continue the negotiations?"

"One at a time, Greta. First, he was very concerned for our son, naturally. He spoke with Ryan, mostly about things that are rather private so I'd prefer not to divulge them here. Second, yes, he has returned to Chaos to continue the peace negotiations."

"Ms. Lau! Did he give any indication of how things are going? Are the strits agreeable?"

"Well, I suppose they're agreeable to some extent, considering they're at the table. We didn't really talk about it."

"But surely you must've had some feeling . . . ?"

"They're in the early stages yet. Admiral Ashrafi, his staff, and the other diplomats there—not to mention my husband—would probably prefer it if I didn't jump to conclusions on their behalf. It's not really my place."

"Ms. Lau!"

"Winton."

"How *is* Ryan? How long will he remain in the residence?"

He watched Sid's tight expression, the fixed eyes on the comp screen. Now his mother either lied outright or confessed he was no longer on station.

If you're good at this job, she'd said, *you'll never have to blatantly lie.*

"Ryan," she said, "is quite safe at this moment and doing as well as can be expected. I have confidence in our security and my husband. The culprits will be caught."

Sid breathed out, audibly. A small, crooked smile creased the corners of his mouth. "Good woman," he murmured.

If the sniper thought he was still on station that might keep them occupied. Hopefully his mother would take her own security seriously too. That gnawed at him. It worried Sid too; he saw the thought playing in his bodyguard's mind as Sid watched the archived 'cast.

He wondered if the captain had counted on Mom Lau's discretion—or savvy. He wondered if the captain saw this transcast or if he cared at all.

"You should come look," Sid said.

"I can hear it fine." He rolled over and stared at the featureless wall so he wouldn't have to watch Sid as Sid watched his mother on the screen.

Then he heard his name but it wasn't some meedee asking a question. The segment must have scrolled to a live 'cast.

Sid said, "Dammit."

Tyler Coe's theatrical voice rang loud and clear from the comp speakers: "Yeah, I was there in the Dojo when Ryan Azarcon was shot at. I saw him dancing with a girl; I think she was dressed like a black cat."

Ryan tossed over and sat up, hitting his head on the bunk above. He swore and leaned out to the narrow aisle between bunk towers. Sid tilted it so they both could see the screen.

Tyler sat in an interview chair, scrubbed, smooth-skinned, and clear-eyed. He said, "I saw Ryan Azarcon push that girl into the bolt."

The bunk seemed to sink a level.

"Give me that," Ryan said, tugging at the comp.

"Wait."

"Give it to me, Sid!"

"Wait a minute!" Sid shoved him one-handed, still intent on the 'cast.

"That's a big accusation," the interviewer said. "How can you be sure in the midst of a flash house?"

"I saw what I saw. Maybe it was wrong"—his tone implied otherwise, of course—"but I'm just saying what I saw. I personally didn't think Ryan was capable of that kind of selfishness—"

But he was capable of another kind?

"—but people do weird things when they're under stress. I'd rather not believe it of him, to tell you the truth."

"Bastard liar!"

All because of the scene in the polly cell. Or some pent up resentment. He'd always suspected Tyler had it in for him, despite the smiles and good humor.

Flake.

Downright publicity whore.

"If Ryan pushed that girl into the bolt, then he'd have to have known from which direction it came. How is that possible?"

The meedee's name was Ben Salter. Ben had always been neutral toward Ryan and his family; he was Paulita Valencia's star associate and Valencia was the most respected meedee in the Hub. At least there was that.

But Tyler said, "I don't know, maybe a first shot landed wide before the one that killed the girl. I'm just telling you what I saw. And I think the pollies should get all the information. I don't think anyone else would really come forward with this, not on Austro anyway. I think the pollies have a right to know in order to help their investigation. Innocent people were killed that shift." His voice wavered. His eyes watered.

"You lying piece of shit!"

"Ryan," Sid said.

"He's saying I *pushed* that girl!"

It wasn't good. Not for him, not for his mother. Certainly not for his father, no matter how you angled it. A tragedy had occurred in the Dojo and it had been his fault in the first place. It was just one step further for people to believe he'd actively done something to cause a death.

The screen split and the Send 'casted his previous statement, him in front of the cams with his carefully scripted words, delivered perfectly. Maybe too perfectly. Juxtaposed beside Tyler's interview, it shed a different tint on his apparent honesty.

He breathed in anger and the cool, dry air.

Beneath his hands were the rough wrinkles of a well-worn blanket. Not the soft silk of a girl's costume.

Blood on the floor.

"Give me the comp, Sid."

"Your mother will take care of it."

"It'll sound better coming from me. It's me he's accusing."

"I don't think you're authorized to 'cast from this ship."

"Bugger it!"

"You definitely won't 'cast in that tone of voice. You'll just give them ammo. Now calm down. It's not irreversible."

"No, it's slander, while I have to sit on my arse."

Sid said, "Ask your father."

Ryan got up and headed for the hatch.

"Where are you going?"

"To ask him!"

"Ryan—"

He yanked open the hatch and turned back, so abruptly Sid barely stopped from crashing into him.

"He said I shoved that girl to her death. If my mother doesn't get on the Send, like *right now,* then I'll find a way to dispute it myself."

"She'll do it. And you need to calm down. You can barely stand."

The edges of his sight blurred and blackened. Runoff from the leap and his drunken bout, he had no idea, but his grip on the hatch handle was the only thing keeping him upright. That and adrenaline.

"Ryan, sit down before you collapse. What did you do to yourself before the leap, anyway?"

He was tired. His joints ached. He wanted an injet of Silver but it was impossible on this ship. He didn't even have any in his one bag. So he couldn't zone. Ever again. It was one situational insult piled on top of the other.

"Look," Sid said, "maybe I can make a few comms once I'm authorized. To the Marines on Austro. I'm pretty sure we can get Tyler red-handed on something." He smiled.

Only Sid could look so innocent while proposing a premeditated bust.

"You'd do that," Ryan said. His nerves settled as Sid continued to smile at him.

"Yeah, you need to ask?"

He didn't return the grin. He should still have had a right to defend himself but nobody in his life seemed to consider him capable. "Think you could get one of your Maureens to kill Tyler while they're at it?"

"Ryan."

"You think I'm joking?"

Something beeped. It was coming from Sid's chest. Sid looked down and pulled out his tags and tapped one. Apparently they'd configured them already, meanwhile *he* still didn't have an outgoing link.

"Corporal Sidney," he said, in his Marine voice.

"Bring Ryan back to quarters, please."

His father. Just what he needed.

"Yes, sir."

"He's making me live with him. In that *little space*. Can you believe it?"

Sid frowned. The tags weren't disconnected yet.

Oh.

His father's voice said, "I assume he's on his way."

"Yes, sir."

Then Sid shut off the tags and put a hand on Ryan's shoulder to steer him out of the room. "Let's make a deal. I take care of Tyler and you learn to keep your mouth shut. For both our sakes."

The walk back had decidedly less interruptions. Maybe Mr. Captain had warned his jets this time (come to think of it, maybe he'd authorized the previous harassment). Or maybe it was because they were fifteen minutes from a leap. The corridors were clear. Sid took him back up to the command crew deck and deposited him in the captain's quarters, then beat a retreat.

It was nice to have friends.

The captain, in his black uniform and standing by the hatch, said, "Do I have to strap you in again?"

He asked it as if it were a common occurrence. Or maybe he thought that one time had set a precedent.

Ryan said, "No."

"We'll come out near Chaos Station. I'll comm you then."

"You don't have to. I've leaped—sober—before."

"I'll comm you when we come out of the leap."

Ryan sighed. "Did you see the Send?"

Your son's been accused of murder. Depraved indifference at the very least. Don't you care?

"Yes, I saw it."

He didn't seem overly worried. Or worried at all.

Ryan said, "Well, can I say something about it?"

"Go ahead. But make it quick."

"I mean on the Send."

The captain opened the hatch. "No you may not."

"He accused me of pushing that girl into the cross fire!"

"Tyler Coe."

"Yeah, Tyler Coe!"

"Consider the source. Don't worry about it. Go put yourself in bed and I'll comm you."

"I'm not going to let that weed say all that shit about me. I can't believe you'd want him to."

The captain leaned a hand in the middle of the hatch. "I don't want him to, but I'm not worried about it. Your mother is capable."

"So am I."

"Ryan, you should already know that if you address every tabloid rumor you'll spend the rest of your life defending yourself. Pick your battles—and your opponents. Only deal with the worthy ones."

"Thanks for the advice. Too bad I didn't ask for it."

"Parental prerogative. Now I really have to go."

Ryan bit the inside of his cheek. "Yeah, you do that."

The man left without a glance.

It was cold.

And he could do nothing but lie down on that bed, bundled in like a child. He stared at the ceiling and waited for the ship to move.

His fingers tapped the sheets. Repeatedly.

The second leap was far softer than the first. Or maybe the difference was in his sobriety. He still blacked out, which was normal for a stationer who had ridden maybe

four leaps in his entire life, but at least he didn't wake up
with the urge to toss, although he awoke with a headache
and the feeling he was forgetting something. Which he probably had. Surface amnesia was common.

The drives were damn noisy. Big growling giant.

He'd kept one arm free so at least he was able to undo the
straps himself once the all clear sounded (a beep from the
walls and a woman's voice), and sat up on the bed smoothing the hair from his eyes. His limbs felt gooey and unreliable, so he just sat there. After a while he thought to check
his watch. Forty-five minutes had passed with him just sitting. He'd totally zoned out without touching a bit of Silver.

Leaps, some people said, were addictive.

But the initial hit was harder and the consequences
rougher. He wanted Silver.

The bedside table beeped. The sound went right to his
brain like a spike. He leaned over and saw a red dot alit on
a back panel. Underneath it flashed "private incoming." So
he poked the dot like he would on a comp icon.

It still beeped and seemed to get shriller. Or that was just
his tolerance level depleting at a rapid rate.

"Dammit!" He slapped the flashing words. The red dot
clicked to green. He said, "What?"

A pause. Then his father said, "Are you cognizant?"

"I have a headache. What's with your damn comm anyway? It doesn't work like normal consoles."

"It's an intercom, not a comp console. Relax. We won't
dock for another half hour but I want you dressed by then.
Eat something light."

"I'm already dressed."

"Presentable."

He sighed. "Why?"

"Your grandfather will want to see you. He's coming
aboard once we dock."

He'd forgotten Grandpa Ashrafi was on Chaos. With the Warboy, whose ship was also docked there. And the symp who'd killed that pirate Falcone and caused the retaliation at the Dojo—did the captain still harbor *him* on this ship?

Ryan thought he might have a few words for that symp.

"Don't wander around," the captain said. "I'll be there in about forty."

It was his father's quarters, but for all intents and purposes it was a cell. He didn't even bother to answer that, just poked the comm until nothing blinked and slid back on the bed.

Lying on his side, he noticed his guitar was secured against one wall, beside the drawer tower, in webbing attached to the bulkhead. His clothing case was nowhere in sight. His father must have unpacked for him.

An excuse to go through his belongings, no doubt.

He must have drifted, because the comm beeped again and he had to open his eyes to reach for it. This time he got it on a first tap.

"I'm on my way to q," the captain said. "I hope you're dressed."

"I'm tired."

"We're going to eat something and you'll feel better. Get dressed, Ryan."

He slapped a hand on the panel. Of course that didn't shut off the comm; he had to touch the words "private incoming" twice to make them go black. Maybe he ought to ask the captain if it had voice recognition and could the captain please program it properly if he wanted his son to live in this damn room.

Quarters.

Whatever.

After a minute Ryan dragged himself up and looked through the drawers, eventually found his clothes and dropped them on the bed before he went to the bathroom. This time he stood outside the stall and waved the water to how he wanted it before undressing and stepping in. No more arctic wake ups, thanks.

After, he changed into something not quite so wrinkled or casual. He knew the protocol, his mother liked him to dress up for dinner too, so he chose a plain red shirt and black pants and even ran a comb through his hair, although he couldn't seem to keep his eyes wide open enough to really care how it looked. Then he wandered out to the living room just as the captain walked through the hatch.

"Will I be able to get on comps at some point?" he asked his father, remembering now that he saw a comp on the couch's sidetable.

"You have your mobile, don't you?"

"You know I'll need the ship link since I'm hell and away from Austro. You have to authorize me."

"Later." The captain went into his bedroom.

Ryan stood outside the screen. "When?"

"When I get a moment. Use Sid's if you want to scan the Send; I've already authorized him. You won't be transcasting so it doesn't matter, does it?"

"Did Mom say anything about Tyler?"

"I don't know." He started to change clothes.

Ryan looked at the kitchen space and thought of the vodka. "She wants me to comm her."

"Use Sid's for now."

Because Sid wouldn't let him transcast either.

They had it all worked out.

"I think I have a right, you know," he said quietly.

The captain came out of the bedroom, dressed in a clean black uniform and with neater hair. His eyes were tired though, almost hooded. They grazed Ryan. "A right to what?"

"To dispute Tyler if I want. To *say* something."

"Figure out what you want to say and maybe I'll look at it. Calling Tyler a bastard wouldn't be smart."

"I wasn't going to do that. I know better, you know."

"There's more going on now than Tyler's little report, you might have noticed. It would be wiser to just let your mother handle it."

That patronizing tone prickled his skin. "You think it looks good that the captain who's spearheading these talks has a murderer for a son?"

His father stared at him, a sudden deep attention that made him regret opening his mouth.

"Ryan, you're not a murderer. What happened in the Dojo was a *pirate* thing. And as far as the Send goes, I never really cared what they thought. Captain S'tlian doesn't care what they think, and we're the ones talking to each other. We're not talking to the Send."

"But it matters."

People looked. People talked. People shot at him and why couldn't his father see that it all counted?

"It matters as much as I make it matter, Ryan. They'd like me to make a big deal of it, like Tyler wants you to make a big deal of it. They want us to worry about everything and validate what they say. But it's all shit."

Maybe it was easy for the captain, locked away here in his ship. He went on, "Some people in the Hub will think bad of you, or me, or your mother. Does that change what's really going on? I'm still going to work these negotiations and sooner or later the rest of the galaxy will get on the bandwagon. It doesn't work the other way. I don't listen to idiots. Now let's go eat."

He said it in his captain's tone. No argument.

Ryan still wanted to pound Tyler's nose into the deck.

But he followed without a word, or tried to; his father

waited for him to walk ahead, to make sure he went forward. So Ryan stuck his hands in his pockets and preceded the captain through the hatch, careful not to trip on the threshold. He glanced over his shoulder to be told which direction. As it turned out it wasn't far, just down the corridor on his left and into a private dining room.

Cream-colored walls greeted them instead of the slate gray of the other bulkheads. Finally some variation; this colorless world had been enough to make him want to toss a can of red paint into the mix not only for the color but for the chaos. In the middle of the room was a three-meter-long table with a faux-wood finish; he could tell by the too-perfect rings beneath the dark veneer, not quite Mom Lau's imported dining set. Shiny bone-white place settings for five sat at one end, with domed, fragrant serving dishes between them. Three of the seats were occupied.

His grandfather sat at one and stood to shake the captain's hand, then without preamble or warning he pulled Ryan into a long hug.

"So good to see you," he said, smashing Ryan's nose into his shoulder. "We were worried."

It was unexpected and embarrassing and hit him dead center like a rock. He took a breath of the admiral's exotic caff scent that had clung to the clothes all the way from Earth, and didn't let it out for fear of what else might leak out of him. His grandpa hadn't seen him in person until he'd gone to Earth but never treated him as anything but a grandson. *He* hadn't seen Admiral Grandpa since Earth, and Earth and all of its tangled memories came back in a rush, as he was held against that warm, uniformed chest.

"Are you well?" his grandfather murmured, loosening his hold just a little.

Ryan still couldn't speak, so he just nodded and avoided the admiral's observant eyes before he gave away all of his emotions and lost control of them completely. It felt too good to be held like that and he couldn't give in to it, not in public.

His grandfather squeezed his arm, maybe in understanding, and over the admiral's shoulder Ryan saw Sid, who stood and smiled at him almost relieved. So the captain had remembered that Sid knew the admiral and offered the courtesy of attendance. Sid was a familiar anchor, made him focus, and between him and Admiral Grandpa, sitting at a table with the captain might at least be tolerable.

But in the last seat was a stranger, a young man maybe his age who stood reluctantly and didn't look any more enthusiastic about being there than Ryan felt. His eyes strayed away from the familial scene and found a blank spot on the wall. Ryan glanced at Sid and let Sid follow his gaze back to the kid, a question. But Sid only shrugged. He didn't know either.

A friend of his father's? The kid looked too young. Unless that was another deep-space deception.

Finally Admiral Grandpa stepped back and motioned Ryan to the empty seat beside Sid. The captain, expression held in as he glanced at the admiral, took the other empty chair across from Ryan and next to the kid.

The admiral was, naturally, at the head of the table.

"A little respite, finally," Grandpa Ashrafi said, sighing as he sat. "Without all the govies, eh?" He smiled. He never quite considered himself a govie, Ryan knew, despite the fact he had enough brass on his uniform to outfit a cruiseship. In his younger years he'd captained the battleship *Trinity* in the war. His dark eyes were alert as usual, his hair shorter than Ryan remembered and sparsely grayed at the temples. But he looked a lot younger than his sixty-plus Standard years, thanks to five tours in deep space and post-thirty suspended aging treatments. It was a common irony that by appearance alone he seemed to be the captain's chronological age—mid-forties—but was old enough to be his biological father. He said to Ryan, "Your grandmother sends her love."

"I got a comm before I left Austro, but I haven't checked since." He couldn't make himself do it, even if he'd had authorization. He almost didn't want to see if Shiri had commed back.

"She's probably inundating you with messages as we speak," the admiral said with a fond smile. He meant Grandma.

"She's bound to miss you," Ryan said, looking again at the unfamiliar face in the room. He didn't exactly want to get into anything personal with this kid here, so didn't say anything more.

The kid was staring at the covered food, but not with much intent.

"Ryan," the captain said. "This is Jos Musey. He's helping with the negotiations. Jos, my son Ryan."

Ryan fixed on him as Jos Musey looked up, hearing his name. He had doll-innocent blue eyes, maybe genetically tampered, it was impossible to tell. Fine-featured, pretty in the way you'd associate with girls, though there was nothing soft in his stare, his expression, or the spare angles of his face. Faint bruising spotted his left cheek and a red, healing scar cut a line down his bottom lip. That evidence of violence set unease in Ryan's stomach above and beyond the steady eyes.

Musey might have been biologically younger, even though something about the way he sat, straight and still, seemed too controlled and too aware—too adult. His dark hair grazed his eyelashes, belying the mature impression, and he didn't wear any sort of uniform that Ryan could see—just plain black.

He didn't blink once as he looked at Ryan. Didn't say anything either.

It was unnerving.

The captain and admiral started talking quietly to each other, leaning to their corner of the table. Sid found his glass of water interesting, maybe eavesdropping on the brass, so Ryan said to Jos Musey, "Hi."

Musey blinked and said, "Hey," because it seemed to be expected, not because he might've meant it.

"So you're helping with the negotiations?" It didn't seem likely.

"Yes."

"Doing what?"

Jos Musey glanced at the captain, as if seeking permission, but the captain wasn't paying attention and Musey looked back at Ryan immediately. "Interpretation. Translation."

He was surprised at the accent. "You're from Austro?"

Musey didn't answer.

Ryan waited, but the pause kept up. Musey didn't seem uncomfortable about it. He just sat there.

Ryan looked at Sid but from his expression Sid had no clue either. Grandpa and the captain still talked. Words like "pirates" and "activity" floated into the sudden silence. Musey's gaze slid over to that side of the table.

"Sirs," he said, "what about the people that were on Slavepoint? Have they been questioned about"—for some odd reason he hesitated—"Falcone's lieutenant? And his protégé?"

The captain looked at Musey and didn't answer immediately. He leaned back. "A few of the prisoners there said a sympathizer transport took them both off planet . . . after we killed the *Khan* and crossed back to Hub space after Falcone."

"Falcone wasn't on the *Khan*?" Sid asked. "Sir?"

The captain looked at him. "No. He was on board a sympathizer ship. Doing business. Arms trade."

"Sympathizer?" Ryan said. "So they *are* in alliance with the pirates."

And yet the captain was going to make peace with them.

"A faction of them," his father said. "Yes."

As if that was supposed to make a difference.

"How can you possibly trust—?"

The admiral said, "The striviirc-na and those sympathizers who are in alliance with their ruling power, of which Captain S'tlian is a part—"

The Warboy, he meant. But now that word seemed taboo. Not *politic*. Or polite.

"—are working on weeding out those dissenters and dealing with them. Thankfully, they seem to be in the minority."

"Oh," Ryan said. "Well then. What a relief."

"Ryan," Sid muttered.

"No, really." He directed his words to his father. "Symps in alliance with pirates, but it's not all of the symps, right? That's reassuring. And the pirates? Their leader is dead, which is great, but they don't seem to be much crippled by it. All it did was make them more pissed."

"It doesn't take much to piss them off," the captain said. "Or you, it would seem."

Ryan ignored that. "And—what—two of their heavyweights are unaccounted for? Let me guess—they headed for Austro after this—what do you call it—Slavepoint?"

"Ryan," Sid said. "Tone it down."

"Why? *I* got shot at because some symp offed a pirate when the Hub had dibs—and my *father's* kept that symp on this boat. People *died* because of it."

They were all watching him, like you'd watch a bereaved person railing uselessly at the heavens.

Admiral Grandpa reached to touch his arm but he sat back, pulled his hands to his lap. Wanted to get up and walk out but he couldn't move, pinned under their stares. His cheeks felt flushed.

He fixed on Jos Musey. "What are you looking at? Why are you even *here*?"

"Ryan," Admiral Grandpa said softly, as if sound would trigger an explosion. "We know it's been rough for you—"

"Grandpa. Don't." The last thing he wanted was a speech motivated by pity and concern.

And to have his grandfather look at him like that. With love.

Sid's silence on his left was enough to make him hear himself. Sid didn't have to say a word for Ryan to know what he was thinking.

Just calm down. You're going to be all right.

Eventually.

If he stayed awake. If he let people help him. If he stayed off the drugs, Sid had said, especially the potent kind on Earth that weren't the best to start with when you hadn't even touched Silver before. Because everyone knew the worst—or best—drugs came from Mother Earth.

His mind kept spiraling back to Earth, more since the Dojo, and it didn't take a shrink to tell him why.

Maybe his mind had never left Earth, though his body had.

He said, "I'm sorry. Okay? I'm sorry." He tried not to look at his grandfather as he said it. "I spin sometimes."

"It's all right," the admiral said.

Ryan waited for the captain to say something, but he didn't. His face gave no clues to his thoughts.

"I'm the symp who killed Falcone," Jos Musey said instead.

Ryan blinked once, and stared. "What?"

"Jos," the captain said now.

Musey still looked at Ryan, unapologetic. "If you want somebody to blame. You seem to be looking for somebody to blame."

Ryan squinted. *"You?"*

A latent accusation. Musey didn't confirm it twice and in that brief silence a uniformed server came in through a side door and paused, making eye contact with the captain.

"Go ahead," the captain said, leaning back.

So the server began to spoon out the creamed broccoli soup and dish out the food for them. All at once so he wouldn't have to return.

None of them said a word.

Ryan's mind buzzed as he watched Musey's expressionless face.

Sympathizer. Symp.

Strit-lover, which was far more derogatory.

Here, sitting down for a meal with them.

The bowls and plates had central warming so nothing would get cold but it wasn't the food giving off that ambient chill. The server poured the wine too but Ryan put a hand over his glass. Getting drunk at this table wouldn't do him any favors. Musey turned his glass upside down before the server got to him. The server edged around the symp rather delicately, as if he were afraid to touch him.

Not surprising.

After the server left, Admiral Grandpa regarded all of them with a small smile and sipped his soup.

"Well, Cairo, your meals have always been eventful."

The captain smiled, wry. Nobody else did.

"Why is he on your ship?" Ryan asked. If they expected

him to be seen and not heard, like at Mom Lau's cocktail parties, that was too bad.

"Because I want him to be, and because he wants to be. As I said, he's helping with the negotiations."

"Then why isn't he on the Warboy's ship?"

"Why does it make a difference to you?" The captain ate, but looked directly into Ryan's eyes. "It shouldn't."

"I'm on this ship now."

"Yes . . . so?"

Nobody was going to step into this argument. Musey was staring at him now, as if surprised that Ryan would even question the captain.

Ryan kept his voice mild and his gaze straight. "I don't want to be on a ship with a symp. I think that's obvious considering we're at *war*."

"Technically we aren't, or haven't you been watching the Send?"

"Yeah, I have. And keeping a symp on your ship doesn't endear you to anybody. You don't seem to get that some people aren't happy with our family right now. Whatever you do affects me and Mom. Or don't you care?"

So much for keeping things impersonal in front of a stranger. There went his words, in the air and flying.

The captain took a breath and set his spoon down. "I care. What I don't care about are ignorant people in Hubcentral thinking they know what it's like in the war when they've never moved their asses farther out than Pluto. If I didn't take steps toward this treaty the Hub would drag their feet for years just to make a decision to cease fire. You, Ryan, have no experience in this area. Don't try to tell me that I don't know what I'm doing." He picked up his glass.

"No," Ryan said, "it seems you know exactly what you're doing. You bullied me and Sid onto your boat just like you're bullying the Hub to make peace with terrorists who blow up our stations and attack our ships. You never compromise unless it's on your own damn agenda."

"I'm not going to have it out with you when you clearly have no idea what you're talking about."

He couldn't stand to be dismissed, even as one part of him knew that the war wasn't really what he was arguing about. "I'm not the only one who sees it. You can't just go around forcing people to comply with your decisions. *Pirates* do that!"

"Your father is not a pirate," Musey snapped.

"Who asked you?"

"All right," the admiral said. "That's enough."

Ryan said, "Nobody seems to have the guts to tell him when he's wrong."

The admiral said, "Ryan, enough."

"It is possible," the captain said, "that you don't have all the facts, considering you've lived most of your life on a station filtered by its own politics."

"Don't patronize me."

"Say something smart and I won't have to."

"Cairo." From the admiral.

"Sorry, sir," the captain said, perfectly respectful in the way you got when you felt the exact opposite.

Ryan knew it well.

"Eat," Sid murmured to Ryan. "Before I slap you."

Judging from the captain's expression, that seemed wise advice. Even though his blood still boiled. And he wanted to reach across the table and hit his father in the face. A few times.

The admiral said, "This reminds me of dinners when you were his age, Cairo."

"Thanks," the captain said.

"At least he isn't throwing cutlery. Must be his mother's influence."

"Sir."

Grandpa Ashrafi hid a smile behind his glass. The captain looked chagrined. Ryan sipped his water, wishing suddenly he had the wine after all. Or something to steady his nerves. Settle his stomach.

Make his father stop staring at him.

The symp, at least, had his eyes on his food.

Sid cleared his throat and made art in his mashed potatoes. "Uh, Admiral . . . how *are* the negotiations going, if I may ask? I saw on the Send that there've been protests on the general dockside here—anti-alien rallies?"

"Yes," the admiral said, frowning. "A small group, but they're loud. So we've decided to hold the talks on *Macedon*, beginning tomorrow. There won't be rabble on our dockside, at least, since the Marines here do a good job of enforcing the military restrictions."

"The aliens . . ." Sid glanced at Musey, who didn't seem to be paying attention anyway. "I mean, the striviirc-na . . . they'd come aboard?"

"They'll be well guarded," the captain said. "And we'll be working over there too, eventually. To be fair."

"Where?" Ryan said.

"To *Turundrlar*."

"What's that?"

"Captain S'tlian's ship."

Ryan stared. "You can't be serious."

Of course they were. Everybody was.

The ship that the Send called *The Hand of Death*. Supposedly that was the translation of the strit name, though humans on the Hub side didn't exactly have a complete strit dictionary or grammatical workup.

His father over on that ship—anything could happen. The symps could break dock and make off with the best captain in the Hub fleet and the admiral of the Joint Chiefs, not to mention a bunch of govie suits from Hub Command. Did nobody think of that?

"It should be interesting," the captain said, like he was talking about a sporting match. "So, Ryan, you see the diplomatic suites will be occupied after all."

That wasn't even remotely funny.

"Speaking of which," the captain said to Musey, "can you inform Captain S'tlian that we'd like to reconvene at oh-nine-hundred next shift?"

"Yes, sir."

"That should give you enough time to take Ryan to medical and then come to the conference room."

Ryan said, "Take Ryan where?"

"My CMO already gave Sidney a physical and I want you to have one before you start training tomorrow."

"Why does he have to take me?" Ryan glanced at Musey, who seemed to be doing his best to memorize the food configurations on his plate.

"Because I've decided he'll be the one to train you."

He didn't think it could get worse, but now he knew better.

Musey didn't seem surprised, at least he didn't react. It was nice of the captain to warn the symp, but not his own son.

"Before you explode," his father said, "it won't be for the full eight weeks. When Jos isn't in the talks with Captain S'tlian and me, he'll orient you to weapons, comps, and basic combat techniques. When he *is* in the talks, you'll be at school."

"School."

"Yes. I don't want you idle on my ship."

He wondered if his mother had a hand in that idea. He looked at Sid, but it was clear he wasn't going to get help from that quarter.

"Why can't I just train with Sid?"

"Because you're not at Sid's level and I don't think you'll deal well in a class of recruits or with my jet instructors."

"But I'll deal better with a symp who murdered a pirate? I don't want this symp to train me."

"Your language," the captain said with a hard stare, "can use some work."

"I don't want this symp to train me, *sir*."

"Ryan," the admiral said.

"I'm not one of your recruits!"

"That's obvious," the captain said, putting a hand on the table, "since I would brig any recruit who bitched as much as you. Four weeks of training isn't a difficult thing to do and you *will* do more on my ship than laze around and scroll the Send. Get used to it."

"Why did you bother dragging Sid here if I'm never going to see him?"

"You're going to see him, Ryan. In off-hours. And after training."

Maybe his father wanted him out of Sid's influence, and wanted Sid out of Mom Lau's.

He saw it then, in one glance that the captain cast Sid before looking back at him.

"You're jealous," Ryan blurted. Fueled by anger or idiocy, he wasn't sure which, but it got more of a reaction out of the captain than anything else up to this moment.

The mask slid, revealing a sharp irritation that could only point to the truth. "I'm what?" the captain said.

"You heard me."

"Everybody heard you," the admiral said. "And both of you are stepping on my last nerve. I try to keep a sense of humor about family but this has been quite a test. You both should be ashamed. Sid, why don't you return to your quarters, you have a long shift tomorrow. Musey, give Ryan a tour of the ship, then bring him back to his father's q when you're finished."

It was so ordered by the Admiral of the EarthHub Joint Chiefs, and none of them, not even the captain now, dared argue with the man.

"I already had a tour," Ryan said to Musey, paused in the corridor on the command crew deck, just outside the captain's mess. That wasn't entirely true, of course. He and Sid had never gotten around to it, except through avoiding jets.

"Good," the symp said, as if he knew. "But you'll get another one."

Musey looked ready to snap. Not like a soldier on parade or anything, his stance was casual enough, but he seemed to expect something that would require retaliation. Ryan wondered if that was normal for a symp (if normal was a word you could apply to symps). Maybe just for a symp on an EarthHub carrier.

"You don't want to do it," Ryan said heading to the lev, "so let's not and say we did."

"Then you can tell the admiral," Musey said, "when he asks. Because he will ask."

"Don't argue about it," Sid muttered, positioning himself between Ryan and Musey.

It was impossible to have a normal conversation with the third wheel rolling along beside them, so Ryan said nothing. The lev opened up, thankfully prompt. Two female officers exited, casting Musey discreet, not altogether friendly looks. Sid got in the lev first and told it jetdeck. Ryan waited until the doors shut with its loud swish-clank, then looked at Musey.

"You're real popular around here, aren't you?"

Musey leaned against the lev wall, apart from them, and didn't answer.

"You talk a lot too. Is that why they beat you up?"

Sid said, "Maybe you should leave him alone."

"I don't know. If he's going to be my guru, then I'd like to know if he's human at least."

The symp's eyes slid off the light bar and landed on him. Sid straightened where he was standing.

Ryan met the stare. "It figures my father would put me with the pariah."

"Why do you do that?" Musey said, in his Austroan accent. Ryan wondered if it was real. Austro had symps, they'd blown up a dock a while back, but he wondered how this one had ended up on a deep-space carrier.

"Do what?" he said.

"Provoke people," Musey said.

"Am I provoking you?"

Musey stared at him. It was impossible to read the symp. He just looked exponentially somber. He said, "You don't agree with what your father's doing? The peace?"

"I didn't say that. Exactly."

"No, you just make bigoted slurs every other word."

"By calling you a symp? Isn't that what you are?"

"And are you a spoiled brat?" Musey said.

Ryan took a step. Sid's hand shot out and grabbed his arm. Sid looked at Musey.

"I think that's enough."

Musey glanced up at Sid but he didn't seem concerned. "It's no wonder people were shooting at him."

Ryan yanked his arm free and went for the symp. But Sid got in the way again. Too fast.

"Settle down!"

Musey hadn't even moved or blinked. Ryan stared at him over Sid's shoulder.

The lev announced the deck. The doors slid open with a

metallic clang. Musey walked out without looking behind him.

Ryan looked at his bodyguard. "You need to talk to my father about him. Please."

"You're unbelievable. You got him going and now you want me to put my neck on the line?" Sid walked out after Musey.

Ryan followed. "I mean it. I'm not going to put up with him."

"You'd better learn. The captain gave you both an order."

"It's punishment. For both of us. You and me."

Sid shoved Ryan's head, not entirely playful. "Speaking of that—*don't* bring it up again, okay?"

"He *is* jealous, you know."

"Just shut up about it, Ryan. And keep your voice down."

Musey was only a few strides ahead of them, parting the way like a plague. The half-dozen jets in the corridor went by with muttered comments Ryan couldn't hear, but he didn't need to. At least with Musey occupying them, most just ignored him and Sid. He thought Musey would just go on ahead and forget Admiral Grandpa's order, but the symp led them right to Sid's quarters and stopped.

Ryan said to his bodyguard, "Can I hang out in here for a few?" Hoping to ditch the extraneous body.

Sid glanced at Musey, sighed a bit. "I don't think you should, Ryan."

"You can take me back to the captain's quarters after."

"That's not what the admiral said."

"So?"

"Look, I'm not in the mood for crossing his orders—or your father's. You don't have to listen to them but I do. They can do things to my career, not to mention my health. I'm sorry."

"How do you sit down with that pole up your ass?"

Sid opened his hatch.

Ryan said, "I'm sorry. I didn't mean that."

"Look, tomorrow's going to be hard. I think I want to crash out. Maybe you should just do this tour and get a good sleep?"

Sid was tired of dealing with the Azarcons. Ryan saw it. He wished they were back home. He even preferred Sid and his mother making eyes across the dinner table to where he was now.

Now it was Musey making eyes—the kind snipers gave before pulling the trigger.

Ryan said, "Well, if you don't hear from me next shift you know what happened." He glanced at the symp.

"Comm me when you get back to quarters," Sid said. He was serious.

Ryan nodded. Maybe Musey was insulted but neither of them cared. Sid would still do his job, however he could, and Ryan found it in himself to smile at his bodyguard for that.

Sid returned it and gave the familiar hand sign. *You're okay.*

Ryan signed back: *For now.*

Sid's lips twisted, wry acknowledgment. He shut the hatch and the corridor enclosed Ryan and the symp in its shadows.

He waited a long moment before turning around to face Musey. "So . . ." Ryan folded his arms. "Give me the tour then."

He told himself this symp wouldn't lead him to a dark corner and kill him.

Musey watched him for a second, as unreadable as the captain, then headed down the corridor the way they had come, without a word. Ryan followed. Every jet they passed on this deck cast them dirty looks and then completely ignored them.

"Why would you possibly want to live on this ship?" Ryan asked finally, after the tenth crewmember went through the ritual glare and Musey said and did nothing. Ryan didn't care for the hate by association. Everybody on this ship besides the captain seemed to despise the symp (small wonder) and if the captain put them together, Musey's reputation would spill onto him. As if he needed that. The fact he was the captain's son must've been the only thing saving him and the symp from being jumped and dumped. "Hey," he said, "are you ignoring me now? Where are you taking me?"

"I'm showing you the ship. I don't have to speak to you. Just look where you're going."

Surly son of a bitch.

Ryan had no choice so he trailed, hands in his pockets. The corridors all looked the same to him—absent of signs or any sort of luxury. Dingy, poorly lit, and newly attacked. Some crew in gray coveralls worked at hatches, control boxes at junction points, and overhead at the pipes. Echoes of machinery buzzing and whining at repairs seemed to bleed up through the decks from the maintenance accesses.

"I can't believe he sent this ship through a leap," Ryan muttered.

"He had to," Musey said.

"Just to get a pirate?"

Musey didn't answer. He gestured vaguely at an open hatch as if to say, Take note. It was the jet lounge that Ryan and Sid had passed before. But Musey didn't stop.

"Why'd you kill that Falcone guy?" Ryan said to his back.

Musey stopped now and turned around. Only one eye

showed blue from the shadows that cut his face. "My life is none of your business."

"My father seems to be interested in your life."

"That's his business."

"I'm on this ship and he says you're going to train me. So I think it's my business."

"It's not." Musey turned his shoulder. "This is the gym on your right. Let's go down a deck."

Musey had the swift, uncanny ability to make him feel ridiculous in his very existence. Something in the symp's tone of voice or the stained-glass blue of his eyes was too quiet and too fearless. Nothing was worth Musey's time, nobody was worth his attention unless he deemed it. And it wasn't the haughty arrogance of the upper tier society on Austro. It resembled that, but it was something else.

More like the captain. Confidence bred from ability, not blood.

How well did they know each other, Musey and his father?

The association made small, angry, and unreasonable spikes scrape at the back of his mind. A thought that wanted to claw its way out and wreak havoc in accusations.

But he was still lost in these vein-dark corridors, still programmed enough to know he had pushed things too far at dinner and he had better not try anything now. He could ditch Musey and ask somebody how to get back to the captain's quarters, but Musey didn't walk ahead this time. He waited and looked at Ryan with that deflective stare.

It would be too much trouble to run, and getting in a fight with the peace talks translator might land him in the brig. He wouldn't put it past his father. So he walked with the symp away from the repair crew and into a secondary lev. The symp said, "Engineering Deck C." Ryan stood on the opposite side to Musey as they descended.

"I'm not all that interested in how these ships run," Ryan told him. "So we can skip some sections."

Musey said nothing, just watched the light bar blinking above the lev doors. They stopped on a rough bump. The doors opened to a long empty corridor, eerily silent, and completely blast-scarred. As if a bomb the size of an elephant had stampeded down the deck, leaving damage in its wake. Perforated skeletal infrastructure showed through half-open interior bulkheads. A burnt metal scent hung heavy in the air, not circulating. No ambient hiss from the vents, no color in the barely lit darkness. No life.

Ryan stayed against the wall of the lev and didn't step out when Musey did.

"What're we doing here?"

Musey had a hand on the door, keeping it open. "I'm giving you a tour."

"I'm not going down there with you."

"I won't hurt you, Azarcon. Be realistic."

But it wasn't Musey that he saw. Over the symp's shoulder was destruction and the smell of new death, and he was not walking into that.

"You sick bastard. Let go of the door, I'm going back up."

Musey stared at him, unmoving. Curious.

"Get your hand off that door before I make you."

"Why are you panicking?"

"I'm not panicking. I don't appreciate your little joke. What'd you plan to do, get me down here then leave me?"

"No." Small frown. "I just wanted you to see what your father does for a living. Then maybe you'd understand why he's talking with the striviirc-na."

"I know what he does for a living, thanks."

"No. You don't. You know what's on the Send, and I think you know that shouldn't be entirely trusted."

"Get your hand off that door, symp." He thought he saw shadows move behind Musey.

How many people had died in that attack at Meridia?

Musey said, "This is what pirates did. Take a long look. You wanted to know why the captain went after Falcone? This is part of the reason."

"Fine. Whatever. Tour's over. Take me back to command deck."

Bloody sadistic symp. Ryan stared at him as he stepped in and let the lev doors shut.

"Jetdeck," Musey said. Then, "I don't know what your problem is with your father, but considering you were shot at on station you ought to be grateful he took you aboard."

"You don't know a damned thing about me, so shut the hell up."

"Are you always this angry?"

Anger and boredom, his shrink had said, *are oftentimes symptomatic of deeper emotions.*

Sid wasn't here now to stop him from pounding the symp, but he folded his arms. Tight.

Musey didn't say anything else, just left his question hanging. It pitched and swayed in Ryan's mind like a dead body on the end of a rope.

Musey deposited him outside his father's hatch and left, no words, not a single look. Ryan took a long breath and stared at the tag scan and since he had no tags yet to open any private rooms on this ship, he had to bang a fist on the thick door. Hatch. Door.

Cripes.

Admiral Grandpa opened it. "Ryan," he said, "glad to see you in one piece."

"Did you think I wouldn't be?" He moved in, forgot the raised threshold, and stumbled.

His grandfather had to grab his arm to keep him on his feet, and laughed. "Careful."

He wasn't exactly swan-graceful, but deep-space carriers made stationers feel doubly clumsy. Damn boat. He glanced around but the captain wasn't anywhere in sight.

"He's in the bedroom," the admiral said. "We just had some tea, do you want a cup?"

The screen was shut. Ryan looked up at his grandfather and sat at the island counter in the kitchen. "Yeah, sure. Did you two fight? Is he still pissed at me?"

His grandfather tousled his hair and went around to the zap plate on the back counter, where the avian-shaped kettle sat. "I can't believe what you did to your hair." He poured the tea with a grin.

"So you did fight. And he's still mad."

"No, we didn't fight. We talked about tomorrow's negotiation session. And I reminded him that he was far more of a terror on me than you are on him."

"I'm not a terror. He just makes me so—mad. He always has to be so *right*."

"A lot of the times he is, even though his methods aren't always—diplomatic. But he's a deep-space captain, not a politician. I believe he is right about the striviirc-na."

The admiral slid over the cup and Ryan put his cold fingers around it. The ship was always so damn cold.

"You and he must be the only ones in the entire government that think so."

Admiral Grandpa leaned on the counter across from Ryan. "We aren't. President James is on our side, he just needed some convincing and a bit of balm on his pride. He doesn't like to be upstaged. The others, like the Hub Council . . . I think they'll come around once they realize it'll be better in the long run. We've got support from most of the major stations in the Dragons, some in the Rim and Spokes.

It's just going to be a long process. We're just at the point with the aliens talking about defining new borders. We haven't even touched upon arms, caches, communications, ship routes . . ."

He thought about Musey being the fulcrum in those discussions and figured his grandfather had to know what was going on, even if the captain might be a bit (voluntarily) clueless about the dangers of relying on a symp. Even if it was just in everybody else's perceptions. People wouldn't get behind a treaty if they knew the translator in the negotiations was the same symp that had murdered a man. A pirate, maybe, but still a man that should've been put through the justice system in the civilized Hub. "What about the Centralists? And that—First Minister Damiani."

"Well . . ." His grandfather didn't seem pleased. "Let's just hope she doesn't get elected."

Ryan sipped the tea, peered down at the tiny dregs collecting at the bottom of his cup.

"But," Admiral Grandpa said, "the problem you have with your father doesn't have anything to do with the war, does it?"

He didn't answer that. He didn't know that he could explain it, if his grandfather followed up on the reply.

"Have you told your parents about London?"

Ryan shook his head. "I don't want the looks."

"What looks?"

"The one you're giving me now. Pity. Disappointment."

"Understanding?"

He shrugged. "Maybe."

His grandfather was silent a long minute. "Try to talk to him. Maybe not about Earth, but just in general."

He reached a finger into his cup and poked at the soggy tea leaves. "How much do you talk to him? I mean, about stuff other than what you have to talk about because of your jobs."

"Less now. That's why I think you should."

"You never told me much about him, even when I was on Earth. I mean, aside from some pictures in your house . . . how come you never talk about him? You adopted him for a reason, didn't you?"

The admiral gazed at him, almost unreadable except he wasn't at work now and Ryan saw the face he used to see in the mornings, in his grandparents' breakfast room on holidays, when the admiral would come in with the dog at his heels and kiss Grandma on the cheek.

Ryan blinked and his grandfather's hesitation straightened out to decision.

"I made a promise to him. Like I made to you. Your father's a very private man and not just with meedees. With his family too, sometimes. You know that. It's not something I care to infringe upon. I don't think I have the right. But you're his son. Some things are different for you than they are for me."

"I can't see what."

"Maybe that'll change. So . . . tell me. What do you think of Musey?"

He couldn't help it; he laughed. More out of surprise than mirth. "Don't even start with that symp. What is his problem anyway?"

"Does he have one?"

"I think he's got more than one."

The admiral seemed amused. "He's been a tremendous help in these talks. Captain S'tlian truly respects him and the way your father's dealt fairly with him has been a big factor in getting the strivs and the sympathizers to the table. Don't stress him out, Ryan."

"Me?" He was honestly offended by that until he saw his

grandfather's sly, habitual smile. "It wasn't my idea to be in his orbit, you know."

The admiral laughed. "Make the best of it, all right? For the sake of peace in this galaxy. And for your father's peace of mind."

"What about my peace of mind? That symp is dangerous."

"You know your father wouldn't trust him with you if he really was a threat."

No, he didn't know that at all. Logically, yes, but what he felt—that was another thing. The captain and the symp both claimed this ship was safer, yet he'd just seen its scarred, exploded innards and been accosted by crazy, unpredictable jets.

"I'd better turn in," his grandfather said. "And so should you; you've got your physical early next shift."

"Don't remind me."

"Comm your grandmother, all right?" He tousled Ryan's hair again on his way to the hatch.

Sid had started that trend and now everybody did it. He'd be fifty years old and they would still mess him up.

After Admiral Grandpa left, Ryan went to the washer drawer and spent a few seconds looking it over. It wasn't like the one at home and he hadn't paid attention when his father had shown him. He figured the biggest button must make it open, and at least he was right. Having it turn on when there weren't any dishes in there would probably give him a couple demerits, on a ship that conserved water output if the timed showers were any indication. Then his father would make him scrub the decks or do the ship's laundry or some other bit of slave labor. He had to watch his demerits, yessir.

And on that thought the screen slid back and he turned around as the captain came out to the living room.

"I'm finished in there if you wanted to go," his father said. He was dressed in an old pair of fatigues and a white T-shirt, and sat on the couch with his slate.

Not a word about the dinner.

Even his silences tended to ignite Ryan's irritation. So instead of starting anything, Ryan just went into the bedroom and slid the screen shut.

He didn't know how his grandparents put up with the captain all these years. Or how his mother did, for that matter. He really had no idea.

He took a timed shower even though he'd had one earlier, but he needed the hot water on his cold skin; blasted himself warm from the body dryer, then rummaged through the drawers in the bedroom in search of his sleep clothes. Outside in the living area loud music played.

At this hour.

It certainly wasn't the sedate background ambience his mother favored, or the Earth classical stuff his grandparents liked. It wasn't cultured or highbrow.

Ryan padded out to the kitchen and had to nearly shout. "What're you doing?"

His father looked up and went to the unit in the wall to palm it down a few decibels.

"Sorry about that, but I work better with it on and I heard you in the shower."

Ryan stared. "You work better with it." He did too, not that his mother or Shiri ever believed him.

"Yes. If I can't hear my comm then I can't be interrupted." His father grinned at the joke, rather uncaptainly. "Do you know this artist?"

A slate sat activated on the coffee table, with a steaming cup of tea beside it. The quarters had a small area rug, blue like the furniture, and the captain was barefoot.

"I think I have their latest upload." Ryan went to the

kitchen, unhinged a glass from the counter stack and tapped out some water from the coldcase unit by the sink. "I thought you'd be asleep already."

"Hell no. I'm used to operating on five hours. More than that and I'm draggy all shift." The captain returned to the couch and sank down, picked up the slate and put his feet on the table. "Besides, there's too much to do for tomorrow."

"Grandpa told me a little. I met the Minister of Alien Affairs one time on Earth at some ambassadorial party, and he's here, right?"

The man had a polite but patronizing view of the strits. He could imagine his grandfather doing damage control on the minister's negotiating volleys.

"Musey's got his work cut out for him with Minister Taylor, trying to interpret his platitudes. Speaking of which, how'd you two get along?"

He sipped his water. "Me and the minister?" Of course he knew better.

"You and Jos."

"Like a moon and a planet." Sarcasm, he couldn't help it.

"Well, you're in one piece."

"That's what Grandpa said. I guess you expected the symp to trounce me."

"Something like that." Another smile. "Why don't you sit down?"

It was a quiet invitation. A completely different demeanor than what was at the dinner table. So Ryan took his glass and went, hesitantly, and sat on the opposite chair instead of beside the captain on the couch.

He expected the captain to say something but the silence stretched. He peered over his glass, across the low coffee table, but couldn't hold the thoughtful stare.

"What? Stop doing that."

The captain leaned back and rested a hand on one of the

square couch cushions, fingering the corner. "You may have noticed that Musey isn't well liked here."

"Yeah, he's got lovely conversational skills. How do you keep him from being killed?"

"I issued an order. They aren't ignored. But I realize that it'll take some getting used to. His unit seems to have forgiven him—he was a jet here, did he tell you?—or at least they don't ignore him, but the rest of the crew . . . it's another matter."

"He was a jet? He's a symp."

"I didn't know he had affiliation with Captain S'tlian—at the time."

It just kept getting better. "You want him to train me and he was a spy? How can you trust him?"

"That's between me and him, but I do trust him. He's a good kid. The crew will come around."

Like the Hub was going to come around about the strits.

"There's a lot between you and him, isn't there?" he said, before thinking he should've kept that one in his head.

"What do you mean by that?" his father said, neutral.

"Never mind. So what if your crew doesn't grow to love him?"

"I'll dump them," his father said.

Ryan stared. "Over one kid."

"Not just over him. Over the fact I prefer acceptance to prejudice."

This was new. "You run a warship. Your jets kill people like him for a living."

"I know it won't be immediate." He sighed. "But that isn't what I mean to say right now. Just be mindful of Jos, all right?"

His father's insistence irked him beyond habit. "So, you want me to be his pity partner?"

"No." His father frowned. "But he needs interaction

outside of the military forum and you're pretty much it on this ship."

"Glad to be of service. Now I know why you drafted me. Isn't it funny that we even look alike?"

The frown deepened. "What?"

"Me and the symp. We both have blue eyes and dark hair. Well, when mine is natural."

"That's ridiculous. You don't resemble at all."

"The subconscious is a funny thing." He drank his water. He wondered if he should chance something harder now.

"Ryan, don't create conflict where there's none. I know it's a talent of yours, but try."

He opened his mouth.

His father continued, "Besides all of that, I think you really can learn something from him. He's smart, he can fight, and if you don't provoke him he can be patient."

"Why do you care so much about him?"

"He's a member of my crew. Sympathizer or no."

That wasn't the entire truth. Ryan stared at him but his father gave nothing.

"Why do you think I'd want to learn how to fight? Or that I need to? I handle myself pretty well as it is."

His father said, "I can see that. But words are your weapons."

He got caught in the accusation, which sounded mild enough until he saw how much his father meant it.

He got up and strode to the kitchen and spun the cold rack until he saw his vodka-spiked juice. He poured some into his glass, which still had dregs of water and ice. No repeat of the toilet tango, thanks.

"I had my shrink sessions on Earth, by the way," he said over his shoulder.

"How did they go?"

"Well, my hats fit looser."

"Ryan, do you think I'm just trying to upset you for no reason?"

"You don't upset me."

"Then turn around and come back here. Without the alcohol."

He considered going straight into the bedroom and locking the screen, but his feet took him back to the chair, *with* his drink. He wasn't going to waste it.

The captain hadn't moved. His feet were still on the table, knees bent and body in a small slouch. As if nothing about him was aggressive.

Pure deception. Unconscious or not, Ryan had no idea.

"I authorized your comp usage, by the way, but no transcasting. You won't be able to link for that. Use ID AzarconR1. Your mother will probably want a comm."

"Thanks," he said. And sipped his drink. "This is all right since I assume we won't be leaping anytime soon."

"You never know. Take your chances."

"The Warboy might pull out of station when you're on his ship, have you thought of that?"

The captain smiled. "Yes."

"Why are you smiling?"

"Because you're concerned about me but you have to be sulky about it."

This was worse than talking to Musey. "I'm just saying. I mean, you're the one with symps running around your ship, and even though some of your crew and the entire Hub might not be happy about this treaty you're going ahead with it anyway."

"You think they'll mutiny?" The smile grew.

"Never mind."

"No, really. That would be something for the Send, wouldn't it?"

"I thought you captains aren't supposed to joke about mutiny."

"No, that's for the crew. Captains can joke all they want."

Ryan pulled on his drink. "You should take the Send more seriously."

"Why?"

Because I have to defend you, he almost said. *Because your family lives with the fallout.* "Because they say nasty things about you, wrong things, and Mom always has to issue statements." He knew his father knew that. He'd overheard enough arguments.

"What do they say?"

"You know."

"What do you hear them say?"

Well, then.

He took a breath. "You think you're above the rules. You run around out here ignoring laws, even from your own father—adoptive father, because for some reason all your files before you were eighteen are closed. And why is that anyway? Your crew is full of orphans and criminals. You torture prisoners of war. You have lovers on ship even though you have a family on station. Now you're harboring a symp. You've probably gone all the way rogue and you'll go over to the strit side with this treaty. Do you get the idea now?"

His father hadn't moved or flicked an expression through it all.

Now he seemed to be thinking about it.

"Well, I don't have any lovers on ship," he said finally.

Ryan said, "Is that it?"

"Did you want me to check off the list?"

He wondered if his father would actually comply. "Yeah. For the record."

His father seemed amused, not uncomfortable. He laced his fingers behind his head and looked up at the ceiling.

"All right. Well, like I said, I don't have lovers on ship. I don't *completely* ignore orders, especially if they come from your grandfather"—he raised an eyebrow, almost talking to himself—"although I do ignore all the dumb ones, regardless of source. You know this war has been going on for longer than you've been alive; if somebody didn't push the government's hand, what do you think your future would be like? Worse, not better. If that makes me rogue then I can live with that. Everything else the Send says . . . what they don't see out here, they make up." He lowered his arms and folded them loosely against his chest. "I think that covers it."

"You torture prisoners?"

"If they need it, yes. I'm not the only one in the Hub. Surely you know our government does it."

Ryan clutched his glass. The ice had melted but the surface was still cold. "How can you say that—so casually?"

"You asked for the truth."

"Strits torture people. *Pirates* torture people. So what if the govies do it? You should be better than that."

The captain leaned over and picked up his cup, sipped. "I don't make it a habit, Ryan. But if someone's got information and I know they have it, but they're being stubborn and difficult, I'll get it from them one way or another—in order to *save* lives."

"There's such a thing as human decency. And laws."

"Rhetoric is fine when you're in an office with a seal behind you. Out here there are practicalities."

One moment he thought the man was easy, and in the next it was another matter.

Yet it all sounded so reasonable over tea, in calm voices.

"What are the good things?" the captain continued.

"What good things?"

"Surely it's not all bad on the Send."

Ryan sipped his icemelt. "No, I guess not."

"You have friends on Austro, don't you? Surely they all don't revile me as a treasonous rogue, and you as the treasonous rogue's son."

"Didn't you hear? I'm Austro's hot number one bachelor. I'm just flowing with friends."

The captain's face froze as if he couldn't quite decide on a proper expression. Then he laughed. "Hot number one bachelor, huh?"

"Don't even."

His father kept laughing.

"Please. Shut up." It didn't help. "I'm serious."

"Apparently so are they."

"Look, just because some—idiotic 'poll' says I'm popular doesn't mean there are, like, actual genuine people out there banging down my door. People think *you're* powerful, or Mom is, so they orbit me for that." He put his foot on the edge of the table and poked a pyramid with his toe.

His father said, "I see."

"Sid's my only real friend, but even then he was ordered to be."

"No, he was ordered to be your bodyguard. I think he's your friend by choice."

The conversation had gone off the scope of what he cared to discuss. He got up and went to the kitchen to dump his glass. Or pour another. He hesitated, thoughts in disarray. Too many choices and not one of them satisfactory.

Retreat to the bedroom, even though that would send a clearer signal of his mental state than he cared to exhibit.

He poured a little more of the vodka and juice, mixed it with ice to give his hands something to do for a few minutes. It also allowed him to keep his back turned.

"Sid's a good person," Ryan said. "You shouldn't be jealous of him."

"Why would I be jealous?"

"Yeah, why."

"He does a good job. I wouldn't want him to fail at it."

Which job, Ryan almost asked. My bodyguard or my surrogate father? But he couldn't do that to Sid. He turned around and leaned against the sink. "You didn't answer one of my points."

"Which one?"

"About your files."

The captain set down his cup on the table, lightly. "They're closed."

"Yeah, so, why?"

His father stood, picked up his cup, and brought it to the kitchen space. He reached around Ryan to place it in the sink. Ryan purposely didn't move. Now his father was uncomfortable, even though it barely showed. But he felt it. Up close he saw the little lines between his brows, a half-suppressed frown.

"My past is private," the captain said. "That's all."

"Even from your family?"

"From the Send. That's why the files are closed. You of all people know how information gets distorted. I'd rather nothing of it was out there to feed the fire."

"But you can tell me. I won't go to the Send."

"Do you discuss Earth?"

Ryan blinked. He shifted away from the captain's close proximity. "We aren't talking about Earth. Besides, everyone knows what happened in Hong Kong."

"But you never talk about it, do you?" His father went back to the living space and picked up his slate. "Music off."

The volume-lowered track blanked to silence. Ryan missed the rhythm and frantic bass. Their voices seemed too loud now. The room too exposed.

His father sat back on the couch without looking up. "I think you should go to bed now, Ryan."

It was dismissal. So when it came down to it, his father still expected him to toe the line like any crewmember.

Toe it, before it was crossed.

He set down his glass and retreated to the bedroom, slid in the screen. An embarrassment-fueled heat spread through his chest and he didn't know why. All that conversation and he was left to feel as if he'd witnessed something unseemly.

Like a bare body or an open soul.

As soon as the beep sounded Ryan remembered he was supposed to comm Sid. The room was dark, the complete black of a place with no windows. He was lying in bed, not sleeping, and the noise made him jump. He leaned over to peer at the comm and reached to poke it, but the light was off.

His father had picked it up outside.

He slid off the bed and went to the screen, got it open a couple centimeters before the voices made him stop.

". . . No, sir," Sid was saying. "They argued."

"About what?" his father said.

"Sir, if I may be candid?"

"Go ahead."

"Sir, Ryan doesn't get why you want Musey to train him and I confess I don't either. We don't know the—we don't know him. Ryan's been through a lot and—"

"I'm aware of that."

"Sir, I'm not sure you are. Earth hit him hard, sir."

"The admiral did brief me, Sidney."

"Sir, please, with all due respect . . . the admiral didn't see all of it. He certainly wasn't at the embassy when it all—happened."

Ryan stared through the sliver of space. His father was

sitting on the couch, he saw the back of his head and his shoulders. He had a hand in his hair, leaning on it. The lights were up in a dim golden glow.

"Speak plainly, Corporal. Is there something more that I should know?"

Sid's voice sounded hollow and hard on the comm. "Sir, his entire life."

"Excuse me?"

"You said I could be candid, sir."

"But not dramatic. Are you saying I don't understand him? Do you think I ought to handle him with velvet gloves?"

"You're not really asking for my advice, sir, so I'm reluctant to really give it."

"Don't be a smart-ass. I'm asking you a question and you damn well better answer it. You think putting him with Musey will stress him out?"

"He's already stressed. He hasn't come down since we left Earth, except when he sailed. That's why he sailed. Musey's an unknown factor and I personally don't get much stability from him either. Putting them together might be asking for it. Sir."

"Or it might knock them out of their respective head-spaces."

"I don't know Musey. Maybe he's honest. But he's violent and I don't want him near Ryan."

"Did he do something?"

"No, sir, but I sense violence from him and I think you should leave Ryan out of it. He's had enough of that."

Ryan tried to stop breathing; it came in short intakes until he clamped down. And remembered to release the edge of the screen. His fingers throbbed.

"They both need to stop running," the captain said.

"Explosions stop movement," Sid said, "but I wouldn't recommend planting bombs on speeding freeways."

"Colorful analogy. But I've got instincts too, Corporal. And my instincts tell me that if we left Ryan on his present course, he'd find any and every excuse to remain inertial."

"Sir, I think you know Musey better than you know Ryan."

The captain's tone was brittle and dark, each word a burnt ember. "So were there things that you should have put in your report about Earth that you didn't, and I'm laboring under false pretenses? About my own son?"

"Sir, reading something in a report never fully describes a situation. Or a person."

"You're saying I'm blind and dumb, is that it?"

"No, sir." A beat. "You have me at a disadvantage, sir."

"Not according to you. Perhaps I should talk again to my wife. She might have a different story still."

"She wasn't there either, sir."

Silence. A long one.

"Sir, I don't need the full eight weeks of training. I'd like to continue my duty as Ryan's guard. At least for the first until he's acclimated, sir. Your crew is rough—"

"I know. But they have orders to leave him alone."

"But he can't be alone here. Sir, that was a large part of his problem on Austro. So I'd like to still be involved. I'd like to train him instead of Musey, at least in the basic combat. Ship regs, I understand, he should be trained by someone else. But I'm more than qualified for the basics."

"You are one bold son of a bitch, Sidney."

"Yes, sir."

"I brought you along for Ryan's sake; I'm not without compassion. I appreciate that Earth holds bad memories for you too, and perhaps you're transferring some of your own feelings to his, but I have some experience with traumatized people. Call it my line of work. I would appreciate it if you didn't interfere with Musey and Ryan."

Another beat.

"Corporal."

"Yes, sir."

"Am I clear, Corporal Sidney?"

"Yes, sir. But the last thing Ryan wants is to be forced into a friendship."

"I'm not doing anything of the sort. I expect them to learn from each other, if they don't kill each other. At the very least. But not if you undercut me. Am I clear, Sidney?"

"Yes, sir."

"Very well. Good luck with the training."

The comm beeped, but this time to acknowledge a disconnect.

Ryan drew a long slow breath as the captain ordered the lights off and settled back on the couch.

Learn from that symp? From that kid his father treated like a second son, for who knew what reason?

He thought about destroying the quarters.

He thought about the gun and knife in the bedside table.

He thought about the booze, and the Silver he no longer had.

In the end he lay in the dark with his arms over his eyes and listened to the sound of nothing on the ship, making his mind nothing, no images, no scents, nothing but the dark and the silence until they squatted in his chest like parasites.

A hand shook him awake. Get up, Ryan, your father's here.

But it was only the echo of Sid's voice, a memory. When he opened his eyes it was the captain's face peering down at him.

He'd slept, finally, a sudden dark oblivion that hung onto

him with claws even now that his eyes were open. He barely felt his father's hand, just realized that it caressed his hair before he blinked and saw the captain across the room, in the bathroom with the door open, looking into the mirror.

So maybe he'd dreamed it.

He smelled eggs and caff. He remembered goldshifts as a child, when Daddy was in dock for a visit, and the wondrous, exotic concoctions on his plate at least twice a day.

His father liked to cook. He'd forgotten that.

"Are you going to wake up enough to have breakfast with me?" the captain asked as he fixed his shirt, and came out to the wide glow of the room. The bathroom light went off as he left its sensors. "To drink something at least. You can't eat before the physical."

Ryan pulled himself to sit up, leaning on one hand, and rubbed his face. "What time is it?"

"Oh-six-hundred."

Bloody hell, military living.

"Ryan?"

"Fine, fine." His stomach gave an embarrassing grumble. Not eat? Yeah right.

He remembered the eavesdropped conversation. He looked up at his father to get some kind of indication, or shoot a glare, but his father pushed the screen aside and went to the outer room.

Breakfast with the parent. Like on station. Maybe his father would work while he ate and nobody would have to talk.

He found a T-shirt that he'd tossed at the foot of the bed, tangled in sheets, tugged it on as he shuffled to the kitchen and hitched up the waist of his pants so the bottoms wouldn't trip him. His eyesight fuzzed and slowly cleared, his blood beginning to circulate. His father sat at the island counter, elbows on top, munching on toast. No slate any-where.

Ryan leaned up and sat and took a sip of the orange juice so he wouldn't have to say anything.

"Caff's over there." His father gestured behind him to the zap plate where the pot sat. "Although you probably shouldn't have it this shift."

"That's fine, I'll get it later."

"How do you feel?"

He shrugged and spread his toast with lemon marmalade.

"What does that mean?—And you aren't supposed to eat."

"It means nothing. And I'm eating, so deal with it."

"You feel like nothing?"

He put the knife down. "Yeah, whatever. Look, I'm barely awake. Can you analyze me later?"

His father watched him, not touching his food now. "Did you overhear me last shift, talking to Sid?"

"What do you think?"

A small sigh. "I think you need to get yourself out of this self-destructive habit of—listlessness."

"Self-destructive. This coming from someone who fights wars for a living."

"Ryan —"

"No. You know what?" His fingers were sticky from the toast. He wiped his hand on the napkin and started to fold it, press on it. "I'll cooperate. I'll go along with your little experiment. Hell, I'll even be civil to Musey if that'll make you leave me alone and *not try to fix me*. I'm not your bloody *project*."

"I don't see you that way, Ryan."

"The hell you don't."

"You're my son."

Ryan stared. He tossed the uneaten toast to his plate.

His father leaned forward. "Don't you think I care about you?"

"Just stop it."

"Why?"

"Because it's stupid. It's bloody head-shrinking shit. I don't need it." He grabbed up his glass and downed half of it until the tart acid burned his throat.

"Ryan, I refuse to sit back and just watch you try to handle what happened to you—what you saw on Earth. And what happened in the Dojo. I'm your father and I won't do it. I know you resent me for a lot of things, not the least of which is because I've barely seen you—"

"I'm over that."

"I'm not going to tell you to get over it. But you're going to get through it."

He gave his father a violent stare. "Is that why I'm here? Because the shrinks on Earth 'failed'? Did someone send *that* to you in a report?"

"Why did you drop out of school?"

Here it went. "It was boring me."

"Are you going to give answers like that for the rest of your life?"

"I didn't even want to study that stuff. That was all Mom's idea."

His father looked at him for so long he almost pitched his glass at him. This was too damn early in his shift to be raking over these rocks, and it just figured the captain would ambush him. He'd been ambushed the moment that sniper took a shot at him in the flash house and everyone must've thought it was a great new strategy to shake out what they wanted from Ryan Azarcon. Just drop things on his head, hard and fast enough until he looked up.

Damn self-pitying shit. He didn't even like to hear himself think.

He got up with his plate and his empty glass.

The captain blinked. "Where are you going?"

"The bedroom. Out an airlock. I don't know. Somewhere so I can eat in peace. I guess I won't be going on station, right? I might as well stake out the safe zones on this ship, since I'll probably die here."

The captain stood, his hand on the countertop. Then his tags beeped. He frowned.

Ryan turned around and headed to the screen.

"Sir," a female voice said, "Captain S'tlian just commed to confirm the meeting at oh-nine-hundred. Admiral Ashrafi and Minister Taylor are on their way now to meet with you beforehand."

"Thanks. Comm Musey, tell him Conference A when he's finished escorting my son."

"Yes, sir."

Ryan looked at the screen and put his glass on his plate so he could free a hand to push it aside.

"Ryan," his father said, behind him, coming closer.

"What." He got the screen open.

A hand touched his shoulder. "Here."

He turned around.

His father pulled out a pair of tags from his pocket, looped on a chain. "These are for you."

They didn't have his face on them but they had the contact pads. Ryan took them and put them in his pocket. "Sid's tag signal, what is it?"

His father didn't break a neutral expression. "VT002. Mine is AZ01."

"Right."

"I'd like us to have lunch. If you want. I'll try to keep my head shrinking to a minimum."

"So after my physical I'm just going to hang around here."

He wasn't sure which was worse, the frustration, anger— or hesitance he now saw in his father's eyes.

"You can comm your mother. Maybe check out the library. Or the school. Now that we're in dock I think they have classes every other shift, on the training deck. The info would be in the ship's intranet. I'm not telling you what to study but at least have a look around. Pick whatever you want. We're linked with Austro University."

He glanced up, conscious of how close—too close—the captain stood. "You don't have to pitch it to me, I get the idea."

"Ryan, just try. That's all I'm saying. And please stop eating, the doctor will want a blood test."

"Yeah." He picked at the crust on his toast.

"You can ask anybody for directions or call up a map from your slate—I loaded the info. Try not to hang around jetdeck or anywhere that's under major construction. I'll see you for lunch? Twelve-hundred?"

"Where?"

"I'll comm you."

Yeah. Now he could be tracked through the tags.

He wasn't expecting it so he couldn't dodge when his father swiftly put a hand in his hair and half tousled it, half caressed it. By the time he opened his mouth to protest or raised a hand to shove away the touch, the captain was gone.

The ship was silent. In dock, in a room encased on every side and locked in by a hatch, the only sound was the chewing noises in his head and his fork against the plate, scooping up scrambled eggs. Physical be damned; he was hungry. He studied the stainless steel and his deformed reflection in the tines, sitting on the bed with the plate in his lap.

Even now, even here, his thoughts slid back amid silence, to Earth.

The embassy.

The Dojo.

The embassy.

Blood and bodies layered in his mind like distorted harmonies.

He got up, went back out to the kitchen and dumped his plate in the washer, drained his glass of juice and grabbed the first liquor bottle on his father's shelf. Just poured a shot and downed that, enough to make his throat burn and his eyes water, forcing his thoughts to the immediate physical buzz.

He wandered around until he found the play unit embedded in one wall near the couch set, then went back to the bedroom to dig into the drawer where his father had packed away his non-clothing gear. He took some slip music back to the player, fed the chipsheet into the slot and upped the volume until sound bounced from the walls and he could hear it even in the bathroom.

Loud music in a mesh of beat, riffs, and ambient thrums.

He took a long shower, waving the cycle three times. Sanity in the mundane. He sang with the music and upped the body dryer until he felt chafed and warm enough to fall back into bed, clothed loosely, under the sheets and almost out. He had a half hour before Musey was due.

But the music cut off.

So much for oblivion. Silence always brought him back.

Then the comm beeped.

Maybe a cancellation. Maybe, in his dreams, it was his father saying, Take the rest of your life off.

He stretched and poked the incoming light on the bedside table, got it the first time. "Yeah?"

Sid said, "Good morning."

Not his father and no such dream. He rolled over to his

stomach and leaned up on his elbows. "No mornings on a ship, Sid. Especially not good ones."

"What, did you wet your bed again?"

He snarled. "Aren't you supposed to be in training?"

"I'm going, I just thought I'd see if you were alive since you never commed back last night."

Night. Sid's dirtside talk, which had infected his own vocabulary after months on planet. You could take the boy off the planet, but couldn't take the planet off . . .

"Didn't my father tell you that symp didn't kill me?"

Silence.

Maybe a little guilt—on his part. Come to think of it. So he added, "Sid, um, thanks for getting in his face. You didn't have to do that."

"You could've told me that earlier." The joke covered it, but he heard the *de nada* beneath.

"I feel so illicit talking to you. Hey, think we can start an affair? What're you wearing now?"

"I'm tapping off, you sick little pus."

"Have you talked to Mom?"

A beat. "No . . . I don't think that would be appropriate. Besides, the link IDs on outgoing comms are archived. I don't think your father would . . . anyway . . . no, I haven't. Have you?"

"I'll comm her after my visit to the torture chamber." He couldn't believe he was saying this: "Do you want me to tell her anything?"

"Ryan, you don't have to."

"I'm asking, Sid."

"Just tell her I . . ." He cleared his throat. "That I miss her. Thanks."

"Okay."

"Now get off the bed and do something constructive today."

"I love it when you order me around."

The connection broke.

He smiled. Then he pulled out his tags from his shirt, separated one and inspected it. Four rows of doubled-up numbers and letters and a thin input display. He tapped in VT002 with the edge of his fingernail.

"Sidney," came the voice, all Marine-like.

Ryan said, "I was just testing it out. My father gave me tags."

"What's your number?"

"Oh, this will make our affair so much fun."

An exaggerated sigh. "Ryan, I have to go."

He looked down at the tag and squinted at the small display. "It's VT001. Hey, a pattern."

"I think it stands for Visitor Temporary."

"That's good to know."

"Just because it says so doesn't mean it's true. I'll see you later, maybe for lunch? It doesn't look like they'll be breathing down my neck . . . the SJI already told me she only wants me for the evaluations and shipboard training. I guess talking to the captain did help."

He wondered if his father had issued that order after breakfast. "SJI?"

"Senior Jet Instructor."

"That sounds worse than Sympathizer Musey. Or maybe not."

"Lunch, Ryan?"

"The captain already shanghaied me for lunch. Dinner?"

"All right."

"Oh, yeah, did you get a chance to comm your Maureens on Austro? About Tyler?"

Sid smiled; Ryan heard it in his voice. "Yeah. Check the SendTertain a little later, hopefully there'll be some breaking news."

"You're my hero."

"Good-bye." Then, "Don't get into trouble."

"On this ship? Nah." He broke the connection before Sid could, just to irritate him, and barely slid himself off the bed before the hatch beeped. For a second he thought it was the comm again, then remembered Musey.

The symp was fifteen minutes early. Of course.

Ryan took his time getting to the hatch.

Musey stood outside in his black shirt and pants, looking almost like a jet, and Ryan wondered if that was on purpose.

"Let's go," Musey said, turning his shoulder.

"I have to put on my shoes."

The symp looked back at him with a barely tolerant frown. Ryan left the hatch open and went to the bedroom. When he came out with his shoes, hopping one on, Musey was still in the corridor.

Poke the symp and he might tip right over.

Ryan got himself in order and stepped out, pulling in the hatch. He didn't miss Musey's eyes going up and down on his less-than-ironed attire.

"I'm not crew, remember?" he said as he followed the symp toward the lev.

"What?" Musey said.

"The way I choose to dress. I don't have to be one of *Macedon*'s clones."

"I didn't say anything."

"I saw you look."

For some reason that seemed to unsettle the symp. He stared straight ahead and palmed the lev call a few times as if that would hurry it. "I really don't care how you dress, but I guess it's a priority with you."

It sounded like a topic Musey didn't want to talk about, so Ryan pursued it. "Nothing wrong with taking pride in your appearance. Where do you buy your clothes from?"

"What?"

"Your clothes. You know, these things we wear on our bodies." He tugged Musey's sleeve.

Musey moved his arm. "I don't know. Some store. On order. On station."

The symp spoke as if the words were in another language.

"Are you really from Austro? Because I don't know a single Austroan that doesn't like to spend cred."

"I'm not."

Musey folded his arms and looked at the lev doors as if willing them to open. Ryan watched the side of his face, where the bruises showed.

"Then why do you have an Austroan accent?"

"I learned it."

"Why?"

Musey breathed out and turned to him. His eyes were a cold blue, the pupils tiny pricks of black under the bright corridor light. "I'm taking you to medbay. That's all you need to know about me."

"What's the big damn secret? I already know you were a spy. It can't get any worse than that. So did you learn an Austroan accent for, like . . . spy work?"

Musey didn't answer.

Ryan took that as a yes. "What's your real accent like? Where were you born?"

"Why are you so curious?"

It was beginning to be fun, provoking this symp. "My father wants us to be boyfriends."

Musey stared at him. The look was worth any grief Ryan might get later. The lev doors opened with a clatter and a man and a woman stepped out, but Musey didn't move and they had to edge around him. Ryan laughed and went in.

"I'm joking. You heard of jokes, right?" The longer Musey stood there, the louder Ryan laughed.

The symp walked in and told the lev, "Maindeck."

"You thought I was serious?"

No answer.

"Damn, you're funny. No wonder people love you on this ship. How do you stand it?"

Still no answer.

"Did I really offend you? A symp?"

Musey faced him, slowly. "And how many 'symps' have you met to warrant that tone?"

He almost didn't speak. But Musey wouldn't hurt him. He relied on that clear fact. "One, counting you. But so? What you people do is all over the Send."

Musey had no reluctance to talk now. "Like the fact you pushed that woman into the cross fire? *That's* all over the Send too."

"Nice to see you keep up with my life."

The lev doors groaned open and Musey went on ahead. "What you do affects the captain."

He followed. "What *I* do?"

Three people passing in the corridor looked at him. He'd been kind of loud. Nobody said anything and their faces ranged from vaguely interested to mildly annoyed. They transferred those looks to the symp.

Musey said, "Yes. What you do and say within earshot of others."

"I'm not the one pissing off govies." He tried to pay attention to where he was going, but after turning a second corner he just gave up.

"Govies are easy to piss off," Musey said. "Just puncture their pride."

"Were you the one who got my father and the Warboy together?"

Musey stopped outside of wide double doors, transparent and probably impact resistant, judging from the faint scuff marks on the thick surface.

"You're here," the symp said, and didn't even pretend that he didn't want to answer that question. "Don't skip out or Doc Mercurio might comm the captain, and since we're in meetings for a couple hours he won't appreciate being called out." Then he just walked off.

Ryan watched him go. He didn't look back. Alone now in the air-cool corridor, arms tucked against his chest, Ryan tried not to feel abandoned. It was silly. He didn't care for the symp's company, much less his approval, and it wasn't like the captain had ordered his son into some experimental procedure. It was just a standard physical and he wasn't going to be a baby about it.

Even though none of the faces in the medbay, as he peered through the doors, were familiar. Nor was the room itself inviting at all. It was sterile white, littered with examination tables that had probably seen more than one violent trauma, and used-looking, dragontine equipment with various pointy extensions that he didn't care to identify. Some units were folded up near the ceiling, others positioned in close proximity to the tables. Everything in the trauma bay was more imposing than any doctor's office he'd ever been in on Austro.

The clientele of his family physician could afford private consultations and velvet treatment above and beyond what was covered by the station health care system. Here the purposeful, gray-clad medical staff that moved from one room to the next, cleaning or carting medical instruments, seemed like the type of people who made you sit in chairs for two hours before hustling you through your near-death experience.

Ryan turned around to walk off—he had eaten this shift

when he shouldn't have, after all, and surely they couldn't conduct a proper examination because of that—and bumped straight into that jet, Dorr.

"Baby Azzz." Dorr grinned. "You ain't boltin', are you?"

Behind Dorr were two other men, both beat up. One was Sanchez.

Ryan wondered if Dorr had done that.

"Go on in," Dorr said.

So he was caught. He wished Sid were here, if only to ward off Dorr's innuendo, because he wasn't sure he wanted to put up with it after going a verbal round with Musey. If Dorr pushed him he might retaliate and end up bruised like Sanchez and the other jet limping behind him.

Ryan turned around and went through the doors, which slid aside as soon as he touched them. No threshold to watch for at least, but he couldn't stop there. Dorr put a hand on his back and propelled him forward.

"Yo, Aki! I brought you a present."

A dark-haired girl emerged from behind a curtained space at the corner of the room, holding an injet.

Ryan let his arms drop. He hoped this gam wasn't going to do his physical. The thought alone made him embarrassed.

"A present, Erret?" she said, approaching with a rather distracting smile.

"Baby Az. Cap's kid. Meet our mainstay, Aki Wong-Merton, Medic Extraordinaire."

Aki laughed. "You need more drugs or something, Corporal? I told you, I don't prescribe for chronic psychochondriacs." She spoke to Dorr but her eyes went to Ryan.

He smiled. She was cute, large-eyed and golden-skinned, and he wasn't stupid.

She returned the look, but didn't seem fooled. "Didn't Dorr tell you? I don't deal with the sassy ones."

"I haven't said a word."

"No," she said, still grinning, "but your thoughts are loud. Why don't you go sit on exam four, over there? I'll comm Mercurio while I deal with Dorr's daisies."

"Daisies," Sanchez said. "This bastard Madison got in the way of my fist, is all."

"Boys," Aki said.

Dorr said, "Plug it, mano, before my foot gets in the way of your face."

Ryan counted four tables from the door and went to it before a fight broke out near him and he got caught in the cross fire. He didn't care if this was the right spot or not and nobody else seemed to either. Aki pointed Dorr and the other soljets—Madison and Sanchez—to exam one and two and ordered them to sit. Madison was taller than Dorr, lankier but muscled, and sounded too laid-back to be much of a threat except to simple tasks. But his knuckles on both hands were branded by black prison tat lettering (if some of Tyler's vids were accurate about that culture), and he wore the same emblem patches on his rolled-up uniform sleeves as Dorr. So they must have been in the same jet unit.

Sanchez, on the other hand, wasn't. Although he seemed to be a higher rank judging from the number of stripes on his collar (barely noticeable as both were black), their arguing grew loud in a matter of seconds, with Dorr the loudest. Aki had a difficult time treating the scrapes, and some of Sanchez's ribs seemed to be bruised judging from his reactions.

It didn't stop him from yelling back.

"You know, Dorr, I'd like to see how *behind* the peace treaty you'd be if you weren't warming the captain's bed while he's rolling in another with the strits."

Both Dorr and Madison reached for Sanchez, shoving Aki out of the way.

Ryan slid down from the table, fast, not quite believing what he just heard or what he was seeing. Aki got between Dorr and Sanchez—brave or stupid—but she avoided a fist from Sanchez's direction and retaliated with a quick jab. Right to Sanchez's ribs.

That stopped him. He yelped and doubled. She spun to Dorr and shoved him into Madison until they were both up against the examination table.

"One more swipe out of either of you and I'll confine you to quarters. All of you. No gym, no training, no lounge. Reason of mental instability. You think I'm joking?"

"What do we need to train for anyway?" Sanchez wheezed. "We're bending over backward for the Warboy!"

"You better train if you wanna walk jetdeck," Dorr said.

"Potty train your mouth while you're at it," Madison added.

Ryan said, "What's your problem with the captain?"

They all looked across at him.

"Stay out of it, kid," Dorr said. Not a shred of humor in his voice.

"It's my father you're all fighting about, jet."

"Stay out of it!" Dorr yelled, turning to him and taking a step.

Ryan backed up, fast. Madison put a hand on the corporal's arm and Aki said, "Erret."

Dorr visibly calmed with the quickness of a dimming light. "Y'know," he said reasonably, setting his gaze back on Sanchez, "if you're so eager to keep fightin', you know where to find me."

"You find that line up your ass, Corporal?" Sanchez muttered, holding his side.

Dorr said, "You don't think we busy enough with Falcone's allies? Even you ain't so brainless that you don't see where we oughtta be expendin' our energy."

"I hate bleeding-heart symps, Dorr, and all their bitching about the injustices of the universe against those damn strits. If they want injustice to stop they oughtta stop bombing stations! Why don't you tell that to our captain?"

"Why don't you get over your sister's death?" Dorr yawned. "You done made up for it in strit bodies—and your moanin' just hit the expiration date of my tolerance."

"Screw you, mano."

"Both of you," Aki said.

Sanchez said, offhand, "Go screw your symp assassin, Wong."

Aki decked him, a fireball of a fisticuffs. Sanchez fell right off the table.

Ryan felt his mouth open.

Neither Dorr nor Madison moved a finger to help.

"Wong!" a voice snapped from behind Ryan.

He turned around and stepped out of the way just as a gray-haired man strode forward. In short order the man threatened Dorr out of medbay and sent Sanchez down the line of examination tables, though Sanchez could barely walk from that smackdown. Then the man looked at Ryan. "Get in my office," he said, pointing to a room on the right.

Clearly it wasn't a time to argue with anybody.

Ryan went.

He watched through the office window as Chief Medical Officer Mercurio (judging from reports Ryan saw on the man's comp when he leaned to look) verbally lashed pretty Aki Wong-Merton for her treatment of Sanchez. She stood with her hands at her sides and no expression on her face, like a jet.

Still—ouch.

Sanchez had deserved it. Dorr had deserved one too, but

nobody seemed willing or able to properly mete out punishment on a jet like him.

What had Sanchez meant by Dorr being in the captain's bed? Surely not literally.

Allegiances, probably. Even on a ship like this, they were divided. Or divided lately, thanks to the captain's actions.

The thought occupied Ryan as he sat on the victim's side of the desk. He didn't turn to look when Mercurio finally came in and shut the office door.

"Ryan Azarcon," he said as he sat in his tall black chair. "A pleasure to meet you. How are you doing?"

A friendly doctor question, which he'd heard before and knew how to answer.

Politely. "Fine. How are you?"

"At the end of my tether with some of the crew. So I hope you won't give me a hard time about this physical examination."

"No, sir." It fell out of his mouth with no effort whatsoever. He'd had it in his mind to bitch about the exam, but not now after that altercation. Mercurio was a commander and probably played cards or something with the captain every Saturday.

The man regarded him with a slight smile, leaning back in his seat with his fingers laced on his stomach. "Glad to hear it. Your father told me that you've taken drugs before. Silver. Anything else I should know about?"

Nobody pulled punches on this ship.

He hoped his face right now was fit for the Send. But maybe that was a giveaway too, when he lied: "No. Just Silver."

Mercurio's mouth twitched, a brief smile. "All right. We'll go with that for now. I have your medical history from Austro, basically you're a healthy young man. Why don't you go next door to this office, there's a private room, and get undressed? There are proper clothes laid out for you there and I'll be with you in a minute. In the meantime, don't flirt too much with Aki. You see how she handles suitors."

Mercurio did everything except take his blood, since he'd gone ahead and eaten breakfast, and that meant he had to come back after fasting for twelve hours. He should've known better; now the doctor would get a second go at him. Aki was nowhere in sight so he ended up returning to his father's quarters, sore and tired and just a little peeved that he had to ask for directions.

Main forward lev, command crew deck, quarters 0001 at the end of the corridor.

At least nobody seemed to care who he was and treated him like a tourist. Must've been because he wasn't attached to a symp or a Marine this time.

Once in quarters he got a drink of juice from the cold rack, first, then went to the bedroom and lay down.

The silence thrummed.

He had to occupy himself if he couldn't sail. In medbay he'd had the passing thought to steal some of their meds and an injet, but everything there was locked in cabinets and people were everywhere. It would be impossible.

He thought about playing his guitar, but it was still too quiet.

So he climbed off the bed and rummaged in his drawer for his mobile. He hooked it on, slipped down the interface eyeband, and blinked the connection. As he worked his way backward to sit on the bed, he calibrated his system to the ship's link codes. His father had told the truth—he was cleared all up the line, though the safety gates were double what he was used to on Austro.

If he tried to transcast he had no doubt this system would flag it and alert the comm officer or maybe even his father.

So he just blinked a rap to his mother's comm and waited the few seconds it took for the sig to bounce in quantum teleportation to the node on Austro. He hoped she wasn't in the middle of her sleepshift. Eventually Marine Perry picked up. He didn't seem surprised to find Ryan on the other end (had probably traced it the moment it lit the comm) and promptly fetched Mom Lau.

He knew the first thing she'd ask.

"How're you getting along with your father?"

"All right. I guess." Not really. But anything more would turn into a bitch session and it wasn't like his mother was an objective listener.

And hard upon that—

"How's Tim?"

"He's in training as we speak. Captain insisted. He says hi but . . . you know, he can't comm you. He misses you though."

His mother was silent. He saw the slightly distorted image of her, combed and immaculate in a soft dark suit. "I understand. How're you doing? Were the leaps okay?"

"Yeah. Listen, Mom, did you take care of Tyler?"

Someone must have passed by her; she was in her office at home, he recognized the leather chair she was sitting in. "What about Tyler?" she asked, distracted.

"That stuff he's saying on the Send. About me—pushing that girl."

"I guess you're lagged out there. Apparently someone tipped the pollies to raid his residence. They found a stash of Silver bullets and harder Earth-born drugs." Her gaze fixed on him. "You wouldn't know anything about that, would you?"

He couldn't help it; he grinned. "No."

"What about Tim?"

"Nope." -

"Ryan, don't lie to me."

"I'm saving you the headache, Mom. Plausible deniability. You know. In case Tyler starts ranting about illegal search and seizure and who might've instigated it."

She frowned. "I don't want you getting involved in things like that, Ryan. I could've easily handled Tyler's statements."

"I said I didn't do anything."

"Listen to me." She leaned forward. "I don't want you taking action in cases like this. Especially no transcasts. Everyone thinks you're still on station and I don't want you doing anything that will tell them otherwise."

A good burndiver could trace his transcast origin back to *Macedon*, that was why.

"So I'm just supposed to sit on my hands. I guess now you and the captain finally agree on something."

"Ryan." She sighed. "You're on his ship now. Don't antagonize him. You haven't been antagonizing him, have you?"

Now she looked worried, as if she thought the captain would hurt him.

"He's annoying me but I haven't beat him up yet, if that's what you're asking. He wants to put me in school. And have that symp train me."

"What?" Sudden angry alarm.

Maybe he should've kept his mouth shut on that last. If she railed at the captain over comm it might just come down on him in the long run.

So he tried to smooth it. "The symp's a kid. He's acting as their interpreter or something so I guess he's trustworthy. Grandpa doesn't seem to mind him either. I haven't really spoken to him much."

Just argued.

"See that you don't. I don't want you near him, Ryan. Or the Warboy, or any of them. If your father puts you there, you just refuse and tell him I said so."

That would go over well. "Mom, I'm not a child."

That opened a floodgate. "Listen to me, Ryan. These aliens aren't in it for peace. They've been blowing out stations and forcing relocation of Hub citizens for years— many of whom end up on Austro and *we* have to take care of them—just because of some gripe that happened decades ago. Those strits got their planet but they still attack the Hub. I don't know what your father's thinking but you stay well out of the way, hear me? Are you listening, Ryan?"

"Yeah."

"Symps only look human, but they think like strits. I don't want you near it."

He'd never thought of her as a warmonger or a racist, but he could see her point. How could you trust the strits? An alliance with them seemed impossible considering history. They blamed non-symp humans for usurping scientific colonies and bases.

Musey didn't seem to blame humans much, as he was still on this ship, but Ryan didn't think his mother wanted to know about his conversations with the symp who'd murdered that pirate Falcone.

Someone spoke to his mother off-comm. He didn't hear anything but a mutter, but her eyes shifted for a long second.

"I miss you," his mother said then, shocking him into focus. "Tell Tim I hope he keeps you safe."

She missed his bodyguard. But she wasn't going to show it over comm.

"I will."

"I have to go, sweetie. Be careful. Comm again soon."

"Okay. You too. I mean, you can, you know. Comm me. Here."

She smiled at him, then the image blanked.

He wondered if she'd ever comm him on this ship. She only used to comm the captain once a month, unless she had an issue to discuss.

He wondered if his room looked the same. She'd keep it like it was, like she had when he went to Earth. He'd told her he planned to come home. All of this would die down and he'd get to go home.

If the Hub decided to back his father all the way. If people stopped being pissed at his father. If pirates were no longer a threat.

He stared at the graphical menu layers on his mobile interface, not really seeing them, suddenly so weighted by the dread of possibly never going home that he lost here and now for a long second.

A message icon flashed at the corners of his eyes, a welcome distraction. Not a live link. He blinked to it automatically. From Earth, dated a week ago. He'd probably received it when the ship was in transit.

Shiri. She appeared in his field of vision, as clear as her voice in his ears. She sounded reserved and sat rather still.

"Hi Ryan. I'm glad you commed me and you're all right. Maybe I shouldn't be sending this but . . . well, I can't help it. I still care and I want you to be happy and you just weren't—happy—when you were on Earth those last few months." Her eyes dropped for a few moments. He didn't move, as if she could see him. "Anyway . . . I wanted to tell you that I did graduate. With honors." She grinned and gave him a familiar sidelong look, a teasing "be proud of me" prompt. "And! I even got an interview with Paulita Valencia's staff." Her eyes brightened and she started to nearly jitter in her seat. "If I land an internship with her or Ben Salter you will hear my scream all the way to Austro. I know what you're thinking too and you can just stop. Shiri, you'll have to go off-planet . . . well, I know that. And I'm prepared. If you can live on some tin can station and not go crazy then I suppose it's doable."

He had to laugh.

"Well, that's it, I guess. Comm back, okay? I mean, I won't mind. I'd like to hear how you're doing. So, okay. I'll talk to you later."

She leaned over and the message folded. He almost blinked at the reply icon before realizing that she'd be able to read its source or at least its path, and know that it came from past the Rim—unless he masked it somehow.

But he didn't know how to do that with any efficacy—or else he could transcast too.

If he could get past the ship's link security.

Maybe he could ask Sid.

This was presuming he ought to answer her. Or even attempt to transcast and risk the wrath of the captain of *Macedon*.

Don't antagonize your father, his mother had said.

Funny coming from a woman who couldn't speak to the captain without arguing about something.

Sid would help him if it was a girl thing . . . Sid was a bit of a romantic.

He wanted to answer Shiri. She wasn't put off by his brief reply. His heart thudded with the beat of how much he wanted to be back in that time, his first year on Earth, when things were new and easy. They'd met in pubs or cafés, shopped outdoors where unpredictable rain chased them into restaurants, or sun warnings in the high summer made them hole up in her dorm with the blinds drawn for a day. Sometimes they didn't feel like lathering on cream block just to walk across the park.

Days melded into nights with a same-day deception, hours stretched out like a slow dawn.

The memory boiled and burned.

Even Sid had liked her, had run her through a million security checks, but in the end he'd liked her. His mother had too, as soon as she found out where Ryan had met her and what Shiri was majoring in.

He'd never told his father about her. Wasn't sure why, now, except it hadn't seemed like the kind of thing he thought his father would be interested in. Like, well, his life.

He disconnected and pulled off the mobile. Shiri had probably gone through the interview already, maybe she'd even won the internship, but she hadn't sent anything more to him. Waiting on his cues.

He had to disguise his comm's point of origin, and his transcast code. Sid would do it for him, if he begged, even though Sid technically didn't want him ever to burndive. The types of people you meet when you dive, Sid said, will make more work for me. So just don't.

And he never had, really, unless it was just stealing music or vid files without paying for them, things that required no interaction with other living people.

But this was different.

He'd ask nicely.

He'd decide first if he wanted to talk to Shiri . . . what would he say?

I'm sorry.

I miss you.

I want to tell you what happened . . .

Do something constructive, Sid had ordered. Spinning about a girl wasn't constructive. At any time.

His father had said, Look around.

So he left the quarters and flagged down the first person

he saw on deck, an older man in a jet uniform and a purposeful stride.

"Hey, can you tell me where the library is?"

The man didn't slow down. "Training deck."

The same as the school. Naturally.

He walked the long, clean corridors (no damage on the command crew deck, at least), watching his dim shadow play on the walls from the bright intervals of lights overhead. Everyone seemed to be on duty or maybe even in bed, ships had round-the-clock schedules like stations. There was always someone awake and someone asleep at the same time, dictated to by shifts, not the sun. That had been the oddest part of living on planet. Up with the sunrise and abed with the night, generally, but once you got used to it there were privileges. Like feeling that warmth on your skin or wearing shades for something more than fashion; or watching your skin change color just from walking outside, not lying under specialized lights.

He used to climb to his apartment rooftop in the summer and stretch out, especially that first year when the sky and its colors completely fascinated him. He'd wear block, of course, and never stay out for more than a half hour at a time, but it had done its work in short order. Your eyes, Shiri had said. I like the way they look against the tan.

He'd never told her his eye color was genetically tampered. But maybe she'd known anyway. All she'd had to do was look him up on the archived Send. There were stories about him from the time he was a toddler. People assumed they knew him when he didn't even know himself. They wanted to categorize him in one sentence.

Austro's Hot #1 Bachelor.

Shiri had never seemed to care about all that.

It was a long time since he'd been with anybody. Or anybody who didn't care who he was or what he could do for them.

That thought got him nowhere, especially when he met a young woman waiting at the lev. She was blond, halfway cute, and her eyes roamed. But he doubted anybody on the captain's ship would seriously step his way; who would, with a father like that?

"The library," he said. "Training deck?"

"You Cap's kid?" she said.

"Yeah."

"You're at the wrong lev."

He looked over his shoulder, down the temporarily empty corridor. "I am?"

"Yeah, you need to go aft. This is the forward deck."

"And aft is . . . behind me?"

She looked at him up and down. She wasn't in jet or command blacks. Gray coveralls instead. "You sure you're Cap's kid? He's got a better sense of direction. And he's taller."

"Are all of you people so smart-ass?"

She laughed. "Pretty much. Go aft, young man."

He hoped she wasn't playing a prank. He turned around and headed aft, wherever that was, just kept walking in the opposite direction, through twists and turns, until he bumped into another lev. If they'd post signs this wouldn't have been a problem. If he'd brought a map maybe that would've helped too.

Well, too late. He wasn't sure he could find his way back, all the passageways looked the same, and the lev opened up promptly anyway, with a startling growl. He got in and told it, "Training deck."

It agreed, and shot down with a bit of a jar. Definitely not Austro maintained.

It stopped and announced, "Maindeck."

"Hey, I said—"

The doors grated open and a pile of crew pushed in. Some were sweaty men and women who had been working on repairs, it seemed. He backed up to the wall, couldn't see over half the shoulders. Somebody said, "Get the next one, mano, we're overcrowded."

"Fattest ones oughtta take the stairs," came the reply.

"There's another lev down that way," said a female voice.

The lev said, "Please clear the doors."

"Yo, back on up, Bucher."

"I'm late for my duty shift, mano, gimme a break."

The lev said, "Please clear the doors."

Ryan gritted his teeth and elbowed his way through the bodies. "I'm coming off, okay?" He got free in the corridor, after some shoves and nasty looks. "There. Now you should all fit."

The doors shut. The jet standing outside—Sanchez's buddy, Bucher—glared at him.

"Thanks, sprig."

He didn't answer; the guy was twice his width in muscle and must have remembered their first encounter. He moved past quickly down the corridor, thinking to find the other lev that the woman had mentioned. All he saw for a few minutes were the same bland corridors with their bland gray walls. Signs of battle peppered the way; bloodstains, blackened pipes, and gouged vents followed him around one corner and the next. Crew dug in at various locations applying maintenance with blowtorches or paint, or otherwise treating the wounds of the ship using tools he couldn't identify.

He turned a corner into a cleaner, empty corridor just as a hatch up ahead opened and out from the room walked an unfamiliar soljet, then Musey and a strit.

He stepped back before he thought, with an instinct to run. *In case of a station attack, please proceed to designated shelters* . . . the biannual school announcement sped through his mind, dredged up from years of drills. Safe behind the corner, he peeked around and watched. Strits had never been to Austro, it was too far in the Rim. The only symps he'd seen (besides Musey) were quick glimpses of arrests when he and Sid happened to go past one of the polly precincts on station. Citizens would stand outside shouting insults. The symps there hadn't looked stritified.

All the images in his head of tall, pointy-toothed white faces came from the Send and propaganda vids.

For a second it seemed like the strit was no more than a human in elaborate costume—it had the same human shape, two arms, two legs, though they were a bit lengthy, and even had hair, though it was silver-white and feathery-long. It wore clothes, just like in the vids, those coiled mummy-like strips—all white—except down the sides that were open and free for the iridescent wings to hang out. Wings under the arms, from wrist to waist, lined with what looked like creases but maybe they were veins.

So it seemed human, until it turned around and he saw its face—the completely black eyes that made it look as if it had no eyes at all, except they reflected the corridor lights in small shards. The intricate silver tattoos covering the area around its eyes and down the edges of its cheeks barely masked the bone structure, which was decidedly not human. It was too bold, too chiseled, created by the hands of an entirely different god.

If strits believed in gods. The Send said they didn't.

White face and white clothing meant assassin. Or assassin-priest, as they called themselves. Kill someone then pray over them, he had no idea. Information wasn't entirely reliable on this side of the DMZ. He heard its voice, words that seemed more of a song than speech, talking to Musey with the jet close by.

Musey was a small, dark body beside the unnatural lack of shading on the alien. They spoke briefly, Musey spouting back the same language, though it seemed much more labored coming from his mouth. Then a third figure—human—emerged from the room, accompanied by another jet.

This one had to be the Warboy. The Send had never captured an image but there was no mistaking the deep indigo tattoo on the right side of his face—a pattern almost as complicated as the strit's—or the serious, almost-strit hardness of his human expression. The white coiled clothing around his lithe form was partially covered by a long black robe. Ample place to hide weapons, though Ryan was sure the jets would've checked him. The Warboy stayed by Musey's shoulder, taller than the strit (who was in fact not much taller than Musey), with long black hair and, surprisingly, an olive-tan, human skin tone. The Send said the homeworld symps had altered pigmentation like the strits, but apparently not the Warboy.

The backs of his hands were covered in similar tattoos. He laid one on Musey's shoulder and muttered something that seemed to make one of the strit's wings flutter in response. The two jets hovered just out of arm reach. They were both visibly armed and notably expressionless.

Then the captain and the admiral stepped out of the room, with a couple aides and a nervous-looking Minister Stellan Taylor of Alien Affairs in tow. The entire group of them started down the corridor toward Ryan's position.

He backed up quickly and walked, looking for an open hatch, trying every other one, but all were locked.

"Dammit."

A corridor junction sat ahead on his right. He jogged to it, glanced over his shoulder.

The group had turned the corner. His father saw him, but didn't say anything.

He took that junction and walked faster still. Deep breath.

Strit on the deck. It was guarded, of course, and it was all for *peace* talks, yeah, but—

His skin crawled. He bit his thumbnail as he walked.

It wasn't an actor in makeup, wasn't a holo image. Of course it wasn't human, that was the point, but it wasn't like looking at a wild animal in the zoo or a pet dog on a leash. Wild animals were still from Earth and pet dogs still ate from your hand, he'd played with one that Sid had grown up with, when they'd visited Texas, and he'd looked into its little dog eyes and knew it recognized him in some instinctual way. He was human, and humans had a long relationship with domesticated dogs. The dog had wagged its tail and licked his face. His ancestors had played with dogs just like Sid's, and there had been a mutual understanding, passed down through genetic memory.

Strits weren't from Earth. You looked in their eyes and they were all black and they had little pointed teeth. They weren't friendly animals, they didn't *think* like animals, they had an unpronounceable language, and *wings*, and they didn't take prisoners of war, everybody said, they just killed you outright if you didn't serve a purpose.

They blew stations and gutted them of valuables, even people, then skipped back behind the DMZ, out of reach. And symps who grew up on their planet were practically alien, they somehow leaped over the human species and landed elsewhere, somewhere without human-type thought, where assassins could be priests and little alien kids were taught how to kill people before puberty.

If aliens even had puberty.

Had Musey grown up like that? How the hell had he fooled anybody on this ship, being a symp acting human?

Because symps *were* human.

Right.

He stopped and leaned against the bulkhead, looked around to figure out where he was going and if he ought to just find a lev and go back to quarters.

Find a lev and find Sid, maybe. Tell him, damn, he'd seen a strit up close.

That was enough to last him a lifetime.

He couldn't fathom having one of them touch him. Or even having a symp like the Warboy touch him, like Musey had allowed. How did you stand so close to killers like that and not want to go the other way?

Of course Sid had killed people in his line of work, plenty of people in the numerous theaters of war he'd been in since he was seventeen on Earth. The captain had killed people too, though maybe from a distance on a ship or a hunter-killer. And something about Admiral Grandpa's smiles always seemed more like a friendly maître d' than a brass-tacked commanding officer. Besides, he'd seen Grandpa in pajamas when he'd stayed over at their house in Virginia one week in Spring Break.

None of them looked—like killers.

Well, what did killers look like? The baddies in a Tyler Coe vid?

Wake up, Ryan.

This was his father's world.

The ship had small echoes in these corridors for such a large vessel. He found himself near a metal stairwell, in a pocket of inactivity, no footsteps or opening hatches or voices from crew on duty. Maybe they'd all vacated this deck because of who else was on it, or maybe he was just in an unvisited part of the ship.

Macedon had recently been through a battle. People had died. *Macedon* was older than his father's command, he

knew that much. It'd had one other captain who'd taken her
out of the shipyard brand-new over three decades ago. The
ship had probably endured many battles, numerous retrofits,
upgrades, patches, and polishes.

He wondered where the dead went.

His damn imagination. He didn't need to be thinking of
that, with an image of a strit's demon-white face and black
eyes already in his head. Childhood fears belched up anew,
now that he was alone, surrounded by steel and cool, ca-
ressing air. As if real life weren't disturbing enough.

He walked, annoyed at himself and his runaway melo-
drama. He was nineteen years old, for crying out loud, and
he didn't need to sleep with a light on. Strits were flesh and
blood, jets killed them all the time, and whatever nightmares
he might get, aliens didn't play into them.

Bodies and blood.

He blinked, looked around, stuck his hands under opposite armpits against the ventilated chill, and considered tapping his tags for Sid, just to ask for directions.

He should've loaded up that damn map into his slate.

Or taken the stairs. Dammit.

His Austro-trained tendencies never looked at stairs as a
route of travel. Levs existed for that purpose. But this wasn't
Austro; a station had signs.

So he turned around and went back the way he'd come,
instead of heading in directions he had no points for, and actually rediscovered the stairwell. Barely lit, dusty thing. He
started down the perforated steps. Training deck was below
maindeck. Right.

Threads of gray smoke floated up past his feet.

He stopped and squinted.

A pair of eyes looked up at him from below the steps.

He moved back up, holding the rail, heading for the corridor again. Almost turned and ran before a voice said, "Hey. You lost?"

It was a human voice, young and male, and the smoke smelled—now that his heart slowed to a normal beat and he paid attention—like cheap cigrets.

He peered down through the holes in the steel.

"Come round," the voice said. "Just down a flight."

He walked, unintentionally clanking his way with heavy steps, and met up with a young guy who sat across a single stair, legs slightly bent to accommodate his height in the small width. The bottom of his right boot was propped against the rail post. One arm rested across that knee with a cig between his fingers. He took a drag on it and looked up at Ryan with bruise-blue eyes in a pale narrow face. His hair was jagged long around his cheeks, unkempt, light blond. He wore black fatigues and a black shirt with the sleeves rolled up, no telltale jet unit patches anywhere.

"You lost, sprig?" he said.

Ryan leaned against the rail a couple steps above him. "No. And don't call me that. Why're you just sitting here?"

"Havin' a smoke. You want?" The boy drew out a pack from his leg pocket and offered it up. His gaze went up and down and back up and he tossed his head a little to clear his eyes.

Ryan felt the stare. He almost accepted the pack but then thought of the hell he'd get later if Sid smelled it on him.

"No, it's all right. I was just going down."

The boy grinned. "Be my guest." He didn't move. And he still held out the cigret pack.

Ryan found his eyes sliding from the *Macedon* tattoo on the boy's right wrist and up to another, darker tat just below the inside of his elbow.

The boy said, "Like it?"

It snapped his attention up to the unblinking eyes. "I don't know. What's it of?"

The boy pocketed the cigs with a little shrug. "My old ship emblem. *Shiva.*"

"The Hindu god of creation and destruction." The tat's image had the three-eyed face and weaponry and even a vaguely phallic shape behind it all, in red. Odd symbol for a ship.

The boy looked surprised and his gaze seemed clearer as he stared up at Ryan.

"That's right. You heard of it?"

"Just the name, from school, not the ship. Why would you name a ship that? Shiva's a god, isn't he?"

"Of creation and destruction. Good and evil. You know, contrasts." He sounded like he was reciting something. "It fit, anyway. What's your name?"

"Ryan."

"Evan," the boy said. "Siddown before you give my neck a cramp. You sure you don't wanna cig? You look like you need one."

No cig, but he could talk to the kid. Evan seemed normal at least. Ryan sat on the step, arms on his knees, and shook his head. "I just saw a strit."

Evan gave an unimpressed sniff. "Yeah, they're on the ship now, aren't they."

"You've seen one before?" If he was a jet, then it was possible.

"A couple times. I been over on the Warboy's ship."

He stared. "And you lived?"

Evan smiled, but it didn't seem to be because of the comment, which Ryan had meant seriously. "Cap can charm a snake, they say. So what're you doing?"

"Doing?"

"On this ship. You don't look like a jet."

"I'm not, I—" Could tell the truth. "I'm here because of my father. The captain."

He waited for the inevitable reaction—kiss-ass or tease.

"Oh." Evan stared at him for a second, letting the cig burn, then he put it to his lips with a kind of slow distraction. "Poor you," he said, around the stick.

Ryan laughed. *That* was new.

"No offense or nothin'," Evan continued, blowing out a fast stream of smoke.

"Don't worry, none taken. So what do you do on this boat besides smoke in stairwells?"

"Keep people happy," he said. "Same as I did on *Shiva*." He laughed.

"Why's that funny?"

"'Cause it is. You wanna go to q?"

"Quarters?"

Evan reached up and behind him, grasped the rail, and hauled himself to his feet. He dropped the butt end of the cig and squashed it with his boot, then jerked his head toward the stairs leading down. "Yah. Wanna?"

"Um, actually I was on my way to the library."

"For what?"

"Just to look around. My father wants me to acquaint myself with the school or something."

"Do it later. I'll even take you, I know all that library shit, I had to run progs on the system. C'mon, mano, I'm bored and you're the next best thing on this ship."

Hell, he was halfway bored himself, and Evan, like Shiri, didn't seem to care who he was.

And it was better than going to school.

Ryan stood and walked down until they were side by side. "Next best thing to what?"

Evan grinned at him. "To screwin' the captain."

He almost stumbled on the last step. "What?"

Evan laughed. "Don't you know the hierarchy of power on ships? The divine right of kingpins?"

"What're you talking about?"

"Alliances. Figure the captain, but if the captain don't want you, figure the favored son."

He stopped walking. Evan went on ahead a few strides before turning around with a question on his face.

"You think you're going to win my father somehow by winning me?"

Evan stared at him as if he'd spoken a different language, then laughed again. "Hell no. Everybody knows you and your daddy are on the outs. Besides, I ain't serious. *Mac* ain't no pirate. I'm just proddin' you."

"Of course *Mac* isn't a pirate."

"That's what I said. Now smooth your feathers and c'mon."

It might not have been a good idea but he went anyway. Evan took him through jetdeck, where his father had expressly said not to go, but he'd been here already with Sid, and anyway, Evan seemed to know quite a few people—personally. He stopped at one girl and backed her to the bulkhead, talking fast and quiet, and Ryan thought he caught more than their mouths communicating. In a few seconds Evan walked off, motioning Ryan forward with a tilt of his chin.

Ryan glanced behind him at the cornered girl, who stared after them with bright eyes. He looked at Evan. "What was that?"

"Just business."

"What kind of business?"

Evan snorted and dug in his pocket and lit another cigret with a finger-band lighter. "What're you, a polly?"

"No, just curious. I have to tell my bodyguard something about where I've been." He smiled to show it was a joke.

"Oh, I seen your bodyguard. He's real cute an' Mariney. He just guard your body and all?"

"I'm not even going to answer that."

Evan laughed. "What a waste."

"Really, what do you do on this ship?"

Evan stopped by a hatch and lifted one of his tags from inside his shirt. "Crew Recreation and Morale. In its broadest sense, sometimes." His eyebrows lowered and his smile went up.

Ryan couldn't believe he was so bold about it. "Doesn't my father, like, forbid that?"

"What, sleeping around? He ain't that much of a dictator. Besides, it gives me protection." He slid his tag through the lock and shouldered open the hatch.

"Why would you need protection?" Ryan glanced behind him before following Evan in, saw a few passing eyes on them and hoped it wouldn't find its way back to his father.

" 'Cause *Shiva* was a pirate and a lotta these jets get on their high heels and look down on me. 'Specially now 'cause all the pirates are actin' up with Falcone dead. Jets fight too many pirates, y'know?"

Ryan kept his hand on the edge of the hatch to keep it open. "You were a pirate?"

"No." Evan turned in the small space of his quarters and half glared at him. "I was *on* a pirate. Not by choice, either. They could give me a tat but I didn't have to wear it inside, right? I don't buy their propaganda shit."

"Oh."

"Close the hatch, mano, unless you think I'm gonna rape you or somethin'."

Well, yeah, he thought, but shut the hatch anyway because he had too much pride in all the wrong places.

The quarters had two bunks and a steeped scent of Evan's cigrets. One of the bunks, which Evan plopped down on, was messy, clothes strewn everywhere, a half-cased pillow at the foot of it. Personal items like a comb, music unit, mobile comp, and a dozen different holocubes bulged out of the web storage on the wall. The second bunk was immaculately neat and only had a couple pouches and a small box in its nearby webbing.

"Siddown," Evan said. "Nothin's diseased in here."

Ryan sat on the unoccupied bunk and pulled his feet up cross-legged.

"Sure you don't want a cig?"

"No, I think I'll get a hit in here just from breathing."

Evan smiled. "You keep bein' funny and I dunno if you even intend it."

"I'm witty that way. You got anything to drink?"

"Sure. What d'you want?" Evan edged forward and dug under his bunk, pulling out a footlocker. He opened the latch. "Beer, fizzy caff, juice . . ."

"Beer's fine."

Evan dug into a cold bag and tossed him an exotic ale.

He tilted the label in surprise. "Where'd you get this?"

"On station, naturally. I don't brew it myself."

He twisted off the cap and sipped. It tasted like outdoors, when he and Sid had gone camping in Virginia forests, the all-encompassing trees and green life that no station could rival, not even in sprawling arboretums like Austro had. "My father must pay well."

Evan snorted. "Nah, I'm just good at poker."

He sipped again, enjoying it, and looked all around, then back at Evan, who hadn't moved his gaze. "So . . . how'd you get on this ship?"

"I don't wanna talk about me. Let's talk about you."

Ryan laughed. "Why? I'm not interesting."

"Yeah you are. Look who your father is. Does that bug you? Is he a hard-ass like that in private?"

For some reason he didn't take offense to Evan's questions. Maybe because they were so honest. "How do I know you won't sell what I say to the Send?"

"'Cause I'll get kicked off this ship or worse. I ain't stupid. Besides, I'm just curious. I never met a famous person before—well, at least not one that actually looked me in the eyes with their pants still on."

Ryan tried not to be shocked, and failed. "Maybe I have stuff I want to keep private."

"Yeah, but you can trust me." The grin appeared again.

Ryan laughed, pulled one of his sleeves down over his hand, and clutched the bottle in the other. "You're—weird."

"I make you uncomfy?"

It was probably obvious. "No, not at all." He drank.

"So you ain't as hard as you act, huh."

"I don't act hard." He felt on the retreat, but it was strangely fun.

"Yeah you do. I read about you. Goin' to flash houses, hangin' with that sail-head Tyler and that glitzy crew."

"How do you know Tyler sailed?"

"Don't they all? And look, you're here with me, ain't you? You like that edge, it gives a sweet cut." He smiled full this time and Ryan saw that one canine tooth was jagged, chipped.

"You read up on me."

Evan said, "Sure. Cap told us his boy was comin' on board and we all better be aware . . . so I looked you up. You're, like, all over the Send, 'specially now with that half-assed attempt on your life."

"Half-assed?"

"Well, they missed, didn't they?"

Nobody had ever said it quite so casually, as if it didn't matter. "So you knew what I looked like and you still asked who I was?"

Evan shrugged. "I wanted to see if you'd lie."

"What if I had?"

"Then I woulda caught you at it."

He stared at Evan for a long second. "And then?"

"Then I'd invite you to my q and see what else you'd lie about. You're like an open bay and it's kinda fun to watch. I seen you on the Send and it's the same when you're in front of cams."

"An open bay? What's that supposed to mean?"

"Things fly in an' out of you an' you don't screen 'em too good."

"I—you think you read me that well and we just met?"

"Yeah. I'm good at readin' people. It was a survival skill on *Shiva*."

"I think it's a little freaky that you've researched me."

"It ain't." Evan leaned to the bolted table between bunks and stubbed out the cig in a small round tray already filled with ashes and dregs. "It's a habit of mine. I like to know who comes and goes. Besides, you're all over the place like your daddy. Why *shouldn't* people read about you?"

Meedees thought the same way. "Because it's nobody's business."

"Yeah, maybe, but people'll still look for it. Pirates look and they found a way to shoot at you. You should be more aware of what's out there." He leaned back against the bulkhead, feet hanging over the side of his bunk. "Can't believe those pirates missed either. They must've been someone's second string assassins."

"I'm glad they missed." It came out snappy. "One of them was a stationer, you know. An underdeck kid."

"I heard that. I heard Falcone's protégé was lookin' to train some of them kids. It was, like, a project of his on Austro."

"What do you mean?" Protégé. Lieutenant. The Send

bandied about the words as if there were a large distinction. The only one he saw was they were alive and their leader was dead.

"Falcone's protégé." Evan watched him with careful attention, as if judging his reaction. "When I was on *Shiva* I met him once 'cause, like, *Genghis Khan* was *Shiva*'s bloodmate in the deep. He went by Yuri and he had to do checks of our operations and report back to Falcone. We're about the same age, bio twenty-one, but he totally bought into the rap. Early." Evan paused and bit the corner of his thumb, paying it particular attention.

"What else?" Ryan said. "Please. This kid Yuri was behind the hit? You know this for sure?"

Evan shrugged. "My guess, Jos's guess. You met Jos, right? The symp? Jos was Falcone's protégé for a year before he ran away and got picked up by the strits. Yuri didn't run away."

That might've explained some of Musey's behavior. Ryan shook his head; it was hard to imagine this world or that the kid sitting across from him had lived in it. And then landed up on *Macedon*. "Why *wouldn't* you get away?"

Evan smiled, as if the answer were obvious. "Pirates who follow Falcone's model, they got, like, a little kid they pick to train . . . for specific work. Indoctrinate, y'know? So they don't *wanna* run away. And then when the kid's good enough they kinda . . . branch out. Create another cell, y'know? Another ship to run with Mother. More than a bloodmate. Like a child. That's the diff between a pirate ship's lieutenant and a protégé. The captain's gotta die before a looey can take the chair, but a protégé . . . if he's good, he gets his *own* ship from the captain. You know the kind of trust that takes? It was like Falcone's *mission* to find a protégé. Someone who's smart, capable, absolutely loyal, and absolutely ruthless." Evan shifted on the bunk and scratched his cheek.

"Theory is, if you train a protégé like that and then he trains one like that, over years you'll have a rock-solid operation with a fleet of ships completely loyal to one big honcho. Falcone's antimilitary model."

Falcone had been a carrier captain. Like his father.

No wonder the Send was hot and bothered about the captain taking on orphans and criminals in his crew, then running roughshod over orders issued by Hubcentral.

"My father knows about this? These pirate . . . tactics?"

"Oh, yeah." Evan nodded. "I mean, I know he's talked to Jos about it and he was right there on deck when Jos killed Falcone. I'd think it'd come up."

Was this why his father was so concerned about Musey's well-being? The symp had been a protégé under the captain's enemy?

All the Hub knew Cairo Azarcon hated pirates. Above and beyond even strits and symps.

"So . . ." Evan continued. "My bet to why nobody's found Yuri? He's got his own ship running the deep. He was this little pirate prodigy. And he was in charge of recruitment on Austro. Hasn't your daddy, like, told you any of this?"

Ryan said, "No." And this Yuri kid was probably the one who shot at him? "How do you know all of this?"

"Jos been askin' me, y'know, him and his contact on Austro. That underdeck symp, Otter. Since I spent some years on *Shiva*. Your daddy's got them workin' on the Dojo thing on the offside."

It hadn't been symps, after all, that they'd had to worry about invading Austro. It was pirates.

Pirates infiltrating Austro's underdeck. Organized criminals with agendas, and yet the Send relegated reports about their activities to the backburner transcasts.

And people moved around the Hub thinking aliens were the largest threat. Just because they got the most attention.

He said, "People died in that flash. Lots of people who had nothing to do with anything. Women—"

"I read."

Ryan slid off the bunk. "I think I better head out." It had stopped being fun.

Evan's attention tightened on him. "Why?"

He glanced at his watch. "I'm supposed to meet my father for lunch . . . soon."

He didn't like the way Evan looked at him. Worse than any meedee. Beyond curiosity. More like he stood in a show window and the only thing stopping Evan from grabbing him was a thin, clear glass.

And how long had Evan been on *Shiva*?

Ryan started for the hatch.

Evan said, "Don't let people see you on the retreat. They'll just advance."

He turned. "What?"

Evan pulled out his own beer from the footlocker, cracked the cap and drank. "Just some advice."

"Did I ask for it?"

"No. People like you never do."

"People like me."

"You know . . . rich, spoiled boys." His eyes baited.

Ryan held the near-empty bottle, stood looking down at Evan and wondered what it was about himself that attracted these kinds of people.

Maybe because he went looking.

He considered just walking out without another word, when his tags beeped.

"Someone's popular," Evan said. "Or in trouble."

Ryan picked up one of the tags and pressed the connect with the edge of his fingernail. "Yeah?"

His father's voice came back. "You can try answering with your name."

Evan laughed.

The air seemed to flex and lose tension.

So he said, "This is Ryan Azarcon, how may I be of service?"

Evan laughed harder.

The captain said, "Where are you, and who is that in the background?"

Evan put his arm over his mouth.

"I'm on jetdeck"—Having wild sex with a pirate, he almost said, but didn't think that would translate well. At all— "just talking to someone. One of your crew. And drinking a beer, which I'm allowed to do since I'm legal."

"Meet me back up in quarters for lunch." The captain didn't sound pleased about the mention of jetdeck.

He was going to get interrogated. Over sandwiches or something. But it was a good excuse to leave. Not that he needed any. "All right. Sir."

The captain broke the connection.

"Yes, *sir*," Evan mimicked.

Ryan said, "I'm going to tell him who I was with and if you get kicked off the ship you only have yourself to blame."

Evan's eyebrows shot up. "I never even touched you."

"I can tell him otherwise."

"But you won't because you're not a liar. Not outright. You just lie to avoid things but not to hurt people. Besides, you really don't want to hide behind Daddy, do you?"

He went to the hatch.

Evan said behind him, "Am I right?"

"Do a crossword or something. I'm not a game."

"But you're a lot of fun. I can be a lot of fun too."

Ryan glanced at him. Pride made him meet the stare on a second look. "I bet."

"If you get bored kowtowin' to the captain just look me up. ED32." And when he didn't answer—"I got the best beer on the boat." Wicked smile.

He did laugh at that, since Evan had probably never seen the captain's stash, and opened the hatch with a yank.

Musey stood on the other side, holding one of his tags.

They both stepped back in surprise.

"What're you doing?" Musey said, hostile.

"Leaving."

Musey's eyes went over his shoulder. Suddenly the symp's hand was on his chest, blocking him from getting to the corridor. "Did something happen?"

"No, but something will if you don't let me pass."

"Evan?" Musey said.

"Relax," Evan said. Ryan glanced behind him and Evan was still lounging back on his bunk. His expression had soured in offense. "We were just talking."

Musey looked back at him, narrow and close. "That true?"

"Yeah, it's true." Ryan made another attempt to get around the symp. "You're his roommate? That's pretty funny."

Musey let him go, though he still frowned.

Ryan stepped back once he was in the corridor, then turned around. He didn't get far before he heard the hatch slam in behind him.

All around him in the corridor passing jets paused and looked. He had no doubt that who he'd been with would get to his father somehow. Maybe even to Sid.

He tried to hide the beer bottle behind his leg, but it was no use. It was impossible to hide anything on this ship.

*   *   *

"Baby Az!" came a voice behind him as he stood waiting, as usual, at the lev. On Austro or on a ship, nothing changed that way.

He turned around and saw Corporal Erret Dorr.

Wonderful.

"Baby Az," Dorr said, sauntering up. "Whatcha doin' with Evan D'Silva?"

"Finger painting."

Dorr's gaze dropped to the bottle in Ryan's hand. "That a euphemism?"

Maybe Dorr was the captain's jetdeck spy. Sanchez seemed to imply it. In which case he didn't have to be forthright. "I'm shocked you know that word."

Dorr's eyes flickered. He put himself only a couple hand spans from where Ryan stood, fingers hitched in his backwaist. "I like to educate myself. So tell me. What went down in D'Silva's box?"

Ryan forced himself not to step back. "Ask Musey, they seem to be friends."

"Uh, yah." Dorr rubbed the end of his nose. "Well, Musey and Evan known each other since they were kids and Evan's sorta got a thing for Jos."

"A thing?" He almost laughed but Dorr was staring at him as if daring him to say something snide. "Why're you interfering with me anyway? Don't you have a job?"

"I'm Cap's other son." The smile meant it. "That makes us brothers, in a way. We all brothers, kinda, though I could do without Sanchez and his crib of cretins . . ." His tone drifted.

"If you're my brother," he said, wishing for the lev, "I think I'd rather be an orphan."

"No you wouldn't," Dorr said, without the smile. "Don't be stupid."

He couldn't move. Dorr had maneuvered around him until he was forced to back into the lev doors.

Dorr said, "Look, Muse is safe, you don't gotta worry about him. Really, aside from the fact he lied about who he was, I still like the little symp. He just a tad messed up, y'know? I'm one of the happy few who gets that about him, and so does your papa. But Evan . . . he ain't no symp and he went pirate for a while. Like, recently. You know that?"

He had the feeling he was being debriefed, and frowned. "He said something about it. I saw the tattoo. But if my father doesn't mind him on this ship, then why should you?"

"I didn't say I minded him. Just watch yourself. His old habits die harder than most when it comes to people relations. And you bein' the captain's son has got some perks. Know what I'm saying?"

"He already told me that. And he's already hit on me. So stop worrying about it, jet, I'm not that innocent."

Dorr's mouth twisted and his lids lowered, mildly offended or setting up for a smart remark, Ryan didn't know, but the scene got compounded when Musey walked up behind Dorr, as silent as a look.

"You ain't that jaded either," Dorr said. "Despite what you think." Then he turned around as if he'd seen Musey approach.

"I'll take him to the captain's quarters, sir," Musey said.

"I don't need an escort."

Dorr said, "That might be a good idea. Thanks, mano." He walked off as if dusting his hands of the situation.

Ryan said, "I can find it on my own."

"I know." The lev doors opened and Musey looked at him, waiting for him to walk in.

He had no choice, or else he'd have to wait for the next ride, so after the two disembarking jets streamed by he walked in and Musey followed.

The symp said, "Command crew deck." Then to Ryan, "After lunch the captain wants me to start working with you."

"So you'll be my *au pair*?"

"Your what?"

"Never mind." He looked up at the ceiling and leaned on his hands against the wall. Evan had been a refreshing change, after all, ex-pirate or no. His association was at least voluntary.

Musey spoke as if it were being pried from his cold dead lips. "I understand you have some interest in comps."

"I guess."

"We can start there. If you want."

Ryan looked at him. "You'll teach me to burndive? Like, high-end stuff?"

Musey said, "No. That's illegal."

"Oh. Well then, I don't have an interest in comps."

"Look, Azarcon, the captain ordered me to train you. Hand-to-hand stuff, gun handling, just basic, as well as tech. To understand it."

"Why?"

He breathed out impatiently. "Because you can't walk around anymore without a clue how to defend yourself. It *helps* if you're decent in a fight. Do you get it?"

"And the tech?"

"Communication. Basic stuff."

"I know basic comm tech. I can even burndive a little. What I want to know is how to burndive a lot. Like, how can I send messages while disguising their origins?"

Musey stared at him.

"You said you're going to help me and that's what will help me."

"How will that help you?"

"Because I don't want to be cooped up on this boat! I

can't go on stations, I don't know for how long, but if I can't talk to people other than my screwed-up family and jets on orders, I'm going to kill something."

"You have someone specific you want to talk to?"

The lev saved him, opened up, and he walked out.

Musey said to the lev, "Hold," and followed him into the corridor. "You have someone specific. Who?"

"Don't work your spy voodoo on me."

"Do you want to stay alive? Don't do stupid things."

He rounded on the symp. Musey didn't even blink. Ryan leaned into his face. "You have no right. You of all people, with your killer Warboy buddy. I know how to stay alive, I've been through"—Stop. Now—"*enough* . . . so I don't need advice from a strit!"

"Sympathizer," Musey said. "Get it right if you want to categorize. Your father's a rogue. You're a brat. I'm a sympathizer. Does that sum it up in your world?"

"Go blow."

"I have orders. They'll try my patience but I'll do them because I respect your father. I respect the fact he's got enough foresight to talk civil with the striviirc-na, so I'll respect that he knows what he's doing with you. But if you push me too far I *will* hit you. And we'll see which one of us gets the reprimand."

He couldn't find anything to say. Too many angry sparks went off in his mind, and he couldn't grasp any of them.

"What's your problem anyway?" Musey said. "So you saw a building blow up. So someone shot at you. Do you have any idea what people *really* see in this war? And yet you bitch and moan over your little traumas."

He grabbed at the front of Musey's shirt and aimed for the symp's face with his other fist.

The next things he saw were the corridor lights overhead.

His ass and shoulders smarted and the bottle had skittered across the deck and spilled.

Musey stood just out of arm's reach, looking down at Ryan as if he'd never moved.

"If you don't want me to do that again," the symp said, "then shut up and do what your father says."

"Screw you. And screw the captain." He pulled himself up, furiously red. He felt it. Worse because he knew he'd deserved it.

"My parents are dead, thanks to Falcone," Musey said out of nowhere, his eyes too steady and too clear. "Yours are still alive and they love you for some reason. Get some perspective."

He walked by Ryan into the lev, which had stayed open, barely touching shoulders when Ryan didn't move.

Ryan couldn't move, not for a long minute. He heard the lev doors clang shut, then turned to them.

His little traumas, the symp had said.

I didn't grow up in the middle of this war, Ryan wanted to say. Wanted to shout.

The war had come to him. Like a stampeding herd of hungry meedees.

He picked up the empty bottle and stood outside the hatch, composing himself because he didn't want his father to see the look that was probably on his face. There would be questions and bothersome comments, and he remembered Sid's voice from months ago, when they were out on a ranch in the middle of nowhere in Texas America, after Hong Kong. Ryan found himself sitting on the back of a rather tall animal called a horse, which smelled and felt a lot different from anything vid could tell you, and Sid said to him, For better or for worse, everyone knows your name and your face because of your parents.

He looked out at the flat brown landscape, some alien world he had to remind himself was actually human, and felt like he was standing at the edge of this planet, one step from falling off. One step outside of anything familiar or safe. And what he really wanted to do was shred himself into little pieces, scatter them to the wind and come out of it with a different face.

Not the face that was all over the Send, from outside that embassy, when he'd thought his grandfather was dead. With the ashes and dust on his skin and his eyelashes, and every time he saw it he remembered how it had smelled.

Cremation, he thought. Ritual burning.

In his ancient history studies he'd read that some of those old Earth civilizations hadn't burned their dead down to the ash, but just so the skin and muscles and juices melted away. The bones remained. Parts of people that they'd gather and bury with jewels and gold.

Parts of people, amid stone dust and steel.

Earth was pure dust. It was in the name, full of the remnants of people who had died, more often than not, violently, across time.

For days after he couldn't shower long or often enough.

For weeks after everywhere he went some meedee eventually found him until it got so invasive and constant even Sid had lost his temper, in a restaurant in London, and decked the man and broke his cam-orb. The EarthHub embassy in Britain had to get involved in that one.

Even the sun burned and he couldn't take it anymore. He'd wanted off the planet before it all came down. Before something else blew up. Before the corpses he saw in his head came to life in the faces of the people around him.

Shiri didn't know. She said, I'm so sorry. And, Let me help. As if it were something that could actually be helped. And when she couldn't help him she said, You have to do

something, I can't be around you anymore. You've changed.
Maybe she regretted it later but she meant it then, and he
yelled right into her face, How can you not?

Lots of people, his mother said on one of her few comms,
saw horrible events like that and just drove on. Look at
when that bomb blew on dockside. The station just went on.
That was what he had to do—go back to school, date his
girlfriend, play games with Sid, and sit with his grandparents at official events where people could say, It must have
been horrible for you (as if it could be pleasant?). The older
people said, If it weren't for your eyes you'd remind me so
much of your father when he was your age.

Most of the time he didn't think they meant it as a compliment. He asked Admiral Grandpa why, and Admiral
Grandpa just said, They don't know your father.

I don't know him, he thought. Do you?

His father sent long-distance condolences, but Earth was,
in the end, too far for him to do anything. People on Earth
didn't like him anyway. Certainly the people who had blown
up the embassy didn't like him. Stop the war, they'd cried to
the cams. The Hub is full of butchers!

He walked the chaotic countries of this planet and nothing felt the same.

And Sid took him out to Texas for the quiet and the peace
from meedees and the Send. He sat beside Ryan on his own
tall horse and squinted at the dry land and the broad unflinching sky. He said, I couldn't take it either, that's why I
went to space.

Sid had fought in deserts.

He knew what it was to burn.

Inside quarters his father had laid the coffee table with
plates and utensils and food in small porcelain dishes.

Expensive and fragrant. Ryan kept going toward the half-open screen. "I need to wash up."

"All right," his father said, behind him, with a question in his voice.

Ryan shut the screen, went in the bathroom and shut the door, ditched the beer bottle in the trash and just sat on the toilet lid. His luck was going to run out. You didn't survive a bomb attack and an assassination attempt and think your life would always be blissful. You didn't front confidence and nonchalance to the public and your family (though whether anybody believed you was another matter) and not crack once in a while, in private. That was the give-and-take. Control was an illusion.

He didn't want to die.

Even though all his life he'd always found the concept of growing old to be a foreign one. And not just because his parents looked barely older than him. The face was just a mask. Inside, he didn't see himself with family and children, living somewhere normal and doing normal things.

He saw himself alone. Dying young.

And there was his father in the living room with some kind of quiche for lunch that he'd made himself, because for some reason the dread captain of *Macedon* liked to cook—as if there wasn't a strit on board or a strit ship in dock or pirates behind every shadow.

Cold. He tucked his hands into his sleeves and rubbed them. Sat there until a knock came on the door, like he knew it would.

"Ryan? Are you all right?"

"Yeah. I'm—coming." He got up, lifted the lid, and stepped away from the toilet so it flushed and his father wouldn't think he'd just been in there looking at the wall. He washed his hands and splashed his face to clear his eyes. Make himself normal. Go out there and just accept that this was where he was now and it wasn't so bad, really . . . nobody was shooting at him. Not with physical weapons anyway.

Evan and Musey and Dorr were another matter.

And Sid was out of reach.

But so were pirates like that Yuri, right?

He took a breath and opened the door. Voices spoke in the outer quarters. As he inched to the sliding screen, he recognized his mother's voice on the other end of the comm.

". . . go this shift?" she was saying.

The captain sighed. "Damiani arrived and we had to break."

"That woman's there now?"

"Yes. 'Reaching out to the far-flung stations,' she says. Really, the Council sent her out here because she bitched about Annexationists making deals with strits. It's going to be fun."

"Centralists have a voice too, Cairo. She's got a right."

"Not if I can help it."

"She's in the running—"

"—and she doesn't want a treaty. How do you think it'll go now? I'm not putting her in a room with Captain S'tlian and the striviirc-na Caste Master. I can barely stomach having her on my ship. It would be disastrous. But that's exactly what she wants."

"Respect her opinion, Cairo. She speaks for a good deal of the Hub, people you can't just ignore."

"If a good deal of the Hub knew what the hell they were doing, this war wouldn't have gone on for so long."

The frustration in his mother's voice went unchecked. "So it's up to you to make the decision for them? We live in an *elective* society."

"Without fair representation. The seat of this government

is still on Earth, a dozen leaps away from stations like Chaos."

"Who have representatives on the Hub Council."

"And we see how effective that is. Hubcentral views deep spacers as either threats or enigmas, it's perpetuated by the Send, and we can't seem to hold our own very well against alien attacks, so we're also costing them cred. It's a ridiculous opinion and Hubcentral solutions *don't work,* Song. Shutting out the aliens isn't working. While we're engaging old hatreds, the pirates are—"

"Stop about the pirates, Cairo. Your mad hunt for them resulted in our son being shot at."

Hard silence. His father's voice was stone. "I see. So we ought to let them kill *other* people because it's safer that way for *us.*"

"Stop twisting my words!"

Ryan shoved the screen aside and stepped out.

The captain turned around from where he sat on the couch, his comp in front of him with Mom Lau's face on the screen. The thrum in the air was a familiar tension, a wire pulled taut between his parents, on the verge of snapping.

And he, as always, would get the recoil.

"Don't let me stop you two," he said, and sat on the chair in front of his set plate. The quiche was still warm and he picked up his fork and cut into it, releasing steam.

"Ryan," he heard his mother say, even though he couldn't see her face, "did you tell your father what I said about the symp?"

"No," he said, loud enough so she could hear. "I was too busy talking with an ex-pirate."

His father stared at him and his mother was silent.

"What ex-pirate?" the captain said.

"A kid named Evan. He told me about Falcone's protégé, Yuri, and how he probably has his own ship and that's why you can't catch him. He thinks Yuri was the one who shot at me. Do you think that? And do you know where he is?"

"Who's this?" his mother said. "Cairo?"

"We don't have anything positive," the captain said, giving him a long look before addressing his mother. "But I suspect this protégé too . . . I've heard of him and he knows I hated Falcone."

Mom Lau was quiet again. Maybe thinking she was right, too right, about what provoked the hit in the Dojo.

"So what are you doing about it?" she asked finally.

"We were in contact with him a year or so ago, but he hasn't answered any comms in a long time."

"You were in *contact* with him? This pirate?" she said.

That would be a nightmare if it got out to the public.

Ryan set down his fork.

"Yes," the captain said, calm. "He'd contacted Otter and Otter told Jos, who told me, that this protégé—Yuri Kirov—offered to turn over Falcone's operation in exchange for complete exoneration of his crimes."

"You're not serious," Mom Lau said. "And you believed him?"

Ryan was thinking the same thing, and stared at his father.

"Yes," his father said, without apology.

"How could you possibly believe a pirate? When you rant about them like—It didn't occur to you that he might be setting you up?"

"Of course it did, but after we tried to set up some sort of meeting to discuss the deal he went incommunicado. If he wanted to take me for a ride he would've followed through. I don't know what happened but—"

"Isn't it obvious?" Ryan asked. "He balked. And now he's pissed that you killed his leader."

Absolute loyalty, Evan had said. Absolute ruthlessness.

"If that's so, we'll find out sooner or later," the captain said.

"If that's so," Mom Lau echoed. "You ought to be hunting *him* instead of sitting dinners with strits. He shot at our son!"

"If so, he missed. And people Falcone trained tend not to miss. Anything."

"How would you know?" Ryan asked. "Because of Musey? He's a symp, so how reliable is he?"

The captain picked up his glass of water and sipped. "Please don't talk to me about things you know nothing about."

"Cairo," his mother said.

"Our son lacks a certain amount of respect, Songlian."

"Well," Ryan said, looking at his father who looked at the comp screen, and the undisguised annoyance on his father's face. "I wonder why."

The captain looked at him. It wasn't a fatherly expression. "I'm going to comm off, Song. We'll talk later."

"All right," she said, with an implicit sigh. "Cairo—"

"Yes?"

A long pause. The captain peered at the screen, questioning.

She said finally, in a clear unwavering voice. "I expect you to bring yourselves safely home."

Ryan watched the tension and a bit of the habitual wall melt from the captain's expression. For a second he almost believed his father was indeed in love with his mother.

But the wall went back up, as smooth as the raising of a voice.

"Ryan will be safe," he said, "and when it's time I'll bring him back. But you know my home is *Macedon* and always will be."

He had compassion enough to sit with strits, but there

wasn't even enough compassion in the man to lie to his wife.

Ryan thought about asking the captain if Sid could return to Austro. He could do that for his mother, if he wanted.

But in the end maybe he didn't have enough love for his mother either. He was too selfish, like she accused the captain of being. He needed Sid on this ship. He wanted Sid here if he had to deal with his father. And when it came down to it, Sid had been his in the first place. Sid had been his friend first.

Like *Macedon* was the captain's duty, first.

And he hated himself for thinking that because his mother was alone on Austro, going about her job with LO Lau in the background saying, I told you so, you never should've married that man or had his child—and with nobody in her apartment but security men who didn't like to talk.

After the captain commed off and they sat for a moment, caught in a guarded, mutual stare, it sank in Ryan's heart how much he did miss her, and how much she probably missed him, even though she didn't say so. Because that was how Laus and Azarcons communicated—in silences, if not in shouts.

After lunch the captain had to go to meetings with "that Damiani woman" so he and Admiral Grandpa could try to convince her to leave well enough alone—the captain said it was good Ryan had plans for dinner with Sid, because he didn't think he would make it. He made it sound like he was going into battle, and maybe he was in a way. Ryan wanted to tell his father that he didn't need to be baby-sat, he could occupy himself just fine with *school*, but he kept that behind his teeth.

An afternoon off sounded like a good deal.

He should've known it wouldn't happen. Just as he finished cleaning up the dishes from lunch, the comm bleeped again and it was his father—again. Saying, "Captain S'tlian and the Caste Master want to meet you. Since we're wrangling with these govies they've returned to *Turundrlar*. Jos will be taking you there."

Ryan was glad he wasn't holding anything fragile, standing there by the coffee table with unsteadiness in his gut. "You're not ser—"

"It's going to be all right, I trust them. I trust Jos."

"Does it matter that *I* don't trust them?"

"I have to go, Ryan. Just be polite. Please. Damiani's already trying to mess this up; don't contribute."

"Captain—"

But the comm disconnected. He hated his father for this. Oh, he hated the man for dumping it like that, like he was just going to walk across the deck to a flower shop or something. He paced to the chair and sat, then got up again with arms against his chest, and decided he was going to refuse. He could refuse, right? What would they do—gag him and cart him over in cuffs?

He wouldn't put it past his father. Or that symp.

People didn't just walk on the Warboy's ship. What if Musey was lying? What if the Warboy had other plans? What a coup it would be to kidnap the son of Captain Azarcon, the Warboy's most dogged enemy . . .

The hatch buzzed and Musey was on the other side of it.

"They want to meet you," Musey said, "and the captain authorized it."

"I know," he said. "But I don't want to go."

Musey still stood there. After a moment he said, "I'll wait while you change clothes."

"I said no."

"Your father authorized it, Azarcon. Comm him if you

want, though I wouldn't recommend it. He's never in a good mood when he has to deal with govies."

"Why would the Warboy want to meet me?"

The symp didn't crack a smile. "Maybe he needs the target practice."

Ryan turned around and went to the kitchen, leaving the hatch open. "That's not funny."

"Go change. I'll wait."

He wasn't going to win this one. "What's wrong with what I got on?" He dislodged a glass and poured the vodka and drank, and it did no good.

"You're going to meet the captain of the striviirc-na fleet, and the Caste Master of one of the most powerful countries on Aaian-na."

Ryan faced him setting down the glass. He'd said the name of the strit homeworld with a pronunciation not even Minister Taylor of Alien Affairs ever got right. Certainly the Send butchered any and all strit words, with a deviant amount of pride.

"How long were you . . . with them?"

Musey shut the hatch and folded his arms. "About five years. Go and change, I don't want to keep them waiting."

"You speak fluent strit?"

Musey stared at him. "Say striviirc-na, not strit. And say Captain S'tlian, or sir, not Warboy. Then you won't get shot."

"I'm just asking. Are all you symps so touchy?"

"Sympathizer. Sheez, Azarcon."

"Well, are you fluent? Because I don't speak a word of their—" Babble, he almost said. "Language."

"I make do," Musey said, with a bare touch of sarcasm. "Since I'm currently working as the interpreter and translator in these negotiations."

Oh, yeah.

It was easy to forget with the symp that he would actually want to help anybody.

Ryan ran out of excuses. Musey was not going to go away.

"Hurry up," he told Ryan, leaning his shoulders against the hatch as if it were built for his permanent use.

Ryan went into the bedroom and picked what he hoped was acceptable attire—a pale blue shirt and tan pants just rough enough in material that he didn't quite look like he was heading for a dinner party. It was also easy to run in, should this meeting come to that.

Musey gave him the once-over and didn't comment, so he supposed it was all right. Not that he cared what the symp thought.

At least he got to walk off the ship.

"Your father will probably be dealing with Damiani for a few shifts," Musey said as they rode the lev down to maindeck. "So we can start your lessons next goldshift."

"My burndiving."

"No," Musey said. "Your combat. You don't need to learn how to burndive. But you need to learn how to fight."

Arrogant SOB.

"So do you think this peace will actually work?"

Musey walked him out the lev and they headed to the main airlock. He didn't say anything for a couple minutes.

"If nearsighted people on both sides just shut up, then yeah. Your father's willing, and so is Niko."

"Niko?"

"Captain S'tlian."

Ryan looked at Musey sidelong. "You call him Niko."

"That's his first name. Nikolas."

"Are you close?"

How close? Ryan wondered. Close enough to betray my father?

Musey seemed uncomfortable, maybe only because they

were within earshot of the crew working on the deck. Once they reached the airlock and the jets on guard nodded them down the ramp, he said, "He trained me."

In what, Ryan thought. To be a spy aboard *Macedon*? Musey didn't say anything else. His eyes cased the dock, even though nobody was around except for a squad of Marines on guard about a hundred meters away at the entrance to the main station. The Warboy's ship was moored beside *Macedon* and in twenty strides they landed up at the bottom of the beaten ramp.

Ryan's gut pinched and his hands sweated, clammy. The dock air went down into his lungs like tiny icicles. He should've worn a jacket. Brought a weapon, maybe.

Talked to his father and told him, Not in a bazillion years will I meet a strit . . .

"I don't know, Musey." He stared up at the round, closed airlock. It was bloodred, battle-scarred, and the point of no return. The Send talked about how prisoners of war on this ship had never made it back.

But Evan said he had.

Musey started to walk up the ramp, no hesitation. "Come on, Ryan."

The use of his first name surprised him. Musey paused at the top of the ramp and looked back.

"Nothing's going to happen to you. I promise." Then he added, "They aren't pirates."

"Says the symp," Ryan muttered. But he walked up to stand beside Musey. "I don't know why they'd want to meet me anyway."

"Because you're his son," Musey said. "And they're curious to know what kind of person he would raise."

For some reason that scared him more than the thought of the Warboy wanting to take potshots at his head.

He was representing what might be good about his father.

Maybe the strits held childrearing to a sacred extreme; maybe they thought if the captain couldn't teach his son manners, then how could he set an example to a government?

He didn't want this responsibility. He didn't want Musey to talk into a commstud and, moments later, have the lock cycle open with a gust of alien air and scents.

Sharp spices, like he'd smelled in Delhi, India—but not. Something deeper penetrated through it; a touch of earth and body that wasn't human, fresh but dark, like the soil beneath the sprawling roots of aged trees.

They went through the inner lock and the scent encompassed him.

Then he stood on the deck of an alien ship, the lock rolled shut behind them with an automated thud and clang, and it was nothing like *Macedon* except in skeletal shape. Strit ships were built off stolen EarthHub specs, so the layouts were similar, but here on *Turundrlar* the walls were calming ivory with red alien designs, like twining thorns and ivy, leading your eye straight from end to end. Corridors were brightly lit as Musey escorted him through one and then the other. They didn't bump into any random strit crew and Ryan wondered if that was purposeful—out of courtesy for him.

He was grateful, at any rate. He didn't think he could keep his composure if a parade of aliens streamed by him on both sides.

Musey stopped him outside a hatch and palmed the call pad. In seconds the little light on the panel blinked white and Musey opened the hatch, pushing it wide with his shoulder. Then the symp turned to him with an expectant stare.

You go first, it said.

Right.

Ryan stretched his fingers at his sides and stepped in, over the short threshold and into a wide lounge.

He saw the strit and the Warboy first, looking exactly the same as his sneak preview in the corridor on his father's ship. They both stood in front of a low table encircled by silken cushions. The light was dimmer here than in the corridor, but still bright without being harsh, a pale bronze glow. It reflected off the strit's silver-white hair and silver facial tattoos.

And its gloss-black eyes.

Ryan heard his own breaths. He hoped he didn't look too panicked as the Warboy stepped forward, soundlessly, and said something to Musey in their own dialect.

He hoped it wasn't a kill order.

Musey answered back, standing just behind Ryan's shoulder, and gave it a small push forward.

Ryan twitched, went until he was within arm's reach of the Warboy. The strit stayed by the table, marblelike face unreadable, skin pigmentation an almost blinding white. The transparent wings, folded elegantly against its sides like a fall of pale silk, were indeed lined by spidery veins.

Or what looked like veins, even up close. But what did he know?

It looked as if it had stepped down from a pedestal, some ancient stone sculptor's work come to life. And yet, when it walked to Musey to greet him with a word that sounded more like a song note, its movements were the opposite of wooden or ponderous.

Ryan tried to stifle a shiver, and looked at the other human in this room besides him and Musey.

Human as it applied to the Warboy was a broad generalization.

The Warboy's tattoo was almost as intricate as the strit's, a curving design around the outer part of his right eye, like script written over script in precise position. Though his skin tone was human warm, his expression was as implacable as the strit's and his irises just as black, dominating the white corners within a fringe of long lashes.

Ryan wished Sid were with him but tried not to let that show. To let anything show. He probably failed. The Warboy stared into his face as if he were reading a Send scroll in Ryan's eyes. He spoke, halting and heavily accented, and Ryan was surprised he understood. Surprised the symp attempted a human language at all.

"Your name, Ry-yan-na," the Warboy said.

Ryan had to swallow, and glanced at Musey, then back at the Warboy. "Um, just Ryan." He didn't explain that Ryanna was a girl's name, for fear of embarrassing the symp. "And yours?" His most polite tone.

"Nikolas-dan," the Warboy answered, pronouncing it just as Musey had: *Nee*-ko-las.

"Nice to meet you—sir." It took no effort now to be respectful. Faced with the man and the alien, and their brazen scrutiny, he couldn't imagine putting his life in danger with the least offense.

He hoped nobody noticed how his hands shook. He put them behind his back.

"Sit," the Warboy said, and went to the low table.

Musey gestured him forward so he went, and sat down on one of the large, soft cushions on an empty side of the table. Musey and the strit filled up the other two. The strit ended up on Ryan's left side so he saw it out of the corners of his eye. The Warboy knelt across from him and he couldn't avoid the stare.

Musey poured what smelled like tea into four round, handleless white cups clustered at the center of the table, then set one in front of each of them. Almost like a ritual.

Then they all looked at him.

"Take a sip," Musey whispered.

If it poisoned him, he hoped his father would be happy. Sending him on this alien ship.

He tried not to smile at the thought, more out of nervousness than anything else, and took a hesitant first sip.

It was a tart tea and made him cough, but a second sip went down smoother and a third one smoother still. A sweet aftertaste rubbed the back of his throat as he set down the cup and smiled at them, his small, standard expression when he didn't want to let on that he was tense as hell.

He didn't think he fooled anybody. The strit hadn't taken his gaze away since they sat down.

The Warboy spoke in his own language, a kind of multitonal song, and Musey interpreted after the entire phrase, with an iron concentration and a clear, steady voice.

"Your father's government doesn't agree with him," the Warboy said, without any preamble and after a single sip from his own teacup.

"No," Ryan said, then fixed the ambiguity, "I mean, yes, you're right. Sir. If you're talking about the treaty proposal. Some of them don't agree."

"Yes," the Warboy said. "You are on the Send a lot."

"Yes," Ryan agreed, wondering that the Warboy watched the news, and it made sense, come to think of it, to monitor what the enemy said about you and what was going on.

He did it too.

Maybe the Warboy watched Tyler Coe vids after all.

"Most recently," the Warboy said, "about pirates in a . . ."

Musey interpreted and provided the last word: "Flash house."

"Yes," Ryan said. Thinking, Yeah? Why do you want to talk about this?

"And they say things about you," the Warboy continued, "that you are . . . popular?"

Ryan shrugged. "I guess."

"Because of your father?" the Warboy asked. "You are popular?"

"I . . ." It was such an odd thing to discuss with this man, he lost his thought for a second. "I guess. Yeah. Sir. And because of my mom, she's kind of important on Austro."

"Do you agree with your father?" the Warboy said.

He was feeling the strit's stare on the side of his face and didn't know how to tell it to please stop doing that. He hated people looking at him like that, like when he just wanted to shop in the market with Sid and some damn rich tourists thought it was *newsworthy* that Ryan Azarcon walked about like a normal person and had to follow him and stare at him, and some even had the audacity to ask for a picture. Or not even ask for a picture, he'd just hear the whir of a cam-orb following behind his head.

And he'd never done anything to warrant that kind of attention, but people gave it because his mother was always in the public eye and his father never was, and they thought their son was good-looking enough to obsess over. Even when he did nothing to dress himself up or make himself presentable, the damn Send still found something fashionable to say about him.

"Ryan," Musey prompted.

He had to look at the strit, since it still stared, but didn't see anything that comforted him in the least, just that alien stillness like those wild animals in nature reserves that didn't seem to know or care that they were circled on all sides by humans. They were still wild and roamed where they wanted, and the rangers kept you far and away, just in case, as you drove by those animals as they sunned near rocks or sat under trees, watching you pass with the easy confidence of predators.

Even the animals that had been born on the reserves for

generations past . . . something in them was still inherently feral. And you knew if you were stupid and went up to them, they'd swipe a paw across your chest, knock you down, and eat you.

The stories they told on the Send about aliens and their penchant for human meat . . .

. . . was obviously rubbish. Humans lived with them.

But his skin still crawled.

He looked at Musey. He hoped Musey could read signals and maybe Musey could tell the strit to stop staring.

"I'm sorry . . . what was the question?"

The alien spoke this time, in a lilting birdlike whistle, except his tongue rolled over consonants, and gradients of sound seemed to reach out from deep in his throat even when his lips didn't move.

It was the full effect of what the Warboy and Musey only approximated with their human mouths.

It was unexpectedly beautiful, and Ryan stared.

"He wants to know," Musey said, "if you hate them as much as you fear them."

So it was a he. And it got to the point too.

Ryan dragged his gaze from the alien back to Musey.

"I'm not—" Afraid of them, he almost said. An automatic defense. Then he bit his lip for a second, pulling on it with teeth. "I mean . . . I don't hate them. I've never met—anyone like them before."

The alien spoke again.

"Maybe if we talked longer," Musey interpreted, "you would truly believe that. But for now we'll have to be patient."

Ryan looked at the Warboy. Nikolas. "The Send says a lot of bad things about you."

"I know," Nikolas said, through Musey. "About your father too. They aren't correct all of the time, are they?"

"No," Ryan said. And quieter, "No."

"He will correct them," the Warboy said. "Do you agree with him?"

"About the war?"

"About the peace," the Warboy said.

"What does it matter what I think?" They were forthright; he figured he could be. "Why do you care what I think?"

He saw the human eyes of this symp, dark to Musey's blue, but while Musey must have still thought in the language of his birth, a language of the Hub, Ryan was sure the Warboy thought only in alien. He held Ryan's stare for a long minute and nobody else spoke.

"You are his son," the Warboy said, so Ryan could understand and Musey didn't have to translate, and poured more tea.

What did that mean? It was an obvious observation.

"Does it matter to you what I am?" he asked, half-wishing that it wouldn't.

"You don't seem to like being his son," the Warboy said, through Musey this time. And Musey watched Ryan with a blatant, curious stare.

"Why would you think that? And why would you care?" They didn't answer immediately and he straightened his shoulders, on the verge of getting up, despite what protocol seemed to demand. "I don't see what I have to do with your political dealings with my father or the Hub. If you're curious about me, fine, but I don't appreciate being gawked at. Or interrogated."

He pointedly didn't look at the Caste Master.

"Your father is serious about this peace," the alien said through Musey, "to allow his son onto this ship."

Ryan heard his own quiet intake of breath. None of them seemed to breathe, but they were alive. He was alive, in that hyperaware state of acute fear. He almost felt all the tiny, individual hairs on his arms, or the soft touch of alien air across the skin of his face and the backs of his hands.

"And are you?" he asked, as level as he could. "Are you serious about this peace?"

"You're here," the Warboy said. "Unharmed."

The tea churned acidic in his stomach. He swallowed. But he held the stare, thinking of his father and the gamble that he'd made.

On his son's life.

And the Warboy smiled.

The clustered cups in the center of the dark table made up the petals on a white porcelain flower. No more tea and no more conversation. Ryan stood with his hands behind his back, clenched together as he watched Musey say good-bye to the Warboy and the Caste Master.

It was a brief few words in that songlike language to the Caste Master, but the Warboy got an embrace.

He tried not to be shocked, seeing Musey engulfed by that assassin. No words were said between them, they barely looked at each other. But the embrace was solid and close, and Ryan didn't miss the way the Warboy's fingers briefly gripped Musey's back before sliding away. There was something almost regretful in the gesture.

Musey let go and turned away, and walked right by Ryan with barely a glance. No cues except the direction of his stride and Ryan had no choice but to follow.

No lingering good-byes or thank yous for him. Were all symps this abrupt?

By the time they hit the station deck outside the Warboy's ship, his breathing had fallen to a more natural rhythm.

"Thanks for that," he said. "I won't sleep for a week."

"They weren't going to hurt you," Musey said, in a subdued tone.

"I didn't know that."

"Your father did."

"I'm not my father. Or you. All I know about them is what I hear on the Send."

Musey paused on *Macedon*'s ramp and looked at him. "Precisely."

"Do you love him?"

That scored one on the symp. A high score. For an unguarded second Musey's eyes seemed to be as transparent as shallow water. But they hardened with the swiftness of habit or practice, and he said simply, "Yes."

Then he continued through the airlocks without a backward glance. "Tomorrow we begin your training. You can find your own way back to quarters."

He did eventually get back to his father's quarters. And sat on his rumpled bed staring at nothing before realizing that was what he was doing. He was surprised Musey had admitted what he had; he was surprised he wasn't throwing up in the bathroom after walking on that alien ship.

He leaned over to the comm and punched in Sid's code. Sid was in training but Ryan interrupted him anyway.

"I just came back from the Warboy's ship," Ryan said.

Sid said, "What the hell?"

"My father's doing. Musey took me. I'm alive." He thought about Silver, but it slid away like a tide. "I feel weird. It was weird."

"Did they hurt you?"

"No. They just asked questions."

When he shut his eyes he saw the Caste Master's black stare.

"Ryan, I'll quit this and come see you. Where are you, in the captain's q?"

"No, don't do that. You'll get in trouble."

"Hell with it."

"Mom would kill me if she knew. She didn't want me going near them." So naturally his father put him on their ship.

"They didn't touch you?"

"No, I'm fine." Now he felt silly. Even though his gut still prickled as if a tiny army were marching in there. Would they want to see him again? Meedees would kill for the opportunity he'd had, and here he was spinning out about it. "Look, I'm just going to take a hot shower or something. Crash out."

"I'll be there."

"To watch me shower?" He could joke. "Why, Mr. Sidney. I do declare."

"Ryan."

"I'm over it. It happened. They didn't do anything and we're in peace talks, right?"

"Don't dive into your father's booze."

"I'm comming out now."

"Just reassure me—you were polite, right? We aren't at war again?"

He disconnected, and laughed, and felt better despite himself. Which Sid had always been able to do, even from a distance.

That late blueshift, after dinner with Sid, he sat cross-legged on the couch in his father's quarters, in his sleep clothes, and practiced his guitar. He could lose himself in it. He was rusty but his fingers remembered the frets, and after a few minutes he picked up a quiet melody from memory, hummed with it since he was alone. He was halfway through the song when the captain came in.

His father saw him there immediately, and his weary expression eased out, a visible relief. "Don't stop on my account," he said, shutting the hatch. "I've never heard you play."

Ryan shook his head. "I only play alone."

"Why?"

He shrugged. "What does it matter?" Especially to you.

"Why wouldn't it matter? I'm curious."

His father went to the kitchen, sliding his comp onto the counter. He spun the cold rack slowly until he met a bottle of whiskey, then dislodged it. He took a small glass from the washer, poured a shallow bit, and sipped.

Ryan said, "Like you were curious to see if the Warboy would kill me when you sent me on his ship?"

If that registered anywhere in his father, the man didn't show it. He just came to the chair across from Ryan and sat rather heavily, said, "You weren't going to get killed."

"If they wanted to get back at you, I was right there. Isn't that everybody's fear? I can't believe you'd risk me like that. Why am I even on this ship? I could do fine on Austro under those conditions." He set the guitar aside and unfolded from the couch.

"Ryan, they weren't going to hurt you. Jos took you over there—"

"Jos is *one* of them."

"Do you really think so? Now that you've spent time with him? Don't fall back on the lazy answers. Or the pre-conditioned ones."

He went to the kitchen and scrounged around for snacks. It gave his hands something to do and gave him some distance from his father. "He's one of them. I'm not saying he doesn't like it on your ship, but his heart is with the Warboy."

"Then why do you think he's chosen to stay on *Mac*?"

"As a *spy*, maybe?" Wasn't it obvious?

"Do you think I'm that stupid? Now that I know where he grew up?"

"I think maybe you—" He found flavored crackers and took down the box from the cupboard.

"I what?"

He turned around, leaned on the counter and buried his hand in the box. "Why do you risk it. Why did you risk me? He could just have easily betrayed you. He's done it before by working for the Warboy on this ship."

"I know him. I'm beginning to know Captain S'tlian. Maybe more importantly, I'm willing to know them. And they're willing to know me. That's what it comes down to. You can't trust somebody until you both start at that place."

He stared across the small expanse in the quarters and into his father's tired gaze. "Are we still talking about Musey?"

"I thought we were talking about the peace negotiations, after a fashion."

The captain was sly. Ryan ate a couple crackers. "Just being willing to know somebody isn't the answer."

"It's where you start."

"The person has to give something, then. Some show of trust."

"Yes," his father said. "So I let you go on that ship. I knew you weren't going to be hurt because I trust Jos, and he trusts that I don't let my crew kill him while he's here."

"Does he know you better than I do?"

The captain sipped his whiskey. "Better?"

"For him to trust you. He must know you. You must've told him stuff about you. Meanwhile I have to pry it from you like I'm a meedee or something."

He wasn't aiming for it, precisely, and maybe the captain really was exhausted to allow his expression to slide and reveal a sharp hurt. But like Musey's habitual control, it was only a glimpse.

"What do you want to know?" his father asked, quietly.

Of course, now faced with it, he could think of nothing to ask. And after a moment the opportunity passed. His father took another sip of his drink and Ryan put away the crackers, and the silence bled between them like a slow reopened wound.

The captain had an early meeting again in the next gold-shift with Damiani and Grandpa Ashrafi. "She wants to meet S'tlian," the captain said, "so she can ask him why he's such a butcher of 'loyal humans.' Her words. Like that will ever happen while I sit at the table." Musey took Ryan for breakfast in the mess hall. A silent escort. The hall was a wide gray room, furiously clean and noisily packed with crew at the beginning or end of their shifts. Clamped black tables and chairs and some benches lining the longer tables, scarred from use, dotted the floor in regular intervals, with the galley at the left and back of the hall. He sat across from Musey at an empty table as they both delved into a pretty decent serving of pancakes, potatoes, and peppered eggs. The non-meats, Musey said, were grown right here on ship in the bioengineering lab. The hall would be less crowded between regular meal hours, he said, but *Macedon* had round-the-clock food availability, unlike most ships. The cook wasn't there in off-time, but pre-made meals were kept lidded and stored in cold cupboards and you could zap what you wanted, when you wanted it.

Food was a nice, neutral topic in a crowd.

"So my father's rich," Ryan said. "I didn't think the military paid so well."

"They don't. He's just smart and gets his cred by other means." Musey watched his face. "Legally."

"What about, like, what he confiscates from pirates and stuff?"

"He usually gives that to NGOs. Hubcentral looks the other way. Not that they could really do anything about it."

"NGOs."

Musey said, "Non-governmental organizations—for humanitarian relief and aid. Especially the ones that take care of orphans." Musey absently turned his cup around on the table. "Hubcentral has programs but . . . it's kind of scattered in deep space and things don't get addressed quickly."

"I didn't know that."

"Well." Musey didn't seem surprised but he wasn't going to harp on it. They were being civil.

Ryan looked at him when Musey was looking at his food and thought about what Evan had said. Falcone had picked Musey for a protégé before he landed a long-term gig with the strits, and then the captain. Musey was *like* this because he'd lived, so far, one hell of an unusual life.

Unusual to Ryan, at least. Maybe not so unusual for other deep-space kids. Musey was far from Austro, even though he kept the Austroan accent—for whatever reason. Maybe it was habit by now. Maybe this ship was habit for him, and that was why he stayed.

"Do you talk to my father a lot?" Ryan asked, watching the face for any hint of expression. Musey gave little, or maybe Ryan just didn't know him well enough yet.

"Lately, yeah. But I didn't much before."

"What do you talk about?"

"Ask him," Musey said, shutting down that line of questioning. He stabbed his food.

Ryan moved on. "So what're you now, if you're not a jet—officially?"

"An LO."

"Liaison officer." Like Grandmother Lau.

Musey nodded and looked down at his plate again, moving the food around.

Ryan said, "Do you like it?"

He hesitated. "I don't have to kill people."

"What's *that* like?"

Musey glanced up at him from under his brows.

Ryan said, "I'm sorry. I guess I'm just curious."

"Yeah. You are." He drained his glass.

Ryan looked around, saw some of the crew watching them. Partially hostile, partially curious.

"Evan said you were on a pirate ship when you were little."

Musey took a deep breath. "Evan talks too much."

"Are you and he like—" Ryan put two fingers together.

"No." He shifted, looked over Ryan's shoulder toward the door. "No."

For whatever reason Musey didn't seem able to even entertain the thought, but it wasn't out of any kind of prejudice. Something about his expression said he'd find a discussion of girls just as uncomfortable. So Ryan changed the subject before Musey bolted on him. "Everyone's afraid the striviirc-na will start encroaching on Hub space if we give them leave to travel our borders."

Talking shop with Musey seemed a safe course.

"Yeah," Musey said. "It's stupid."

"Why?"

"Because Niko's fleet is the only thing that keeps Hub ships from *their* borders. Not to mention the pirates. They like us running around fighting each other too. If people like Damiani had their way, they'd own the stars all the way to Aaian-na. That's the only way Hub humans wouldn't see the strivs as a threat—if the strivs were beaten."

"Hubcentral humans."

"Yeah. But . . . even though some of the stations and

colonies out here are on-line with your father, they'd just as well be on-line with a conquered alien world. Just as long as nobody fought anymore near their homes."

"It's a lot of old hatred. Resentment." Ryan moved his eggs around. "And fear. You have to understand that. Doesn't the—Nikolas—understand that?"

"Yeah, he does. Some sympathizers and strivs on their side aren't for the treaty either. But he's going to try. We have to try, at least. Right?"

Ryan didn't get to answer. A body shored up by his chair and a hand messed up his hair roughly. He dodged his head and glared up.

"Baby Az," Erret Dorr said, smiling down at him, "look who I brung. It's my new boyfriend, Maroon Siddy."

Sid said, "In your dreams."

"Too true." Dorr laughed. "How'd you know?"

Hartman was there too, and Madison, still bruised, and even Aki Wong-Merton. They all seemed to know each other well, probably they were friends (amazing that Musey had friends on this ship), and Ryan found himself smiling at Aki as she took a seat beside Musey with her tray of food. She smiled back.

"Doc Mercurio misses you in medical. When are you going back?"

"When I'm forced," Ryan said.

"Y'all are too glum," Dorr said. "I saw this black cloud over yonder table and figured it must be Musey's company. So I thought, Better bring over my bad self and my new boyfriend and lighten things up. You gonna finish them pancakes, Jos?"

"No," Musey said, shoving over his tray. He looked put out by the crowd, but he seemed used to it.

"I'm not your boyfriend," Sid said. "Give it up." He sat beside Ryan and elbowed him in greeting. He didn't seem damaged by his association with these jets. So maybe Dorr's influence was considerable indeed. Or maybe Sid was actually teaching them a thing or two.

"Jets don't give up," Dorr answered. "That's the diff between us 'n' Maroons."

"That and your smell," Sid shot back.

Their table got loud fast.

"He outnumbered and he still sassin' us, Dette," Dorr said to Hartman.

"Brave macaroon," Hartman said, with a grin.

Sid winked at her. Aki was laughing, and Ryan thought it was amazing what a mouthy jet could do to a conversation.

"So what y'all bin talkin' about that you look so unfunny?" Dorr asked.

"The war," Ryan said. "Pirates."

"Ah." Dorr waved a syrupy fork. "Screw 'em."

"I meant to ask you," Ryan said, "what did that jet Sanchez mean about you being in my father's bed?"

"Not what you think," Madison said, inspecting his knuckles.

"I'm loyal," Dorr said. "That's what that mutinous punk meant. Don't worry, I got my sights on him. You just stay out of his way."

"Should've taken him out long ago," Musey said.

"Every ship needs a few," Dorr said. "Like dogs got fleas."

"Mutinous, though?" Sid asked. "Isn't that dangerous?"

"If he was real dangerous he wouldn't be breathin'," Dorr said.

"What do you consider real dangerous?"

Dorr smiled. "Me." Then he shrugged. "Sanchez likes to spout. It lets us know what the less advanced crew might think and helps us keep tabs so if it ever gets outta hand we know who to boot. But his groupies ain't as prolific as he makes it sound. Ships got hierarchies, mano. Politics. It ain't only reserved for Hubcentral wanks."

"Comforting," Sid said, but his face said the opposite. "The captain's going to deal with that, isn't he?"

"Jetdeck takes care of jetdeck," Hartman said. "But feel free to kick him, Maroon, if he crosses your path."

"Yah," Madison said. "Comm me and I'll even help."

"Ryan," Musey interrupted, "why don't we head to the shooting gallery?"

He understood why the captain hadn't wanted him roaming jetdeck. It wasn't because of jets like Dorr, who insinuated himself into your routine as if all the galaxy was a VIP invitation.

"Jos don't like a crowd," Dorr said. *Teasing* the symp.

"Not one with you in it," Musey replied, standing. Dorr laughed and Musey tipped his chair back, a sudden movement that made the corporal grab the edge of the table in reflex.

"You going to be all right here?" Ryan asked Sid. Among wild, chair-tipping jets.

"Yeah," Sid said, with a grin. He could hold his own, apparently, and these jets seemed to respect that.

Ryan was learning.

Musey put the gun in his hand and raised it to aim at the standing holotarget in front of them, across the firing range about ten meters away. The symp's eyes passed critically over Ryan's stance before he shifted Ryan's shoulders, lifted his elbow, and made sure his grip was secure.

"This feels weird," Ryan said. But kind of familiar. Like the games he'd played in Austro's cybetoriums, except this gun was a real weight, even though it was a training weapon. It felt, Musey said, just like the real ones.

"It's your first time," Musey said. "Now line up the laser sight and fire."

He did that. The target registered a glancing blow on the left arm.

"Try not to flinch," Musey said.

Easier said than done, holding something that could—if it were real—kill a man.

"And relax," the symp added.

The second shot missed completely. "Shit."

"Straighten your shoulders," Musey said.

He remembered asking Sid to show him how to fire the bodyguard sidearm. Sid never had and now Ryan knew why. After a few more shots it started to be fun.

It was like a violent sort of etiquette class. There was a proper way to stand, hold the weapon, aim, breathe. All the things you had to pay attention to before it became second nature. Ryan popped off a couple more shots, one of which hit the target's crotch. He turned to Musey with a proud grin.

"That'd disable the bastard." He thought it would get a crack of a smile out of the symp, but Musey just stared at him.

Somebody's tags beeped. Turned out to be Musey's. He tapped them and stepped away, waving at Ryan to continue practicing. It sounded like it might've been Evan on the other end of the comm, but Musey went out of earshot, down the range.

Ryan squinted and shot at his pirate-dressed holotarget. He spun the gun around like he saw in the vids and pictured Tyler Coe's face on the image.

"Captain's son," somebody said, on his left.

He turned, took a step back automatically, glad he did when he saw Sanchez there.

He looked toward Musey but all he saw was a black-shirted shoulder. Musey was leaning against one of the partition screens between target stations, his back to Ryan.

"What do you need that symp for?" Sanchez said. "I just want to talk to the other Azarcon."

"Well . . . now you've talked to me." He fingered the gun, acutely aware it wasn't real.

But Sanchez was all smiles, nonthreatening, as he picked up his own practice weapon and stood at a neighboring station. "Need help with this?"

Ryan said, "No. Thanks."

"Here, watch." The jet edged over to Ryan's station and fired his weapon three times.

The target registered three dead-on hits, one in the forehead and two in the heart.

Ryan said, "Nice. Now get out of my light." He wasn't in the light, as the lights came down overhead rather bright, but it seemed like the thing to say.

"Mouthy," Sanchez said.

"It's one of my more charming traits," he said. And saw Musey had noticed them and was heading over now, semifast. Face unreadable and fixed on Sanchez.

Sanchez seemed unperturbed. He leaned to Ryan and whispered near his ear, "I hope that symp teaches you well. I have a feeling you're gonna need it."

Ryan tilted his chin back. "Go ahead and see how far you'll get."

"I'm not going to touch you," Sanchez said, his smile large and white as Musey reached Ryan's side. "I just want you to be safe. Captain's son and all. Take good care of him, Muse."

Musey didn't say a word, just stared at the jet.

Sanchez set his practice weapon on the target console and wandered out of the gallery.

Ryan breathed then, not aware that he'd been holding it in.

"Pirate," Musey muttered, resetting the target.

"What do you mean?"

"He says one thing, but means another. I don't know why the captain hasn't dumped him. He hates that kind otherwise." Musey concentrated on calibrating the holo settings, as if trying to exorcise a thought in menial detail.

Ryan put a hand on the console, "What do you know about my father and pirates, Jos?"

Musey raised the gun one-handed and shot five rounds into the target's face before it took a step. "Ask him."

Musey said he had some documents to translate for the captain and Nikolas, for whenever the talks would resume once First Minister Damiani was done bitching at the captain and the admiral (Musey's words), so he took Ryan to the library with the clear suggestion to "do some work on your own for a couple hours."

On their way there Evan joined them, on his way too or maybe purposely planned since Musey seemed on edge after Sanchez's pop visit. Ryan wasn't sure Evan could be much protection against a jet, but Musey left them at the door of the library with barely a glance, apparently satisfied that his charge was safe.

Evan stuck hands in his sweater pockets, as if he didn't know what to do with them if they weren't holding a beer and a cigret.

"He's full of jokes and jollies," Ryan said to Evan, by way of greeting.

"I know. You should see him do an impersonation of your father."

Ryan laughed. "Really?"

"No." Evan grinned. "But wouldn't that be funny?"

Beyond funny, they agreed.

And it was easier then, now that they had a mutual target for a couple inside jokes.

They found a workstation in the corner of the large library, sidestepping the broad, currently deactivated tactical table that dominated the center of the deckspace. Jets probably used that; there was a holoarm bent up near the ceiling. The other smaller stations were sparsely occupied by crew, not all of them jets, tapping at comps or talking softly to them. Some of the people huddled in small groups. At least one couple was half hidden behind a privacy screen, making out.

Evan said, "A good place to go if you have prudish berthmates."

The library was between training deck and jetdeck, accessible by both, with private rooms off to the side where the school was conducted. One sprawling fishbowl window showed a class in progress, lined up at tables with their open comps, a dropscreen linked to another class (at Austro?), and a uniformed instructor at the head of the room. Evan explained that the captain encouraged the crew to gain credits and eventually diplomas or certifications, above and beyond what was required to perform their duties on ship. If you wanted to take an art course just for fun that was okay too. *Macedon* paid for it, so many of the crew, especially the younger kids, took advantage of it.

"Not too many of us went to formal school, like if we were at relocation colonies or you know . . . adopted by pirates," Evan said.

"I read about that. On the Send," he said, before thinking that sounded kind of funny. Like discussing a vid. "I mean, about the relocation colonies." He'd read about it in passing. It had never seemed very urgent to him.

Evan didn't comment. He was probably thinking, Typical rich stitch.

Ryan couldn't argue it either.

He unclamped a chair from a nearby cubicle and set it on the deck beside Evan, in front of a single comp. "So deal me more dirt about Musey. I want something on him when we start combat training, so he doesn't damage me too badly."

Evan laughed so loud they got told to shut up.

Ryan whispered, "What's with you two anyway? He your boyfriend?"

Evan grinned. "Uh, no. Jos? If he ever admitted he liked *anybody* I think I'd die of shock."

"Why's he like that, anyway?"

"He'd kill me if I told you. Just . . . put two and two together. I told you Falcone had him for a while." Evan looked toward the comp and poked at it absently to activate it. "It doesn't really matter though. I know he's cool about it, the way he can be, even though he doesn't say anything. Or do anything."

"Just because he hasn't killed you?"

Evan laughed. "Actually, yeah, with Jos . . . if he doesn't shove you or smack you around that's pretty much acceptance in his head."

"I couldn't live with that."

"No?" Evan rubbed the knee of his fatigues. "Hmm."

"So how'd he kill that pirate anyway?"

Evan ran his finger down the comp screen, highlighting menu icons in a fire trail. "Stabbed him in the neck."

He hadn't expected the answer, or the way it was just tossed into the air.

Evan looked at him with a small, amused smile. "Why're you so appalled?"

"I don't know . . . it just seems kind of . . . cold-blooded."

"Jos can be pretty cold-blooded."

He believed that. Falcone must have hurt Musey bad.

It was rotten of him to pry, especially to use Evan for a source. Since Evan seemed to like his company, or was lonely, or something. Ryan looked at the comp. "So . . . show me this thing. Does it access the Universal Library Files?"

"Yeah, and you have limited access to the Send too. They're holo optional. But you can't transcast from these units."

"Oh."

"Have you checked the Send lately?"

"Actually, no. Too busy running around with Musey."

Evan smiled. "Apparently everyone on Austro is wonderin' if you're okay and why haven't you been seen on their decks. They're sayin' maybe you were more injured at the Dojo than anybody let on."

He felt his teeth grind. "I don't give a damn. I'm sick of the Send. What, is Tyler Coe saying I lost a limb or something?"

Evan laughed. "Mano. Azarcon. You gotta have a sense of humor about it. Just think. All those stupid wanks on that station makin' up stories about how you're holed up in your room. And here you are on your daddy's bad-ass ship havin' convos with ex-pirates and symps."

"Well," he said, having to grin, "when you put it like that."

"Poor little meedees," Evan continued, "scurryin' about with their little cam-orbs in search of a story. Imagine if there weren't no war or no Azarcons. They'd have to pick their noses to find somethin' newsworthy."

He couldn't stop laughing. "*Nose* worthy."

The couple making out on the other side of the cubicle had the gall to peek over and say, "Keep it down."

Ryan said, "Aren't you two done yet?"

They weren't combat jets so they didn't take issue with him. Evan leaned close, his voice dropping. "Do you know how to burndive?"

"A little. But it doesn't matter here, my father hasn't authorized me to transcast. The ship would flag me if I tried." His eyes grazed over the comp icons but he was careful not to blink code at the holo prompt that would connect his optical implants. "I wanted to send back some comms to my ex-girlfriend but . . . there's that point of origin issue. She can't know I'm on ship."

"There are ways around that," Evan said.

"I don't know how. My burndiving skills don't extend that far. Especially not using a carrier link."

"Musey knows how. He spied for years on this ship and sent reports to the Warboy."

"I already asked him and he said no. He's on my father's orders."

"Maybe you didn't ask him sweetly enough."

"Evan, I don't think he'd go against my father for anything. Besides, you want to get me into trouble?"

"Nah." Evan smiled, showing his jagged tooth. "But it'd be a lotta fun if you could drop insults to meedees and mess up their 'casts, don't you think?"

He laughed. "Yeah."

"Highlight some words about that half-sprig Tyler. I mean, what else are you gonna do on this ship to amuse yourself? Might as well screw with the meedees. They do 'cast a lot of shit about you and your family."

"As long as my father is who he is, that won't change."

"That's 'cause people got all the wrong info." Evan's eyes brightened and he leaned to the comp, tapping into it.

"What're you looking for?" He leaned forward on his elbows.

"Since Jos can't help us, we can help ourselves."

The "us" part didn't spook him much, but he wondered at it. Maybe Evan was just bored.

"Part of my job," Evan said as he poked at the screen, "is to review what's been looked up in the files and stuff, so we can get an idea of what the crew's interested in and we can place orders when we get to port. Like games and specialty vids, that kinda thing."

"Wouldn't it all just be porn?" Ryan grinned.

Evan laughed. "Surprisingly, nah. But I know my way around this system. Okay, look here." He pointed to a series of links and ran his finger down the screen, slowly scrolling them.

Links to comp tech information. Back door progging, holointerface shortcuts, and buildable templates . . . the basics of burndiving.

"Hey," Ryan said. "Brazen."

"You know it. If you're a good enough progger you can burndive, and this stuff is *officially* here 'cause some of our techies wanna improve their skills. Cap's comm officer can dive. She tailed Jos a couple times."

"Really?" He reached over and poked some links, scanned the info.

"I learned a little just from following some of these manuals and trying them out on my comp back in q. I haven't told Jos, though, so don't say anything. He'll probably think I wanna sabotage the ship." Evan smirked. "But I ain't that good. It would take a lot. If you know some stuff already I bet you can pick up the rest. At least to mask a comm sig."

"I think I can." He chewed his lip. "I want to copy some of this and take it back to my mobile."

"I'll get you a cube. Or do you prefer chipsheets?"

"Any or."

Evan got up and wove his way through the workstations

to a supply room near the back. Ryan shifted into the vacant seat, bloomed a separate window, and looked for the holo setting icon. It was much faster this way. He found the icon in the corner and blinked twice at it. The ship library engulfed him then, a smooth transition from real-world to comp-world that he'd only found in the latest upgrades of the tech.

Sweet setup, Daddy.

He darted around the columns of choices to acquaint himself with the system; it wasn't much different from the library units he'd used on Earth or Austro. So he voiced a search for *Falcone*.

It wasn't a long wait. A blurt of links sprang across his sight in ghostly lines.

FALCONE, VINCENZO MARCUS—CAPTAIN.

GENGHIS KHAN—SHIP.

PIRATE—ORGANIZATION.

He ran his gaze down the list, watched them highlight yellow as his implants scan-connected, then blinked back up at the first item. It flicked open to an encyclopedic paragraph.

. . . notorious captain of the pirate ship Genghis Khan, *he was formerly a decorated commanding officer of the Earth-Hub vessel* Kali. *Born on Kane Station July 29, 2132 EHSD, he entered the Navy Space Corps Academy at 16 . . .*

Ryan scanned.

. . . and was posted as senior helmsman on Kali *at age 20 . . . was the captain of* Kali *by age 30 at a time that is widely considered to be the height of the deep-space war . . . was disgraced at the Battle of Ghenseti in 2162 EHSD when—*

"Ryan."

He blinked out hurriedly and looked up past the faint images of the words that ghosted across his vision in afterburn.

A quick glance at the screen showed the second window still blank since he hadn't manually accessed anything, except for basic icons, so he patted it to shut it down.

"What were you looking for?" Evan asked, passing him a chipsheet.

"Stuff about Falcone. Like why my father hates him so much."

"He does bad things to kids like Jos." And me, was the implicit suggestion. Evan gazed at him in mild offense. "I guess it's kinda weird for you to think about. 'Cause you grew up rich with your schools and your bodyguard."

"It wasn't perfect," Ryan said, and turned around to transfer the files he needed. He slid in the chipsheet and tapped away. "Besides, it's not my fault where I was born."

"Sorry," Evan said, moving closer to his shoulder, a hand on the back of his seat. "What're you doing later this shift?"

Ryan didn't take his eyes from the screen. "Don't you have to work?"

"Duty's a little loose now that we're in port. I mean . . . I get my work done but nobody's going to bark at me if I slack. Technically I can probably get a pass to go on station. It's not like I'm a jet or considered essential personnel . . ."

"I can't go on station. Anyway, I'm having dinner with my father."

"Oh."

He ejected the sheet once the information was transferred and stood, rolling it up, then tucking it into a cargo pocket on his pants. He blanked the comp. "Thanks for this, Evan. I'll figure out a way to comm Shiri now. Shiri—my girl-friend."

"Thought you said she was your ex?"

Ryan smiled at him. "Maybe not for long. So thanks."

"Yeah, sure, no problem."

He wasn't sure when the atmosphere had changed, but Evan didn't move back to allow him room into the aisle.

"Look, Evan . . . I hope you weren't helping me because you thought I'd . . . you know. That isn't how I do things."

"I didn't." The blue eyes darkened, angry. "Thanks. See ya around." Now he moved off toward the exit.

What now?

So much for being upfront.

They got out to the corridor and Musey was just walking up.

"Hey," he said, pinning on Ryan. "Want a break? Did you look around at the school?"

"Not really," he said, before he thought it might be more preemptive if he lied.

"Why not?" Musey said.

"'Scuse," Evan said, walking right past without stopping.

Musey grabbed his sleeve. "What's wrong with you?"

Ryan tried to melt himself into the bulkhead, or edge by, but the way was blocked. He could turn around and go the other way but the symp cast him a look that said, I'm not done yet.

On the captain's orders, still.

"Nothing's wrong," Evan said. "I did Junior a favor and now he thinks I wanna *do* him."

What was there to say to that? Nobody said anything.

Evan tugged from Musey's hold, blushing. It was doubly obvious against his pale skin. "So, like, the pirate's always gonna want to screw the new kid. I get it. Even when the pirate's just tryin' to do an ordinary favor 'cause he likes the kid. Just friends. I got that loud and clear, Azarcon, and besides, you ain't even that hot."

He said as calm as he could, because he wasn't going to

make the situation worse, "I misread. I'm sorry. You just seemed to get strange."

"I was trying to apologize. Never mind. Pirate self gettin' in the way."

"Stop saying that. You're not a pirate."

"Yeah I am. He's a symp. I'm a pirate. Ask the crew, they'll tell you quick enough."

His voice was getting loud. Other people way down the corridor noticed.

Musey said, "Leave it."

Evan stared at him. Ryan watched them and it felt, curiously, like how it was when his parents fought. Like he knew there was history there and probably deep emotion, but the armor on their words was too thick, damaged and holding.

He looked away at the scratched surface of another hatch. So he didn't see what happened, he just heard the sudden change of tone in Musey's voice.

"I have to talk to Ryan, but I'll see you later."

It wasn't dismissal, but more like a question that had too much embarrassment inside to signal itself.

"Yeah," Evan said, sulkily appeased. "Later, Azarcon."

Now he looked back and the air was clearer. He said, "Sure."

Evan left, completely ignoring everything around him, including the other crew, and Musey said, "He's kind of manic."

"I don't blame him. It's a bitch on this ship, isn't it?"

That got an unexpected smile out of the symp. Musey had two dimples on his cheeks that made him look about half his chronological age. The expression died rather quickly.

"I saw that," Ryan said, honing in. "The symp can smile."

"Only off-shift," Musey said, with a straight stare. "And every other Saturday."

Back in his father's quarters, which Ryan was beginning to think of as his own now (testament to the subtle indoctrination of ship living, in his opinion), he checked his comms and spent some time sifting. One came from Dr. Grandma Ramcharan, which made him smile because she reminded him about doing all the things a young man his age ought to be doing, especially when it came to "women on his father's ship"—as she knew there were many: be kind, be respectful, and be especially careful.

It was good advice. The last thing he wanted was bedbug rumors floating to his father.

Another comm blinked from Shiri. She didn't take it personal that he didn't comm back, but she wasn't going to harass him either, since she knew this was a rough time right now. She just wanted to tell him that she'd landed the internship with Paulita Valencia on Mars.

He wanted to congratulate her, seeing her excited expression and the way her eyes lit up so they seemed more crystal than dark. Damn, she was cute, and a great kisser, and it was getting on in months since the last time he'd really touched a woman . . .

When he thought about it, memories of the flash house sprang to mind. Which was just screwed up, and made him annoyed with himself, so when he checked the rest of the messages and saw the long list of meedees hammering with requests for interviews, he thought of Evan's off-the-cuff idea: Wouldn't it be fun to mess with them the way they messed with him?

When he got in these moods, it seemed like a fun proposition.

What did he think of Tyler's accusations? What did he

think of the news that Tyler had been arrested for possession of illegal narcotics? Why wasn't he venturing out in public again, was he going to let the pirates "win"?

As if this was all a contest.

Delete. Delete.

If he learned to really burndive, where he wouldn't get caught, he could infiltrate these 'casts and exploit the truth instead.

He could talk to Shiri.

He could wreak vengeance on people like Tyler Coe without having to depend on Sid or his mother.

Silly notions, maybe. And at this point—moot.

His father commed him on his tags to cancel dinner. He was still in meetings with govies and their aides and too much caff, and he sounded stressed and somewhat pissed. Ryan said, Okay, and got off comm as soon as possible.

It was beginning to feel more like Austro after all—the parent missing meals because of work, and more stressed at certain times than gratified by their job.

So he commed Sid for dinner and suggested just lounging in the q with music and junk food he'd stolen from the galley (captain's son's privilege; the cook couldn't tell him no, especially when he turned on his smile), and Sid was there in ten minutes flat.

"I'm so tired," he said, heading straight for the couch and stretching out with his feet hanging over the end.

"I thought you said you were teaching them new tricks." Ryan grinned across the coffee table from where he sat on the deep blue chair with his comp, his feet on the edge of the table and a bowl of salty chips handy.

"You ever try to train a dog? It's tiring. Dumb animals just run in circles." Sid waved his hand.

"Don't insult the dog species. I like dogs. I wish Mom had let me get one."

Sid laughed. "Could you imagine a dog on her marble floors? She'd make it wear knit booties. Silver to match the decor."

The image was too much, and they were both tired. It took five minutes of laughter before Ryan could speak again, and he had to avoid Sid's gaze.

"I know you're wary of comming my mother because the outgoing sigs are traced . . ."

"That's not the only reason."

". . . Well, I have an idea. I'm comming her now and you can talk to her from my comp authorization."

Sid looked at him, then pushed himself up on both hands. "Ryan, I don't know if that's so—appropriate. Considering where I am right now."

Too bad he hadn't thought of that a few years ago, when they were on Austro.

But—no. Ryan wasn't going to start that train of thought barreling down the same old track. "It's already done. I'm sending a live rap."

Sid stared at him, wordless.

"Well, it's not like you can sleep with her from this distance." He tried to make it wry. "You can talk. Just don't argue. If I want to hear my mother argue with someone I'd just make the captain comm her."

"Ryan . . ."

Mom Lau's face bloomed on his screen. She seemed surprised to see him and looked like she was preparing for bed. She was at home, he recognized the organza curtains behind her shoulders, wore no makeup, and her hair was down.

"Hi Mom."

"Ryan—is something wrong?"

"No." He allowed a tiny smile and looked at Sid. "Someone just wants to talk to you." He got up and moved away from the comp.

"Ryan, what are you—?"

Sid went over and sat down, a little slow. Ryan kept going toward the bedroom but he heard the brief silence from both of them.

Then his bodyguard said, somewhat hesitantly as if he didn't know how she would react: "Hi Song . . . how are you?"

"Tim," his mother said, so surprised she seemed at a loss for words. That was quite a thing for Songlian Lau. "Tim, it's so good to see you . . ."

Ryan thought about loitering by the bedroom screen to eavesdrop, but he glimpsed Sid stretch a hand and touch the comp image with light fingers.

So Ryan slid the screen shut to give them privacy and picked up his guitar.

First Minister Damiani kept his father busy for the next seventy-two hours. They, plus his grandfather and Minister Taylor and assorted other govie types, locked themselves in one of the conference rooms on maindeck and Ryan maybe or maybe not passed his father at lunch break. He kept it polite and his father kept it distant, consumed by other matters presumably. In any event, the captain was Not Pleased by this delay in the peace talks in order to address Damiani's concerns, and it was wiser to contain their breakfast conversations to "hello" and "good-bye." Ryan was often in bed before his father came back to quarters, either from his meetings or his time on bridge or in his office catching up on ship work, most of which involved the constant repairs.

Since the Warboy and the Caste Master were still on their ship, Musey had plenty of time to spend on Ryan. The symp wasn't one for public places, so he usually kicked Evan out of their quarters and kept Ryan in there—for the comp work (weapons training and basic hand-to-hand fighting were all in public. Ryan got bruised and humiliated both, in short order). So, after perusing the files he'd gotten with Evan in the library, he tried to steer Musey toward one topic in his lessons.

"I don't care exactly how a comp is built or what. I just want to know how to *use* it."

Musey leaned back in his desk chair and squinted at Ryan, who sat cross-legged on Evan's bunk with his comp in his lap.

"I'm not going to teach you to burndive, for the last time, Azarcon."

"Just a little. Just basic stuff, nothing that would pass as a felony in court. Come on!"

"No."

"Musey . . ."

"Why do you want to know so badly?"

He threw in his hand. "There's a girl—"

Musey looked at the ceiling, shifted, and tossed his slate on the desk.

Ryan sighed. "Look, I know you're Mr. Teflon about that stuff, but some of us like to have a social life."

"Is this you trying to convince me?"

"Jos." By now they occasionally used each other's first names without belligerence. "Jos, I'd really like to talk to her, but I won't unless I can mask the point of origin, right? Please. I asked Sid but he said no."

"Small wonder."

"He's all afraid my father will boot him." Sid had not been the romantic that Ryan had hoped he would be. Either that or some of the jets' uncompromising attitude with a capital A was rubbing off on him. Being on this ship seemed to do that to people.

"*I'm* afraid your father will boot me," Musey said.

"He can't. You're kind of indispensable."

"You've never seen your father actually command, have you? Nobody is so indispensable that he won't humble you if he thinks you need it. I've even seen him call Dorr on the carpet."

"Musey. How will he find out?"

Musey shook his head.

"I'm going to learn one way or another, you know. I'm not dumb, I can read, I can do math. You either teach me to do it properly so I *don't* give myself away somehow, or I go off and try it and blow it all by mistake."

"Your father would skin you."

"I'm not afraid of him." He stared right into the symp's eyes as he said it, the way he noticed Musey did when he wanted to make a particular point. "Look, you aren't as angelic as you like to play it. We just keep this between us and nobody's got to know. If I do get caught I'll tell the captain I figured it out on my own. He knows I know a little already."

"You're not going to burndive, Ryan." But it didn't have the previous conviction.

He said, to nail the deal, "Yes. I will. It's up to you whether I do it safely or not."

"I could just tell your father and he'd confiscate your comps."

"Like I won't be able to access another one? Short of locking me in my room . . . you know, I slipped Silver by my bodyguard. For months."

Musey stared at him. "Well," he said slowly, "your bodyguard's a Marine, not a jet."

"No. I'm just stubborn that way." He smiled, big eyes, bitten lip, his sweetest expression. It worked on Shiri most times. Even Sid.

Musey wasn't Shiri. He looked like he had the worst job in the universe and wasn't even getting paid.

Which was true.

Musey said, "The very basics."

He tried not to gloat. "That's all I want. Code mask. Maybe a little diversionary tactics—?"

"Don't push it. I ought to take you in there and leave you."

He laughed, leaned over, and touched Musey's arm. Musey flinched slightly, not visibly, but Ryan felt the muscle twitch. He kept his hand there, anyway, to make his point. And Musey didn't break his wrist, which he knew the symp could do without any effort. So that had to mean something.

"I promise . . . I'll be careful." He met Musey's quiet, introverted gaze with a genuine smile.

Musey looked at him for a long moment, then slowly removed himself from Ryan's touch.

"You need to spend less time with Evan," he said.

He and Sid had dinner this time in the mess hall, with Dorr and Hartman and other regulars: vapid-looking blond Madison, a flight crew team that appeared to be friends of Musey's (surprise in itself that Musey had friends outside of the jet circle), Evan of course, and Aki.

Ryan sat beside the girl and flirted, but she seemed more interested in Sid and kept asking him what Earth was like. Sid didn't seem to mind at all and even told her about his grandmother's ranch and how he'd grown up riding *horses*. That perked everyone's interest, spacers that they were.

"He fell off a lot," Ryan said.

"Not as much as you did," Sid said, teasing, but would a girl from a space station know how hard it was to actually *fall* off a horse?

Aki found it funny.

Musey was the only one who didn't appear interested,

but Ryan could read him a little better now; Musey just never liked to *look* like he was listening, but he always was, and in this case he seemed enamored of Earth as well, in the way he fixed on Sid in regular intervals throughout the conversation. Or maybe he was enamored of Sid and his hazel eyes and lightly freckled nose, like Aki seemed to be.

Sid and his ol' boy Marine charm.

It got boring fast.

Ryan turned his attention to the broad wallvid, high in the corner of the mess hall. It played at a low murmur and had been cycling the SendTertain when they'd sat down, showing music bites in colorful layers.

Now it had his father's face on it with a split screen of a female meedee and a scroll of words.

Ryan sat up straighter, hitting Sid's arm.

A crewmember shouted, "Vid, eighty-five!"

Every eye in the room turned to it and the increased sound burst hollowly out across the hall as the voices died.

". . . death now allows some of his previously compartmentalized files to be declassified. Naturally the military does not advertise this fact and had it not been for Mr. Pompeo's research for his work, currently entitled *Azarcon A–Z: the Unauthorized Biography of Cairo Azarcon*, many of these details would not have come to light. Just hours ago Arthur Pompeo sat down with Paulita Valencia on Mars for an exclusive interview. Here is what he said . . ."

The meedee's face was replaced by the same old man who'd accosted Ryan on Austro, sitting in an Earth Victorian-styled chair in what looked like someone's living room but was probably just a set, softly lit and fully powdered under the lights.

"Oh, shit," Sid said, echoing Ryan's thoughts.

Pompeo said, "While there isn't anything explicit in the late Falcone's early files to show his affiliation with Cairo

Azarcon, one only has to line up the dates and relationships to see the connection. I'd like to say, however, that I am releasing this information for the government's benefit, and for the benefit of EarthHub's citizens who now depend on the captain in these negotiations with our longtime enemies."

"Right!" Dorr shouted to the screen. "You fat old dirtside arse!"

Ryan didn't take his eyes from the transcast, feeling pushed down into his seat by an undefined weight.

Half the mess hall got on their feet in outrage.

"Shut up!" Ryan shouted, his voice echoing. They looked at him, noticed him, realized he had every right to yell.

They quieted. Ryan dug his fingers into his legs.

Arthur Pompeo continued, interspersed with quick shots of Paulita Valencia's dark-haired elegance and alert gaze: "Early in 2163 EHSD, Vincenzo Falcone broke out of the Kalaallit Nunaat military prison. With help from other crooked officials he wasted no time in establishing himself on the Arms—"

This dirtsider was so ancient he still called the Dragons by its old name.

"—as a pirate of considerable wherewithal and deadliness . . ."

"Damn well sayin' a eulogy," Evan muttered.

". . . in organizing what was previously a scattered group of rogue ships into a purposeful fleet of marauders that systematically combed through our colonies, relocation camps, and stations often on the heels of strits who had passed before and thus weakened our defenses. He took advantage of the war situation because he knew carrier battle group movements and could even anticipate deep-space ship schedules."

Valencia interrupted. "But what does this have to do with

Captain Azarcon? By the dates we're discussing, the captain was no more than a teenager, chronologically, and a young one at that."

"Yes. The captain's past has never been released to the public and any attempts I've made to elicit his participation in my research have been summarily stonewalled. But we do know that he was officially adopted by then-Captain Omar Ashrafi in 2169 EHSD, at the age of eighteen. Though this isn't illegal, it is unusual for someone who is considered a legal adult for two years to now be legally made a relative of a rather, shall we say, influential man. One who has the power to bury dirty comrades and classify information. It is no secret that Admiral Ashrafi, in his days as a deep-space captain of the battleship *Trinity*, was instrumental in bringing Falcone to justice after the massacre at Ghenseti, and was perhaps the most vocal when Falcone escaped."

"That's no surprise," Valencia said, with subtle irony. "Falcone, as a fellow captain, had left Ghenseti unprotected in order to chase after his own idea of vengeance on the striviirc-na. Many captains were doubly offended by his piratical actions later on."

"And now we get to it." Pompeo smiled slightly. "Who did he attack in those first years of piracy? Now that his early files have finally been declassified, we know that in late 2163 EHSD Falcone attacked a colony *near* Meridia— the general coordinates put him near Meridia, even though the actual name has been conveniently deleted. Meridia's colony manifests have always been classified by Hub Command, which cited that they were there under a military industrial initiative and both the military and the corporation refused to release details of the colony's demise or of its workers and their families. But one might find it interesting to note that it is Admiral Ashrafi who signed the order to seal those files."

"Implying what?"

"Pointing to the *fact* that he only had them sealed after he returned from his deep-space run, in 2169 EHSD. Six months later Cairo Azarcon's adoption files surfaced and were presented to the Navy Space Corps Academy for perusal prior to admission, stating that he came from an orphanage in some far-flung Rimstation, one that had been attacked by strits and their records, again, conveniently destroyed."

"I'm afraid I still don't follow you."

Pompeo sighed. "Cairo Azarcon did not come from any long-forgotten Rimstation. It's my belief he was born on the Meridia Moon, in *that* colony, and *when* Falcone attacked Meridia, Cairo Azarcon was taken by the pirate and lived aboard that pirate ship. Six years later he was rescued by Ashrafi in a documented battle in early 2169 EHSD, out in deep space—a battle, I may add, that crew from the replenishment ship *The Nile* confirm did include an exchange of fire between Falcone and Ashrafi. It is not incredible to believe that Ashrafi's soljets boarded the pirate and arrested crew, as soljets are wont to do—in fact they did, because pirate prisoners were soon deposited at the nearest military outpost in that region: Argos Station. I have checked the station files and confirmed it to be so."

He sat back as if he had just discovered the cure for a deadly disease.

In that brief pause Ryan remembered to breathe, though what he really wanted to do was pelt something at the screen.

"Mr. Pompeo," Valencia said. "If Ashrafi had attacked Falcone, even to board *Genghis Khan*, why wasn't Falcone arrested at that time? How was the *Khan* allowed to escape?"

Pompeo waved two fingers, as if dismissing the question.

"According to reports submitted by *The Nile*, two pirates came to the *Khan*'s defense. *Trinity* was forced to retreat with what prisoners they could get. Unfortunately, Falcone had not been among them."

"But still, Mr. Pompeo . . . you must realize these claims about where Captain Azarcon was, and when, are circumstantial at best. We are talking about a decorated officer in the EarthHub Armed Forces."

"Who has no past and has never come forward with one. What is he, an amnesiac? Why is the man so stubbornly private over the smallest details, such as where he was born? All of my evidence points to one thing in my mind, and I have only begun to scratch the surface of it: Cairo Azarcon spent time on a pirate ship in his years as a teenager, became an adult on said ship, and perhaps even fully participated in that life. It makes sense in light of his reputation for accepting criminals and fugitives into his crew. I'm also quite sure that this comes as no surprise to those in the military and citizenry of the Hub who are familiar with his rogue tactics in the past years of this war."

The screen segued back to the meedee, who Ryan now realized was standing outside of the Chaos military dockside. The label flashed at the bottom of the screen.

"Mr. Pompeo further asserted that he will continue his investigations and any new information would certainly be included in his forthcoming biography. So far neither Captain Azarcon nor Admiral Ashrafi offered to make a statement with regard to these claims. If they prove true, this can greatly bolster the position of noted Centralists like presidential candidate First Minister Judy Damiani, who is right now aboard *Macedon* to discuss the process of these peace talks—the details of which have been, to this point, also kept secret."

Unbiased meedee reports, his *ass*.

"Screw it," Dorr said. "They ain't seen rogue yet. We oughtta go rogue on Mr. Pompous and his cartoon claims."

Ryan couldn't move for a long second until he heard Musey reclamp his seat to the deck. He looked up and Musey was heading out the door. He got up before Sid or anybody could stop him and ran after.

"Where are they, Jos?"

"Go to quarters, Ryan."

"It's true, isn't it? That old fart is actually telling the truth, isn't he?"

The mess hall was on maindeck, and so were the conference rooms, which he realized was Musey's target. But Musey only went so far before turning on him and putting a hand on his chest. Full stop.

"Ryan. Go to quarters."

"Where are *you* going? You can't just barge in—"

"I'm not going *there*. Niko's hearing this too. This affects everything. Right now the captain's getting the news and he's in the same room as First Minister Damiani, who's also probably getting the news, and the last thing he needs is his kid bursting in with emotion. But I need to get to *Turundrlar*—"

A hatch opened up down the hall, behind Musey.

The captain stepped out and started off in the opposite direction, toward the lev. Purposeful. Trailed by an armed jet and a tall silk-suited woman who had to double-time it to keep up.

"I want answers, Azarcon!" she said, unmindful of anybody else who might be within earshot. "I won't allow these talks to go forward until you provide me with—"

Admiral Ashrafi came out from the room. "Lower your voice, Judy."

"I will not lower my voice. I will not stand here and accept his silence or your agenda. Not anymore, Admiral."

"There is no agenda, besides a desire to reach a peaceful resolution. You seem unable to grasp that, Minister."

"Maybe because the government is tired of being lied to or run roughshod by your deep spacers. And why haven't I met the strits yet?"

The admiral said, "You won't with that attitude."

Ryan tried to get around Musey but the symp pulled him back, half around the corner. Kept him rooted with a hard grip. He tried to break from it and couldn't, tried to move Musey and couldn't. It was like shoving against a rock, despite the symp's slender stature. So he just stopped fighting and watched, feeling his blood boil.

Damiani said, "Captain, this won't be resolved with your jet between us. We need to sit down and discuss—"

"What?" his father said, stopping to look at her. "Would you like to use my so-called dangerous history to drag these talks into oblivion? I won't allow it."

"This is exactly the issue. You won't listen to reason."

"I'll listen to reason, Minister, not gossip and excuses. Your government, most of whom couldn't identify deep space on a starmap much less set foot here, would like us all to keep fighting the aliens because it fits into your ideals and prejudices. Out here is reality, which you seem determined to disprove even though we've spent hours discussing the fact that space is black. Yet you insist on calling it blue. I feel no need to waste more time on it. These talks will go forward with or without your support. If you'd like that to change then you had better consider dragging your friends off their little planet and into my territory."

Her voice was stony. "Space is not your territory, Captain."

"It is when I'm in it. Or else why did you send me here?"

The lev opened up as if he'd commanded it and he walked in without a backward glance.

The jet got in after and stopped Damiani from following, standing right in the way. Admiral Ashrafi set a hand on her shoulder. "Let's you and I go back to the room for a few minutes. We have more to discuss with Minister Taylor."

"You won't succeed in bullying me," she said. "Or double-teaming me."

The lev doors shut, swallowing his father. The admiral steered Damiani back to the conference room and only then did Musey let Ryan go.

He moved toward the lev. Musey caught his arm again, not as hard but it still made him turn.

"Be careful," Musey said. "Let him explain before you say anything."

Ryan didn't have a reply. He tugged out of the symp's grasp and went for the lev. His mind rattled with a dozen different worries, cycling like a whirlwind.

His father spent years with a pirate. *The* pirate.

Did Mom know?

Was this why they always fought?

The Hub was never going to get behind him now . . .

And—

How could he let us find out from the Send?

Your father isn't a pirate, he told himself on the interminably long lev ride up to the command crew deck. He leaned against the wall and measured his breaths, got himself together because what that old man had said couldn't be the entire truth. Like everything else on the Send, there were other truths.

His father hadn't kidnapped children, raped women, destroyed ships. Maybe it had been like Evan said—skin, but not blood. They could tattoo you but they couldn't make you believe it.

His father and his damn silence.

His father's reputation was undisputed. Stories like that didn't spring from a well of nothingness. His crew was hard, he had to be hard to lead them. He had to be hard to hunt strits down and kill them. He didn't care that most of the Hub considered him a relentless rogue. He hated pirates too, and why shouldn't he, if he'd been victimized himself? But people who were abused had a higher risk of abusing others, wasn't that the statistic? Weren't you always the most bitter to those you resembled?

But his father was an orphan. Like Musey, like Evan. Like probably half his crew, because he did recruit the criminals and the fugitives, the people everybody else had dismissed. That had been no lie. But he didn't compel them to be slaves and murderers as pirates did. Pompeo twisted it, but now that *he'd* seen it, what was so wrong with taking kids nobody else wanted? Everybody needed the same basic things—food, shelter, and community. Affection.

Family.

And he was stuck with his, you couldn't pick it, you couldn't leave it, and if he had to be honest with himself, he'd fight for it too. His family. His father, who the Hub was going to hate if they didn't already, just because some nosey old coot of a tabloid journalist wanted a swan song before he croaked.

Screw them all.

His father could be a bastard, but he was a good bastard and he wasn't a pirate . . . even if he had been a pirate a bazillion years ago.

Pirates didn't make breakfasts for their son. Or restrain themselves from putting their mouthy son in the brig.

Pirates didn't hold back from murdering people who stood in their way. Maybe Judy Damiani needed to consider that.

He almost missed his stop, leaning against the wall, looking at the ceiling, thinking. Thinking. The doors opened up, he didn't notice until the last minute and almost got his arm stuck as he made a mad dash out to the corridor before the lev shut again.

He opened the hatch with his tagkey. Music blasted out at him, his own selection that he hadn't removed from the unit earlier this shift.

His father was in the kitchen, leaning against the counter with his arms folded and eyes to the floor, and the music was so loud he didn't even look up when Ryan shut the hatch.

But he looked up when Ryan shut off the song.

"I think they can hear that back on Earth," Ryan said, when the captain said nothing. And when the silence persisted, "Are you avoiding comms again?"

Normal conversation, almost. He didn't know how he did it.

"What?" The captain stared at him.

Ryan couldn't think of a thing, under that look.

The captain turned his back, faced the sink.

Ryan said, "So it's true."

His father shrugged. "As far as that goes."

"Are you going to do something about it?"

"I suppose I'll have to now." He unclamped a glass from the shelf.

Frustration leaped up at an alarming rate. Provoked by his father's false nonchalance, or just . . . maybe he expected a more violent reaction from the captain. Something that would strongly deny everything that meedee had said.

Like: I never did those things, Ryan.

It was skin, not blood.

"You have to do something. The man's essentially saying you're a pirate."

"Yes, and he'd like me to get on the Send and address it so he can rebut. He's playing gunslinger."

"So address it. Isn't this one of those battles you have to fight?"

"I haven't yet decided." He spun around the vodka and juice, dislodged it, and poured. Sipped, then took a longer drink.

"This is affecting the negotiations, you know you have to deal with—"

"You don't have to tell me what it's affecting. I'm well aware."

The cold space between them seemed farther than the span of the quarters. It wasn't all his doing. So he took a step closer. Forced his voice calm. "It's affecting me too. Are you aware of that? Or is it that you just don't care? You let me find out from the *Send*."

The captain went by him with his glass and sat on the couch. He drank the vodka and Ryan saw then, in the precise way he refused to look up, that it had been an act of will alone that got him from that conference room to the privacy of his quarters without breaking expression.

Because it was breaking now.

Ryan didn't know what to do with his hands.

"Your grandfather," the captain said, rather carefully. Well enunciated. Not quite looking his way. "Your grandfather and I knew at some point it was all going to blow wide. We'd just hoped it was after I was dead."

"You were on that ship with Falcone."

The captain nodded.

"But you were a kid. Like Evan. How can they blame you?"

"You do. Don't you? You should see your face."

"I . . . those things. That they do to people. You did those things?" He couldn't help it; the thought disgusted him and there his father sat, like a stranger.

"Depends on what things you're talking about. But you

got your answer now, right? Mr. Pompeo's fed your curiosity and the curiosity of billions of people who have nothing better to be concerned about even when it's staring them in the face."

"You have to let them know you're not like that."

"Ryan, I could be sainted tomorrow and it wouldn't make a bit of difference. They want the smut. I refuse to play into it. Plus, in a real way, I am like that."

"You're not."

"How do you know? Your biggest gripe is that you don't know me."

He couldn't argue with that, but he couldn't class his father in with people like Falcone, who had taken Musey as a child and sold Evan to another ship. Not when he saw both of them on his father's ship, by choice, when they had no right to be here.

"I am like that," the captain repeated, his eyes on the table and the glass in his hand, turning slowly. "Those things Damiani accused me of, the things on the Send reports; those are pirate traits. Where do you think I learned them? I do run roughshod over people I think are fools. I'll blow a ship instead of negotiating with it if I think the point would be better taken with a missile, and I have tortured people to get information. I've done it personally, before I ever met your grandfather, and I've ordered it as a captain on this ship."

"But it's still different," Ryan said. Wasn't it?

His father didn't hear him. Not quite. "I'll go ahead and deal with a pirate if it'll serve a mission I'm running, without consulting anybody, and I'll damn well talk to a strit on peaceful terms without the government's by-your-leave. I've murdered people on my own deck for disobeying me too many times and I killed plenty for Falcone. I learned from him that you're alone out here and you lead as you see fit. The Hub doesn't see it that way; they'd rather lead from the ground. And I hate them for it, almost as much as Falcone did. Is all of this what you'd like me to tell the Send? Is this what you want to know about me, Ryan?" The eyes lifted and speared him through.

"I don't apologize for my behavior. I don't regret the things I do, and maybe that's a pirate trait too. Falcone used to say that a lot—never regret and never second-guess. And I haven't. I don't. I don't regret marrying your mother, but at the same time I don't regret leaving her on that station for years at a time. She knew I was on the command track when she met me and she knew I was a ruthless son of a bitch. Should I apologize? Should I apologize to the lemmings of the Hub or those ignorant bastards back on Earth? I won't." He drank, a fast gulp that made him blink.

Ryan didn't know what to say to put a coat of reassurance on anything. He wasn't even sure that it was needed. Truth was more important at this point.

His father didn't seem to mind that Ryan was mute. Maybe because he didn't want to hear what he thought his son might say. So he said himself, "I can't even bring myself to truly apologize to you and you're perhaps the one I've hurt the most. Maybe you're my only regret, but even then . . . I never told you. And I never would, if I wasn't forced."

His father set the glass aside on the table. In the thick quiet it made a ringing sound. He didn't raise his eyes, just rolled up his right sleeve and exposed two tattoos. His *Macedon* service tat, the profile of Alexander the Great backed by a sixteen-point black star.

But above that, near the inside of his elbow, was a different image. A stout black horse with a flowing mane and flaring red hooves. Like the emblem on that hidden gun and knife in his father's bedside drawer. The worn weapons of steel and leather.

"*Genghis Khan*'s emblem," his father said. "I've got another one—here." He touched above his heart. Then he looked at Ryan, almost a question. Almost afraid. "Only the protégés get marked on the heart. For blood. He didn't just give me orders . . . I asked."

The room was dim and the silence full of shadows.

Ryan sat down on the couch next to his father because he didn't want to shout. He didn't want to stand his ground anymore. Not in this. Up close, his father's eyes were weary and—young. The past wasn't so distant for him. Not out here and not in there, inside of him.

"I'm not as unforgiving as the Hub," Ryan said, "or as bitter as your wife." His father couldn't speak and didn't move. And that immobility captured Ryan deep inside, so he wanted to hold it somehow if only to help his father resist it. He said, "I'm your son, Dad. *I'm your son.*"

He cleaned up the mess from lunch, which was still in the sink, while his father disappeared into the bedroom and slid the screen shut. He welcomed the menial task. It allowed his mind to shut down and the knot in his chest to unravel. His father hadn't touched him, had looked at him as if he'd wanted to, but opted out. And Ryan didn't know what that was about. Why things were different now just because now he wouldn't have—minded.

Maybe it was for the same reason Musey didn't like to be touched. Maybe it all surfaced again for his father and it was too difficult to allow yourself to be touched.

Ryan washed the dishes manually just to hear the water run, to do something with his hands.

The comm buzzed on the couch's sidetable comp. It kept buzzing; his father wasn't picking up. Ryan wiped his hands on his pants and went to it, saw the familiar incoming tail marker—from Austro.

He sat on the couch and poked the icon, told himself to be neutral no matter what his mother said.

"Ryan," she said. "Where is he?"

His newfound neutrality went out the airlock.

"Mom, I don't think now's a good time."

"What has he said to you?"

Obviously more than he'd ever said to her. She was angry in the way you got when someone dropped a bomb on your preconceptions.

"Mom, let's not do this now."

"I want to speak with him." She tapped her desk; she was in her office. Arthur Pompeo's transcast had caught her at work and now it was going to be a frenzy for her to get home, if she was even going home this shift. The meedees would be beating down her door. "Get your father on comm."

"He's not a pirate, you know."

"Is that what he said? Has he explained that Pompeo is completely lying?"

"He'll 'cast when he's ready. You know, sometimes the last thing you want to do is get up in front of people—"

"This isn't about what *he* wants to do, Ryan. Dammit, for once, it's about what he's *obligated* to do and never does. He should've warned me. He could've told me this man had approached him."

He could've *told me*, her eyes said.

"Pompeo talked to *your* mother, you should be yelling at her. You know she probably fed the story about his 'rogue behavior.' "

"What did he say to you, Ryan? About Pompeo's claims?"

It wasn't his place. So he kept his mouth shut.

"Ryan."

"Mom, you married him. You had me with him. Whatever some meedee says shouldn't get in the way of that. He meant it when he married you, or else why am I here, now, on his ship? Whatever he doesn't want to talk about shouldn't make you think he's bad or lazy or mean. Maybe *he's* hurt, Mom. Can't you think of that?"

She didn't answer him. Because she was hurt too.

"Some things you just can't talk about, Mom. With anybody."

"I understand that," she said, but she didn't really.

She'd had a time limit on him after Earth.

Get up, get your girlfriend, go to school, and get over it. Not that she didn't love him.

But it was easier to love somebody when they did what you wanted.

His father still didn't emerge, even a half hour after Ryan cut the comm with his mother and just sat on the couch letting it roll over him.

His thoughts were busy, too many of them clamoring for his attention, but he still jumped when the hatch buzzed. The captain wasn't going to answer that either so he opened it himself.

Admiral Grandpa said, "Where is he?"

Ryan let him in. "Back there." He pointed. "Grandpa, I don't think he's being a coward about it. I mean, about not wanting to go on the Send. I think he's just afraid he'll make it worse somehow."

"Either way, he's going to have to say something. This isn't the type of thing you can ignore."

It was true. "He was Falcone's protégé—like that pirate they think shot at me. Did you know that?"

His grandfather had eyes on the bedroom screen but

pulled them back to look at him. Looked at him for a long second as if seeing him after years of absence. "I knew where he came from and I know in general what it was like—on Falcone's ship. But he's never been willing to actually discuss it with me. What exactly happened to him."

It was an odd comfort to know that he wasn't the only one who met up with his father's reticence. He knew his mother had, but she had been impatient about it.

He tucked his arms against himself. "What . . . what about his family? What happened to them, do you know?"

His grandfather rubbed the bridge of his nose. "They were killed at Meridia when Falcone raided it. I've looked into it and his parents' bodies were found, and one brother, but the other brother's body was never recovered. Which doesn't mean he's alive . . . it just means . . . he was never recovered."

He'd had uncles. And grandparents. Who'd had no idea he would ever exist. "What were . . . how old were they? His brothers?"

Brothers.

"Bern was the eldest by two years. Paris was quite a bit younger than your father, by eight years. He's the one we can't confirm. Cairo was the middle child."

Bern, Cairo, and Paris. Old cities on Earth. So his grandparents had either been from there, or had a sense of humor, or just liked the way the names sounded.

He felt the admiral's hand on his arm.

"Ryan . . . ask him about it sometime. Later. He might tell you."

"You can't tell me?" There had been other people in the galaxy with the last name Azarcon, who were his direct relatives, and he wondered if they all had his father's sense of humor, or his, or that loudmouthed almost-arrogance that his mother always pinned on him as an Azarcon trait.

"He needs to tell you," the admiral said. "I've respected his silence and I think I should respect his decision to talk, if he talks to you." His gaze shifted. "He will talk now, at any rate, at least to the Send." The admiral went to the bedroom screen, knocked. "Cairo. I hope you're writing your statement."

The screen opened. The captain stepped out in his dress uniform. A black, ironed affair with small stripes of elemental color on his chest—gold, silver, bronze. Red and blue and deep earth green. A pin of golden wings on the opposite side, lest anyone forget he was a fighter pilot first.

Ryan knew the intention—it would be difficult to see a pirate in that getup. He wasn't even armed.

He tugged at his collar and started for the hatch, barely glancing at the two of them. "If I have to wear this damn starch then the entire galaxy had better pay attention."

The mess hall was packed. What crew could fit in there planted themselves on chairs, tables, and benches. Others holed up in quarters with their comps or commandeered spots in the lounges and wardrooms and library, anywhere with a vidscreen. That was what he and Sid saw on their way around the ship until he remembered to comm Evan.

Ryan didn't want to be around the entire crew when his father made the statement, and Evan said Captain S'tlian and the Caste Master were out there with the captain, the admiral, their jet escort, and both Minister Taylor and First Minister Damiani. And Jos had gone as interpreter, Evan said. Jos had disappeared onto *Turundrlar* since Pompeo's speech, talking to Nikolas about the captain. Reassuring him, maybe. If anyone was going to understand the captain's past, it would be the Warboy who'd practically adopted Falcone's *second* protégé.

Still, "pirate" was a sore word among *Macedon*'s crew,

considering who they'd been persecuting for the past few months.

Given the choice, Evan said, he'd prefer to be in quarters by himself. So he invited Ryan in. Sid went perforce.

Evan lit a cig and held an open bottle of beer, the comp on an unclamped chair between the bunks. He made room so the three of them could lean back against the bulkhead and watch the transcast, albeit with their legs hanging off the side of the bunk.

Right now the cams showed a milling crowd of meedees and station officials and a blank podium just inside the military dockside doors. In a second box on the split screen, a single male meedee chuffed on about Arthur Pompeo and his claims, stirring the fire before the brimstone came down, filling the dead air.

They waited.

"Do you know what he's going to say?" Sid asked, arms folded.

"No. I didn't ask. He dressed and—went."

Evan leaned over from Ryan's right side and half smiled. "I have an idea what he'll say."

"What?" Sid said, looking at Evan sidelong.

Evan grinned and raised his middle finger.

Sid said, "Ha!"

Ryan shook his head. "No, that'd be my statement. My father's far too diplomatic."

Sid said, "It's starting."

Someone stepped up to the podium, a woman in a dark suit and a pin on her lapel—a black circle with a gold outline of the station overlaid.

"Chaos Stationmaster," Evan said.

She gazed out at the crowd as if counting heads, while four jets, Dorr, Hartman, and Madison among them, filed in first and stood in front of the hastily erected backdrop. It had

EarthHub's sun-and-nine-planets displayed on a black circle, ringed by close-set silver stars. The seal represented all of the Hub, even the stations in the Dragons. Ryan figured it was also his father's choice to have that and not *Macedon*'s banner in prominent frame.

He remembered to unclench his fingers.

Admiral Ashrafi was the next to stand on the dais, flanked by the Warboy and the Caste Master, wearing tiny earcomm pickups. Next to them stood Musey with a commbud on his lapel for interpretation into those pickups. At that point you could hear individual breaths from the meedees. For many of them it was probably their first time seeing a live alien. Ryan was sure the jets, who held rifles and stared out at the crowd in a constant roving of eyes, weren't the only security on that dockside.

Sid confirmed it by pointing out the units he recognized merely by where they stood and what subtle equipment they had on their bodies, easily missed by an untrained eye.

Minister Taylor and First Minister Damiani, who still didn't look pleased, walked up rather quickly and stood to the side almost out of frame—maybe they'd have a turn at the mike, though Ryan hoped not.

Finally the Chaos Stationmaster gestured for the lights to come up in advance of the transcast. They hit her with a vengeance. She squinted, raised a hand, and asked for them to be turned down. Then she said simply, "Ladies and gentlemen, Captain Azarcon," and stepped out of the way.

In deep space, despite technical rank, it was his father who would be given an admiral's treatment—out of respect for his years on the front line of the war. And because people wanted to hear from him first, since deep-space captains rarely made statements to the Send. They weren't politicians and prided themselves on that fact.

But not this shift. Now he had to speak and he had

EarthHub's attention in a way Damiani could only dream about.

The captain stepped up to the podium with no visible hesitation, laid both hands on either side in a pose of relaxed authority, and gazed straight out at the cams and the lights without squinting. His eyes looked large in the pale angles of his face. They were dark, steady, and unreadable.

The meedees erupted as one.

"I'm going to say a few words and then open it up to questions."

He had no slate, no prompter, and no earcomm. It went out live and free. The meedees fell silent, though someone coughed here and there.

"Quite a few months ago, perhaps even a year in Standard time, Mr. Arthur Pompeo approached me via comm to request my assistance in a project of his—my biography. He cited all sorts of reasons why this would be beneficial to a man in my position, as he said—'a captain of galactic note.' He said that as a decorated officer in the EarthHub Armed Forces it was my duty to present to the citizens of the Hub— and to history—an unequivocal picture of my heroic accomplishments. His words, not mine."

Projected humility. It seemed he truly believed it too.

"I told him, in no uncertain terms, that I was not a hero and what things I had accomplished were between myself and those who wished to bestow upon me whatever recognition protocol devised. But I had never set out to achieve such recognition, nor did I feel I owed it to anyone to expand on it for the sake of notoriety. My duty is foremost to my crew, the military, and the citizens of the Hub. That is the order in which I prioritize my professional life and I don't apologize for it. The lives of my comrades and those under my command depend upon it, and since for years we were the ones fighting the war on the citizens' behalf, I think such an order should go undisputed. I told this to Mr. Pompeo.

"He responded that he was going ahead with the biography anyway, with or without my approval. He proceeded to contact my wife Songlian Lau, Admiral Omar Ashrafi and Dr. Hannah Ramcharan, my adoptive parents, and many other people with whom I'd served over the years. He even had one of his associates harass my son on Earth after the terrorist actions in Hong Kong, asking for rather personal details about our relationship. My son was recovering from trauma, but Mr. Pompeo had no compassion for that."

Ryan hadn't known the meedee Sid had decked in Britain had been one of Pompeo's men. He was even less sorry about the abuse now, especially considering Pompeo's false sincerity on Austro months later.

"Now many of you may believe that you have a right to know about my personal life because of my rank and career, but I want to make clear, right now and for the record, that I didn't choose to be a captain in the EarthHub Armed Forces—I didn't study, work, fight, and kill the enemy on your behalf—because I wanted to bare my soul to the galaxy. I don't see why that ought to be a prerequisite for my position as a commanding officer.

"Many of you were, and are, affected by the war. Many of you were, and are, aware of my actions, as well as the actions of other men and women in my position, to put an end to the war. We have fought on many fronts and in many battles. You may consider these peace talks to be yet another front, another battle, hopefully a bloodless one and hopefully the final one. I do.

"Because like many of you, I grow tired. I was also affected by the war at a very young age. It is no secret that pirate activity increases when the conflict between the Hub and the striviirc-na increases. Pirates capitalize on our busy fleets—and merchants, stations, and colonies pay for it. Thirty-four years ago, my home was so affected. Like many of you, I lost my family."

He shifted. His hands slid a bit down the sides of the podium and he bent a little toward the mike, visibly swallowing. Ryan wasn't sure if it was a premeditated move, but it broke the stiffness, imbued some candid emotion.

"No, I rescind that. I didn't lose them. It wasn't a matter of voluntary or mutual abandonment. My family was killed. In short order I became an orphan. I know from the inside out what many children experience because of our dogged insistence on perpetuating this war. I know, from the inside out, the debilitating crush of grief. And I grow tired. I grow tired of pirates who use our lost children to their own ends. The striviirc-na were not our only enemies, and yet we became so involved, so bloodily single-minded, that the future of EarthHub fell by the wayside.

"Not long ago I woke up to that. I hope the rest of Earth-Hub will wake up to it. The striviirc-na are not our enemies. In the past few weeks I've come to realize that many of their concerns are the same as ours. How can we stop the bloodshed? How can we build back our hopes so they won't be destroyed again? How can we insure a safe future for our children?

"Pirates can be more effectively fought if we work together. Merchants, stations, colonies that are preyed upon year after year by pirate ships . . . I grow tired, the same as you, of death reports. Many of my crew were orphaned as children and youths. They fell into crime to stay alive, or were manipulated by adults into the life. Yes, I take them aboard *Macedon*. I feed them, clothe them, and train them. Because others do not. I don't look at the circumstances that brought them to my attention—their criminal files, their drug use and violence, whatever the case may be. I look at the circumstances that compelled them to those lives in the first place, events that were out of their control. I give them an opportunity to change the course of their lives—for the better."

Ryan felt Evan shift beside him.

"Many of you are wondering about my past. You've heard Mr. Pompeo claim that I was a pirate in my youth before I was a student at the Navy Space Corps Academy. And I suppose if I came right out and laid claim to that allegation, all of my subsequent deeds—my 'heroic accomplishments,' my 'captaincy of galactic note'—would amount to nothing in your eyes. My efforts to form a truce with our longtime enemies so that we may map a future in which our children need not fear to *live* . . . I suppose my efforts that way would suddenly be spurious, suspicious, and ill-meant?

"I hope not. I fervently hope that the citizens of Earth-Hub—who live on stations, colonies, and merchant ships that I have protected to the best of my ability across the star systems—would not be so narrow-minded or judgmental . . . or bloodthirsty."

He straightened, took a breath, and released the podium. He stood in silence for a second and swept a hand back over his hair, which had fallen across his forehead like a black, misfired arrow.

"My family was slaughtered by pirates. I was twelve years old and I witnessed their murders. I was taken aboard a pirate ship. You have all read accounts from people, both victims and victimizers, of what occurs aboard those ships. I have no intention of going into detail about what was, for me and many others like me, a devastating experience. I trust you all to respect my wishes in this, for the sake of my family."

Ryan saw the flashes of light popping on his father's face and thought this respect would be highly unlikely past a shift or two, but at least there would be that shift of a pretense of privacy.

"Admiral Ashrafi brought me out of that experience and gave me the opportunity to build new and good experiences. I have a wife and a son, whom I love a great deal. I have a crew with whom I share a mutual respect. I'm a father as well as a captain. As a father I want to protect my son, and as a captain I know exactly why he needs that protection. And for these two simple reasons, I look to end this war."

He placed his hands back on the podium and stared out at the meedees, not at the cams. The next arrow, the verbal one that counted, fell with perfect precision in timing and tone. He said it almost casually and directly to the galaxy.

"Thank you for your patience and respect. Now I will take any questions you may have."

Ryan was aware of their eyes, the closeness of the quarters, and Sid's arm against his arm—not quite comfort, because why did he need to be comforted?—but it was an unspoken thing, support maybe, because he'd watched his father stand in front of billions of people and admit . . . maybe not everything, but enough. It was enough.

And he knew from the inside out what face his father would have once he was alone with himself, out of uniform, out of sight, and it was tiring just to think about. Holding that face. Holding it in. Wanting to shout that nobody had a right.

Nobody had a right to make you afraid.

He'd lost the right not to be afraid when people shot at him. When a building came down. When his world's color changed to red. Suddenly all you felt was afraid, with sporadic moments of forgetfulness.

And that tired you too, until you didn't want to do anything but lay flat and forget it all completely. Forget that you were supposed to be afraid, that you *were* afraid, and that there had even been a time when you were oblivious.

His father wasn't his father anymore. Not just.

He was a twelve-year-old boy watching his family murdered.

That was the private face.

That was the thing you could never talk about, because then it would want to surface in more than just words.

Ryan slid off the bunk and left Evan's quarters, alone. His father was still talking to the meedees, addressing their bombardment of questions. About the negotiations and the striviirc-na and the war. And he knew what it was like to speak and not hear yourself, to make sense and not feel it because all your emotions were somewhere else, away from the lights and the constant questions. The expectations and the judgments.

To live in that world you had to detach yourself from it.

But sometimes that bled through to the rest of your life and you wanted to completely detach yourself. You kept people at arm's length, or brought them in only on your terms; you went to parties and sailed and tried to forget it all. You went on a ship whose schedules you controlled, whose comms kept you safe from too many messy in-person entanglements.

You played by other people's rules, whoever they were—meedees, dead enemies—the people who made you feel alone and fooled you into thinking it was necessary. Or worse, that you preferred it. That you even liked to be that detached.

But he never *liked* it. And he knew, now, neither did his father.m

So he waited at the airlock for his father to come home, so that *he* would be the first thing his father saw when he walked up that ramp.

DIVE

A month later, April 15, 2197 EHSD, I read on the Send that EarthHub had a new president: Centralist First Minister Judy Damiani.

EarthHub President Judy Damiani.

And she was so damn pleased with herself. Her smiling face and single hand waving to the masses in her inauguration transcast was accompanied by the proud statement that her winning the votes proved that "the loyalty and solidarity of Hub citizens will always prevail over the wanton actions of deep-space Annexationists."

"Damn election musta bin fixed," Erret Dorr said, at one of our habitual mess-hall meals. "I sure as hell didn't vote for her skinny Centralist arse."

My father had pretty much ignored her after his now famous transcast, especially when she'd gotten up on that podium after him and made public, before he was ready, the items of discussion in the peace talks—which included a reparations resolution for alien colonies taken and plundered by the Hub. Naturally that didn't go over well, especially blurted out with no bracketing explanation.

She'd known by then that my father would not allow her to contribute her view on the matter to the striviirc-na or Captain S'tlian, despite pressure from the Hub Council or Hub Command, the latter of which Admiral Grandpa officially represented in the talks. Minister Stellan Taylor of Alien Affairs, who was supposed to be the diplomatic mouthpiece for President James, sided with my father in theory, but with his boss at the end of his political term, Taylor knew which side of the galactic government currently bore the most weight, and it wasn't the Annexationists.

So now—Centralist President Damiani.

Captain S'tlian and his Caste Master had returned to Aaian-na a week after my father's transcast—not entirely pleased with Damiani's lust for the limelight and her untamed mouth, which she had counted on. They supported my father and liked dealing with him and Grandpa, through Jos, but the "loose-armed Hubcentral reps" (as Nikolas put it) were another matter. Jos said the Caste Master had his work cut out for him on Aaian-na too. Opponents raised arms on both sides, apparently.

Minister Taylor and his staff stayed at Chaos Station for "any eventualities." The next spate of meetings were scheduled for June 1. Damiani and my grandfather (and their army of govie suit support) leaped back to Earth three days after *Turundrlar* pulled out of dock, to "consult" with the Council (and campaign to the masses, at least in Damiani's case). Grandpa said the break would give him a chance to do some damage control back on Earth, with the other govies.

Operation: Assassinate Pompeo, Erret called it.

That wasn't what Grandpa meant. But he had to present the current terms to President James and try to iron out "the Azarcon upset," as the PolitiSend coined it.

People always wanted a catch phrase.

My father's statement had stunned the Hub—for about eight hours. Just enough time to grab some sleep, wake up, and see that nobody's opinions had really changed on the galactic level. Sure, now more than ever most of the stations and merchant ships in the Rim and beyond supported the peace talks, but the captain's reticence about divulging details about his past still rankled Hubcentral and those within their immediate reach. Which meant a lot of people on the Earthward side of the Spokes still thought deep spacers were odd and suspicious, and worst of all too independent, and apparently these paranoid Hubcentralists counted more than everyone from the Rim to the Dragons.

Grandpa's damage control didn't ultimately help.

Damiani thwarted any attempts to put a decent face on the talks by reminding everyone in all her transcasts that symps and strits were notoriously wily and couldn't be trusted, and preemptive action was much more favorable than trusting to a long, drawn-out peace process that was spurious from the instigators up (meaning my father). My father had known her expedition to Chaos was part of her overall campaign strategy. I even suspected the timing of Pompeo's statement, but there was no proof that he was directly aligned with the new administration.

Proven victorious, Damiani gobbed on about how one of her missions as the new president was to "reassess our deep space priorities"—which my father interpreted to mean that she planned to use deep spacers and their affairs as a scapegoat to the troubles in the Hub as a whole, including pirate activity and the war. Never mind it was a deep spacer spearheading the peace. That too was suspicious because deep spacers (and captains) didn't have a right to spearhead anything on behalf of "loyal Hub citizens and their elected representatives."

Pax Terra's Governor Allison, who held sway over a good deal of merchant votes in Hubcentral by being their homeport, had more moderate views about the cease-fire, but cautioned all citizens to still be aware of those "in our midst who might seek to capitalize on the quiet. Vigilance will be our reward." Sympathizers and sneak attacks, he meant. As if Pax Terra, so close to Earth, had ever been even sniffed by striviirc-na.

Musey called Damiani a bigot. Erret Dorr volunteered to go on a clandestine mission and assassinate her at the same time he brought down Pompeo, in a kind of two-for-one deal (the captain said No, even though he was tempted). Sid said she was dangerous, and my mother considered her realistic.

"I think your father needs to be more cautious," she said to me over comm, as if I could do anything to truly influence him. We still had breakfasts and dinners together, unless he got up too early, worked too late, or I was invited to socialize with the crew. Dorr and Lieutenant Hartman made an effort to baby-sit me on occasion, though I think it was just their excuse to taunt Sid (or flirt with him, I could never figure out which). Sid got harassed in the gym sometimes, but he never let it get past jetdeck because that would've made it worse. He handled himself, anyway; some jets walked around bruised after their "workouts" and kept the name-calling to a minimum.

My mother would've given the captain a lecture if she knew what his crew was like around me. Sanchez's unit never outwardly touched us but they made their disdain known through dirty looks and following us around dark corners. I didn't walk the corridors alone below maindeck on Sanchez's shift and neither did Musey and Evan, which was on Dorr's orders because there wasn't much point in instigating things. Not that any of the crew would really hurt me, but I didn't trust it on certain off-shifts when they were allowed to drink. I offered to talk to the captain about it but Dorr said to leave jetdeck to jetdeck, unless it got bloody, and in that case it wouldn't matter because Sanchez would be dead.

Besides, my father didn't need one more thing to worry about. It was better if we policed ourselves.

Macedon, now newly refurbished, went back out on patrol of the Demilitarized Zone, but more for pirate activity (especially any that might point to that Yuri person) and wayward sympathizers who weren't loyal to the Warboy. Naturally the Send reported any ambiguous actions by Hub captains in the deep—actions that had nothing to do with the cease-fire, but impacted public opinion of it. They zeroed in on activity that lent itself to interpretation (the treatment of prisoners aboard ship, long absences from port, comms made to "questionable" people). The spotlight may have hit my father in the face, but the diffused glow cast wide on all of his comrades.

I went to school when I wasn't being beat up by Musey, or now Sid, in "training," badgered (or protected, depending on your opinion) by Dorr, or hit on by jets that didn't much like my company but thought posing a sexual threat would rattle me without too much condemnation (they knew I wouldn't run to Daddy). It didn't rattle me; one thing good about Tyler's parties, I got used to roving eyes and octopus hands. Sid thought it was all funny (to a point, and then he got into fights on my behalf), and made an issue of saying how proud he was of the fact I was studying *something* other than my fingernails.

Partially to cast off the scent of my burndives to Shiri and partially because I was honestly interested, the courses I took through *Macedon*'s link to Austro University were centered around galactic law and history, with a minor in music theory. For *this* the captain allowed my commsig to be masked (his comm officer set it up), so it appeared as if I were still on station. It was easy enough to use that excuse to slip a few other comms into the mix, but tailored to Mars. So school was good for something, though I didn't tell Sid that.

Evan called it fortuitous timing.

Musey called it just a matter of time—before I was caught. And then, he said, he'd be happy to eulogize me.

Oh, but he was good at the burndives and his code tactics were smooth and easy to remember. He said Niko's brother had taught him, and for a second I thought he'd talk a bit more about it, like he seemed halfway willing to do if I asked him about Captain S'tlian, but of the brother he said nothing except that the man was dead.

Musey knew, of course, what I was doing in the dives. He even asked me how it was going with the girl, marked improvement on his general outlook on relationships, according to Evan. I didn't aim that high; I thought he just wanted to know if I was being careful.

In my first lesson he'd said, "If you foul up and get caught, I'll make you regret it."

My first comm to Shiri reminded me why sometimes we got into shouting matches, and why I loved being with her and missed her these past few months. She was no sycophant. She didn't let me get a word in at first. I lay back on my bed, hands behind my head, and looked at her in leisure through my mobile as she sped on about how wonderful Paulita Valencia was, how generous and confident and smart. She was learning so much, she said, at Valencia's news studio on Mars—and wasn't I impressed that she'd actually made it off Earth? Oh, yeah, and she was so happy to finally be talking to me in real time.

Then she paused, took a breath, and took me in with an easy, appreciative look.

"I missed you," she said.

The girl could lay it on, but she was sincere, and if I didn't say something back she was going to reach through the comm and strangle me.

"I missed you too," I said, "when I've had time to think."

"You're such a romantic," she said.

"Well, since you're not here to have sex with me, what do you expect?"

"Ryan!"

I always loved to tease her with insults. She said it was my sandbox mentality.

"So what's it like now on station?" she asked. "Now that your father's said all that and Damiani rules the roost?"

She had some odd idioms. By all that she meant about his past with Falcone, which the meedees after the press conference had actually not pursued to his face (it didn't last, but at least by then he wasn't in front of cams and he could ignore the comms). She also meant about the negotiations, which they *had* asked about. Extensively.

Shiri still didn't know I was on *Macedon*, nobody off-ship knew but who had to know, and I couldn't tell her.

"How do I know you won't take what I say to the wonderful Ms. Valencia?" I was only half teasing.

She looked back at me, serious. "I'd never do that without your permission, Ryan. Nothing about you has come out from her, right? She respects your father."

"Not enough to ignore Pompeo. Or ban him from her network."

"Well . . . you have to admit, it's interesting. She limits his hyperbole, anyway."

"Interesting wouldn't be my word. It's my father's life that SOB is messing with."

She was silent for a second. "A man in his position does have to be accountable, though."

"For the work that he does, not his personal life. And he can't be accountable for what was done *to him*."

She never worried much about pissing me off. She knew I liked to engage and she had an uncanny ability to judge how far to take it. "Well," she said, "what *did* he do while he was with Falcone?"

"You're saying he's a pirate."

"No, Ryan, *he* said he was a pirate."

"I don't think you were listening to the same transcast. He was *kidnapped* by pirates. Why does that make him one?"

"He spent six years with them. As a prisoner? If so, then why didn't he just say so?"

"Because maybe it's not so black and white like meedees want to make it."

She frowned a bit at my disdain. "My point exactly. Therefore he's accountable to the public and his government to justify his actions."

"You wouldn't say that if you knew him. He's only mean to fools, especially the dangerous ones."

"Do you know him? You used to always complain about him."

"I didn't *complain*."

"You bitched, Ryan. About him or your mother or Sid."

Well, I had. "Before or after Hong Kong? I bitched about everything after Hong Kong." I could tell her that, I could say it. I saw in her eyes that she wanted to ask more.

"Have you been talking to him regularly?" she said instead. Maybe scared I'd bug and run if she pursued that line of questioning, like I had on Earth.

It was easy to lie, and I didn't like that. Not to her. "Yeah, we talk. He comms all the time. And he's not a pirate."

"The entire galaxy can't know him like you do."

"So they should reserve judgment. Actions speak louder, anyway, and they didn't complain about it when he was winning the war for them."

"Some people still did. The word that came in about what was going on out there . . ."

"Dirtsiders have no clue about deep space, Shiri. Nobody farther than the Spokes dislikes my father."

Broad generalization, but essentially true.

She hated being called a dirtsider. She had nothing to say to that, but I read the flash of anger on her face. She didn't like my stationer attitude, even when I was right. Or especially when I was right.

"So how *is* it at Austro now?" she said. "By the way, it's nice to see you're still a jerk sometimes."

I laughed, even though she meant it, and ignored it after that. "It's mad. You can imagine. Damiani's a wrench, I swear that woman and her Centralist fanatics . . ."

"She's not a fanatic. Don't you think she has some valid points?"

I wanted to say, Yeah, if I was still on Austro and hadn't met the strit and symp in question. I didn't quite link with all the gossip about the fact they were murderers and shit— even though they probably were—because they'd stood behind my father at that press conference, stood by him now despite rampant arguments in the Hub about his credibility.

"Damiani's points would be valid if they were stuck on top of her head," I said.

"Don't be glib, Ryan."

"She's an alarmist. They all are. They think the strits are just doing this to get the Hub to sit back, and then they'll attack. Like the strits have been *lying* about the fact their resources are strained."

"Well, can't they? Possibly?"

Not according to Jos. It was true that another bout of war was the last thing Captain S'tlian wanted. "I just don't agree with how Centralists think the only way the war will end is if we take away all the strits' spacefaring tech. That's a little extreme. And paranoid."

"Granted." She half smiled. "But extremism aside, the moderate Centralists have good points. Do you think it's a good idea to decommission our arms? What about pirates?"

"Moderate Centralist. Oxymoron. Surely you don't mean members of the Family of Humanity?"

Terrorists that they were, who touted Centralist politicians like Universalists touted Spiritual Harmony.

"Ryan."

I'd had this discussion with my father, so I gave her the answer he'd given me. "The idea behind it is to decommission them against each other. Not against the pirates. If we pooled our resources against the pirates we'd clean up the trade and travel routes in no time at all. Merchant ships *will* get on board for that."

And they were. Too bad the strongest opposition was coming from the Centralists on Earth and that was still the seat of the Hub government. Austro's weight was considerable, but so was Pax Terra's, Earth's closest and largest station, and the way votes worked, a station was a station, no differentiation between deep space and Hubcentral. Plus the military, which made up a considerable chunk of the votes, was still being paid by Hub Command—in Hubcentral.

"Territorial claims?" Shiri persisted, since she couldn't argue my other point about merchants. "Giving back moons and colonies? How realistic is that?"

"We'd taken them at gunpoint to begin with. Are you just arguing with me to be a devil's advocate or do you really not condone the treaty?"

She smiled. "You sound suspiciously like a meedee with that question." She still thought I shouldn't have dropped out.

"It's in the blood, if not the diploma," I said.

"I'm not sure if a treaty, with all of those terms, would be the best thing. I mean, they're even asking for a release of prisoners of war. Meanwhile we all know they don't *keep* prisoners of war, at least not admittedly. So we should just hand over their symps while they kill Hub citizens?"

"They have a different approach to things like that."

"You mean inhumane."

The Hub had bitched when Musey had killed Falcone too, because that kind of justice went against their traditional sensibilities that said it was far more civilized to spend cred on imprisoning a man who'd escaped once already. It was pride, not humanity, that fueled their reactions.

Strivs and symps were much more expedient. "Do we hold them to the same standards as humanity? That's what got us into the war in the first place."

"Tell that to the families of those prisoners."

Shiri had Centralist tendencies. I never would've thought. Even though she was an Earther born and bred, she had always come across as more outward thinking.

"You're a lot more militant now," she said, in a quieter tone and with a closer stare.

"I was thinking that about you. Since when aren't you willing to see the other side?"

"It's scary, Ryan, to think about the strits flying around out there without being caged somehow. It's hard to trust that."

That was what it came down to, all the time. Fear.

"Like it's scary to have my father, the so-called pirate, in command of an EarthHub carrier? The problem with Centralists is they want to control everybody and see everything, meanwhile they won't get their own asses off their planet and their minds beyond the Spokes."

Her frown deepened. "It's our planet too. All of humanity's. Stationers and deep spacers that don't consider Earth a part of things—that contributes to the division too, you know. There're deep-space extremist factions just like there are on Earth."

"Yeah, and Earthers call them captains, while putting them out here to defend their green pastures."

"I think you're clouded because it's your flesh and blood being attacked. I'm *not* a Centralist, any more than you're a symp, despite how you sound." She sat back and folded her arms casually.

I didn't put any weight to it, in case she followed up. "Getting shot at does that to a person."

She watched me for a long second. "I'm so sorry, Ryan," she said, in a different tone. "I wish you'd stayed on Earth, then that wouldn't have happened."

Stayed with her. She didn't move her stare and I had nothing else to look at.

"It might've still happened, Shiri . . . just . . . on planet."

"Do you think, um, you'll ever head insystem again?"

I had to do something before it got too far into hopeful promises and expectations. Considering where I was. So I didn't answer except with a slow, devious smile.

She shook her head and pointed at my nose. "I know what you're thinking, Azarcon, so stop it."

"What am I thinking?"

"You're a rotten little boy."

I widened my grin. Gave her the eyes. Piled it on thick because I knew so much sweetness would sicken her, and she'd laugh and forget about wanting to talk about where I might end up in a month or two. "So when're you going to leave Mars and come farther out?" I asked.

"When you invite me for an exclusive interview." Her smile matched. "With your *father*."

I groaned. "That hurts me."

"I doubt."

I'd forgotten how sharp she could be. I was slipping. "You must irritate the hell out of Valencia."

She smiled, all false candy and sunshine. "I'm going to land a major story by the end of this year, I promise you."

"Not with my father."

She said, "Then what're you good for? Get off my comm already."

I missed her. Especially on this ship, where the women looked at me as if they could chew me up and spit me out without breaking stride. Not that they were butch, but I didn't want to get involved in that culture, not here, not with my father looking over my shoulder and jets who liked to brag.

"Take care, Ryan," she said, smiling genuine now, and put her hand on her comp screen.

I couldn't do the same, with my mobile, but I smiled back. "I'll comm you again."

"You better."

"Even though the only reason you care is because I'm an Azarcon." Bait. Just to see how she'd react now.

"I'd kiss you if I was there or you were here," she said, "and then I'd slap you."

We tried to have dinner together at least three times a week, my father and I, just alone. Breakfasts were usually a rush job because he needed to be on the bridge now that *Macedon* was back on patrol, and because govies from Earth had no sense of timing and liked to comm him at 0500 to ask him for updates from Aaian-na.

He said, Until some things are signed and action backs it up, the Warboy is still patrolling the DMZ, so don't think about attacking them.

Damiani didn't like that, but my father said the last thing he was going to do was spy for her under the guise of administrative interest.

The Family of Humanity had a new political dartboard and my father's face was on it. Of course Damiani didn't *support* those extremes.

She just fed them.

Politics, my father said, wasn't one of the things he cared to discuss at our private dinners. Instead he wanted to know how my school was going and if Sid was fitting in and did I think Sid would be happier assigned back to Earth? He said Admiral Grandpa was asking.

We were in the captain's mess, but without the formal place settings and interrupting servers. It was just me and him in casual clothes and a simple meal. I pushed my pasta salad around on the plate.

"Do you want to send him back to Earth?" I asked him.

My father never said much to Sid, which suited Sid fine, but I couldn't help thinking it was because my father didn't want to accidentally say something that he'd rather not. About Mom Lau.

That was something we never talked about either. Sid and Mom Lau.

"I won't kick him off the ship," he said, "but he might prefer being somewhere—"

Where he was needed. Because I seemed to be going along all right with my new school and my new friends.

"I don't think he minds being here and working with the jets," I said. "Besides, I'm going to need him when I go back to Austro." I had every intention of going back to Austro, once things settled down.

And I still, selfishly, wanted Sid around. Just because I couldn't imagine being somewhere without him, not after seven years. Not when we still understood each other's hand signs and sometimes all we had to do was look at each other and nobody else got the joke when we laughed.

The captain looked at me and sipped his water. "I don't want to depress you, but I don't see that happening anytime soon."

"It doesn't—depress me. But . . . I can't live on this ship. Not, like, forever. It's not my life."

Maybe that insulted him, or hurt him, but lying about it would be worse.

"I understand," he said. He picked up the napkin from his lap and folded it into a neat square and placed it beside his plate. "How about some dessert?"

"All right."

He was going to shelve the discussion, but it wasn't over. He liked me here. He even talked about giving me my own quarters on the command crew deck because he didn't want to crowd me. I didn't request it; he wasn't much in his own quarters so I had the run of it most of the time.

He stood to go to the captain's galley and get the dessert, but his tags beeped when he was halfway to the door. His tags always seemed to beep during meals.

On the other end was Lieutenant Hartman. "Captain," she said, "we have a situation."

He slid open the galley door and motioned the cook there to bring out the dessert plates. "What is it, Lieutenant?"

"Corporal Sanchez, sir. Dorr had planted a mirror tracking code in Sanchez's comp that would siphon his actions to Dorr's, and he was, well, in a dive to Austro."

The captain's face froze. "Burndiving for what purpose?"

"Well, apparently he's been in contact with a Centralist rep on station. Someone from the Merchants Protection Commission, not a higher-up."

"Centralist."

"Yes, sir. Would you like me to bring him to your office for questioning?"

The cook came out with a couple plates of chocolate cake. My father let him pass but he wasn't looking that way. He rested his hands on his waist and turned to the wall, chin lowered.

"No," he said. "I've had enough. Is he in brig now?"

"Yes, sir."

"Get him to medbay so Rodriguez can remove *Mac*'s tattoo. Then get his ass off my ship."

With *Macedon* in transit?

"Yes, sir," she said, without hesitation.

He added, "We're meeting up with the replenishment ship *Oasis* in two hours, Lieutenant. See to it."

"Yes, sir," she said, and commed out.

I didn't touch my cake. "What would you have done if we weren't rendezvousing?" I knew the answer, but I sat there hoping my father might surprise me.

He didn't. He rejoined me at the table and edged his spoon into the dense chocolate. "I'd have found somewhere out of the lanes and jettisoned him. He's had enough warning and he didn't heed it."

The punishment for mutiny on ships at war was summary execution.

Except—technically we weren't at war.

And technically Sanchez didn't commit mutiny. He was just disobedient and shot off his mouth a lot.

But you didn't split hairs like that on deep-space carriers. Not on my father's, anyway.

I had learned.

I was surprised to hear my father's voice in the living room when I came out the bathroom after my shower. It was already 0730 and the captain was usually on the bridge or in his office, doing his captainly things. Some instinct or tendency to eavesdrop made me pad quietly to the screen, which was open halfway, and lean my shoulder against the inside panel, out of sight from the kitchen. I saw my father's arm and the back of his right shoulder from where he sat on the couch, and it didn't take long to figure out that my parents were talking to each other over comm.

". . . about that, Song?" my father was saying, with an

uncharacteristic, implicit sigh in his tone. "You feed them information and they'll just want more."

"Maybe they deserve to have more," Mom said. "Cairo . . . all this time. And you never thought you could trust me enough to tell me? You didn't even pick up my comms until now, so how am I supposed to feel?"

"It wasn't about trust. It was about not wanting my private life in everybody's living rooms."

"Thanks a lot. This strategy's worked well for you over the years, hasn't it? You'd rather the coward's way out and have me learn about this—from a *meedee*? And Ryan—what you did to *him*—"

"Ryan is fine. We talked. He's fine."

"You talked."

"Yes, you know, I don't chain him up in a dark room and kick him on off-shifts."

I heard myself in that comment, and I thought so did my mother.

"Don't, Cairo."

"I'm sorry. I really am. That you feel you have to deal with it in public. You never understood—there're lines that don't need to be crossed in a public forum, and it's you that have to dictate where they are. Not them."

"Don't tell me my job. When my husband, a public figure, makes a declaration such as you have, there is no other way to deal with it but in the public. Or else they think you're hiding something."

"I am hiding something. I'm protecting my personal life from a rabid galaxy that has no right to know—"

"They have a right, Cairo! They pay for your ship!"

I heard the shield go up. "They don't pay for my ship," he said.

"Pretend for one second that you actually work for Earth-Hub."

The captain's voice hardened. "EarthHub. Not the government. I don't care what they have written down, once we're out here staring down the torpedo tube of a strit battleship, the government is not in the equation. They're canceled out of it, Song. That's something you stationers and dirtsiders don't get. I spent hours trying to get it through Damiani's head, but she was so adamant in her ignorance."

"You treat your relationships just like your captaincy, do you know that? Not everyone thinks like you—or should! Other people *exist* in your personal equation."

"If they want to survive out here they'd better think like me. You don't want me telling you your job. Well, don't tell me mine. And that's what Damiani and her ilk want to do. They'd like me to tell Aaian-na that we'll have a *mutual* cease-fire on *our* terms. How does that make sense? How does that get us anywhere but back where we started, stomping all over an alien race? It's pride. Dirtsiders and Hubcentralists are ignorant and proud. It's a rotten combination, Song."

"You should know about pride, Cairo. I wasn't talking about the government or the strits. I was talking about us."

An audible breath. "Song . . . there hasn't been an us for years. Haven't we recognized that already?"

Silence.

"Because," Mom said, in a quieter voice, "you've given up. It's no longer important to you. I don't know that it ever was."

"It was," the captain said. "But never as important as what I do. You knew that, Song. I told you. I can't . . . I never could devote myself to the extent you wanted."

"Now I know why."

My father said, in a tight voice, "Yes. Now you know. And I looked the other way with you and Sidney because of it. So don't talk to me about pride."

I should've shut the screen at that point, picked up my guitar, and minded my own business.

But I didn't. Couldn't.

"What happened, Cairo," Mom said, a hitch in the words. "Help me—understand you. For once."

"There's nothing . . ." the captain started, on automatic, it seemed. He was quiet for a long time. I thought he was forming his thoughts but when he spoke it was clear he was fighting—for composure. "I learned from the bastard. So what does that say? That I enjoyed some of it? That some of it was *worth* it? I can't—that isn't something—who I am . . . as a captain, a person . . . tied up in that. Like I *owe* him something. But I don't. I know I don't. Except when I think about how it was and I'm back there. I hated it. But I still can't make myself remove these damn tattoos or even cover them up now like I did when I was in the Academy. I can't toss the weapons he gave me because . . . in a way I don't want to forget. And it's nobody's bloody business, Song. Not even yours, or the admiral's, or Ryan's. It's mine." A long beat. "It's mine. Do you understand?"

"No," she said. "I don't understand why you think you need to handle this by yourself. I don't even understand who you're talking about. Who is this 'he'?"

No sound from my father.

"Cairo. Falcone had a reputation—"

"Justly deserved. Let's leave it at that."

Of course she wouldn't. But she tread gently, it was in her tone. "Is that why you let that symp kill him?"

"I didn't let him. He just did it. And I'm not going to punish him for it. He had reason."

"Why didn't you?"

"Because I'm not living in it to the extent he is . . . at least, I wasn't . . . and I felt no immediate need. I had the man in custody and he knew what I'd become despite . . . or because of . . . his—work." A surprising burst of laughter. "That last conversation was worth it to let him live. He tried to goad me and take credit for my success as a captain, you know, because he trained me. That's partially true but I know not all true. So I told him that if it *were* true then he only had himself to blame for being in my brig. That got *quite* the expression on the old bastard's face. He never liked my humor."

"You actually find that funny?"

He sounded like his normal self now. "But it is, Song. I looked in his face finally and laughed. He wanted to murder me. It was perfect. It was over. I don't need meedees exhuming all of that, or the government pawing through it because they don't want anyone's attention on forging a treaty."

"You think that's what they're doing, that they don't have real concerns on the matter—or how you're handling it?"

Humor still infiltrated his voice. "That *is* what they're doing, Song. I've been talking to them for the past couple months. And after being trained by a pirate, I can see easily enough when people are lying. That's one of the reasons they don't like me. They can't lie to me."

She sighed. "How is Ryan?"

"I think he's finished his shower and might be eavesdropping on us."

I took a step back. Looked at the ceiling. My father said, "Ryan, come in here and say hello to your mother."

I considered going back to the bathroom just to prove him wrong. But not after that conversation. I went out and my father turned slightly in his seat to look up at me. My mother's face showed on his comp screen on the table. She saw me too as I came up behind the captain.

"I'm glad you two haven't killed each other," she said, her own demeanor fallen back to a familiar place.

"No, he lets his crew do the dirty work." I smiled and tried not to see him as he looked at me, knowing that I'd heard every word between him and my mother.

After a moment he turned back to her. "Why don't you speak to your smart-ass kid? I have to get on bridge."

Smooth. He didn't have to talk to me if Mom Lau had dibs.

"I wonder where he gets it from," my mother said.

I sat next to him on the couch. "Let's have lunch, Dad. Even if the strits give an unconditional surrender in the next hour. Okay?"

The captain said, "If they did, we wouldn't. But since they won't, I will." He got to his feet and picked up his slate from the table. "See you later." He didn't quite smile at me as he went out the hatch.

That was probably the fastest retreat the captain had ever executed. It was like he had a time limit or volume capacity for intimate discussion, and then he had to discard it and start over from a comfortable place of controlled distance.

I wasn't surprised that I recognized it.

Maybe that was just the way it was, like Evan said about Musey. You just got so far with him and then you had to stop, because there wasn't a person or a tool in the universe that could get past that wall, that defense.

Those memories.

If you didn't want artillery to fall around your head you just had to sit outside in silent siege and wait for the bridge to come down.

My mother must've known that too well. She was silent, watching me. Her hair was swept up and stuck through with silver pins, but tendrils flew free. I could imagine the flurry in her offices. It was always flurried. "Ryan. How are you?"

What she actually asked was how exactly were the captain and I getting along? She always wanted updates.

"Are you going to have to do damage control for the rest of our lives? Maybe he has a point, Mom. Just don't address it."

"I have to address it, Ryan. Even if it means divulging just a little in order to deflect the rest from attention. Did you hear what he said?"

"Yeah." Had heard it a lot earlier than her and still didn't quite know what to think of it. It had sounded like my father was talking about someone else's life.

"Falcone trained him. He was a pirate, Ryan. Full-fledged for those years he was in their custody, if I heard right. It doesn't matter if he wasn't willing in the beginning. People won't like that a man with countless loads of arsenal at his disposal—"

I waved my hand. "I get it, but why does that cancel out all of the *documented* good he's done?"

"In a perfect universe it doesn't. But perception is what counts. You know that. A pirate association discredits him, to say the least. And therefore the peace process."

"I want to do something about it."

Her gaze flickered. "What do you want to do?"

"I don't know. But people should know him—" Like I do, I almost said. What I did know of him. When he wasn't being a stubborn despot.

"It's best if you stay out of it."

"Mom . . . I don't know why you and Dad don't get it. But I can't stay out of it. I'm in it already. He said as much to me, way back when, and I think it applies across the board, not just when it's convenient for you."

She looked surprised.

"I'm Austro's hot number one bachelor"—a twist of a smile—"and Cairo Azarcon's son. But to the Send and the galaxy at large I'm hiding like a little girl in my room. I'd rather be useful. If people are so interested in me, the least I could do is say something worthwhile."

"What would you say exactly?" she asked slowly.

I chewed my lip. At least she was listening. I said, "I don't know. Yet. Exactly." If I could even handle the pointed spotlights. Because they wouldn't stop at my father. They'd ask about my own experiences—you didn't volunteer yourself to the public without expecting that. I'd have to have an answer for them that still somehow protected me.

"I suggest you think more about it," she said. "But I can already tell you what your father would say."

"I know." Therein lay the rub.

Her eyes slid sideways to something on her desk. "I have to go now, sweetie. Okay?"

I smiled at her. "Okay. I miss you." It came out as something you say to people over long distances, but as I said it I realized it was true. I wasn't sure what exactly about her I missed, since she'd never been much for affection or confidence; maybe it was just because she was my mother.

She cleared her throat, touched the screen lightly. "I see your hair's growing out finally. And your father says you're back in school. I'm pleased, Ryan. Try to finish this time."

"Comm me later, okay?"

She smiled. "All right." I knew she meant it this time. "I do have to go."

It didn't take long for her to disconnect. She wouldn't get maudlin over comm. That was one thing we had in common, all three of us.

My father came to see me spar with Musey. Not that it was much of a contest; mostly it was humiliating, but oddly fun once I stopped caring how much people laughed. We were in the ring, which was actually square, in the sparsely occupied gym. It was a sizable area with a multitude of different torture implements, designed to stretch, enhance, or tear muscles. I wasn't one for working out. The exercise bags attacked me, the track around the rim was too monotonous, and the people who used it all regularly were far too fit. I supposed it was important for upkeep on jets and to divert an overabundance of energy, especially when they weren't fighting battles every other shift, or preparing to fight one.

Sid and Evan stood off to one side of the ring, their backs to the hatch, shouting encouragement to me (Evan, the traitor, alternated between me and the symp). As soon as I saw my father walk through the gym entrance Musey clipped me across the cheek and I fell sideways against the rope barrier. I was wearing headgear but it still made my brain reverb.

I groaned and staggered up, adjusting the padded section on my face.

Musey approached, somewhat concerned. "You all right?"

"Yeah, yeah."

"Helps to pay attention," he said.

I tried a sucker swipe at his head, but he saw it coming somehow and dodged, grabbing my passing arm to fling me to the mat.

"Damn!"

"You're improving," he said.

I got up, slower this time, and stretched my aching back. "Don't patronize me."

"I'm not. It took less than a distraction to get you down a month ago."

"Like a strong wind," Sid chimed in, as if anybody had asked him.

Evan laughed, then went quiet and moved aside as my father approached.

I glared at both of them.

No help from the familial quarter either. He was smiling. "Shower and let's get some lunch. I've got time."

"Okay." I leaned my arms on the ropes and made faces at Sid, then held out my gloved hands. "Here, do something useful."

"Yes, Your Highness." He mock scowled. But he tugged the straps open for me so I wouldn't have to use my teeth.

Musey crouched down by the ropes to talk quietly to my father, too quiet; I couldn't hear anything. Evan kept a polite distance, but he watched Jos. I wondered if he could read lips. Sid pulled off my gloves, then reached up to undo the cheek guards.

Someone's tags beeped. I looked down inside my T-shirt but it wasn't mine. We all checked and it turned out to be my father's. He tapped it.

"Azarcon."

"Sir," the woman's voice came through, sounding oddly strained. "Check the Send. *Now.*"

"Their timing is impeccable," he muttered. "As usual." He looked over to the vidscreen up in the corner of the room and called it on.

A male meedee stood in front of a polly barricade, on some deck that didn't look like the one outside the dockside on Chaos, where most of the latest reports had come from in preparation for the upcoming reconvention of the peace talks.

Words scrolled across the screen, even as my father snapped at it to increase the volume.

But he didn't need to. The headline burned into my eyes.

AUSTRO'S SENIOR PUBLIC AFFAIRS OFFICER AND WIFE OF CAPTAIN CAIRO AZARCON, SONGLIAN LAU, KILLED BY A SUICIDE BOMBER ON HER WAY TO A ROUTINE PRESS CONFERENCE IN MODULE 7.

The room was a tiny space, and everything in me narrowed to a dark, blistering point.

The first night after the attack on the embassy, I didn't sleep for long. I remembered hearing Sid and my grandfather talk in the outer room of the hotel suite we'd secured since our apartments in the embassy were destroyed, while I sat up in the bedroom watching the Send. The students they'd arrested shouted into the cams about "the butchering EarthHub" and "their butchering captains." The meedees called it a symp terrorist act, but these kids didn't look like symps, they were my age.

That night I dreamed I met my father, after seven years, and when he hugged me I blew up and killed us both. I knew you weren't supposed to die in your dreams, but I died a lot at night after that day in Hong Kong. Little bits of me went out hour after hour until I'd developed such an acute insomnia that Sid couldn't even stay up with me anymore.

It was stressful to sleep. It was painful to be awake. We traveled back from Hong Kong through Asia and Europe and Sid found me in the hotel bathroom in London with a bloodstream full of street drugs. No high-end Silver distillations, this was my first and last taste of Earth's alternative. It hadn't been intentional. I didn't remember any of the immediate event, except convincing the room server to buy me whatever was on the corner and slip it in my hand the next time I ordered food service.

I remembered waking up in a private hospital room with Sid beside the bed, his head by my arm, asleep. I never worked up the courage to ask him how he'd found me, but I didn't really need to; I saw it on his face for weeks when he looked at me.

I always thought I'd die young.

Stupid, he told me, with tears in his eyes. You selfish, stupid kid.

My grandparents put me in therapy and when I refused to cooperate with that, Sid took me to the middle of nowhere. Pretty soon the memories didn't burn as much, but I needed off the planet. And I made them promise never to tell my parents.

Never. Not in any official reports, or unofficial ones.

Surprisingly, both my grandparents and Sid agreed. Maybe because they knew how serious I could be now.

No, Sid had said. I think you should tell your parents yourself.

Never, I thought. I could never hurt them that way.

But there was another way to hurt somebody. I knew it now.

In silence.

"Ryan, come down."

Sid looked up at me from the gym floor, up through the blue ropes of the ring where I leaned, sitting on the mat with my cheek against them. It was hard to breathe and I shook. About five meters away my father paced, talking on his tag-comm to somebody, a hand resting at the back of his neck.

Sid reached through the ropes and took my elbow. "Come on, get up. Come down here."

His eyes were glassy and dazed, fighting to stay focused. I pulled away and hauled myself up, nearly fell right over to his feet trying to negotiate the ropes, but Musey came up quickly and seized my arm and guided me down as if I would break.

As soon as my feet hit the floor Sid grabbed me with both arms and held on. Over his shoulder I saw the transcast and its repetitive shots of the exploded hallway where it had happened. He held me so tightly with my cheek against his shoulder that I couldn't breathe. My heart hammered, struggling. I heard his tiny gasps, raking for his own breath, and felt how he shook. Eventually I put my arms around his back and tried to say something that would make him feel better, but nothing came out. Not even tears.

I just stood there.

And I heard the ship's drives as it moved through space, heard it so loud when for the past few weeks I'd learned to ignore it, I'd gotten used to it like I'd gotten used to being safe. The craziness was Out There, in all the rest of the galaxy, not here where it could touch me.

And I'd been right. It hadn't touched me at all this time.

Musey and Evan hovered, wordless.

Then my father stopped talking on comm and came up as if to cut in to a dance. His expression was tight, pale, and expectant. But he stopped because I looked away, I didn't know why I did it, but I did, and Sid's grip was so hard around my ribs I knew there would be bruises.

Maybe Sid heard my father, or felt his presence, but he didn't move and I didn't want him to move, my body had become a dull ache, felt too warm as if all of me was going to slip away and run down like rain to an open gutter. Sid started to whisper something against my hair that sounded like, "I'm sorry."

Hong Kong. London. The Dojo. Now this?

But I was still alive. I was so alive it hurt.

I went to quarters alone, sending Sid away because I couldn't look at him either after a while, and the captain wasn't in there. I shut myself in the bedroom and stood looking around at its now familiar gray walls, the expensive blue sheets on the bed, some of my clothes strewn haphazardly across it.

Illusion. Nowhere was safe.

I paced, sat, ended up on the bed with my hands up in my sleeves and my leg twitching, feeling sick but not in any way that could be relieved. My hands wouldn't stop shaking, they turned cold, and I didn't know if it was the air in this ship or my own dried sweat or both.

My heart was a mausoleum, and it was crumbling.

I didn't know how long it took the captain to come in. I paced—five or six strides from one end of the bedroom to another, repeated. I occupied my mind with failed attempts to think of nothing but blank walls. I splashed my face with water, went out and paced again, finally turned up the music and sat on the couch and listened to its harsh beats and vocal screams, loud and mangled mirrors to my own emotions.

He came in and ordered it off, but I ordered it back on. He sat next to me and pulled me to his chest, but—no.

He yelled the music off and grabbed my face in his hands, forced me to look at him even as I dug my fingers into his wrists.

"Ryan."

That was all he said, and stopped. Not a bit of emotion sloughed off him.

"Shouldn't have happened," I said.

"I know."

"You should've protected her!"

He didn't say anything to that. Maybe he felt guilty. I still couldn't read his expression. He wouldn't allow himself to crack.

Well, damn him for it.

I shoved his hands away and stood. He got in my way, gripped my arms.

"Let go of me!"

"Listen—Ryan—I want you to listen."

"What for? What the hell is left? *My* safety? It's a fucking *joke*!"

His eyes searched mine as his hand went into my hair, smoothing it back.

"Don't." I tried to avoid his gaze but he moved my head up with his fingers in my hair and I couldn't help it, everything welled up and started to spill. "That was meant for *me*."

"No," he said, shiny fissures in the blacks of his eyes. They opened to little rivers of light. "No, Ryan . . . it was meant for me."

He didn't want to, but we were going back to Austro. I got my wish to go home again. It was probably the reaction the killers had expected—a suspension of the peace negotiations and two Azarcons in their sights. My father said he'd been in contact with the pollies on station, and what was left of my mother's security (two had died with her, in the explosion), and demanded to know what the hell had happened.

He told me while I was still quiet.

She'd been on her way to the press room from home, to make a routine statement in answer to a number of meedee questions about the upcoming talks and whether she'd spoken to the captain recently. Security had mapped the route (different each time), with all the safe locations along the way predetermined, and a minimum of traffic to contend with from outsiders.

A woman posing as a legitimate meedee had approached her, asking questions as if she were really interested, and my mother, being the way she was, had stopped to at least tell the woman that she would address the questions in her statement.

And the woman had rushed her.

Security shot her when she was within a meter, but she was on a time bomb.

She *was* the time bomb.

And now there were funeral arrangements, and advance security details, and the obvious expectation of more meedees once the ship docked.

My father was sending ahead a platoon of jets on a Charger APC to work with the Marines and pollies on station, for both the investigation and the logistics of our arrival, and the security details for the funeral. Because he didn't trust Grandmother Lau to take care of things. He told me Sid had requested to go and he'd granted it.

"How could you do that?"

He said, "Because Sidney asked. And I believe he needs to do something or he'll—"

"Be killed. Over there."

His voice was gentle and I didn't want to hear it. "He's not a target."

But it was the pattern of things.

"Who did it?"

"We don't know yet."

"Pirates again? Are they still mad at you?"

His mouth tightened. "Suicide isn't their style ... Ryan ... please."

I didn't know what he was asking.

I said, "When we find out who did it, I want them dead."

He stared at me for a second, as if we were time-delayed. The two of us on the couch with the thrum of the moving ship all around, and the further we went the sicker I felt, and the angrier I got.

"Promise, Dad."

He reached over and stroked my cheek briefly, then let his hand drop. It seemed like metal nails drove down my throat and into my lungs.

He wasn't going to make promises he might not be able to keep. He never had.

"You should go and say good-bye to Sidney," he said. "I'll be here when you come back."

I banged and buzzed the hatch at Sid's quarters until he opened it, bleary-eyed. The Send chattered behind him from the comp. The same cycled shit. My mother's face from an archived 'cast, the exploded hallway with a swarm of pollies choking it up. The speculations: pirates. Anti-peace factions like the Family of Humanity. Even though terrorist groups rarely targeted specific individuals. That was more the realm of governments. I dragged my gaze to Sid's duffel, packed and ready to go.

"No," I said.

"I'm going to make sure they don't screw it up."

"There's no point!"

"I'm *going* to see you there. When you come in with your father."

My body felt full of splinters. They stabbed behind my eyes.

"You need to stay here," he said. "You're safe on this ship." He picked up the duffel. When he looked at me his eyes were red and dry. It was his bodyguard face. Except for the eyes.

I hadn't been without him for the last seven years. It might've occurred to him too. Before he left he pressed his lips to the top of my head, as if I were a child.

I waited for the news to hit that Sid had been killed in another assassination attempt or freak accident, but it didn't come. Captain S'tlian and the Caste Master sent their condolences, Jos said, and I stayed completely off the Send. I didn't even feel like talking with my grandparents and I didn't trust myself to speak to Shiri.

My father didn't rush *Macedon* back to Austro like he

had the last time. He kept Musey busy translating his intentions to continue the negotiations, despite everything. Maybe he needed to do that, like Sid needed to be busy and I needed the music turned up and my solitude uninterrupted. In the hours between leaps I sometimes sat with Evan in that dusty stairwell, in silence, because Evan seemed to understand that crowds and words were cumbersome and annoying.

Soon enough we arrived on Austro and my father came in from a long shift on bridge, looking like he had made that double leap from deep space on foot. He sat me down at the kitchen counter while he drank a cup of hot caff, and told me that as soon as we stepped out of the military dockside our faces were going to be transcasted. And then everybody would know that I hadn't been on Austro. Not that it mattered now.

"I can handle it," I said, even though I had no idea if that was true.

"All the arrangements have been made," he said. "It's being held in the Universalist Chapel in Module Three and we're leaving in two hours. The meedees will probably not accost us, out of respect, but they will 'cast."

"You said that. And I said I can handle it."

He sipped his caff. "All right," he said. "Better get ready then."

I slid off the chair and went to do that.

I thought the captain would wear his dress uniform, but he didn't. Whatever protocol was, he emerged from the bedroom in a black suit like I wore, no rank or insignia or anything otherwise military. I followed him out, in silence, all the way down the rackety lev, doubly loud because we were in dock and the drives were quiet. It seemed to echo my nerves.

On maindeck we picked up a jet escort of six, nobody I recognized offhand except, surprisingly, Musey. Hartman's unit, including Dorr and Madison, was on Austro. I made eye contact with Jos and he acknowledged it with a bare blink. He was an excellent sniper, I knew, and I wouldn't have been surprised if he'd asked the captain to be on the detail, negotiations or not. The captain would want his best jets with us.

I felt better with Musey at my back.

But that went away when we stepped down the ramp, off ship, and headed toward the tall dockside doors. My father walked beside me, we were flanked on all sides by jets, but the dread embedded in my gut and began to chew. My hands shook, but I didn't want to put them in my pockets in case I'd need them free for a quick movement. I tried not to breathe too fast, even though we came up on the exit at a brisk pace.

My father paused and he gripped my wrist.

"Stay behind my shoulder," he said.

"All right," I answered, a bit hurriedly. And took a long breath.

We stopped at the doors. One of the jets in front of us muttered something into his commstud and the doors to the station concourse began to open.

Even before they were fully apart, the bursts of cam lights went off in our faces, like muzzle flash.

Pollies, Marines, and jets all made a fence line on the walk-route to the private podway that was our destination. Behind them were the authorized meedees, and behind them, far back and cordoned off, was the public, craning for a glimpse. Above all our heads a stream of wallvids scrolled our own images back at us.

I looked up to avoid the immediate, consecutive glares of

the lights and got caught in my own gaze. Someone had mounted a 360 cam up on the edge of one of the screens (the airborne cams were forbidden on the route). I saw myself walking close behind my father's right shoulder, surrounded by black, and we were in black, a fast-moving body of darkness. My father's face, plain for all the galaxy to scrutinize, was a pale mask. Mine looked dazed, my eyes too large and too blue, the ends of my hair so obviously fake and yellow, washing out the color of my skin.

For a second I felt as if I were up on that screen looking down at myself looking up, and I paused, blinking, and stared ahead at the Marines. Maybe Sid was here.

A hand went around my back. I thought it might've been Musey but my father suddenly pulled me smoothly against his side and held on, forcing me to keep pace with the group.

The executive tunnel came up, but the crowd didn't diminish until we were through the doors to the small, white platform where our scarab-shaped pod idled, alone.

A squad of jets was there already, and quickly opened the doors and guided us in. I sank down against the deep, plush gray seats, and folded my arms against my stomach. My father gripped my shoulder.

"Are you okay?"

I nodded. Musey and three of the jets piled in next to us, while the other two went up front. Once the door slid shut all the noise outside dampened and we sat suctioned into silence.

I wiped my eyes. Stress tears, nothing more.

I didn't object when my father's arm found its way around my shoulders. It was something to lean into so I wouldn't slip to the floor of the pod; it steadied the small shivers that threatened to collect into uncontrolled shakes.

Halfway there, and no incident yet. I still couldn't breathe fully.

Musey had a pickup in his ear and seemed to be listening to something. But he didn't say anything, so I supposed they had it all covered. I tried not to pick a thread loose from my sleeve cuff.

The pod finally stopped and we climbed out, jets first, then my father and I. It was a short walk through an empty corridor to the three mirrored executive levs. More station Marines surrounded us until we were safe inside. Even though they must have secured the compartment and probably the lift shaft all the way up to Module 3, I didn't breathe out until the doors opened on our floor.

It was quiet here. The privacy of the rich—carpeted halls, pale painted walls, and molded ceilings—ultimately a thin skin, because just outside the heavy, carved doors were more meedees, lined in the public corridors all the way to the Universalist chapel and its stained-glass portico. Artificial light overhead filtered through the shapes of stars and moons and deep blue spacescape, the four panels all connected by a thread of gold that represented the human soul.

My mother hadn't been particularly religious except on holidays, and even then she vacillated between traditional observance, ancestral, and the most common on Austro, which was Universalist. She would've liked the aesthetics of the place, though.

It was like a vid premiere as our heavily armed entourage marched briskly toward the portico, flashes chasing our heels. Some young voices from the civilian crowd yelled, "We love you, Ryan!" It made me look, surprised, confused that anyone would shout such a ridiculous thing, especially now, but I didn't stop, not with my father on one side propelling me along and Musey behind me making sure I didn't balk.

Once inside the chapel I heard my father breathe out,

then catch himself, as the doors shut behind us and we were suddenly engulfed in the quiet of the sanctuary.

Tall arches bent above us, fluted steel with warm brown, faux-wood jackets. Heavily carved images of pointed stars and round, ringed planets decorated the higher beams, trickling down to more abstract lace patterns and historical leaf motifs, all intertwined like the gold thread on the glass. Wide pews, velvet seated in bloodred, pointed the way up to a slightly raised dais that was backed by a blue glow and blended speakers to project the music.

It was peaceful and vaguely morbid in its emptiness (the other guests hadn't been admitted yet), and at every exit stood an armed jet.

Sitting on the dais was a sealed, silver casket tube.

I stood frozen at the bottom of the aisle, my father's hand around my arm, the soft music a sudden heavy pressure in my head.

Then a door to one of the private side rooms opened and a dark-haired woman strode out. For a split second I thought it was my mother and twitched in shock, but as she came farther into the cone of sconce light I saw it was Grandmother Lau. Her black hair lay flat against her skull in a long sheen. She was shorter than me even in heels but didn't give the impression of needing to look up for anything.

"You have nerve to come here," she said to my father, her face a pale sculpture of anger.

"I have a right, Yvonne." His hand slipped from my arm.

"Yes, your precious rights. They caused this. And even this—" She gestured to a jet. "Armed guards in a place of worship."

"Would you rather a security risk?"

"*You* are the security risk. You even dragged her son into it."

I bit the inside of my cheek, looked past her shoulder at the casket.

She spoke out of sorrow. It was on her face in high relief.

"Yvonne," my father said. "Not here. Not now." He put a hand between my shoulders to guide me to the front row.

"Captain," she said, before we could walk past, "what will make you stop? *Ryan*'s death next time?"

He turned to the side so abruptly she took a step back and put a hand on the edge of one pew. He was almost toe to toe and his voice didn't rise above that distance. "Not now. And not in front of my son. Back the hell off."

I couldn't see his expression, but Grandmother Lau's face seemed to stiffen and become fixed on her grief and anger. Years of accusation lined her eyes. She looked over his shoulder at me and I didn't know what else she saw there but it made her turn and head down the aisle, past the jets who didn't move; she had to walk around them.

We made it to the front row and sat. I leaned forward and put my head in my hands, feeling boneless and too warm. A headache started to spread from behind my eyes to the back of my skull. I wasn't going to last the service; it was already beginning. I pressed the heels of my hands to my eyes.

Someone touched my hair. I looked up and Sid was there, in his dress uniform and a somber little smile, though his eyes were dazed and distant. Not a scratch on him.

I stood and hugged him for a long minute as the sounds of the guests arriving broke through the silence.

No matter who spoke I couldn't raise my eyes. They remained fixed to a point on the thick, patterned carpet between my feet, my hands clenched in my lap. I sat between my father and Sid and tried not to make any sound at all. Some part of my mind drifted up to the high ceiling, up there among the echoes of the soft string music and stifled sobs.

My father laid his hand on the back of my neck and didn't remove it until it was his turn to speak.

Sid didn't say anything, or move much, but I heard him sniffing and he lifted one hand to his eyes a lot. I didn't care who saw or what they might think, I reached over and took his hand. It was as cold as mine.

I glanced up into his eyes. He was momentarily surprised, but he clenched my fingers and it eased the tightness in my chest just a little.

I didn't really hear anything that anybody said, and in Grandmother Lau's case that might've been a good thing. I felt her eyes on me. The service was a blur of saddened voices that reached to all my corners and settled, as if I'd never be rid of them. But eventually even my father sat down again and in that pause, when the crying from behind me carried loudest in the brief silence, I wanted suddenly for all of it to be over, to be alone, to hear finally that the people responsible were dead and burned to ashes.

I didn't know if I could make the walk back to the ship, once again past those meedees.

"No rush," my father said as we heard the crowd file out of the chapel behind us. The jets were going to stay, there was a platoon of security all around, so I stood when we were alone, just my father and Sid and I, and went to the casket to touch its cool surface.

They hadn't laid it open because a bomb had killed her. Ripped her apart.

I sank to my knees, then just sat on the carpeted steps leading up to the thing that held my mother, the remains of her. It wasn't even good enough to hold the scattering of my emotions. They all just seemed to race away like the spidery cracks in a sudden broken glass. One touch and the shards would fall around my shoulders and cut me.

*   *   *

Sid walked with us now, on my opposite side, with my father still on my left. We retracked all the ground from the chapel to Module 7, back toward the solid thought of home, the ship, and I never wanted to go somewhere so fast as to back inside my father's quarters, away from the meedees. Now they yelled questions at us as we passed through the edges of the concourse toward the dockside ring, their momentary lapse of respect completely forgotten now that the funeral was over, never mind the grieving.

Who was behind the murder, did you know?

What was the current state of the negotiations?

What had Ms. Lau's mother said to you at the service?

Did you blame yourself for her death?

I was tempted to yell back, if only to shut them up, but our fast pace didn't allow it and I couldn't look up into the glare anyway. My father didn't say a word.

Behind me Musey suddenly shouted, "Heads up!"

I flinched from Sid's sudden grip on my arm as he yanked me back and low. I looked up and saw a balloon, a pale blue shape floating over the crowd toward our security team. Then all I saw was black as two uniformed bodies and Sid in his dark blue surrounded me and my father and shoved us along on an abrupt detour.

I glanced back at the majority of our security as the balloon suddenly popped, raining bright bits of confetti.

Then the shots started. They sounded like they had in the Dojo.

Somewhere at the back of my mind I knew what was happening. They'd seen an anomaly, and you didn't take chances. Security had mapped out numerous safe points along our route in the event of an attack or some other threat and that was where we were going, at a mad rush, my father and I, Sid, Musey, and another jet I didn't know. Walls blurred by, our feet pounded, and behind us the staccato crack of rifle report echoed up and down the deck.

"In here," Sid ordered, dragging me down a side corridor, one I didn't recognize on this station. But we were still on the main level.

A round shape rolled across the deck in our path. Sound whooshed to silence and my sight shorted out with a painful flare. Something hard banged my shoulder, then my knees, and my brain screamed signals that I was no longer on my feet. I scrabbled to get up even as a shadow emerged from the blurry edges of my sight. One of them seized my collar and dragged me hard across the floor, nearly choking me. I went with it since it was probably Sid or Musey or my father. All the noise fed back into my brain like static.

Gunfire went off close to my head. I jerked back on instinct, blinking, seeing a body fall in front of me, the one that had held me.

"Sid!" I leaned down, grabbed the person's shoulders, and looked close through the sparking black spots in my vision—but it wasn't Sid. It was another man, older, a stranger.

I recoiled and looked behind me where smoke fed out from the corridor I'd just left. I didn't see my guard or my father.

Dead?

I went cold. My heart thudded with effort.

Someone whipped me around by the arm and yanked me ahead. I saw a glimpse of blond hair and pale blue eyes.

I fought him, using fists and feet, driven more by terror than technique despite hours of Musey's instruction. But it worked. He stopped, letting me go, and turned around so I saw his face up close.

Another stranger.

I tried to twist and run, but his hand shot out like a

missile and knocked my head back. I hit the wall, losing momentary motor function just long enough for him to take me up again. This time I felt the bite of a rifle muzzle against my side. His other hand reached around and groped up the front of my shirt, sending spikes of panic through me, but he stopped as soon as he felt my tags. He ripped them off and threw them to the floor.

"Go on," he said into my ear.

I went, hot wet lines tracing down my face from the smoke. With the tags gone I couldn't comm the ship and they couldn't track me.

I didn't know where I was but I knew where we were going as soon as he yanked me up short in front of a waist-high steel grille in the wall.

Austro's underdeck tunnels.

He shoved me through first, hit me to keep me down while he yanked the grille back to the wall on its magnetic clamps, then dragged me up again and manhandled me further through the transsteel innards of the station. My head rang, my eyes had barely adjusted to regular light after that flash and now saw nothing but black and faint orange spots from overhead. Somewhere something dripped and all around smelled like cold metal and stale air.

Finally he stopped and pushed me sitting against the wall. Damp went through my clothes and straight to my bones.

I took a ragged breath, looked up as he crouched on his haunches across from me, his back to the moisture-streaked wall and his rifle across his lap. He was young, or seemed near my age, with a cherubic roundness to his features and a pale smoothness of skin that you normally saw on children. His lips were puffy and chapped, used, his eyes a kind of corpse-cold blue. Bleached of life. Evaluating.

He shifted and dug into a pocket on his right thigh, came out with a file of cigrets, extracted one, and lit it with a fingerband lighter. His eyes didn't stray from my face. He took a drag and blew the smoke upward, his other hand still gripping the rifle.

"Shout anything and I'll kill you," he said, in a lazy tone I'd heard before from junkies. But his eyes were too clear for him to be drugged or habit-driven.

I didn't say a word. My ears still rang.

His clothes were threadbare, dirty white fatigues and sweater, a black T-shirt over top with some sort of flaking bird design on the front, in yellow. He scratched his chest with a half-gloved hand and looked down the tunnel.

"Don't worry, they're not dead. It was a thunderflash, not a bomb."

I stared at him, tucked my arms against my chest. "Who . . . who was that other man?" I asked.

My captor said, "Another pirate. But I didn't want his help anymore."

Another pirate.

"Did you kill my mother?" Pirate or no, my muscles tensed, wanting to spring across the gap between us and beat him senseless.

But he said, "No," with a quirk of his lips, part smile, part disdainful smirk. "That was the govies," he added.

Before I could open my mouth he leaned forward and tapped my foot with the nose of his rifle. "I was supposed to kill you a few months ago, but I didn't." He said it as if it were some sort of secret between us.

The sniper. Pirates.

I shifted. "Then what am I doing here now?"

"I'm saving your life—again."

"You could save it by putting me back with my father."

"Out there?" His eyebrows went up and he laughed.

"That'd kill you for sure. No, I think we better sit this out for a bit."

My leg wouldn't stop twitching. I chewed on my sleeve cuff. Prayed abstractedly the way nonbelievers did, but nothing stayed long in my mind. Fear hunted hope, and thought and bravery, and drove them to the ground.

"Relax," the pirate said. "I told you I didn't kill your mama. They *want* everyone to think it's pirates. But it was them."

"Why?"

"Treaties don't always get signed at official tables, Azarcon. Other parties tend to do deals more directly." He got to his feet and motioned me up with his gun. "Let's go talk to your papa."

He took me through more tunnels until I had no idea where we'd entered. Graffiti decorated some of the walls, sharp-angled gutter hieroglyphics that seemed ready to crawl from their surfaces and taint you with dirty color. Everyone on Austro knew stories of the underdeck population—murderers, thieves, runners for drugs and guns. It all flowed in the undercurrent dead air of these hidden decks, despite numerous polly raids. People shipped here after their stations or ships were blown in the war, but forgotten somewhere in the bureaucracy of relief aid systems, ended up underdeck. Orphans, traumatized veterans even, and doubtless pirates on the run.

Like this one. He knew the tunnels. He pushed me through the shadows, avoiding the echoes of limbless voices, until we squeezed past color-coded intestinal support columns and into a three-by-two-meter rectangular nook, hidden well from the main tunnel. It was darker here and I almost tripped over a blanket that lay on the dank floor. But

I didn't miss seeing the comp that sat shut on an overturned plastic bin, illuminated by a watery yellow cyalume stick.

I stared at the comp.

The young pirate slung his rifle on his shoulder, shoved me on the blanket, and pulled out wire cuffs from his back waist like a polly. He drew my wrists to a pair of horizontal pipes running the length of the wall and tied my hands to it, then dragged over another bin to sit on in front of the comp. Its razor shell wasn't beat up and showed no identifying labels. Custom-built from the insides out, and as he flipped it open and tapped away he seemed more than familiar with it.

Pretty soon he said, "*Macedon*, I want to talk to your captain. He should be back on ship by now."

How did he know *Mac*'s comm frequency?

A female voice on the other end of the comp said, "Identify yourself."

"No," the pirate said. "Tell the captain I have his son." He leaned back and smoked. The visual must have been deactivated.

In a matter of minutes my father's voice came over, steady though it was shored by rage. I wished I could see his face or that he could see mine. "Where's my son?"

The pirate aimed his rifle at me to warn me. "He's right here. I just saved his life."

Hesitation. Maybe from surprise. "Explain yourself."

"My name's Yuri Kirov," the pirate said.

That caused a long silence.

I stared at him, but he ignored me.

"I'm going to talk, Captain," Kirov said, "and you're going to listen because Ryan is right now in front of me. Unharmed, for now. Don't trace my sig, I can tell if you do and that'll piss me off. You don't need to know what I look like right now either, so don't ask me to turn on the visual. And—"

"I've ordered a lockdown of this station, Kirov. You're not going anywhere."

Kirov paused, staring hard at his comp, sucking just as hard on his cig. I shivered.

"They went for that?" he asked, with mild interest.

My father said, "They had no choice. It's my jets on their deck. So you'd better spin me a good story if you don't want to be shot on sight."

If he was concerned for me it didn't come through in his voice.

Kirov said, "I was in contact with a boy in the underdeck named Otter about a year ago, who was in turn in contact with a symp spy aboard your ship. I'd offered to deal Falcone in exchange for exoneration."

"I remember."

"Obviously that didn't work. I had to cut contact when Falcone got suspicious. I'm telling you this because I want you to understand . . . I still want out."

"You want out. Falcone's protégé. You've kidnapped my son."

"I *saved* him. It was Centralist fanatics who killed your wife and they were going for Ryan next. To wear you down."

"And I should believe you because—?"

"If this was a vengeance thing, Azarcon, I'd just kill you direct. They want to intimidate you without making you a martyr."

"And you're looking out for my well-being, as well as my son's? I don't see my son here with me, Kirov, and I'm fast losing patience."

I tugged at my cuffs but they just pinched tighter. The pirate licked his lips. "You should understand, Captain. The old khan talked about you. You don't get anything for free in this galaxy."

I stared at the faint light reflecting in the pirate's pale eyes. They were fixed on the screen.

My father's voice was a cold snap. "I haven't yet heard anything that ought to make me lenient when you're captured. And you will be captured, Kirov, if it means combing this station for a year."

Yuri Kirov smiled faintly. "After your symp killed the old khan, I got told to assassinate your son. You know how it works among pirates, don't you? It was expected. But I didn't kill him, obviously. In fact, I saved his life. I killed my own station contact instead. Some rich stitches got in the way but . . . oh, well."

"If you're expecting gratitude you'll have to wait."

"I don't expect anything but a fair shake. I saved your son's life that shift and I've just done it again. Pirates didn't kill your wife, Captain, it was govies."

"You keep saying that. Repetition doesn't make it true."

"I slept with the woman who ordered it. She's one of the leaders in the Family of Humanity cell on Austro but her day job's a rep for the Merchants Protection Commission. I been running intel on her since New Year's and you might like to know she's had contact with one of your jets."

Sanchez. My father said nothing, but I heard his thoughts.

This pirate was telling the truth.

Kirov continued, "Centralists and Family, it's an old sordid rumor, isn't it. She wanted to get you back here and finish it off with Ryan. Then where would you be? You know my reputation and you know I could get that info. I think you even know exactly how it's done, don't you?"

"I want to speak to my son."

Kirov dropped his cigret on the floor and heeled it out. "Not yet. You look into my claims and find out I'm right. Then you'll know I'm being honest."

"That won't prove anything except you're a manipulative bastard, which isn't news. I do know your reputation. I know you're operating as a pirate, even though you claim you want to come clean. Well, it would help your case if you released my son immediately."

"I can't do that. Number one, the people who killed your wife are still out there making plans to get Ryan, and if they can't kill him they'll kidnap him and try to manipulate you—like I'm doing, except they won't be as nice. So you really don't want me to let him loose. And number two, I need insurance that you won't hunt me down. Because you won't right now, Captain, since I have him and I can see what you're doing on station through the Send. I want you to find out the truth about the Family of Humanity. You might be surprised—or not—where the links go. The fact I'm even talking to you ought to be a clue. Some people really don't want this treaty, Captain . . . I can count three factions offhand and that makes for some acrobatic bed business. In more than one sense."

My father's voice sounded raw from strain, or restraint. "I suspected Damiani had personal contacts within the Family. Are pirates the third partner, is that what you're confirming?"

"No, Azarcon. You confirm it. It'll sound better coming from a decorated captain. Then we'll talk about your son. You know I'll keep my word. Honor among protégés and all that."

"I've not agreed to a thing."

Kirov's voice hardened, the first sign of emotion, impatience. "I want out, Captain. If you expose this triumvirate and grant me asylum and exoneration, I'll release your son. It's a simple symbiosis. Otherwise I have no choice but to stay where I am—with Ryan. And deliver him to the people who wanted him in the first place. Trust is a luxury I don't have in abundance. I think you understand me."

A long beat. "How will I contact you with my information?"

Kirov reached to touch the comp. "I'll know by watching the Send. Your actions are well documented lately, aren't they?" He tapped the screen and shut down the comp. Then he speared me with a quick, half-lidded grin. "Your papa plays hardball, big-eyes. It totally turns me on."

And he laughed.

At least I knew my father was alive, and I could only hope Sid and Musey were too. I watched Kirov and his comp, hoping he'd step out to take a piss and I could stretch over there and maybe send a message to *Macedon*.

He caught me looking.

"You want to see what your papa's stirring up dockside? Should pass the time." He brought the comp to me and sat down close—too close—held it on his lap and tapped it on. His hands moved fast, opening a link to the current transcast.

I thought about bringing my foot up to kick him, but he looked like he could handle himself and I'd just end up bruised, or worse.

The Send report flashed on the screen, a torrent of information and diatribes, all of them directed toward my father.

"... locked down the station in an unprecedented and, many say, unwarranted move. His jets occupy the dockside, his officers are in the stationmaster's office, and the captain himself has declared that he will 'disable' any ship that attempts to break dock without authorization from *Macedon*. All of this because his son has gone missing, in the wake of his wife's death. Is it grief fueling these martial actions?

Will the next step in the captain's regime be forced inspection of all ships at port?"

"Wow," Kirov said, mocking or not, I couldn't tell. "He must really love you." His eyes scraped over me. "I guess I'm not surprised."

"You're pissing him off, is what."

The pirate laughed. "What an honor."

Conversation was better than silence; maybe I could get something from him. "If you know his reputation, then you know he doesn't respond well to blackmail."

"This isn't blackmail. It's dealmaking. I know your father can appreciate that. We had the same teacher, after all."

I couldn't stop my mouth. "Difference is he doesn't live in it still."

"What do you know?" His eyes darkened in irritation. "I bet I know more of what makes your papa tick than you. Shit like that doesn't vent so easy." He waved his hand. "Anyway, I can bank on his care for you. I don't think he'd risk your life."

"You would really kill me?" I glanced at the rifle lying on his opposite side from me. "How far do you think you'd get if you killed me?"

His expression froze to a mask. "I don't have to kill you to hurt you." His hand reached out and stroked my hair back.

I wrenched my head away, breath stuck in my throat. I couldn't look at him now.

"Don't be so repulsed. Your father did the same in my position." A snort of laughter.

"No he didn't."

"We had the same training, big-eyes. If anything mine was better, since the old khan learned from his mistakes. Lost two protégés, though he never liked to count the last one. That kid ran away too soon."

"Just shut up."

More laughter, sounding like the kind you gave when you didn't give a damn. High, reckless, and jaded. "You're perfect," he said. "Perfect and pretty, if someone cleaned you up a bit. And you grew a few cents and gained some meat. And fixed that weird haircut."

"You like to hear yourself speak, don't you?"

"I'm just wondering what kind of geisha Cairo Azarcon's son would make. Oh, if I was still in the world I might take you on."

I wasn't sure I wanted to know the extent of that suggestion. Blood was laboring to my hands, my wrists were so sore.

"Ooh, look. The viper's out." Kirov turned up the volume on the comp.

President Judy Damiani came into frame, on Earth or Mars it seemed, judging by the blue sky behind her in the distance.

"This is the sort of behavior from deep spacers like Captain Azarcon that cannot be tolerated in any degree. Trade has been halted because he's taken it upon himself to act as Austro's authority, bulldozing as usual over the governor, the stationmaster, and the police commissioner. He's been ordered by Hub Command to relinquish control and work with station authorities to find his son, but he's refused. If anything proves his pirate tendencies it is this latest action, and I for one am not comfortable having such a man on speaking terms with the aliens."

I looked at Kirov. This was all his fault. My father had just lost his wife; he wasn't going to risk losing me too.

I didn't want him to risk losing me either. But now he was risking everything.

I pretended to sleep. The pirate had to sleep too at some point, or take a piss or a walk or find somebody to screw . . .

something, while he thought I was defenseless, tied to the pipes, and out of commission.

My arms were numb by now. I let it spread to my chest and the roiling storm going on in there. Panicking would accomplish nothing and I refused to give the pirate the satisfaction. Even when he tried to elicit conversation about my mother. I just turned my cheek to the damp wall and shut my eyes. Eventually I did doze, awoke, saw his back turned as he leaned on one of the pipe columns, peering out to the main tunnel throughway. I shut my eyes again but stayed awake, listening to him shift.

After a long while he approached. I kept my breaths regular and deep, chin to my chest. I felt him test the cuffs, tighten them, then he patted my head with a little laugh and moved away. His footsteps disappeared in the distance, echoing.

I opened my eyes and looked for the comp. He'd left it on the blanket by my feet, shut down. I stretched and dragged it closer with my heel. I couldn't reach it with hands so I kicked off my shoe, stepped on my right sock and pulled it off too, then toed the comp until the pressure flipped open the screen. "Icon options," I told it.

Nothing happened.

Damn, it was on a voice pattern.

Frustration threatened to burn my eyes. Think.

He hadn't activated it with his voice. Which meant there was an alternative key. A manual one.

I stared at the screen and the keypad. Common activation sets, I knew, thanks to Musey. Feeling more than a little foolish, but mostly desperate, I toed some combinations on the pad. Gingerly and painfully, my chin against my right arm, which was stretched at an uncomfortable angle now.

The eleventh try made the screen blink and colorize, then a security message popped up.

Of course it would be passworded.

I didn't need to get the password now. I just needed the holo-option, and that was an icon on the screen that was there as soon as the comp went live. I toed it and brought the comp as far up toward me as I could, stretching to look at the screen and connect my implants to the option. Once the icon lit I blinked the common Morse that sent me from the real world into the comp one.

Now I *saw* the password gate, the menacing red cannons that I had to disarm. In my head was a list of codes to break down and select in blinks, piece by piece, from the universal language of letter-and-number items. Put them together in the right order and that would disable it, if I only found the correct one.

Between Musey's training and my own criminal curiosity, I tackled it with sweating concentration, trying to keep my ears open for footsteps.

But I should've known better. Pirates like him didn't make noise and with my sight occupied, it was difficult to truly listen.

He didn't warn me, he just ripped the comp away without letting me blink out.

It felt like a dozen knives stabbed into my eyes.

I yelled and pressed my forehead to my arm, tears running down now like they were being chased. Kirov shouted above me, then his hand came down. I tilted over but he grasped my hair and wrenched my head up.

"What did you do?"

I tried to blink the tears away, but the world was black.

My eyes were wide open but my world was black.

I heard him pace, as pain tears tracked down my face in continuous rivers. Forced disconnections in burndives were an absolute no-no, especially if you had implants.

I was blind.

I tried not to panic but it wasn't working. My head reeled from too many fast breaths and my hands started to tingle. From hyperventilation or the cuffs, I wasn't sure.

Kirov said, "Shut the hell up with your breathing," as if that would help.

I kept my lids tightly shut but the pain didn't let up. My eyes felt like they were melting from their sockets.

I concentrated on the hope that any minute now my father would come and get me. Please.

Kirov muttered a litany of threats until he finally seemed calm enough to deal with me. He grabbed my jaw in his hand and his breath hit me in the face, cigret raw.

"You are one lucky boy, you didn't break my password gate. *One lucky boy.*" His fingers squeezed, almost forcing my mouth open. "You still can't see nothing?"

"No," I said through gritted teeth. "You bastard."

He shoved my head with a disgusted growl and moved away, taking the cigret scent of his clothes with him. "You're gonna do us both in, manito. Your daddy's gonna kill me for letting you be blind."

His voice trailed off in thought. I heard the spark of a fingerband on the end of a cig and the smoke smell got worse.

"Let me go," I said. "He'll go easier if you just let me go."

I doubted it. Unfortunately so did Kirov.

"Shut up," he said.

"He's linked with that symp Otter. How long do you think it'll take him before he finds you down here?"

From the pirate's silence I knew he was thinking of it too.

"Dermo," Kirov muttered. Footsteps started to track again from one end of the small space to the other. "Do you know what'll happen to me if your papa doesn't take my deal?"

I didn't answer. He wasn't looking for one.

"I'm dead," he said. "The Family or the pirates or some Centralist agency, they'll figure it out when I don't show up for them. I *need* your papa, dammit. He's the only one would listen to me—"

He stopped abruptly. His footsteps went away, then paused. Silence sank deep for a second before softer footsteps padded toward us. From the main tunnel.

I didn't hear him approach, just felt the gunpoint against my neck and his lips against my ear. A rough hand clamped over my mouth.

"Don't speak."

It could be my father's jets, or Otter, and Kirov was getting desperate. I didn't think I had a long shelf life in his hands.

So I bit at his skin and wrenched my head away, yelled, "HELP ME!"

"Idiot!" Kirov rasped. He let me go and stood, moving away from my side.

The steps came closer, it was hard to tell how many. A female voice said, "What the hell, Yuri? Where've you been?"

Someone he knew.

"Is that Azarcon's kid?" the voice continued, alarmed.

Another voice, male, said, "You're supposed to kill him!"

Oh, *shit*.

I started to struggle. It wasn't brave. I was a strung piece of meat flailing on its last breath as Kirov said, "Change of plans."

"Since when?" the girl said, clearly suspicious.

A gunshot went off. Then another, right after.

I froze.

Two dull thuds sounded on the cold deck.

No more voices.

Except one. Kirov said, emotionless, "They're dead and it's all your fault."

They were kids he'd trained in the underdeck, he said. They were destitute, indoctrinated, and pirate loyal, and they'd helped him track me back in February so he could stage the hit at the Dojo. Who looked at homeless kids on deck? Not rich stitches who didn't want to be reminded of their obligations to humanity. He'd told them and Falcone's lieutenant that it had gone bad because of my security, not because he'd shot the one of them who'd been his partner in the flash.

He'd brought me to this hidden nook to avoid them, so he wouldn't have to explain that all the things he'd taught them about pirates was shit, they weren't looking out for the best interests of the throwaway kids; in fact he wanted to leave the pirates now. But he couldn't tell them that.

But I'd opened my mouth and ruined it. Now he didn't just leave them. He killed them. And there were bodies.

So we were moving. And if I said a word he swore to the stars that he would shoot me. He dragged me by the arm with my hands cuffed behind me. My feet, one shoe off and bare, scraped on concrete and splashed in shallow puddles of things I didn't care to identify. My own sweat permeated my nose, and the scent of an environment where people passed through but nobody cleaned.

I stumbled for a third time. I was sure my one foot was bleeding by now from scraping the deck. It burned with pain. He yanked at me but I resisted. "Forget it!"

He shook me hard. "You *want* to die?"

My heart pounded, so loudly it seemed to travel through the tunnels like the station was pumping it.

"Don't do this, Kirov. Think. He'll help you if you let me go." Brave, empty words. I didn't want to die. I didn't want to end up lying dead in these cold tunnels and have my father or Sid find me. No. I saw it behind my eyes and the tears that ran now weren't all from the physical pain. I couldn't see him but I faced him, and I knew all he had to do was shoot me and it would be over.

It wasn't smart to taunt a person so willing to kill. But he went to all this trouble because he believed my father could help him. He was that desperate for a second life and who else would listen to him but Cairo Azarcon?

"He'll help you," I said. "But not like this."

"You're blind," he said. I heard him pace. "He won't forgive that."

I wanted to convince myself when I said, "Docs can fix it. And you might be surprised what he can forgive. Don't you think he knows what happened to you?" My nose was running now in the cold. I tried to wipe at it with my shoulder. I tried to listen for sounds of him putting his gun away, or brace myself for violence. I said, "I'll speak for you. I'll make him listen."

"You're a liar," he said into my face, suddenly close and intimately soft. "You're going to get me killed."

He must have seen that he was running out of options. Even if my father did what he asked he'd have to deliver me back, damaged. And no amount of dealmaking would make my father see the light in that outcome. Not in Kirov's pirate mind.

I felt his hand stroke over my hair, once. Then he moved away.

His sudden silence sent a tunnel of fear burrowing through my gut. I backed up.

He let me.

I'd misjudged him.

He was too desperate.

And I didn't see it coming. I just felt the bolt hit me in the chest and, oh, Mother, Mother, it burned.

Sound went in and out like distorted echoes through a mike. Shouts rode in the cold air. It was too cold, too dark, and my cheek lay pressed against something rough and unforgiving. I breathed in that darkness and wondered if this was what they'd felt. Those people at the embassy. In the Dojo. The girl I'd held in my arms.

My mother.

I breathed and it was their pain I felt, all of them, wrapped around me in a shroud. A hard pain that dug its jagged edges into my chest like it wanted to exhume my soul.

I breathed and the sound filled my head, struggling.

A voice from far away in the tunnel said, "Roll him over. Gently."

It came from far but hands touched me immediately. Close. Like they knew me.

They rolled me over.

The pain unearthed me and flung me to the fire.

Open your eyes, Ryan, please open your eyes.

It was a song in my ear, whispered just under the heavy thrum of the ship's drives. I was used to the ship now, its music was an odd lullaby that said we were moving. Skimming stars and cheating time, deep spacers like Erret Dorr liked to say.

"Ryan. Open your eyes."

My father's voice. It was an order, but I wasn't one of his jets. I didn't have to listen.

"He's trying," Sid said. "At least he better be."

Sid would knock me awake if I didn't do what he said.

Thin horizons of dusky light bled into the dark. Shadows

moved. A little more daylight and the world began to awaken, come alive, and reveal itself.

It wasn't daylight, it smelled like medbay, and my immediate world consisted of my father and Sid, one on either side of the bed, looking at me. Their faces were blurred, but not from tears, and everything was more gray than I remembered.

My lids were heavy. They drifted shut again.

"Ryan?" My father's voice, closer. A hand touched my shoulder. "It's okay, your eyes are healing. If they hurt that's the residue from the bot-knitters. Doc said it'll be a while before your sight clears."

If it would ever clear. I peeked at them again. Nothing had changed. It was a shadowy picture.

And I remembered.

I remembered Mom was dead.

The tears burned.

When I was still drugged and groggy my father told me that Doc Mercurio had removed my optical implants in order to try to repair the damage from the interrupted burndive. So I'd never be able to dive again. It wasn't a great loss. But my eyesight might never return one hundred percent. They didn't know; we had to give it time. Bot-knitters were intricate, industrious little nanoworkers, but the eyes were a complicated biological mechanism.

Like my heart, which was also healing. Physically.

Only Sid and my father were allowed to visit but it didn't much matter. I slept a lot, made up for all those bouts of insomnia I'd taken with me from Earth. The first thing I asked for was the date.

"You were out for forty-eight hours," Sid said, when my father was elsewhere.

"Only forty-eight?"

My body felt like it hadn't moved in a month.

"A long forty-eight," he said. He sat at the side of the bed and even with my blurred vision I saw his unkempt hair and the way his shoulders slumped as if gravity alone fatigued him.

My voice croaked. "Where's my father?"

"On the bridge. He'll be back soon." He poured me some water from the bedside table and held it for me as I sipped the straw.

It was a private room in medbay and the door was shut. Silence, except for the drives, insulated us.

"What happened?" I asked, and tried to brace myself for the answer.

Sid moved the edge of the blanket, dissecting it with fingers. "I got a concussion from that thunderflash, but everyone else made it out okay. Otter and his gang underdeck found you and then helped us track Kirov before he could split the tunnels."

"Otter's in a gang?"

Sid shook his head, rubbed an eye. I may have slept but he probably hadn't. "He *runs* a gang. Musey said the symps on Austro recruited Otter a few years ago to work for the Warboy. But he's a tunnel rat through and through, and when he isn't running ops for symps he's terrorizing the pollies."

"He knows comps too."

Sid sounded amused. "He's an enterprising kid."

"Maybe I can meet him sometime. To thank him."

Sid didn't say anything. I couldn't see his face clearly through the damn blur.

"I don't think we'll be going back to Austro anytime soon," Sid murmured finally.

"Why not?"

"I think it'd be best if your father explained. We got that pirate at least, he's in the brig being interrogated."

None of that sounded good.

"It was my fault," I said.

"What was?"

"What Kirov did. My being blind. I tried to dive a message on his comp and he caught me, and that panicked him when I couldn't see after, and then he shot these kids because I yelled out—"

"None of this is your fault, Ryan."

"I didn't help." I felt like digging out the irritation from my eyes. "I could've helped—something."

Sid was firm with me. Angry, but not at me. "He's a pirate and if he shot somebody he's the one killed them."

"He wanted my father to help him. He was telling the truth about the Family of Humanity and Mom, wasn't he?"

After a moment, Sid said, "Yes. He knew that Centralist woman's comm codes. We confiscated her comp and Musey extracted her correspondences."

"Don't let my father kill him."

"Why not?" *He* wanted to kill him. It was plain in his voice.

"He can help," I said. "Maybe he'd testify, maybe that'll screw up Damiani if there's a solid tie between Centralists and the Family of Humanity."

Maybe that would help the negotiations.

Maybe it wouldn't be fair for my father to kill Kirov, because at one point they'd been in the exact position, wanting to leave a life, except Grandpa Ashrafi hadn't turned his back.

"Look what he did to you," Sid said, quiet.

"But I'm alive," I said. "Aren't I?"

*   *   *

I ordered Sid to bed. He didn't want to go but the sick and infirm hold a curious power over even the most stubborn Marine. If he didn't want me to distress myself on his account he'd do what I said.

So he went.

I slept, and when I woke up again my father was there, in Sid's spot. A gray film still lay over everything.

He leaned down and hugged me, gently, as if we'd always made this sort of contact. It didn't matter. Right now it felt like we always had. I figured he held on because he thought I needed it, but the seconds stretched and it wasn't for me.

Then he straightened up and said in a slightly hoarse voice, "How do things look?"

I squinted at his expression. "Grim. Are we going back to Chaos?"

He breathed out and fingered the blanket by my arm. "Not yet . . . I don't know when we'll be able to dock at a Hub station. After Austro, Damiani ordered me recalled to Earth. For a court-martial."

"What? Can she do that? Can't Grandpa—"

"No. He can't. She has a right. I took control of the station without authorization. It was just the excuse she needed to rope me in and put the negotiations on permanent hold."

"But what about the Rimstations and merchant ships . . . they'd back you. They already back you, some of them."

"They don't get a vote in Hub Command."

His voice was flat. He stared at a point on the pillow by my head for a long moment, but then he looked at me in the eyes, leaning closer so I could see his stare and he could put his hand in my hair, touch me. He said, "I couldn't risk it when Kirov took you, Ryan. You were gone. I didn't really care to squabble with govies about protocol. If one ship had left with you on it, you would've been lost."

On a pirate ship. That was his fear. And his actions made
him a pirate in the government's eyes.

Or maybe he was just a parent who had the power to protect his child, and used it.

My father wasn't going to Earth on Damiani's order. He
was heading to deep space, for now, and Musey said Captain
S'tlian would supply *Macedon* as long as they continued
their alliance against the pirates.

That was more than fair, considering my father wasn't
finished with pirates yet. Or negotiations—corrupt govies
notwithstanding. If some stations and merchants, colonies
and bases in the deep didn't want to fight anymore, my father was going to settle something between them and the
striviirc-na, and what were Damiani's allies going to do
about it?

Rogue, the Send said. It was all over the Send. Rogue
Captain Cairo Azarcon who had a pirate in his brig that he
refused to deliver to justice, and he left a shaken Austro Station in his wake.

My father called it regrouping.

Kirov had a lot of knowledge in his head—about pirates
and all of their allies. Evan was right; Falcone had trained
Kirov well in a lot of areas, not the least of which was intel
gathering, but with it came a good deal of indoctrination. He
wasn't particularly cooperative, was extremely distrustful,
but Musey said a few shifts in *Macedon*'s brig might change
his mind.

I thought, The pirate wanted out for a reason. He *wanted*
to help, he just didn't know it yet.

If we built a strong case against Damiani's ilk and sent it
under the wire to Admiral Grandpa, it might eventually take
the WANTED sign off *Macedon*'s hull.

We real popular, Erret Dorr said. You never feel more alive than when somebody's got a gun to your head.

They visited me. Musey, Evan, Erret. Even Lieutenant Hartman and Aki, who got me anything I wanted if I just asked her when she passed my room or checked on my chest bandage. I binged on chocolate for a week. Doc Mercurio told me this wasn't what he'd meant by a physical exam, but if I got sick on candy he'd use that as an excuse. So I stopped.

Musey and Evan brought me music in a hand player, with earbuds, and Musey said there were a few tracks in there from Aaian-na, if I wanted to listen. They had a stringed instrument sort of like a guitar and he thought I might be curious. Courtesy of Nikolas S'tlian, he said, who had asked what I was interested in and wished me a swift recovery.

"It's pretty good," Evan summarized. "But it's a bit quiet for my tastes."

Quiet didn't sound too bad to me.

Musey said, "I'm sorry we lost you on deck," as if I were a hat that had fallen off their heads. His earnest concern made me smile.

"Well, at least you found me. If you talk to Otter let him know I'm grateful."

Musey nodded, hovering at my right while Evan sampled some of the medbay food at my bedside, making faces but eating it anyway.

"So," Musey said. "Get better. If you still want to learn more hand-to-hand."

"Only if you teach me."

"Who else?" he said. "I'm on orders." One side of his mouth twitched and he patted the blanket by my leg, briefly, before turning and leaving the room without even a goodbye. Like a real symp.

Evan wiped his hands on his shirt and grinned at me.

"Better watch out, next thing you know he'll be asking you on a date."

That made me laugh and it hurt my wounded chest, but I didn't care.

Two weeks of solid mending and I was ready to move. Stubborn Marines, jets, or captains had nothing on stubborn rich sons. I was out and walking about, albeit like an old man, using the bulkheads as a guide and prop in my blurried progress through the decks. They all volunteered themselves to watch over me in shifts, like I was some sort of favored pet too stupid to find the litter box on his own.

"Get out," I said finally to Dorr, whose turn it was, as he followed me to the bathroom in my father's quarters. "Enough. Get out."

"Don't you need help? Can you see to aim for the bowl?"

I was all ready to be mad before I realized he was joking. Punk jet.

"I may not be able to see well, but your fat head is a large enough target," I said.

He laughed and tousled my hair. I didn't care, since ultimately he left—after threatening me to keep my new tagcomm handy in case I needed anything.

Once I was alone I squinted at the ship's map in my comp, memorized which levs went where, and went down the decks to the brig.

My father was going to kill me, but that would be later. For now I rode to the bottom of the ship, far away from even the loudest sounds of the drives. The brig was truly buried in the belly of *Macedon*, where crew and captain could forget about you if they didn't like what you said or did. The jet at the monitoring station in the cold, steel-ridden room looked surprised to see me but I said, "Captain okayed."

Sons hath their privileges. And it was fascinating what a

smile, big eyes, and an appeal for pity toward the injured could do to a jet's resolve.

"Just don't go too near the cage," she said.

I didn't intend to. Despite the barrier between us, I kept a meter distance between me and Kirov, as he leaned on the gate.

"I heard you were alive," he said. "Congrats."

I stared through the bars at his flat blue, moisture-rimmed eyes. The light was bright in his cell and I saw him more clearly than I had in the underdeck, even with my damaged sight. He was bruised on his face and arms, his hair looked darker, matted and long, and he still wore the same clothes he had in the tunnels.

"Congrats to you," I said, with as steady a voice as I could manage. Even with the barrier between us I half-expected him to jump through and grab me to finish his work. "You're holding out here."

"It ain't so hard. I like jets." His mouth pulled in a smile, half-hearted.

"Why don't you just cooperate?"

"For what?" His gaze slipped to the side as if he was bored.

It wasn't boredom. I saw it now in the way he chewed on the edge of his thumb, creases formed at the sides of his mouth as if he was trying to stop something distasteful from falling out. It was a despair so ingrained it occupied the slightest of his looks or movements. Even if my father came here personally and opened the gate, this pirate would doubt the intention.

"You thought he could help you," I said. "He still might. If you help us."

Kirov snorted and didn't answer. He turned and went to the single cot in the cell and dropped down on it, feet up on the mattress, knees bent.

"The only reason you're alive," he said, "is 'cause some stroke of luck made them find you in time. You don't think your papa realizes this? I killed you for all intents and purposes. I meant to. Now go away, Dead Man."

He was young, or at least he looked it. Evan's age. Maybe my age. He had the snarky attitude of someone too used to associating at arm's length.

"Where are you from, Yuri?" I asked.

A moon colony like my father?

"Do you have a family?" I asked.

Like my father's brothers?

He tilted his head on the pillow and stared at me. Even from a distance, and with my blurry sight, I felt his sudden sharp attention.

He didn't answer. Maybe he couldn't. Maybe I'd hit some spot in him that nobody had yet aimed for, or maybe I'd missed completely.

It didn't matter. He was going to be on this ship for a while, and I was going to come back.

I was in my room playing my guitar because I could shut my eyes and do it, just feel the strings and hear the music, when Sid visited. He sat on the other side of the bed and leaned on one hand, and I opened my eyes and saw him up close with a little less blur and grayness than a week ago. He looked like he'd lost weight in those weeks since Austro and some permanent lines had appeared around his eyes that weren't from laughter.

But he still smiled for me. "When're you going to grace the ship with a live concert?"

"Ha ha. Never."

"Ah, c'mon, when you feel comfortable we can put you out on station and you can earn some extra cred busking on the deck."

I laughed, but then we both remembered that the only station we could dock at lately would be one deep inside striviirc-na territory. Sid looked down at the bedsheet and sighed.

"Well," he said, "it's a thought."

"Sid." I watched his face, dreading what I might see there. "You know . . . you're not really caught up in this. I'm sure my father would let you go to one of *Mac*'s sister ships and they could take you back to Earth. To your family. Your mom."

He looked at me, surprised. "I'm not really *in* this? You've been my family for seven years—and counting, Ryan."

"I mean . . . you're an EarthHub Marine. And you were ordered to accompany me. They couldn't hold that against you."

"Ryan . . ."

"Maybe it'd be good for you to be away from the Azarcons for a while. We tend to draw fire." I tried to make it light.

He wouldn't be, not now. "But it's my duty to be here, Ryan, and I'll always be here if you ask."

It wasn't just duty. I saw it in the way he looked right into my eyes. Like he always had, unperturbed by anything I might throw at him.

"What about you?" he said. "You can always go back to Earth and stay with your grandparents. If you didn't want to be on ship. I'd go with you."

It was an option. But he'd have to go as my guard again, because Earth wasn't safe. Especially now. And going to school, camping, riding horses, and tanning on roofs seemed more than a world away. I thought about being away from my father. Or my odd mix of friends that I had somehow made on this ship.

I couldn't do it.

I think he knew my answer, but he wanted me to hear the question.

I said, "Joanne Martin commed me. She said Mom left her estate entirely to me."

He nodded; it wasn't anything that surprised him, but any mention of my mother always made him quiet.

"I want you to help me."

"Of course," he said, without hesitation, without even asking for details.

That was Sid.

My grandparents on Earth crowded in front of their coded and secured comm so they were both in the frame, and both of them could tell me they loved me and I was going to be all right, and even if Grandpa himself had to send an assassin after Damiani he was going to see my father and me in person sometime in the near future.

"Take care of your father," Dr. Grandma said, which I thought was odd until I thought about it, and she continued, "He needs more than the Hub's support right now."

"I know . . ." One day, I figured, I was going to sit down with my grandparents and ask them what it had been like, to live and put through school an eighteen-year-old Cairo Azarcon. I had the feeling they would talk to me now, that my father wouldn't mind the additional stories to whatever he might tell me himself. What had he looked like when Grandpa took him off Falcone's ship, and how had Grandpa ever convinced him to toe the line long enough to graduate from the Academy?

Had he thrown him into it and ordered the education, like the captain had done with me?

When had they started to love him as their own son?

It must have been something extraordinary for my

grandparents, who'd had two daughters through their own blood, to take on a headstrong pirate orphan.

Maybe they didn't see it as so special, though. Maybe it was just something they couldn't ignore, that my grandfather couldn't deny when he was on a battleship in deep space, seeing the ramifications of the war on families across the Hub. Maybe he even felt a little responsible.

Maybe my father did, and thus his crew. Filled by Dorrs and Hartmans, and Museys and Evans.

"I'm glad you two at least are together," Grandpa said.

Especially because Mom was gone.

The distance between our comms seemed too far, when I remembered those sun-drenched breakfasts in their home in the summers.

My room in my father's quarters seemed cold by comparison.

Then I heard the hatch open from the outside room and my father's voice called out, coming closer, "Ryan? Are you in here? Let's go to dinner. The cook's outdone himself for you."

And that was familiar. That was the warmth that picked me up and set me exactly where I belonged.

I told the captain at one of our recent dinners, "I want to do something about these war relief agencies that aren't properly helping people. Maybe with all the cred Mom left me. Maybe I can set up some sort of fund, I don't know. I'm still working out the logistics. But people need to know . . . you should tell people . . ."

"Tell people what?" my father said.

I rubbed my sore eyes. They were healing, but slowly, and they still ached if I didn't shut them every few hours. I took a deep breath to test the healing there and the tightness in my chest was a little less than it had been.

"How it is out here," I said. "The truth. When Kirov talks . . . you have to help him so he wants to talk . . . we could let the Hub know for sure what Damiani did. What the Family of Humanity are into and their connection to her."

"Intel is often slow in coming," he said, "and slower still to be compiled and transmitted, especially now that we're cut off from official channels."

"Official channels never bothered you before."

He smiled. "True."

"And if you transcast or drop news, if Musey sets it up or something so you can burndive, they won't be able to stop you, or charge you, or anything. I mean . . . you're already rogue, what're they going to do?"

He watched me. "I'm not sure mine is the best face to put on things right now. Maybe once things settle down."

Oh.

I pushed my food around on the plate. "Maybe."

"I haven't given up," he said.

"I know."

"Many of my comrades are still on board with the peace, and we're going to make it work in the Dragons. Eventually, hopefully, once the truth comes out . . . we'll be able to return to Austro. And Earth." His tone tread lighter. "You won't be stuck on this ship forever."

"Dad," I said, "that's not an issue for me."

He took a sip of his water. "Oh?"

"I mean, sure, I'll want to go back to Austro at some point. Or Mars. Or Earth. Anywhere. But . . ." Hiding out on planet or in an executive tower wasn't going to help me anymore. Or help anybody.

"But?"

I set the fork down and rested my hand on the table by my plate. "Yuri went into piracy because Falcone recruited from a relocation camp. He told me. Evan's been showing me stats of pirate attacks on camps and merchants, dating right back to when you—at Meridia."

He tilted his chin at a slight angle, interested but cautious. "What are you thinking?"

"There's got to be some way to help these people. And the kids. The government's not doing it properly. Jos told me about NGOs. And . . . Mom left me a lot of assets. And cred. We can transcast. We can make it known . . . what it's really like in those places. Like where you come from."

I didn't know what was in my words, particularly, that made his stare so wide and his eyes so curiously bright, despite their dark color.

But I told him what I wanted to do, and how, from what I'd hashed out with Sid and Joanne Martin, across comms, and how in some way I planned on never forgetting that I'd had blood-related uncles and grandparents with the same last name, and maybe the captain could fill in those blanks. And maybe there were things he didn't know that we could find out. Had he asked Admiral Grandpa about any of those files?

"No," my father said. "I actually never had. At the time . . . I'd just wanted to forget. Maybe that sounds odd, but—"

I told him it didn't. At all.

And then I told him about Earth, and why if we ever went back I'd want him to go with me.

To Hong Kong. And to London.

To that hotel where Sid had found me.

It was my first time saying it aloud, and I had to admit that maybe it hadn't been unintentional, maybe I'd just been weak and selfish and too weighted. But I looked that memory in the face like I looked at him. One started to fade, like some pains do, and the other stayed fixed, like love or decision.

* * *

I commed Shiri a week later and I admit I took some pleasure in her shock.

"All this time you were on *Macedon* and you didn't tell me. Are you okay?"

"That seems to be all you've been asking lately." I tried a smile on her and touched the edges of my eyes, habit now when they pained me.

"You have to stop getting into trouble and then I'll stop." She stared at me as if she could gauge my health through the comp screen. "I'm so sorry about your mother, Ryan."

I nodded. I wasn't going to get into that in private or in public. Not for a while. Or ever. "I'm comming because . . . if you still want to impress Paulita Valencia and land that story, I can set it up."

She stared. I looked back and wondered what she saw now. Maybe it was my altered vision, but Shiri seemed closer than a comm's usual perspective, her eyes darker and more intense.

She said, as if she thought I was teasing her, "Your father's going to talk to me? Really?"

It would make her career.

"Not yet," I said, taking a deep breath. It settled my heart and sharpened my words. "But I will."

ABOUT THE AUTHOR

KARIN LOWACHEE was born in Guyana, South America, and grew up in Ontario, Canada. She holds a creative writing and English degree from York University in Toronto and taught adult education for nine months in Canada's tundra community of Rankin Inlet, Nunavut. Visit her on the web at www.karinlowachee.com.

VISIT WARNER ASPECT ONLINE!

THE WARNER ASPECT HOMEPAGE
You'll find us at: www.twbookmark.com then by clicking on Science Fiction and Fantasy.

NEW AND UPCOMING TITLES
Each month we feature our new titles and reader favorites.

AUTHOR INFO
Author bios, bibliographies and links to personal websites.

CONTESTS AND OTHER FUN STUFF
Advance galley giveaways, autographed copies, and more.

THE ASPECT BUZZ
What's new, hot and upcoming from Warner Aspect: awards news, bestsellers, movie tie-in information . . .